# His offer was tempting.

Emily gave Will an apologetic smile. 'Thanks for the invitation, but I can't meet you for dinner. Tonight, tomorrow night or any other night.'

He rose to tower over her. 'You know I won't give up,' he said softly, his face expressionless although his eyes burned hotly.

'You should.'

'I won't.'

'Why not?'

'Do you want me to go into detail? Here, in a public place?' He threw a pointed glare at their surroundings. 'However, if that's what you want, I'll be happy to discuss our unfinished business...'

**Jessica Matthews's** interest in medicine began at a young age, and she nourished it with medical stories and hospital-based television programmes. After a stint as a teenage candy-striper, she pursued a career as a clinical laboratory scientist. When not writing, or on duty she fills her day with countless family- and school-related activities. Jessica lives in the central United States with her husband, daughter and son.

**Recent titles by the same author:**

A HERO FOR MOMMY
DR PRESCOTT'S DILEMMA

# BABIES ON HER MIND

BY

## JESSICA MATTHEWS

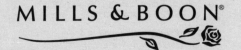

MILLS & BOON®

To Veda, a true-blue friend.

My special thanks go to Patricia MacDonald RN,
for sharing her neonatal nursing experience,
and to Betty McGinnes, CT(ASCP),
for her cytotechnology tips. Any errors are my own.

*First published in Great Britain 1999
Harlequin Mills & Boon Limited,
Eton House, 18-24 Paradise Road, Richmond, Surrey TW9 1SR*

© Jessica Matthews 1999

ISBN 0 263 81697 4

*Set in Times Roman 10½ on 12 pt.
03-9906-46471-D*

*Printed and bound in Spain
by Litografia Rosés S.A., Barcelona*

# CHAPTER ONE

'MEET me for dinner. Six o'clock.'

Will Patton's familiar tenor voice, coming from out of nowhere, caught Emily Chandler by surprise. An instant later a sense of fatalism filled her. She should have expected this conversation since she went through this every time he appeared on her unit.

She scrawled her name at the end of the nurse's note, closed the medical record and slid it into its appropriate slot. 'No, thanks, Doctor,' she said light-heartedly to camouflage the self-consciousness his attention produced.

'Why not?' he asked, leaning one hip against the counter where she was trying to finish her charting before her shift ended.

'I'm busy.' She stole a glance at him, fully aware of his mysterious, roguish looks—dark eyes, equally dark eyebrows, jet-black hair and the faint scar running along his right temple.

His lean jaw squared slightly and his eyes flashed with something akin to exasperation, yet his tone remained even. 'Tomorrow night, then.'

She leaned back, schooling her expression to hide the inner turmoil his piercing gaze caused. She'd seen for herself how nothing, no matter how trivial, escaped his notice. He'd never relent in his pursuit if he knew how thoroughly he rocked her composure. Her best and only defense was to act as if unmoved by his interest.

Conscious of the two staff members who were walking past, she reminded him in a whisper, 'We agreed to keep our relationship professional. Strictly doctor-nurse.'

Considering the subject closed, she reached for another blue notebook, but his large hand shot out and held it in its slot. 'Agreements can be renegotiated.'

One broad shoulder was so close she could have rubbed her nose against his coat. A faint scent of his cologne teased her senses. 'If both parties are willing. The key word being *if.*'

A ward clerk hurried past and Will released his hold on the chart. 'Come on, Emily,' he said in a low voice. 'What harm would dinner cause? I take colleagues out all the time.'

His offer was tempting, but she knew how easily the most innocuous of circumstances could become complicated. She gave him an apologetic smile.

'Thanks for the invitation, but I can't meet you for dinner. Tonight, tomorrow night or any other night.'

He rose to tower over her. 'You know I won't give up,' he said softly, his face expressionless although his eyes burned hotly.

'You should.'

'I won't.'

'Why not?'

'Do you want me to go into detail? Here, in a public place?' He threw a pointed glare at their surroundings. 'However, if that's what you want, I'll be happy to discuss our unfinished business…'

'No!' She sighed. For the past three weeks he'd been tenacious about initiating personal conversations during their relatively private moments at the hospital. She'd rather have had back the days when they hadn't exchanged more than a polite and impersonal greeting.

An inescapable truth filled her with resignation. Will

meant what he said. He was a man who didn't like loose ends, and if he claimed to have unfinished business with her then she didn't have a chance of holding him at arm's length for long.

She squared her shoulders, vowing to be equally persistent. Will would have to wait until her brother's problems were behind her. She could only handle one personal crisis at a time.

'I'll check my schedule for the next few days,' she conceded. 'But I won't promise anything.'

'Fair enough,' he said. 'See you tomorrow.' Turning on one heel, he left without waiting for her farewell.

Before the odour of hospital disinfectant erased the pleasant combination of his aftershave and masculine soap, Molly O'Donnell, a buxom, red-headed nursing colleague on the maternity unit, plopped beside Emily and pulled a sheaf of notes from the side pocket of her purple scrub pants.

'Why don't you just tell the poor man yes?'

Emily stared at her friend. 'What?'

'Tell the poor man yes,' Molly repeated. 'He's been asking you to dinner for weeks now. The least you can do is put him out of his misery.'

Emily dismissed her friend's comment. 'He can go to dinner with one of the other nurses.'

'He could, but he won't. He hasn't given any of us a second glance since he arrived in Crossbow three months ago. It isn't because us northern Texas gals aren't trying to catch his attention either.'

'Try harder,' Emily ordered, 'then maybe he'll leave me alone.'

Molly drew her eyebrows together in a puzzled frown. 'But why, Em? You're a free woman. You broke up with Don Springer before Christmas. You don't have to observe a mourning period. If Dr Patton's interested, don't let all that masculine appeal go to waste!'

'I'm not interested in another relationship. Casual or otherwise.'

'Good gosh, Em. He only wants to take you to dinner. If you ask me, you two would make a great couple.'

'Looks can be deceiving,' Emily said ruefully. 'Besides, I'm not the kind of woman he's searching for.'

'How do you know? You haven't said more than two full sentences to him unless it concerned one of his patients.'

'I just do,' Emily said. 'And until I get the problems with my brother straightened out I don't need any more complications.' She returned to her record-keeping as a sign the subject was closed. She'd made up her mind and didn't intend to justify her decision with a lengthy explanation. Her reasons were too personal to share with anyone.

'I still can't see how going to dinner with a man like Will Patton could be a complication,' Molly grumbled.

'It is,' Emily said flatly. 'Take my word for it.'

Molly sighed. 'Considering how handsome he is in that dark, brooding sort of way, a night with him would liven up a girl's life. According to the rumors, he was quite a hellion in his younger days.'

Emily was surprised by Molly's tidbit of information. 'He doesn't strike me as a hellion now.'

'No,' Molly agreed, 'but maybe he's simply suppressed his youthful energy, waiting for the right time and place. If so, unleashing that passion could make for an exciting evening...' She winked.

The subject of passion hit too close to home. 'Helping Kevin with his homework is all the excitement I want to handle right now,' Emily said.

She immediately changed the subject. 'Do you want to walk tonight?' she asked, mentally crossing her fingers and hoping Molly would cry off. Their exercise program, intended to invigorate her, had failed miserably. However, she was receiving one benefit. She fell asleep the moment her head hit the pillow.

'Yeah. Wanna go after work?'

'No, I have a doctor's appointment.'

'It's about time you took my advice,' Molly declared. 'You haven't been perky the last few weeks.'

'Overwork and stress will do that to a person,' Emily said dryly. Although she downplayed her constant fatigue, she hoped it wasn't a symptom of something more sinister than the conditions she'd described. 'I'll tell all when I see you afterwards.'

However, Emily's nonchalance had faded a few hours later as she waited for the results of the lab work Dr Ferguson had ordered. She'd been given the opportunity to go home and wait for his phone call, but had decided to remain in the patient waiting room instead.

Her trepidation increased with her summons to Dr Ferguson's private office. Sitting on the chair in front of his desk, she studied the golf memorabilia lining the walls in order to keep her mind from jumping to conclusions, but each passing moment made it more difficult to remain optimistic.

Both impatient and nervous, she rubbed her sweaty palms against her jeans, before playing with the ends of her hair. The door opened without warning and she flung her braid over one shoulder, instinctively stiffening her spine to brace herself for the worst.

'I believe we have our answer, Emily.' Emmett Ferguson walked into the room, his voice as merry as his fifty-five-year-old countenance. He was tall and slender, had gray hair—and bushy eyebrows to match—and wore his glasses perched on the end of his nose.

She managed a smile. 'That's good.' She took some comfort in his pleasant expression. Surely he wouldn't deliver bad news wearing a smile.

He sat behind his desk, laid her chart before him and peered down at her. 'You, my dear, have some decisions to make. First of all, you'll have to choose another physician because I won't be able to treat your condition.'

Her fears of leukemia mushroomed and her heart skipped a beat. 'You won't?'

'Sorry. I haven't practiced obstetrics for the past five years.'

*Obstetrics?* Emily frowned. 'What are you saying?'

'You're pregnant. See for yourself.' He handed her a sheet of paper.

Emily stared at the page bearing her own name— she'd checked for good measure—unable to believe the fateful words. 'Are you sure this isn't a mistake?' she asked hoarsely.

'No mistake. The report confirms my suspicions.' He studied her over his glasses. 'Being pregnant isn't the end of the world. I can think of worse things that could be wrong with you. You can, too.'

'I know. It's just so…shocking.' Emily had always subscribed to the philosophy that a husband should come before children. Granted, she'd done a lot of impetuous things in her life, but it didn't seem fair to get caught the first time her principles had wavered.

Dr Ferguson patted her hand. 'I'm sure it is.' Although he hadn't specifically mentioned her unmarried state, she knew he'd referred to it.

She managed a grin. 'I was prepared to hear about

infectious mono or leukemia, not a positive pregnancy test.'

He closed her chart, leaned back in his chair and steepled his fingers. 'Pregnancy has a better prognosis. However, I'm surprised you didn't realize your own condition. Working on the ob-gyn ward, you surely know the signs.'

'I'm used to dealing with the end of pregnancy, not the beginning,' she said wryly. 'Also, I've had a number of issues come up at home in the past few weeks so I assumed my exhaustion and loss of appetite was stress-related.'

'Understandable, I suppose. As you can see, the rest of your lab work—white count, chemistries, and so on—falls within normal range. Your hemoglobin is a little low, but a mineral supplement should bring the level up nicely. In the meantime, decisions have to be made about carrying this baby to term.'

She nodded.

'I would urge you to discuss your options with your partner. He's an important part of this triangle.'

Triangle was an apt description. Even if she lived to be a hundred she'd never forget the evening of the Christmas Ball. In her mind's eye she pictured her child's father in his tuxedo, standing out in a sea of other distinguished people.

Her son could grow up as his carbon copy.

'Regardless of his decision, I'm keeping this baby,' she said quietly.

His face became thoughtful. 'I'd say you're about ten weeks along so that will make him or her an early September baby. Your obstetrician will give you a more specific date after he examines you.'

Emily rubbed her forehead as the changes in her future—her family's future—ran through her mind.

'Which brings me to the next point of discussion,' Dr Ferguson said. 'I recommend you see Dr Patton.' He smiled. 'Being relatively new in town, he doesn't have a lot of patients vying for his attention yet.'

Emily tensed. This was a complication she hadn't considered. 'I'm afraid that isn't a good idea. Our personalities…clash.' She winced at the relative untruth, but hoped Dr Ferguson would believe—and accept—her explanation.

'Will can be gruff on occasion,' he admitted. 'He also seems to take life too seriously, but from what I've seen and heard about him he's an excellent physician. If he's given you a hard time in the past it's because he's concerned about his patients. Trust me. You'll be in good hands.'

She wouldn't argue that point.

'I know he's an excellent doctor,' she began, 'but history is the problem.' At Dr Ferguson's puzzled frown, she blurted out, 'He's my baby's father.'

'How did your appointment go?' Molly asked later that evening as they strode through the mall as part of their fitness routine. Emily couldn't afford a health club membership, and since today's February weather was blustery they—like many others—took advantage of the shopping center's controlled atmosphere.

Emily stopped to tie her frayed shoelace in front of a clothing store's window display. The red and silver foil hearts arranged on the glass and scattered along the floor complemented the garments designed especially for the season.

'I have to find another doctor. Dr Ferguson can't handle my case any more.'

'Omigod.' Molly's green eyes grew wide. 'What's wrong?' Unlike Emily, Molly always wore the latest fashions, even in exercise apparel. Today a pair of black Lycra leggings, a lime-green pair of shorts, a black shirt sporting a huge Nike logo on the front and a top-of-the-line pair of designer trainers covered her voluptuous frame.

Emily straightened, sorry for distressing her friend. She tugged her oversize red T-shirt down over her hips and brushed a speck of lint off the knee of her black fleece jogging pants. She caught her reflection in the storefront window and wished for a portion of Molly's overly generous curves to pad her modest ones.

'It's nothing serious. Well, it is, but it isn't.' She paused. 'I'm pregnant.'

'You're what?' Molly's surprise shone on her face like a beacon.

'I'm pregnant,' Emily repeated.

'Omigod. When? Who?' Molly's disjointed questions jelled. 'Don't tell me it was Don.'

'It's not Don.' At least fate had smiled on her in that regard. The thought of him being her baby's father sent a cold chill down her spine.

'Then who?' Molly demanded. 'I *know* you aren't seeing anyone. In fact, the only man who's expressed an interest in you is—' Molly cut herself off. Her expression became incredulous as if the ramifications had struck her like a bolt of lightning. 'Don't tell me you're having a clandestine affair with—'

'Will Patton,' Emily supplied. 'It isn't an affair. At least, I wouldn't classify one time as an affair.'

'One—? Omigod. I have to sit down.' Molly made

her way to a bench in the middle of the walkway and sank onto it.

Emily followed.

'I can't believe it.' Molly shook her head. 'You, Miss Conventional, had a one-night—'

The title Molly had bestowed on her reminded Emily of what had got her into this predicament. 'Don't say a word,' she said sharply. 'Don't you dare make that evening sound cheap. It was an extremely therapeutic experience during a very difficult time of my life.'

Molly apologized. 'I'm sorry. I know what you've faced these past two months. It's just that I'd never expected you to do something so...so...'

'Impetuous?' Emily asked.

'Yeah.' Molly tucked a lock of her page-boy bob behind one ear. 'When did this happen?'

'December seventeenth.'

'The seventeenth?' Molly's eyes widened to saucer-sized proportions. 'Why, that was—'

'The night of the Christmas Ball,' Emily finished. A couple, their arms entwined, strode into her line of vision. She remembered what it had felt like to be wrapped in Will's embrace.

'Good gosh, Em. He only started working in Crossbow last October. He might be a professional, but after two months you hardly knew the man.'

Emily hid a wry smile. That fact hadn't changed much over the past few weeks.

'Whatever possessed you?'

Emily fingered the hem of her shirt, before smoothing it over her thighs. 'He had his car and offered me a ride when I wanted to leave. He was very kind.'

'So you paid him back by sleeping with him?'

Emily glared at her friend. 'Absolutely not,' she said

stiffly. 'We didn't plan to spend the night together. The idea just developed.'

Molly scoffed. 'That's what they all say. However, you haven't convinced me that he didn't take advantage of you. You weren't in the greatest mental state at the time.'

'Gee, thanks. Now you make me sound like I was on the verge of a nervous breakdown.'

'Stronger people have broken under less stressful conditions. I don't know how I'd react if my uncle was throwing his weight around and making a bad situation worse.'

'I'll admit to being frantic over trying to avoid a nasty custody battle. Our whole family—Gran, Kevin and myself—was in an uproar for the longest time.'

'Which proves my point,' Molly said. 'You weren't thinking clearly. On the other hand, Dr Patton should have shown more restraint.'

'Please don't be so hard on Will. Everything we did was based on a mutual decision. He wasn't to blame.'

'You're defending him?' Molly sounded aghast.

'He was going through a difficult time too.'

Molly crossed her legs and leaned back, as if making herself comfortable. 'I'll withhold judgment for the moment. However, I'm especially curious how you managed all this without giving me the slightest clue.'

Emily drew a deep breath. 'It all started as soon as I left our table…'

Emily strolled down the corridor of the Crossbow Country Club in search of a quiet place. The Christmas Ball committee's innovative idea of providing both country and western and rock and roll music at the hospital's annual holiday dance had proved a success. Staff members and their guests filled each party room, and the noise level was deafening.

She should have been cold in her midnight green halter dress, but the large number of people had raised the club's ambient temperature to a balmy degree. She'd even discarded the lacy shawl covering her bare shoulders and back because it had become more of a nuisance than a help.

Thinking of nuisances, her tight skirt, even with the slit extending from her ankle-length hem to above her knee, made walking a difficult task. Taking dainty steps when she was used to long strides was more trying than she'd imagined.

To her joy, she discovered an empty lounge at the far end of the building, complete with soft lighting and Queen-Anne-style chairs arranged in small groups for intimate conversations.

She slid off her black pumps and carried them to a corner opposite the door. Choosing a seat with its back to the entrance, she sank into its depths with a grateful sigh.

As she relaxed in the peaceful surroundings the smile she'd worn all evening faded. Pretending to have fun while her mind drifted onto her personal crises required more energy than she could summon. She was starting to feel the effects of constantly presenting a cheerful front to her family and friends.

Emily closed her eyes, intending to allow herself half an hour before returning to the party. Without conversation buzzing around her, she shut down her conscious thoughts and allowed her other senses to take over.

At one point she picked out the muted wail of a Garth Brooks tune before a rendition of the latest number one pop rock song overpowered it.

Next she focused on the plush carpeting underneath her nylon-clad toes and the mixture of ladies' perfume and men's aftershave that clung to her.

Fifteen minutes later voices interrupted her solitude. She peered around the chair's wing and saw a gorgeous, statuesque blonde standing next to Dr Patton. Her expensive peach-colored silk creation contrasted with his black tuxedo, as did her fair complexion against his dark one. The combination of her exquisite features and his rugged countenance made them a handsome couple.

Emily felt a stab of envy.

As she debated whether she should make an exit, the woman's words seemed to echo in the room. Emily couldn't stop hearing their conversation any more than she could voluntarily stop breathing. She froze in her chair, willing herself to be invisible as the woman spoke clearly.

'I can't marry you.'

'You can't?' Will sounded surprised.

'No, I can't. I thought I could, but I can't.'

'What do you mean, you thought you could?'

'Just that. I thought I could. But—'

'But what?'

'Please don't make me say it.' It sounded as if she were begging.

'Come on, Celine. I want to hear why you changed your mind.'

*Celine.* Emily wasn't surprised by the glamorous name. It certainly fit the woman's alluring appearance. She'd always considered her own unremarkable girl-next-door image to be as ordinary as her name. Maybe she'd dye her light brown hair a rich chestnut shade the next time she visited Pearl's Beauty Boutique. If wishes were horses, she'd have the money to fix her retroussé nose as well. People like Celine always had straight noses, which made it easy for them to look down upon others.

'I didn't change my mind,' Celine said. 'When you proposed I asked for time to think about it, and I have. My answer is no.'

'I see.' He paused.

'You're just too structured, Will. You live your life by a timetable.'

'I'm amused you think so.' Emily imagined him stiffening his spine. 'Being an obstetrician, my day doesn't usually run according to schedule.'

No kidding, Emily thought. Where was the glamorous Celine getting her ideas? Didn't she know babies arrived when they felt like it?

'I don't mean your daily activities. I'm referring to the way you have your whole life mapped out. One-year goals, two-year, five-year, ten-year—the whole nine yards. There isn't any room for spontaneity.'

'So you want unpredictability.'

Emily shook her head in derision. After the twists and turns she'd experienced lately, she'd embrace predictability with both hands.

'Don't make it sound like a dirty word,' Celine snapped. 'You plot your future and form strategies for everything. Unfortunately, life doesn't go according to a blueprint. Someday, when your contingency plans fail and you're facing the unexpected, you'll fall apart.'

This woman obviously didn't know him well, Emily thought peevishly. She'd never met a more calm physician when facing an emergency.

'Gee, thanks,' he said wryly. 'Your confidence in me is overwhelming.'

Celine touched his arm. 'I know how hard you've

worked for everything you've achieved in your life and I know you won't stop until you make every goal a reality. Your determination is part of what attracted me to you in the first place.

'Unfortunately, I feel like I'm just a pretty bauble you picked up along your way to the top. A trophy, so to speak.'

'You do yourself an injustice,' he said.

Her voice softened. 'You want someone who'll help you in your quest, but to be honest I don't want a husband who wants me because of my society background or because I'm a senator's daughter. I want someone who wants me because I'm Celine Meyeres.'

He didn't answer.

'Look at yourself, Will, and you'll know that marriage between us would be a huge mistake. You're not even upset.'

'You'd rather have me rant and rave?'

'Be honest, Will,' she said gently. 'You're too much in control to share more than just a tiny part of yourself. I, for one, want more. I'm selfish enough to want your whole heart and soul.

'Our marriage would be simply a means to an end,' she added. 'A contract to give you what you think you should have at this stage in your life.'

'If that's what you think—'

'If you're honest, you'll admit that you only proposed because the obstetrics group wanted to bring a stable, married man into their practice.'

'That's not true.'

'Oh, Will. I know you're fond of me and I'm fond of you, but fondness isn't love. We're both selling ourselves short if we're willing to be satisfied with such a mild emotion. Don't choose a wife based on your preconceived idea of what you want her to be. Act on your desires. You're thirty years old. Surely you've seen or met someone who's caught your eye.'

'I thought I had.' He sounded irritable.

Emily imagined Celine's smile of pleasure at his compliment.

'We had some good times,' Celine said. 'I won't forget those. I wish you well—you deserve it. Goodbye, Will.'

A cramp in Emily's fingers signalled her involuntary grip on the chair. Part of her wanted to rush out and chastise the woman for her mistaken judgment while another part urged caution. This wasn't her problem to solve. Besides, Dr Patton was the strong, silent type. He wouldn't appreciate her interference, however well meant it might be. She waited for several minutes, straining her ears for the slightest hint of their presence. Hearing none, she rose, slipped on her plain black pumps and started to make her way to the door.

A few steps later she stopped short. Dr Patton sat in a high-backed chair, his expression thoughtful and, oddly enough, also vulnerable.

'Ah, excuse me,' she said hesitantly under his surprised gaze. 'I…um…didn't mean to overhear, but I was in the corner when you and your…um…date arrived. I…um…tried not to listen.'

His skepticism was apparent.

'I'm sorry. I couldn't help it. The sound carried.' She paused. 'If it's any consolation, I know how you feel.'

He stared at her with the piercing scrutiny she was beginning to recognize so well. She'd felt it on more than one occasion at work. 'You do?'

'Yes. I broke up with my boyfriend a few weeks ago.'

'Under those circumstances, I'd say you can empathize more with Celine than with me.'

Her face warmed under his sarcasm. 'Actually, he precipitated it.'

His disbelief was obvious and she felt compelled to explain.

Emily sat in the chair next to his and crossed her legs, hearing the rasp of her nylons brushing together. Suddenly aware of the provocative picture she presented, with the slit in her skirt revealing a good portion of her thigh, she planted both feet on the floor.

'We'd still be together if he hadn't given me an ultimatum. I was supposed to choose between him and my family.'

'And your family won.'

'It wasn't a contest.' Taking umbrage at his comment, she rose stiffly. 'Never mind. It's a long story. You're probably not interested.'

'Actually, I'm still trying to figure out why you think you know what I'm going through.'

'My brother has had trouble with discipline since the middle school term started last fall,' she began. 'It's nothing terribly serious, but my uncle has taken a sudden interest in Kevin's upbringing.

'You see, Uncle Bert lives in Dallas and is trying to enter local politics with a ''get tough on juvenile crime'' platform. By straightening out Kevin's life, he'll build his image in the process. He believes Kevin needs a man's firm hand so he's threatening to take over Kevin's guardianship.'

She drew a deep breath. 'My lawyer thought Gran and I would have a better chance of defusing the situation if I got married. Don and I had been dating for nearly a year so he was the logical choice.'

'And he let you down.'

'Afraid so.' She hesitated, unsure if she'd offend him by asking more questions. But an idea had popped in her head and refused to go away. Nothing ventured, nothing gained, she thought, clenching her fists to hide her nervousness.

'*Did* you propose to Celine because Dr Moore offered you a partnership?' she asked.

'Do you always ask personal questions?' he fired back.

She stood her ground. 'Only if it's something that I need to know.'

'Are you sure it isn't simple curiosity? Sheer nosiness?'

'Not at all,' she assured him. 'It's important. I just can't explain why. At least, not yet.' If ever, she added silently.

He hesitated, as if debating whether or not to answer. 'Being married wasn't a condition of the partnership,' he said eventually, sounding tired. 'I'd known Celine for about a year and it just seemed like the timing was right.'

'I see.' So much for her hope that he *needed* a wife as much as she needed a husband.

His eyes grew wary. 'I answered your question so you can answer mine. Why did you ask?'

Emily shrugged, as if she considered their conversation insignificant. 'If Celine's comment was true, I thought we could help each other.'

He lifted one brow. 'Oh?'

To hide her desperation she said in a light-hearted tone, 'You wouldn't consider marrying me, would you?'

# CHAPTER TWO

EMILY would never forget the surprised look on Will's face as long as she lived. His eyes filled with panic, as if he didn't know how to extricate himself from the awkward moment.

Knowing she couldn't stand to hear his polite rejection, she took pity on him and rose. 'Hey,' she said carelessly, moving her head so her long crimped hair swung onto her bare back. 'You asked, and I answered. Forget I said anything. The question was inappropriate and I apologize for putting you on the spot.'

Intent on escape, she pivoted on one heel and headed for the door. Two steps later Will's grip on her elbow brought her to an abrupt halt.

'It's not that I don't think you'd make a wonderful wife,' he began, sounding apologetic. 'I'm sure you would. It's just that…' he didn't finish his sentence, plainly at a loss for words.

She squared her shoulders, not willing to show how much she hurt inside. 'I know,' she said, giving him a faint smile as she stared up at him. 'I heard Celine's comments. You want someone like her—a senator's daughter. Someone with society connections who can help you reach the top.'

Will grimaced. 'When you say it like that I sound shallow and heartless.'

'I'm only paraphrasing Celine. If you want someone who's strictly silk and satin, I say go for it.'

His gaze was searching. 'What will *you* do?' he asked.

23

She flashed him a bright smile. 'Call my uncle's bluff. In any case, don't worry. I can take care of the situation.' She'd disentangled her way out of problems before. With luck and clear thinking she could do so again.

Wanting to flee before she lost her cheerful composure, she said, 'If you'll excuse me, I have to meet my friends before they think I've been abducted. I promised someone a dance.'

She turned away, but not before she'd caught a glimpse of his bleak expression. Suddenly hesitant to desert him, compassion fathered her impulsive offer. 'Would you like to join us?'

He started to refuse, then nodded. 'Sure. Why not?'

'Great.'

Placing his hand on the small of her bare back, he escorted her to the door. She hadn't realized how tall he was—a full head above her.

Her dress suddenly seemed far too skimpy. His touch made the skin on her exposed shoulders and back tingle with feminine appreciation and anticipation. Instinctively, she knew Will wouldn't dance with the same puppy-like enthusiasm as Gaylon Powers.

Deep in her thoughts of dancing in Will's arms, she didn't notice Don standing on the threshold until she'd walked within arm's reach. He, too, wore evening attire, but his brown hair was ruffled, his bow tie hung askew and his top two shirt buttons were undone. The scent of alcohol clung to him and obviously contributed to his belligerent attitude.

'Well, now. Isn't this a cozy sight?' Don sneered, swaying where he stood.

'You're drunk.' Emily tried to glide past him, but he grabbed her wrist in a painful grip.

'If I was I wouldn't be able to see what you're doing,

and I can.' He faced Will. 'I suppose she's told you her sad story.'

'Let her go,' Will ordered. 'We're leaving.'

Don chortled. 'Leaving for where? Or, should I say, for what? It had better be your place because you can't go to hers. She can't offend her granny or the boy, you know.'

Emily gasped. She twisted her arm free and retreated a step. 'Go home, Don.'

He ignored her to address Will. 'Be warned, though. She's a tease. You won't get far with her unless you put a ring on her finger. Miss Prim-and-Proper wouldn't want to act like a *real* flesh-and-blood woman. No-siree. She acts like she's high on a pedestal, far above the rest of us mortals.'

Don shook his head. 'Like I told her, she's got to make it worth a man's while if she wants him to support her whole family. No one in their right mind would do it, and I...' he stabbed himself in the chest with one index finger '...am in my right mind.'

'Really?' Will said, his voice cool. 'I wonder.'

Don motioned to Emily. 'Come here, doll. I'm more than willing to kiss and make up.'

He swayed for an instant before he lunged forward, his intent to grab Emily clear. However, instead of gripping her arm, his fingers curled around the edge of her bodice. A split second later the hook holding the strap around her neck gave way. The front of her dress sagged.

Catching the scrap of fabric before total humiliation encompassed her, Emily wished the floor would open up before she died of embarrassment. She glanced at Will and was surprised to see his jaw clenched.

'Step aside, Emily,' Will ordered.

Don tapdanced like a boxer in the ring. 'Mr Smooth

Moves is gonna fight me for your honor, Emily.' He leaned closer to Will. 'Let me know if it helps you score with her. I'll try it myself.'

Before Emily could move, Will's fist smashed into Don's mouth with enough force to upset his balance and send him sailing across the floor.

Don rose on one elbow, touched his upper lip and stared at the blood on his fingertips. 'I'm bleeding,' he said in surprise. He moved his jaw. 'You knocked a tooth loose.'

'Count yourself lucky it was only one,' Will ground out, removing his coat.

'You won't get away with this,' Don warned.

Emily stood frozen as Will flung his jacket over her shoulders. As if she were a child, he helped her slide her arms into the sleeves while protecting her modesty at the same time. His heat and scent surrounded her, making her realize how cold she was both physically and emotionally. She shivered.

'Let's go,' he said, holding her free hand to help her step over Don's sprawled form.

'I'm so sorry,' she began. An urge to weep swept over her.

'Don't be. He had it coming. Besides, it wasn't your fault. It's a shame he tripped over the loose seam in the carpeting, isn't it?'

'You'll live to regret this,' Don called out, but Will ignored him. Instead, he ushered Emily past as if they were on a leisurely stroll...

'Afterwards,' Emily said, remembering how she'd fussed over his bruised knuckles, 'Will sent someone to tell you that I was leaving.'

'But he obviously didn't take you right home,' Molly said.

'No. By the time one of the doormen brought his car around I was shaking like a leaf. Will took me to his place for a cup of coffee so I could pull myself together and fix my dress. I couldn't risk Gran or Kevin seeing me like that.'

'But you didn't stop with a cup of coffee.'

Emily gave a faint smile. 'No. And don't ask for any specifics because I won't give you any.' Those memories were too private to share—memories best reviewed on those occasions when she was alone.

'And now you're pregnant.'

'Yes.'

'Honestly, Em. Trouble follows you like a shadow.'

'Tell me about it,' Emily said ruefully. 'I know what you're dying to ask, and the answer is yes. I intend to keep this baby.'

'Are you going to tell Will?'

Emily sighed. 'Yes.'

'Before or after you break the news to your grandmother?'

'Before. He's the father—he should hear it before anyone else.' She grinned. 'Other than you, of course.'

'Good.' Molly sounded satisfied. 'That will save me from doing it.'

Emily stared at her friend in horror. 'You can't tell him.'

'Wanna bet? The least he can do is propose.'

She shook her head. 'I'll refuse.'

'Have you gone nuts? You asked him to marry you when you hardly knew him and now that you do—in the biblical sense—you won't even go to dinner. You have a much better reason for tying the knot now.'

Emily hesitated before she lifted her chin in defiance. 'He wants a wife with bluer blood and softer hands than mine.'

'Tough. I'm not going to let you assume all of the responsibility when he was a willing party to the whole thing. Besides, you're not the only one affected. You also have Kevin and your grandmother to consider.'

Emily winced at the prospect of telling her family about her predicament. She'd always preached responsibility to her brother and now he'd have proof of how her actions didn't line up with her words. She'd simply make it a lesson in reverse—it would be a perfect example of how one impetuous act brought long-lasting repercussions.

'I know, but we'll manage.'

'What about your uncle?'

'After he visits this weekend and sees how well Kevin is doing he'll forget about us again. Though, to be on the safe side, I'm not going to tell Gran or Kevin until after we see him,' Emily decided. 'In any case, you're jumping ahead of yourself. I don't expect Will to pop the big question.'

'He certainly can't if you refuse to be around him for more than a few minutes at a time. If he knows what's good for him, he'd better propose.'

'That's the whole point, Molly. I don't want him feeling obligated. Now, if you don't mind, can we drop the subject? I want to be home by six.'

Molly frowned, but she obeyed. While they walked for the next hour their conversation touched on every subject imaginable, except for the one preying on Emily's mind—how to tell Will.

When she got home she feared her family would notice her preoccupation, but they were too busy with their own agendas to see that she wasn't as attentive as usual. Gran rushed through supper to hurry to her garden club meeting while Kevin grudgingly researched Dwight D. Eisenhower for his Social Studies assignment.

By the time Emily reported for duty next morning, she still hadn't thought of a good way to approach Will on the subject of his impending fatherhood.

'Are you going to tell him today?' Molly asked at their mid-morning breather.

'I don't know exactly what I'm going to say, but I'll think of something when the time comes.'

'Well, think fast. Regina Johnson is on her way in and he's delivering her. JoAnn wants you to assist.'

The prospect of working with Will, while knowing his child resided within her, brought panic. Although she'd assisted him many times since their evening together, she'd always treated him with the respect and deference due to him and he'd reciprocated. Other than his persistent invitations to dinner, neither had mentioned their lapse—not even when they were alone.

Today that would change.

'Why me?' she asked, silently bemoaning her fate.

'Luck, I suppose.' Molly winked.

'But she's Dr Hudson's patient,' Emily recalled from the woman's previous history. The forty-two-year-old first-time mother had been admitted on two previous occasions with premature labor. Magnesium sulfate had stopped her contractions and allowed her to continue her pregnancy.

'He's out of town for a family emergency,' Molly said. 'Dr Patton is covering for him until next week. As soon as I'm finished with Mrs Larkin I'll be in to help. It shouldn't be much longer.'

'Thanks.' Emily strode into the birthing room and

quickly transformed its parlor-like appearance to a delivery suite.

A nurse's aide brought Regina in a wheelchair while her husband, Tom, kept pace at her side. 'This could be the real thing,' Emily remarked as she helped the woman into the birthing bed.

Regina clutched her huge stomach and pressed her lips into a hard line as another contraction seized her. 'Are you sure? I still have three weeks to go.'

'I suspect you're close enough,' Emily said. 'We stopped your labor before to give your baby enough time to develop. He's probably mature enough now to survive on his own.'

She pointed to a neat stack of protective clothing. 'If you need help putting anything on, let me know,' she told Tom. 'Don't forget, ties go at the back.'

While he donned a gown, hat and bootees, Regina's gasp caught Emily's attention. She turned to find the bedding drenched.

'Oh, my,' Regina exclaimed, her skin turning an embarrassed shade of pink. 'What a mess.'

'Perfectly normal,' Emily said, working to change the sheets. 'Since your water's broken, you'll definitely be having the baby now.'

'I wish Dr Hudson were here,' Regina moaned. 'I don't want to do this without him.'

Seeing the stubborn set to Mrs Johnson's chin, Emily spoke with conviction. 'Dr Patton is one of our best obstetricians. Don't worry about a thing.'

'I still want Dr Hudson,' Regina whined. 'Nobody's as good as he is.' She drew a deep breath and began to huff as another pain lanced through her midsection.

Emily turned to reach for a pair of gloves, but as she did so she saw Will standing near the foot of the bed.

'You're here.'

His mouth twitched as if he thought her inane comment humorous. 'In the flesh.' Skirting her, he approached Regina's side. 'I know it's disappointing to have someone other than your regular physician deliver your baby, but I'll do my best. You have my word.'

'Thanks,' Tom murmured, apparently satisfied by Dr Patton's little speech.

Regina lay against the pillows and managed a faint smile. 'I'm holding you to your promise,' she said pertly.

Will didn't seem insulted by her comment. 'Fair enough. Now, I'll check to see how far your cervix is dilated. Once your water breaks I'll attach an internal monitor to the baby's scalp to see how he's doing.'

'It broke a few minutes ago,' Emily said as she inserted an intravenous fluid line in Regina's forearm.

'Well, then,' Will said, 'time to go to work.'

Regina moaned and her husband's eyes appeared panic-stricken above his mask. A lock of brown hair hung out from underneath his surgical cap. 'She doesn't look so good.'

'Regina's doing fine,' Will assured him. 'I've reviewed her records and spoken with Dr Hudson at length. She should sail through this without a problem, but if I see any signs of distress we'll do a C-section.'

Tom nodded, plainly relieved to know of the alternative plan. Emily handed Will a pair of large latex gloves and, after pulling them on, he quickly examined his patient.

'He's in position,' he told the bystanders as he affixed the lead to the baby's scalp. 'You'll be holding your baby by lunchtime.'

Emily studied the monitor. The peaks indicating the

heart rate flowed across the screen in a normal, steady rhythm.

Will laid a hand on Regina's abdomen during her next contraction. As soon as it had ended he said, 'Let's give her some oxytocin.'

'No drugs,' Regina gasped.

'It isn't a painkiller,' Will soothed, motioning for Emily to follow his instructions. 'The medication will strengthen your contractions and won't bother the baby a bit. The sooner he arrives, the better for both of you.'

'OK.' Regina wiped her forehead with the back of her hand. Emily administered the oxytocin, then handed Tom a damp washcloth to cool down Regina's face.

Her contractions grew stronger. After several minutes of waiting, Will positioned himself at the foot of the bed. 'Now we're in business,' he said. 'Baby's crowning. Hang in there, Regina.'

Emily had been feeling nauseous since she'd woken up that morning, but what had previously been an uncomfortable sensation in her stomach suddenly rolled to a full boil. This is a fine time to develop morning sickness, she thought.

Perspiration began to pour off her forehead and heat emanated from her entire body. Taking deep breaths to bring her riotous stomach under control, she paced as she swiped at the sweat with one sleeve.

Will turned his head to study her. His eyebrows were raised above his mask in silent query. Caught, she halted in her tracks. Darn! He was certain to ask questions.

He turned his attention back onto his patient. 'Push, Regina. Come on now, *push*.'

Emily scanned the neonatal equipment standing at the ready and compared it to her mental checklist of requirements. Only Molly was missing. Wondering why her supervisor hadn't sent someone to help, she was ready to reach for the call button when Molly rushed in.

'Sorry I'm late,' the redhead said under her breath. 'This place has been like Grand Central Station.'

Emily sent Molly a grateful glance before she swallowed hard to fight the growing knot in her stomach.

'You're just in time,' Will answered, guiding the baby's head into the waiting world. Immediately he suctioned the secretions from its mouth and nose, before delivering the tiny shoulders and then the rest of the body.

'A boy,' he announced, placing the mewling infant in the blanket Emily held in her arms. 'He looks healthy, too.'

Emily ignored her stomach as best she could while she carried the Johnson baby to the radiant warmer. As she walked those few steps she rubbed his back to stimulate his breathing. Within seconds his lusty cries of outrage filled the room and she crooned softly until he settled down to stare at this strange person who'd entered his world.

'Do you have a name picked out?' she asked, fighting her queasiness. Keeping the baby under the heat source, she replaced his wet blanket with a dry, warmed one.

'David Alan,' Tom said proudly.

While Will carefully delivered the placenta and checked it for completeness, Emily performed a one-minute-after-delivery Apgar score based on little David's heart rate, respirations, reflexes, tone and color.

'He's a nine,' she reported, glad to see the score was high on a scale of ten.

She prepared an identification band and attached it to his small ankle, before repeating the Apgar score. Next she trimmed the cord and applied erythromycin eye ointment to both of the baby's eyes. Then she weighed and measured David, rewrapped him in another fresh blanket and passed him to his father. The injections of vitamin K and hepatitis B vaccine could wait until after he'd met his parents face to face.

'Anyone else waiting in line?' Will asked, stripping off his soiled gloves to wash his hands.

Molly shook her head. 'Not unless we've admitted someone in the last few minutes.'

Experiencing another sudden wave of nausea, Emily wanted to shout for joy. She couldn't wait to leave the room. Rivulets of perspiration ran down her cheeks and her hands shook.

'OK,' he acknowledged. While he gave young David a cursory examination Molly moved in closer to Emily.

'Are you OK?' she whispered.

'Sort of.' Emily gritted her teeth, determined not to lose control until she'd taken care of her patient. Concentrating on her tasks seemed to help, at least until the time came for the samples for Pathology to be labeled and readied for transport.

The sight of the blood and tissue sent her stomach into a roller-coaster loop. Determined to hide her distress, Emily dashed into the hallway and into the small nurses' restroom directly off the lounge, tugging off her mask and clamping her mouth closed along the way.

She made it just in time.

Emily retched until her stomach emptied. Kneeling in front of the commode, she rested her elbows on the cold porcelain rim and propped her head in her hands. She felt too miserable to check out who was responsible for the sound of running water.

Someone lifted her thick braid and placed a cool, wet

washcloth against her neck, before thrusting a second one in her right hand.

'Thanks, Molly,' she murmured.

'You're welcome,' Will answered.

Startled, Emily's elbow slipped and she banged her funny bone on the curved rim. Pain shot up her arm and she gasped.

He handed her a Dixie cup of cool tap water. 'If you're finished, why don't we go somewhere where you won't hurt yourself?'

'I'm fine right here.'

'Yes, but I'm not.' He leaned against the sink and placed one hand on the opposite wall. 'This room isn't designed for double occupancy.'

The door swung open, striking Will's polished wing-tips. He shifted his feet as he glowered at the intruder.

Molly peered inside. 'Em? Are you OK?'

'She's fine,' Will answered.

'I can speak for myself,' Emily grumbled.

Will crossed his arms. 'Go ahead.'

'I'm fine,' she told Molly.

Molly didn't appear convinced. Lines of worry creased her freckled face and her green eyes showed concern as her gaze traveled back and forth between Will and Emily.

'Why don't you sit in the lounge for a while?' Molly suggested. 'You'd be more comfortable.'

'My thoughts exactly,' Will said. 'This room isn't big enough for one person, let alone three.' He shot Molly a pointed glance, as if suggesting she left.

'Can I get you something?' Molly asked. 'A soda?'

'Don't you have patients to care for?' Will asked her in no uncertain terms.

Molly visibly bristled. 'Yes, but—'

'Then don't let us keep you,' he said.

'Before I go I intend to say my piece.' Molly poked a finger in his solar plexus. 'You'd better…'

Sensing a tense moment ahead, Emily flushed the toilet, hoping to drown out the ultimatum she suspected Molly was trying to deliver. Molly's comments were bound to pique his interest if not confirm his suspicions.

While Molly stormed away, Will grabbed Emily's elbow to help her on her feet. Without a word he guided her into the lounge and toward a vinyl-covered sofa.

Emily sank into its depths, still clutching the Dixie cup as if her life depended on it. Out of the corner of her eye she saw him sit at the other end, close enough for her to reach out and touch if she so chose.

For a few seconds she sat in silence, testing the opening phrases she'd rehearsed during the night. Unfortunately, none of them sounded right.

His voice shattered the stillness and, unprepared, she jumped.

'You have something to tell me, don't you, Emily?'

# CHAPTER THREE

EMILY tried to gauge Will's mood.

His face remained impassive and his dark eyes held a silent query. The slight lift to one of his eyebrows indicated expectancy.

The scene reminded her of a child being brought to task by a parent who knew the truth and was simply waiting for an admission of guilt.

She swallowed hard.

Will leaned closer. 'Why don't we try this? I'll ask the questions and you can answer yes or no.' At her feeble nod he began.

'Are you pregnant?'

Her shoulders slumped as she stared at her fingernails for a long minute. Then she met his hot, piercing gaze. 'Yes.'

He nodded once, his countenance still impassive. 'Were you going to tell me?'

'Yes.'

'When?'

'Today.'

'How long have you known?'

'Since yesterday.'

'And yet you turned down my dinner invitation?' He sounded incredulous. 'It would have been the perfect opportunity—'

'It would have,' she agreed, 'except I didn't find out until I saw Dr Ferguson after my shift ended. I needed time to think.'

'And what did you think about?' A sudden tension seemed to grip him.

She drew a deep breath, reading between the lines to his underlying question. 'I intend to welcome this baby into my home. I'm sure my family will do the same.'

Satisfaction flickered in his eyes.

'You may not care for my decision so—'

'Actually, I'm very happy with it.'

She stared at him in surprise. 'You are?'

'We *are* talking about my son or daughter,' he said, as if reminding her.

'Then you're not afraid the baby isn't yours?' At three o'clock this morning the thought had occurred to her. Like a recurrent nightmare, it wouldn't go away.

His mouth twisted into a wry grin. 'I recall that night well, including every little *physical* detail. I'm the father—no doubt about it.'

She blushed at his subtle reminder of how he'd been the first man she'd slept with. 'Even so, we haven't been together for over eight weeks…'

He shook his head. 'You haven't been out with anyone in all that time.'

'How do you know?' she demanded.

'I made it my business to know.'

Her jaw slackened. 'You spied on me?'

He shrugged. 'I asked a few discreet questions.'

Irritated, Emily rose and began to pace. 'A few discreet questions?' she parroted. 'And what did you discover?'

He began to tick off the points on his fingers. 'You're single. You live with your grandmother and brother. After your parents' death nine years ago, when you were eighteen, you and your maternal grandmother were awarded custody of three-year-old Kevin. You worked your way through college and nurses' training and worked in Dallas for a while before you came to Crossbow two years ago. A year later you transferred to the birthing center when a position became vacant.'

She held her hands on her hips. 'A few discreet questions, my eye. Sounds like you have a more complete dossier than the FBI.'

'FBI? Is there something else you're not telling me?' he asked, a smile teasing the corners of his mouth. 'Perhaps you're a wanted woman in three states?'

'Don't laugh,' she said crossly. 'You know what I mean. By the way, you don't seem as surprised as I'd thought you'd be.'

'Would you rather I lost my temper and threw things?' he asked mildly.

His comment reminded her of something he'd told Celine. Perhaps the woman had known him better than Emily thought she had. She narrowed her eyes. 'Have you been talking to Dr Ferguson?'

'Have you?' he countered.

'Of course I spoke with him,' she snapped. 'He wanted you to handle his referral. I had to explain why his suggestion was impossible.'

Will steepled his fingers as he appeared to consider her comments. 'I haven't talked to Emmett lately, at least not about you. To answer your question,' he said, changing the subject, 'I'd noticed you seemed tired and less like your vivacious self. I guessed at the reason why.'

'How long ago?'

He lifted one shoulder in a shrug. 'A few weeks.'

An idea clicked into place. 'Is that why you suddenly started inviting me out?'

'More or less.'

'If you wanted to know if I was pregnant, why didn't you just ask?'

He raised one eyebrow. 'So everyone could hear?'

Aware of her lack of co-operation when he *had* tried to talk to her, she was certain her skin had turned a bright hue. Even so, she was relieved by his restraint. He could have easily forced the issue on several occasions.

'In any case, I've had more time to adjust to the idea of parenthood than you have,' he said.

'That's nice because the news caught me totally by surprise. I thought we'd—you'd—been careful.'

'Accidents happen,' he said, his tone curt. 'The only foolproof method is abstinence.'

'Well, now that you know,' she said brightly, 'don't worry about a thing. I plan on sticking to our original bargain. I won't make any demands.'

He muttered an expletive that took her by surprise, although she recovered rapidly.

'Since we've settled everything, I have to get back to work now.' She pivoted and made for the door, but he reached it before she did and blocked the exit.

'Nothing is settled,' he ground out. 'Sit.'

'Hold on,' she said, her irritation over his high-handed tactics growing by leaps and bounds. 'If I stay any longer I'll have to make it up over the noon hour.'

'You aren't skipping lunch,' he stated, eyeing her slender frame. 'You can't afford to skip any meals.'

'But—'

'But nothing. I'll talk to your supervisor and explain the circumstances.'

'No!'

'She's going to find out anyway,' he said. 'Your condition will be obvious sooner than you think.'

Emily found both his perception uncanny and his practicality aggravating. 'Please don't say anything to anyone, at least not for a few weeks. I'll meet you tonight and explain. Name the place.'

'And risk you not showing up at the appointed time?' He shook his head. 'You've done things your way for the past few weeks by pretending we were strangers. No more.'

'That was the arrangement,' she reminded him, hating the note of desperation in her voice. 'We agreed to one night with no strings attached.'

He crossed his arms and stood with his feet apart. 'Now we *have* strings, so the original deal is off. It's time for a new bargain.'

She narrowed her eyes in suspicion. 'It is?'

'Yes, and we're going to iron one out as soon as possible.'

'Not now. I'm on duty.'

'Then clock out.'

'Yeah, right,' she scoffed, tossing her head. 'Unlike you, I need every cent of my paycheck.'

'Child support is something else we need to discuss.'

'We don't have to decide that *now,* do we?' She glanced at her watch and did a mental calculation of her remaining time. 'I can give you another fifteen minutes. Whatever hasn't been hashed out in that length of time has to wait until this evening.'

'Agreed. Now, sit.' He softened his tone. 'Please.'

Emily sat. This time, however, Will remained standing.

'The way I see it,' he began, 'we only have one logical choice.'

She tensed. 'Which is?'

'To get married. I'll organize a license and a justice of the peace for next weekend.'

She crossed her arms. 'I won't accept.'

He didn't seem surprised by her refusal, only curious. 'Why not?'

'Because I know the qualities you want in a wife. I don't have a single one. In case you've forgotten, you want someone like Celine, not a working girl.' Her weakness for beautiful underwear was the closest she came to the silk-and-satin type of woman he favored.

'You're the only one carrying my baby,' he pointed out. 'To me that's a very important element in your favor.'

She shook her head. 'A relationship would never work. We hardly know each other.'

'We got along well at Christmastime.'

'One night doesn't make a marriage,' she snapped. 'Besides, we were both…hurting.'

He shot her a glare. 'OK, let's consider the alternative—we remain single.'

'Yes, let's.'

'Considering the situation from your angle,' he said, 'being an unwed mother doesn't carry the stigma it once did. However, people will question your wisdom. You're twenty-seven—old enough to avoid the impetuous and ignorant mistakes of a sixteen-year-old.

'I'm sure you could weather any gossip, but you're facing a custody battle. Don't you think your uncle will use this as an example of how you're unfit to give proper guidance to Kevin?'

Emily bit her lip. Her uncle *would* use her condition to his advantage. He hadn't become the largest sporting goods distributer in Texas by being Mr Nice Guy. He made a career of ferreting out his competitors' weak spots. She'd simply have to make sure that he didn't find hers.

'It might,' she admitted. '*If* he knew. We're getting together next weekend to re-evaluate our options, and as long as Kevin's behaviour is above reproach my pregnancy won't be an issue. However, I'm not foolish enough to give him any extra ammunition. If you don't say anything, no one will know.'

'Not until your pregnancy becomes obvious. What will you do then?'

'As I said, my uncle is only concerned about his image. As long as Kevin's doing well in school, nothing else will matter.'

Will raised one eyebrow in apparent disbelief.

'Then consider this from my angle,' he said after a short pause. 'My responsibilities to this community include finding ways to improve the quality of the birthing center. If my personal life is suspect, people will question my professional life, which in turn will reflect on the hospital. My future could be at stake.'

'*Could* is the operative word,' Emily said. 'I'm not jumping into marriage on the off chance that the scenarios you described *might* happen.'

He started to speak, but she forestalled him. 'You've given several persuasive arguments, but I don't think we should rush into damage control. Chances are good there won't be any harm done.'

He rubbed the back of his neck in obvious exasperation. 'Ever heard of prevention? Crisis management isn't the answer. As for luck, a person makes his own— whether it's good or bad.'

'But why look for problems when none may exist?'

'The field of medicine is all about looking for problems before they present themselves,' he reminded her.

She softened her tone. 'I sympathize with your concerns and your worries over your reputation, but I honestly believe both of us are strong enough to survive any gossip. After all, don't most people consider an unwanted pregnancy as the woman's fault?'

'You're making a mistake.'

'Perhaps. As for your past coming back to haunt you, this is Crossbow, not Denton.'

'We're sixty miles away. News travels and rumors make the rounds faster than a cold virus.'

Emily rubbed her eyes, wishing she could wave her hand and make all her troubles disappear. 'I know you've spent a lot of time thinking of all the angles. However, I need one question answered. Would you be proposing if I *wasn't* pregnant?'

'Under normal circumstances a courtship comes first,' he said, as if informing her of how the procedure worked. 'We haven't had one. Yet.'

It wasn't likely either. Pregnant or not, she wasn't the type of woman he wanted.

'So although I admit I wouldn't be proposing I'm sure I'd be trying to get to know you better.'

She met his gaze, assessing his sincerity. He seemed earnest, but she found his statement hard to believe.

'I appreciate you wanting to do the so-called "right" thing,' she began. 'A few weeks ago I'd have jumped at the opportunity because I thought marriage was the answer I needed. Since then I've learned differently.'

'Our child needs us.'

'I don't deny it. I won't ban you from his or her life.'

He paused. 'As you said, I've spent a lot of time mulling this over and weighing our options. The solution I've suggested is the most beneficial to everyone.'

'I disagree. Once you've salvaged your reputation

you'll realize that you're saddled with a wife who doesn't meet your standards.'

'What if we agreed to a temporary marriage?' he asked.

Her temples throbbed as the stress of the past twenty-four hours manifested itself. Her brain felt overloaded, first by Dr Ferguson's news and now by Will's high-pressure tactics.

Emily held up her hands in surrender. 'I really can't deal with all this right now. I have to get back to work.' Escape was more like it. She needed time to pull her thoughts together.

As she reached for the doorknob he grabbed her wrist. 'At least think about my proposal.'

She rubbed her forehead, too tired by his onslaught to argue. 'OK, but don't hold your breath waiting for me to agree.'

His face remained solemn. 'I won't.'

Will returned to his office, utterly frustrated. How could Emily reject his offer? He'd weighed the alternatives and had arrived at what he considered the best solution.

Emily might prefer to wait until a problem surfaced, but he didn't. He'd much rather form a strategy to avoid them altogether, which was what he'd done. A reasonable woman would have jumped at the chance to avoid gossip and to pass some of the responsibility onto the father.

Apparently, Emily Chandler wasn't a reasonable woman. It was a surprising revelation, considering how calm and efficient she was at the hospital. To be honest, he'd expected her to ask *him* for assistance. Supporting her family on a nurse's salary wasn't easy. It would be more difficult with the added expense of an infant.

Regardless, all wasn't lost. He had the few weeks before her condition became obvious to persuade her to accept his suggestion.

With that decided, he focused his attention on the steady stream of patients. At four-thirty he performed his last scheduled exam for the day.

'Our suspicions were correct,' he told Lynnette Fairchild, who'd exchanged her paper gown for her street clothes. 'Your pregnancy test is positive.'

The twenty-four-year-old brunette grinned. 'That's wonderful.'

Unbidden, he pictured Emily hearing similar news. He doubted if she'd shown the same level of excitement as Mrs Fairchild.

'I'm sending you to the lab for some basic prenatal tests,' he said. 'Do you know your blood type or your husband's, by any chance?'

'No. Sorry.'

'Well, we'll find out soon enough.'

'Does it matter?' Lynnette asked, her smile dimming.

'If you're Rh-negative and your husband is Rh-positive, you may be a candidate for Rh-immune globulin after the baby's born to protect future children. It's nothing to worry about, just something to deal with as a precautionary measure.' He made a mental note to check on Emily's status since he was A-positive.

'Oh.' She appeared relieved.

'When you come back next month for a check-up we'll arrange for several blood tests to screen for genetic abnormalities. Some physicians call it a multiple marker screen or an AFP-3. The three procedures will give us an idea if there are any neural-tube or ventral-wall defects, as well as trisomy—like Down's syndrome.'

'And if something's wrong?' she asked, her eyes showing concern.

'There are other, more definitive procedures we can do, like an amniocentesis or chorionic villus sampling, but you're young and healthy so the chances are good you won't need those tests at all.'

Lynnette clutched her small handbag. 'I did a lot of stupid things when I was a teenager. I wasn't what you'd call a ''good'' girl. I haven't had any problems but—'

'We routinely run checks for chlamydia, gonorrhea and other sexually transmitted diseases,' he said, trying to allay her fears. 'If we detect anything infectious we'll treat it.'

'My last pap smear wasn't good,' she said. 'Will my pregnancy make a difference?'

Her results from three months ago had revealed mild dysplasia, but the classification didn't warrant any intervention other than a repeat pap.

'Hormones can affect the cell structure,' he said. 'If the cervical cells appear cancerous on this smear we'll evaluate your choices.' He mentally reviewed her options, but elected not to overwhelm her on her first visit. 'Any more questions?'

She shook her head and he continued, 'If you want to celebrate tonight, remember—no smoking, no drinking, no drugs.'

'I've been trying to stop smoking,' Lynnette admitted. 'I'm down to two cigarettes a day—one in the morning and one at night.'

'Very good. Smokers are known to have low-birth-weight babies who also have a tendency toward respiratory infections.'

'I've heard,' Lynnette said wryly. 'Which is why I'm working to give up my habit.'

'Don't forget to take a vitamin supplement every day and be sure it contains extra folic acid. If in doubt ask the pharmacist. Eat healthily and exercise, but don't overdo it.'

'OK.'

'I'll see you in a month. Before you leave, my nurse will give you some leaflets to study. If you have any questions or start bleeding or cramping, call me immediately.'

'I will.'

He stepped outside and signaled his nurse, Tina Allen. 'Give her the usual bag of goodies,' he said, referring to the packet containing product and general information in addition to samples of vitamins and acetaminophen. 'Is Gene still here?'

Tina, a slim woman in her early fifties, nodded. 'He's with a patient right now. I can let you know when he's available.'

'Thanks.' Will turned toward his office and sank into the comfortable executive chair behind his new desk. He reached in the top drawer for a handful of steel-tipped darts. Facing the well-used board on the opposite wall, he let the first one fly while he wished away his craving for peanuts since the small bowl on his desk was empty.

When all six darts graced the various rings of the board he rose, yanked them out and returned to his desk to repeat the process.

The day had been unusual, to say the least. He didn't know how he felt about having his suspicions regarding Emily confirmed. Part of him took pleasure in his accurate assessment, while another part was awed at the prospect of being a father.

He heaved another dart. Emily had tried so hard to avoid him these past few weeks. Initially, he'd fought the desire he'd felt whenever he'd been in her presence because he didn't like the way his response had become automatic. To compensate, he'd often been more curt with her than necessary.

However, his attitude had changed one morning three weeks ago when he'd noticed that the circles under her eyes had darkened and her step hadn't had its usual bounce. He'd found himself watching her, puzzled by the loss of her usual sparkle. Suddenly, the light had dawned.

Immediately, he'd changed tactics—asking her to dinner, being more personable. If she'd had something to tell him—and he'd thought she might—he'd wanted her to feel as if he was approachable.

The picture of her draped over the commode was a complete reversal of his memory concerning the Christmas party. He'd carry the vision of her on that night for a long time, if not for ever.

That had been the only time he'd seen her light brown hair unrestrained. It had hung in long, crimped waves against her bare shoulders and back, like a cape over her dark green halter dress. At work she wore her hair tied at her nape or in a basic braid.

Her shapeless uniform didn't do her justice either. He recalled how her Christmas dress had fitted her slim form like a surgeon's glove. He'd never dreamed how provocative a slit in a woman's skirt could be. Those glimpses of her shapely leg had raised his blood pressure several points.

As the night had worn on he'd seen, touched and tasted much more than he'd expected. Unbidden, his thoughts turned toward the past…

Emily sat at the kitchen table, wearing his maroon terry-cloth bathrobe. Her dark green dress lay in her lap as she stitched the torn strap together with the black thread he'd found in a pocket-sized sewing kit. The cup of coffee he'd prepared stood in front of her, sending a white whirl of steam upward.

He sipped from his mug, lost in his thoughts. Celine's refusal hadn't come as a complete surprise, but even so he felt a keen sense of disappointment. Her character assessment had been somewhat correct, but making plans and taking control of his life had brought him this far. He didn't intend to change now.

Glancing at Emily, he saw her hands were now still.

'I'm not a tease,' she said without preamble.

'I didn't think you were.'

'I don't put myself on a pedestal.'

'You don't have to explain yourself to me,' he said. 'Your ex-boyfriend was drunk. I usually don't believe a person's ramblings when he's under the influence.'

'But I want to explain,' she protested. 'I *need* to.'

He fell silent, understanding her feelings.

'I'm not a prude,' she said, slinging her hair over one shoulder. 'I'm very discriminating.'

Will sipped his coffee. 'A smart move in this day and age.'

'That's what I think too.' A tear glimmered in her eye. 'Then why do I feel so bad?'

'It hurts when someone you thought you loved turns on you.'

She licked her lips. 'Is that how you feel? After Celine?'

He held the mug to his mouth as he took stock of his feelings. 'Yeah. I guess.' He did love her, although it hadn't been in the heart-wrenching, all-consuming way she'd wanted. Logic, not emotions, ruled his life.

Obviously Celine wanted the opposite and was smart enough to know she couldn't change the habits of a lifetime.

'I have this strange urgency to prove Don wrong. Is that crazy?'

The same idea had crossed his mind. He'd like to disprove Celine's harsh character assessment. He admitted having a tendency toward planning and deliberation, but to accuse him of lacking any spontaneity at all was totally inaccurate.

Decking this Don fellow had been a case in point. He wished Celine could have seen the entire episode.

He shrugged. 'Sounds reasonable to me.'

Emily glanced at the dress on her lap, then placed the wad of fabric on the table. She rose.

Her voice was whisper soft. 'Will you help me?'

Will froze, unable to believe her invitation. 'Help you what?' he asked, wary.

'Prove that I *am* a flesh-and-blood woman. For the last ten years I've made every major decision in terms of how it would affect my family. Now I want to make one just for me.'

She loosened the belt. The fabric parted, revealing slight curves and skin that had been kissed by the sun in months past. 'Please?'

He swallowed hard. Logic dictated his refusal, but Celine's accusations echoed through his mind.

*Structured. Controlled. Predictable.*

His resolve wavered.

Emily came closer until she stood only inches away. Electricity seemed to sizzle between them. 'I want a night to remember.'

'You don't have to do this,' he reminded her.

Her dark brown eyes bored into his. 'Yes, I do. All

I'm asking for is one night, no strings. Tomorrow we'll go back to a professional relationship and forget this ever happened.'

Seeing her stand in front of him, soft and sweet, he doubted if he'd ever forget.

His throat felt dry. 'Why me?'

'Because I feel safe with you.'

Need swept through him like a tidal wave beyond control. He reached out and touched her cheek. Her soft skin drew him like a puppet at the hands of a master. He rose, inhaled her sweet scent, then bent his head to taste the coffee on her lips.

'You're sure?' he muttered, realizing his need for comfort was every bit as great as hers. Logically, he should step back and take her home, but he'd never claimed to be a saint.

She sighed and melted against him. The belt loosened completely as she flung her arms around his neck. 'More than ever...'

Will shifted position in his chair, hearing the vinyl creak under his weight. Just thinking about that evening made his body turn traitor. Even after six weeks his self-control bordered on non-existent where Emily was concerned.

He'd originally thought he could relegate that evening to the past, chalking it up to a pleasant interlude. Unfortunately, it hadn't turned out the way he'd expected. He wanted her now as much as he had after he'd pressed her luscious body against his.

Having been ruled by his passions and desires as a child, he hadn't wanted to give in to impetuous impulses again. He'd organized his life and planned his future.

Now everything had turned upside down. The straight path he'd charted had developed a huge curve.

He didn't intend to bury his head in the sand and ignore potential trouble. 'Be prepared' was his motto and he'd reaped the benefit enough times to make it worth his while.

Regardless, he didn't intend to shirk his obligations. The family he'd intended had simply come much sooner than he'd anticipated. His plan to be firmly established in his career before a child arrived had gone awry but, as Celine had so aptly reminded him, life didn't always run according to blueprint.

To be honest, the thought of Emily having more of his babies wasn't distressing at all. He also felt a measure of pride at being the man she'd chosen to be her first. The idea of Emily having a relationship with another man, of someone else raising his child, was simply inconceivable.

Idly he saw the darts he hadn't remembered throwing clustered around the bull's-eye. Gradually, a new plan of attack formed in his mind and he smiled. Emily Chandler's days of running from him were over.

# CHAPTER FOUR

EMILY answered the knock at the door and instant panic rose in her chest. 'What are you doing here?' she asked in a stage whisper.

Will stood on the small step, his collar turned up against the brisk evening air. 'Isn't it obvious? You said we'd meet tonight and talk.'

'I didn't mean here at my house.'

He lifted one shoulder in a casual shrug. 'You left before we could arrange a time and place. I took matters into my own hands.'

'Fine,' she said hurriedly, wanting to end this conversation as quickly as possible. 'How about the Pizza Hut? Seven-thirty?' An hour and a half should be enough time to erase the traces of her nap, tie back her untidy mass of hair and hide the circles under her eyes.

'Who's at the door, dear?'

Emily heard her grandmother's quavery voice coming from the kitchen. 'It's for me, Gran.'

Helen Oakland appeared in the hallway, holding a long-handled wooden spoon. She smiled and her eyes twinkled at the sight of their male visitor. 'Invite him in, Em. Don't keep him out on the porch.'

The cool breeze coming through the open door seeped through Emily's sweatshirt and she grudgingly stepped aside to allow him entrance. 'Say hello, then leave,' she muttered.

He crossed the threshold. 'But I just got here,' he mumbled back, smiling at her grandmother.

'Then think up some excuse. You're a smart man.'
The tension building behind her eyes was growing to
monumental proportions. She had Kevin's problems to
contend with, and from Will's innocent expression he
had something up his sleeve as well. Given his penchant
for planning, which she'd experienced at first hand, she
knew this wasn't a friendly visit. He had some ulterior
motive in mind.

'Gran, this is Dr Patton.'

Will reached out to take the elderly woman's wrinkled
hand. 'Please call me Will. I'm a friend of Emily's.'

Oh, God. He's going to use Gran to get what he wants.
Inwardly, Emily cringed. Outwardly, though, she pasted
on a smile.

Emily's grandmother beamed at him. 'I'm Helen
Oakland. What brings you out tonight?'

'I came to invite Emily to dinner, but I see I'm too
late.'

'We were just sitting down at the table,' Helen said.
'You're welcome to join us.'

'That's kind of you—'

'But he can't,' Emily interjected on a desperate note.
'He's... He's....' Her mind failed her.

'Actually, I'd be delighted to try some home cooking,'
he said, plainly ignoring Emily's unspoken plea to leave.

'You don't have any family around here?'

'Not a one,' Will replied.

The delight shining from Helen's face matched the
sun in its intensity. She had always encouraged Emily
to go out more and the idea of an eligible male falling
right in her granddaughter's proverbial lap was something she clearly applauded. Wondering what would
come next, Emily rubbed at the tension line in her
forehead.

'Emily?' Helen asked. 'Where are your manners? Take the poor man's coat. I'll have Kevin set another place at the table.' She bustled off, calling out instructions.

Emily draped Will's jacket over a hanger and stuffed it unceremoniously into the closet. 'You were supposed to dream up an excuse for leaving.'

'And miss out on your granny's cooking?' He sniffed the air. 'Not a chance.'

'Tonight isn't a good night for a social call,' she began, thinking of Kevin's black eye.

'Then you should have accepted my dinner invitation,' he said smoothly, finger-combing his windswept hair.

'Everything's ready,' Helen called from the kitchen.

Will moved forward, but Emily placed a hand on his forearm. 'Please. Don't say anything about…you know what. I don't want to give Gran something else to worry about right now.'

'Then I hope you're giving serious consideration to my earlier proposition.'

'Please?' she whispered.

The bleak expression in her eyes made him feel guilty for making her think the worst about his unexpected arrival. 'I didn't come here to cause an incident. I came to meet your family.'

A new wrinkle formed on her forehead. 'Why?'

'Why not?' he countered.

'Em!' The changing voice of a young male punctuated the air. 'I'm starving in here!'

'I'll be on my best behavior,' Will promised.

She must have sensed the futility of an argument because she didn't say a word. Instead, she shot him an exasperated glare, then led him into the cozy kitchen where bowls of Salisbury steak, mashed potatoes, green beans and a salad waited on the table.

'This is an unexpected pleasure,' Will said, moving toward the chair Helen indicated. He wasn't surprised to see he'd been placed next to Emily.

Will held out his hand toward the boy across the table. 'You must be Kevin. I'm Will.'

The boy was a twelve-year-old male version of Emily. Their hair color, cheek-bones and jawline were the same, although Emily's possessed a softer edge. Even their eye color was a similar shade of brown, although Emily's had more flecks of gold and green.

Kevin blinked in obvious surprise as he tentatively shook Will's hand. Actually, only one eye blinked. The other had a distinct purple ring around it and the eyelid was nearly swollen shut. 'Pleased to meet you,' he murmured several seconds later, as if finally remembering his manners.

'Shall we sit down?' Helen asked brightly.

Emily took her place beside him. Her mouth was pinched and her face pale. For a fleeting moment he regretted barging in unannounced, but as he watched her he soon realized that the food, not his presence, was making her feel ill.

'How's school, Kevin?' Will asked, helping himself to the meat before he passed the bowl. 'Let's see. I'm guessing you're in sixth grade?'

'Yeah. It's OK.'

'It must have improved from when I was your age,' Will commented. 'I hated school.'

Kevin's good eye nearly bugged out of his head. 'You did?'

Will nodded. 'Everything was boring and I got into a

lot of trouble. If I hadn't met Abe Darnell I'd probably be in prison today.'

'Really?' Kevin's interest was palpable. Helen seemed intrigued while Emily's expression revealed wariness.

Will nodded. 'I'll tell you the story some time when you're bored and have nothing to do.'

Helen passed the plate of dinner rolls. 'Speaking of boredom, I wish Emily's job was less stressful. She goes full steam all day long. Aren't they going to hire more nurses?'

He glanced at Emily. 'I don't know.'

'Well, it's terrible how they're running the staff ragged,' Helen declared. 'Em comes home at night too exhausted to eat. Something should be done before her health suffers.'

'Gran.' Emily's voice held a note of warning. 'Will isn't involved in the nursing staff decisions.'

The perfect opportunity to enlist Helen's help stared at him, but he wouldn't disregard Emily's wishes. He had to build trust between them in order to achieve his objective.

'If it's any consolation,' he said, 'different times of year are busier than others, not just at the hospital but in private practice too. This is one of them.'

Emily nodded, her gaze telegraphing relief. 'That's what I keep telling you, Gran.'

'As for Em being tired,' he continued, 'I'm sure she'll revert back to her perky self soon.' He stared at Emily's half-eaten portions, which had been small to begin with. If this meal reflected her eating habits, no wonder her grandmother fretted over her.

He placed his fork on his empty plate and wiped his mouth with a paper napkin. 'That was delicious. The best I've eaten in ages.'

'You're welcome to come any time,' Helen announced, brushing a small pile of crumbs into her palm before she scooted away from the cloth-covered table. 'I hope you like banana cream pie, Dr Patton.'

'Will,' he corrected. 'And, yes, banana cream pie is one of my favorites.'

Helen gathered the dirty dishes together as she rose. Before Will could offer to help, Helen issued her orders. 'Kevin will help me clear away the table. Emily, why don't you show Will into the living room?'

Emily froze. 'I'm...I'm sure Kevin and Will can visit for a few minutes. You don't mind, do you, Will?'

He smiled, aware of her stalling tactics and Kevin's long-suffering sigh. 'Not at all.'

'Come on,' Kevin said, his tone indifferent. His chair scraped across the linoleum floor before he rose to lead Will into the small room. Immediately he grabbed the remote and clicked on the Discovery channel. 'Wanna watch TV?'

Will noticed a partially built model of a space station, a sewing machine with doll-sized clothes stacked nearby and a basket of yarn containing various sizes of knitting needles. The model belonged to Kevin, he guessed, although he had a hard time deciding which hobby belonged to Emily.

'I'd rather visit with you.'

'You would?'

Will was amused by Kevin's astonishment. 'Yeah. What do you like to do?'

Clearly suspicious of Will's offer, Kevin clicked off the television before he lowered himself onto a well-worn easy chair and sprawled bonelessly in its confines. 'Stuff.'

Will smiled, recognizing himself at that age. 'What kind of stuff?'

Kevin shrugged. 'Computer games. Astronomy. Building things.'

'Then you have a computer?'

'Yeah. In my room. I'd like to get hooked up to the Internet, but Emily won't let me. She's afraid I'll see porno pictures or spend all day chatting with some fruit-cake.' His disgust over her reasoning was obvious. 'She doesn't understand how hard it is to do reports without getting all the neat stuff off the Net.'

'If it's OK with Emily, you're welcome to access the Web from my computer for as long as you like.'

Kevin's whole body came alert. 'Cool. There's a thirty-minute time limit at the public library.'

Will mentally scored a point for himself. 'You men-tioned building things. Is the space station yours?'

Kevin slouched again. 'Yeah. It's the Mir. When I get to high school I want to take woodworking classes.'

'Wise choice. How are you at repairs?'

'Pretty good,' he said proudly. 'I usually take care of stuff around here. I even replaced an electrical outlet, but it was tough, with Em hovering over me.'

Will smothered a smile. 'I'll bet.'

'She was afraid I'd electrocute myself, but I told her I'd be OK since I'd shut off the power. I'd tried to ex-plain about currents and ground wires, but it didn't help. She jumped at every little noise and looked like she was ready to start doing CPR.'

Will nodded sympathetically. 'It takes time to get used to the idea of someone growing up. Especially if we're talking about a person we've cared for since he was a baby.'

Kevin cocked his head as if pondering this new concept. 'You think?'

'I'm sure of it.' Will motioned to the dolls' clothes. 'Does your grandmother make those?'

'Nah. Em has a friend who goes to craft fairs every spring. She helps Tanya with her sewing.' Kevin fell silent for a minute. 'How long have you known my sister?'

'Ever since I moved to Crossbow four months ago,' Will answered truthfully. He didn't feel it necessary to divulge the fact that, discounting the night of the Christmas Ball, he'd only visited with her on a semi-personal basis for the last three weeks.

Kevin's eyes narrowed. 'That's all?'

Will didn't take offense at the youth's questions. He understood how protective Kevin must feel toward his sister, being the so-called man of the house. Even so, he didn't intend to describe their relationship in detail.

'Have you ever met someone and immediately you became good friends?' he asked, thinking of the events that had culminated in the creation of their child. 'That's sort of how it was between Emily and myself. Things just clicked.'

Kevin nodded, as if he could relate. 'I didn't like Don. I couldn't figure out what Em saw in him.'

Will didn't hold too high an opinion of Emily's former romantic interest either, but held his counsel.

'He kept trying to boss me around like I was a little kid.'

Will sensed a trap. 'I'll try not to do the same.'

'You're only being nice to me so you'll get on Emily's good side.'

Honesty seemed the best policy. 'Partly. More importantly, though, I think you can use a friend. Someone who'll listen and who isn't part of your family. Someone objective.'

The expression on Kevin's bruised face revealed more than mere words. He was obviously burdened about something and equally unwilling to talk to his sister about it. Will knew better than to press for any particulars; Kevin wasn't ready to confide in him.

Will changed the subject. 'Do you have a dog?'

'Nah. We don't have room for a pet. I don't want one, anyway.'

'Too bad,' Will said lightly. 'I'm hoping to get a golden retriever.'

'A kid at school has an Irish setter,' Kevin volunteered.

'Nice animal.'

Silence descended and Will waited for Kevin to initiate the conversation. He wasn't disappointed.

'School's boring,' Kevin announced. 'The teachers are dweebs and the kids are mean.'

'What makes you say that?'

Kevin touched his swollen cheek-bone and avoided Will's gaze. 'They say stuff.'

'Stuff' was definitely Kevin's favorite word. 'What sort of things?'

He shrugged. 'It doesn't matter. They're all dumb, anyway. Who needs 'em?'

'Is it everyone or just a few?' Will asked.

'A few.'

'If you ever want to talk man-to-man about it, I'm available.'

Kevin shook his head. 'I don't need anyone to talk to. I can handle things myself.'

Will kept his tone light and nonjudgmental. 'Getting a black eye is an interesting way to handle things.'

'At least I won't be around those jerks after school for a few days. I have detention.'

'What happened?'

Kevin hesitated.

'I'd like to hear your side. If you want to tell me, that is.'

Kevin chewed on his upper lip. 'Somebody stole three mice off the science lab's computers. The principal announced a locker search if they weren't turned in. A couple of the guys acted like they were up to something so I checked my locker and found the stuff.'

'Then what happened?'

'I sneaked all three pieces into the science teacher's mail box outside his room. After school I heard Judd and Eric bragging about what they'd done.'

'Did you tell the principal?'

Kevin appeared horrified. 'And be labeled a snitch? No way. Mrs Rogers wouldn't believe me, anyway. Judd and Eric live in the *good* part of town. Their folks are pillars of the community.'

Will heard his sarcasm and remembered similarly frustrating experiences. Once again he felt a special kinship to the boy. He'd even battled with a teacher named Mrs Rogers, and said so.

'No kidding?' Kevin asked, intrigued by the coincidence. 'Could it be the same lady?'

'Probably not. I didn't grow up around here.' He thought a moment. 'She'd be nearly retirement age.'

Kevin's good eye sparkled. 'I'll bet it's her. She's got gray hair.'

Will hid his smile at Kevin's deductions. He almost wished it was the same Mrs Rogers. He'd enjoy walking up to her as living proof that the young man she'd labeled as a candidate for reform school had become a physician.

'Does Emily know about the stolen equipment?'

Kevin shook his head. 'Just that I was fighting. Again. Don't tell her either. She has enough to worry about.'

'Your uncle?' Will guessed.

'Yeah. It's my fault, too. I may have ruined everything for Grandma and Emily. Maybe I should just give in and live with Uncle Bert.' Kevin's voice matched his glum expression.

'Do you *want* to live with him?'

'Nah. He's always harping at me about stuff. He's gonna go ballistic when he finds out about today.'

Will hesitated. 'What if you explained the situation to him? I'm sure he'd understand your actions. He was a kid once too.'

'No!' Kevin was horrified. 'He'd tell Mrs Rogers and the guys would make my life hell.'

Will sympathized. The boy had to choose between the lesser of two evils—not an easy prospect.

'I shouldn't let those jerks get under my skin,' Kevin admitted, 'but they do.'

Will remembered a group who'd known which buttons to push to send him over the edge too. Abe had taught him how to control those feelings and now he saw his opportunity to pay back the man who'd helped him.

'If you want to, call me the next time you have a problem with Judd and Eric. I'll help you sort things out.'

Hope flared in Kevin's undamaged eye. 'You will?'

'Sure. Provided I'm not in the middle of delivering a baby or in surgery. Even so, I'll come as soon as I can.'

Will shifted his weight to gain access to the wallet in the back pocket of his khaki trousers.

'Here's my phone number at the clinic,' he said, handing Kevin a business card. 'If you want to talk I'm usually at home in the evenings.'

Kevin slid the card in the pocket of his jeans.

'I don't know about you,' Will said, pleased with his success so far, 'but why don't we see what's happened to our pie?'

'Why are you dawdling, Emily Ann?' Helen asked.

'I'm not dawdling. I'm doing the dishes.'

Helen nudged Emily away from the sink. 'Then you're procrastinating. Although I can't imagine why you would when there's a handsome fellow waiting to see you in the other room.'

She thrust a tray with two slices of pie into Emily's hands. 'Take this and enjoy yourself.'

'I can't. Uncle Bert's coming tomorrow night and I'm worried over what he'll say when he hears about Kevin's detention.'

'All the more reason to take a break,' Helen said firmly, before giving Emily a gentle shove. 'Go keep your young man company.'

'He's not my young man.'

Helen waved her hand. 'Whatever. Oh, and remind Kevin it's time for homework.'

Emily strode toward the living room, determined to send Will on his way as soon as possible. She wanted to keep their encounters strictly professional and to stomp out the sparks she felt in his presence.

She'd fight her attraction with everything she possibly could. As much as she'd like to be the woman he wanted—the partner he dreamed of—she wasn't. Nor would she pretend otherwise.

For that reason she refused to consider being his wife, even temporarily. She'd be devastated when their relationship ended. The pain of him leaving her for someone like Celine would eclipse any effects of gossip she'd ever endure over her unmarried and pregnant state. She wasn't a prideful person, but she possessed enough to know that she couldn't deal with people's pity.

She met Will and Kevin at the door. Kevin reached for the tray with the two servings. 'Thanks, Em. We thought you'd gotten lost or forgot about us.'

Forget Will's presence? Hardly. Emily pulled the tray out of Kevin's reach. 'Sorry. Your piece is in the kitchen. You can eat while you're finishing your homework.'

Kevin uttered a long-suffering sigh. 'Do I have to? Will and I've been talking.'

Emily hid her surprise. Her brother had never willingly spent time with Don. 'Afraid so. Your report is due tomorrow.'

Will grinned. 'I'll see you before I leave.'

Apparently satisfied, Kevin left while Emily placed the tray on the scarred pine coffee-table. 'It sounds as if you two found something in common.'

Will took the saucer and fork she offered before he sat on the sofa. 'Did you think we wouldn't?'

Emily shrugged. 'I didn't know what to think. What did you guys discuss?'

He swallowed his bite, then grinned. 'Stuff.'

She groaned. 'Oh, God. Don't tell me you're hooked on Kevin's vocabulary.'

'It's a fairly all-encompassing reply that doesn't say

anything. Though, to answer your question, we talked about his interests, school, that sort of thing.'

Emily stared at him, incredulous. 'He actually mentioned school?'

'Yeah. He's having a tough time with a few of his classmates.'

'I gathered that from what the principal and counselor have told me.' Her eyes narrowed. 'What did you say to get him to unload on you? You're basically a stranger.'

'Maybe it's because I *am* a stranger that he felt he could confide in me. Or maybe it's because I'm a good listener. In any case, I might be able to help him. If you'll let me.'

She placed her half-eaten dessert on the tray. While she applauded his gesture she questioned his motives. 'Why are you bothering?'

'Because I want to.'

She wasn't convinced. 'Oh, really?'

He stretched out his long legs. 'Whether you like it or not, I'm part of the family.'

She stared at him, incredulous. 'You're what?'

'Kevin is my son or daughter's uncle,' he said, sounding patient.

Emily glanced at the doorway, afraid to find her grandmother or brother overhearing the conversation. 'Keep your voice down!'

'So I have a vested interest in what goes on,' he continued, slightly above a whisper.

She jumped to her feet and planted her hands on her hips. 'I have enough problems with my father's brother. I refuse to dance to your tune as well.'

Will sat up straight. 'Don't lump me in the same category as your relative. Whether you like it or not, whether we ever get married or not, we're tied together because of our child. I want what's best for him or her.'

'I want what's best for him or her too,' she snapped.

'Then let me help in whatever way I can. The extra stress is bad for you and the baby.'

Once again he was right. Her stomach was either nauseous from hormonal changes or knotted with nervous tension. At this rate Will Junior would starve to death.

The telephone rang in the distance and its abrupt silence reminded her of the other people in the house.

'I don't want to discuss this here,' she began. 'We don't have any privacy.'

'We'll have to tell your grandmother some time. She already suspects something's wrong.'

'I'll tell her the whole story, but not now.'

He rose. 'Fine. Get your coat.' At her hesitation he added, 'I won't keep you more than an hour.'

Emily met her grandmother in the hallway, aware of Will behind her. 'We're leaving—'

'Your uncle—'

Emily stopped in mid-sentence. She rubbed at the painful knot forming in her stomach at the mention of her relative. 'What were you saying?'

'Bert just called. He won't come until next weekend because he's meeting with his managers.'

Relief coursed through Emily. 'What luck! Kevin's black eye won't be so obvious and we won't have to tell him about his detention.'

Helen smiled. 'I thought you'd be pleased. Now, what were you going to tell me?'

It took Emily a few seconds to pull her thoughts together. 'Will and I are going out. I'll be back in an hour.'

'Have fun,' Helen said.

Within minutes Emily was sitting in Will's car. 'The

Pizza Hut is the other direction,' she pointed out, as he turned right instead of left.

'I know. We're going to my place. It's more private.' He paused. 'Is that OK with you?'

Emily's mouth went dry. She hadn't expected to go to his home, but a busy restaurant wasn't the best place to discuss their personal lives. Memories of her last visit sent her pulse racing, although she couldn't say if it was due to anticipation or anxiety.

She cleared her throat and spoke nonchalantly. 'Yeah, sure. Your place is fine.'

As Will escorted her into his living room a short time later awkwardness assailed her. She knew so little about this man and yet she was having his baby.

'Would you like something to drink?' he asked.

She wasn't thirsty, but she needed a few minutes alone to collect her wits. 'Water, please.'

When he'd disappeared, Emily studied her surroundings. The room was neat, but a faint sheen of dust covered the surfaces. Newspapers were stacked haphazardly beside the sofa and a glass bowl of peanuts graced the end table. The furniture was spartan, the colors dated.

A small table in one corner held state-of-the-art computer equipment while a well-used target holding five darts hung on the wall beside it.

Emily turned to sit in the wooden rocking chair just as he strode in, carrying a glass of ice water and a bottle of light beer. She took the cup, conscious of how their fingers brushed, then settled herself against the cushions.

'Peanuts?' he asked, holding out the dish.

Her stomach flip-flopped. 'No, thanks.'

He took a handful before he took a seat across from her on the divan.

'We really don't have anything to discuss,' she said. 'Everything is under control with my uncle now.'

'Maybe.'

She frowned at his noncommittal reply. 'You don't think so?'

He lifted the bottle to his lips and took a swallow. 'I've never met him so I can't say. The question is—will he accept *your* report on Kevin's progress at school?'

Emily fell silent. She could imagine Bert calling the school and browbeating some poor secretary until she spilled everything she knew. 'It's a risk I have to take.'

He placed his bottle on the end table next to the bowl of peanuts. 'That's my point. You don't *have* to take the risk.'

'If all you're going to do is try to coerce me into marriage, please drive me home.'

He straightened and held up his hands as if in surrender. 'You're trying to satisfy your uncle. I'm simply giving you a way to appease everyone.'

'I know you're looking out for everyone's best interests, but I'm not convinced your solution is the best one.' As he started to speak she continued, 'However, I said I'd think about it and I will. Just don't push. OK?'

'Fair enough,' he said. 'By the way, have you chosen a doctor? Both Dr Moore and Dr Abernathy can work you in by the middle of next week.'

Anger and horror clashed in her mind. 'You made an appointment for me?' She enunciated each word.

'Not officially.'

Her anger dropped one degree. 'Good—because I want to see Susan Hathaway.'

He hesitated. 'Isn't she in family practice?'

'Yes. So?' she questioned.

'Is she good?'

'I've been happy with the way she takes care of her mothers. The baby will need a doctor anyway.'

His mouth fell into a straight line as if he didn't care for her decision, but he was powerless to do otherwise. 'I'd feel better if Gene or Charles were involved...'

She refused to budge. 'I wouldn't.'

Silence descended and for a few seconds Emily heard the house creak. 'OK,' he said, his disappointment obvious, 'but if you develop any complications I reserve the right to call in a specialist for either you or the baby.'

'We already have one. *You'll* be there,' she reminded him. Then, touched by his vehemence, she added, 'I have faith in you. You'll help her take care of us.'

'Yes,' he said, sounding possessive. 'I will.'

# CHAPTER FIVE

'I CAN'T believe this is happening again.' Heidi Detrich lay against the pillows, her facial color matching the white sheets. 'I'm supposed to *enjoy* the first few months of my pregnancy.'

Emily sympathized, wishing her own stomach would co-operate. Dramamine had helped, but not to any great extent. She'd have to try suppositories next and she wasn't thrilled with the prospect. To add insult to injury, she hadn't slept well since Will had taken it upon himself to visit every night for the past week.

Satisfied with the steady drip of glucose and electrolyte solution, she injected the vitamin B complex and vitamin C into a second port. 'You've experienced severe morning sickness before?'

Heidi nodded, clutching the emesis basin. 'I suffered the same way with my first baby. In fact, that's how I knew I was pregnant. These women who sail through their first trimester without a problem make me ill.'

'Were you admitted to the hospital?'

Heidi nodded. 'I stayed for about a week. She called it the same thing, too, but I can't remember her exact words.'

'Hyperemesis gravidarum,' Emily supplied. 'Quite a name, isn't it?' She cleared away the used cotton balls and alcohol pads, then discarded the syringes in the biohazard container.

'Yeah.' Heidi closed her eyes.

'Do you have a boy or a girl?'

'Girl. She's staying with my mother because Rick can't take off work. Lucy's three and quite a handful.'

'I'll bet.' Emily closed the miniblinds against the morning sun. 'While you're here all you need to worry about is getting your rest. We won't give you anything by mouth until tomorrow, but the IV solutions will bring your fluid balance back where it should be.'

Heidi's smile was wan. 'Good—because I'm tired of feeling rotten.'

Emily gave her a sympathetic smile. 'In the meantime, just relax and enjoy being pampered. I'll close the door to filter out some of the noise. Visitors aren't always considerate of our ill patients.'

With that, Emily returned to the nurses' station and began jotting her notes in Mrs Detrich's medical record. She'd have to be alert for changes such as jaundice or elevated blood pressure.

Susan Hathaway strode out of another patient's room, exhaustion adding extra lines to her face.

'I thought you went home,' Emily said, watching the fifty-year-old physician sink beside her and scrawl her instructions in another chart.

'Fat chance,' Dr Hathaway said with a tired smile. 'I have an office full of sick people to see before I can call it a day.'

'I hate to ask you this when you're swamped, but are you accepting new patients?'

'My life isn't always this hectic. Yes, I'll add an occasional new person to my list. Why?'

'I'd like to make an appointment.'

'Routine or emergency?'

'Routine.' She paused. 'I'll have Dr Ferguson's office send my records over.'

Dr Hathaway glanced at her, her eyes narrowing as she clearly pondered the reason for the change.

'I'm pregnant,' Emily said in a voice meant for the other woman's ears only.

Dr Hathaway's puzzlement cleared. 'I see. Tell my receptionist about our visit and she'll schedule you in my next available slot.'

'Thanks.'

She rose and stretched. 'Call me when the rest of Mrs Detrich's lab results come in. You know the number.'

Emily nodded before she went to check on another new admission, Dolores Gonzales. 'How are you doing?' she asked the thirty-year-old woman.

'OK, I guess. Do you know when Dr Patton will be in to do my surgery?'

'You're scheduled for noon so you shouldn't have much longer to wait.'

Mrs Gonzales clutched the hand of her husband. 'I'm so nervous about this. What if it doesn't work?'

From the records Emily knew Dolores suffered from an incompetent cervix. She'd miscarried twice before, and to prevent her from losing her third baby Will intended to intervene surgically. With Mrs Gonzales fourteen weeks into her pregnancy the time was right.

'Nothing is absolute,' Emily said, 'but the cerclage, or band of sutures that Dr Patton will place around the cervix, will keep the amniotic sac from protruding and rupturing early.'

Dolores swiped at her eyes. 'If I lose this baby…I don't think I can go through this again.'

'I know it's distressing, but don't give up hope. This procedure works very well in helping women with your difficulty carry their babies to term.'

Dolores nodded. 'That's what Dr Patton says. I guess

I just need to hear it over and over again before I'll be convinced.'

'Understandable. Have you noticed any bleeding or cramping lately?' The symptoms Emily described would contraindicate performing the procedure.

'No.'

'That's good. I'm sure Dr Patton has told you to avoid any sexual activity.'

Dolores glanced at her husband and gave him an apologetic smile. 'Yes. It's been so strange. First we're supposed to work hard to get pregnant, and then when I am we have to stop.'

'It doesn't seem fair, does it?' Emily commiserated. 'But having a baby to fuss over will make up for those nights of frustration.'

Dolores nodded, her smile tentative.

'I'll be back to check on you in a little while.'

Will arrived a short time later, looking handsome in his black trousers, white shirt and black and white striped tie. At first Emily couldn't stop her heart from skipping a beat. In the next instant she found his fresh, spotless appearance irritating when she felt like death warmed over.

'Hello, Em,' he said evenly.

'Doctor,' she said primly under his searching gaze.

He raised one eyebrow. 'Didn't sleep well last night?'

How could he tell? she thought a trifle waspishly. She'd seen huge circles under her eyes on the last trip to the bathroom, her skin color was blotchy and her clothes felt too tight. She handed him Mrs Gonzales's chart. 'No.'

'What's wrong?'

'Everything. Nothing.' She didn't feel like going into detail about her nausea, which was growing to mammoth proportions. She'd never realized how so many different smells could set her stomach rolling.

She'd been making excuses for missing meals so her grandmother wouldn't learn how little she was eating or see how her food didn't stay down.

'I saw Susan Hathaway as I was coming in,' he remarked.

Emily wasn't fooled by his offhanded manner. He hadn't mentioned the subject since he'd first brought it up a week ago so he was obviously anxious to hear if she'd made arrangements for a prenatal exam. The irritable imp on her shoulder warned her not to succumb to his polite manipulation.

'That's nice,' she said tersely.

'Testy today?' he asked.

'Why wouldn't I be?' Emily demanded. 'We're short-staffed, my head and feet ache and I can't eat or drink. Also, a certain doctor is constantly underfoot.'

He blinked, clearly taken aback by her sharp tone, and she immediately regretted her remarks. Ever since the night Gran had invited him to supper he'd dropped by once a day to say hello. He'd even spent Sunday afternoon with Kevin as they'd scoured the city and surrounding ranches for a golden retriever pup.

She rubbed her eyes and her shoulders sagged as low as her spirits. 'I'm sorry. I shouldn't take out my frustrations on you. Yes, I saw Dr Hathaway. She'll take me as a patient.'

'Good. Let me know your—' He stopped short as another nurse strode by, waiting to continue until after she'd passed beyond hearing distance. 'Appointment time. I'll arrange my schedule accordingly.'

Emily's jaw slackened. 'You want to come?'

He peered at her. 'Would you rather I didn't?'

He *was* the baby's father, she told herself. He had a moral right to be present. 'I really didn't give it much thought.'

'I want to be there.' His voice turned soft, almost like a caress. 'Never forget that.'

Of course he would, she scolded herself. He's worried about his child. 'I'll phone this afternoon and let you know.'

'Good. How's Mrs Gonzales?'

'Tense. She's afraid she'll lose this baby like the others. I did my best to encourage her.'

'Then I guess it's my turn.' Will disappeared into her room and returned ten minutes later. 'All systems are go,' he said. 'I'll run over to Surgery and see how soon my OR will be ready.'

Within a short time the surgery staff arrived for Mrs Gonzales. By the time she returned it was after one o'clock and Emily was ready for a break.

'You'd better eat something or you'll end up in the hospital,' Molly warned. 'Like Heidi Detrich.'

'I would if I could keep anything down. I've drunk enough tea and nibbled on enough crackers that I can't hardly stand the sight or smell of either.'

'Have you weighed yourself lately?'

'Yeah. I've lost a few pounds.'

'Only a few?' Molly seemed skeptical. 'When do you see the doctor?'

'In two days. On Friday.'

Molly leaned closer. 'How are you doing otherwise?'

'If you're asking about Kevin, my uncle will be in town on Saturday. I think he'll agree that Kevin just went through a bad spell and isn't on his way to a life of crime and violence. Bert's political career won't suffer.'

'And Will?'

Emily sipped the lukewarm tea and grimaced. 'I hate to admit it, but he's been great. Kevin and Gran like him too.'

'What about you?'

'He's a nice guy,' she said, avoiding her friend's gaze. Actually, she considered her adjective an insipid choice. Will was wonderful. He'd worked a miracle with Kevin in a week. Her brother was calmer, acting more at peace with himself and less like a bomb ready to explode.

Celine had judged Will to be structured and controlled, and Emily agreed to a certain extent. However, while Celine had considered those as character flaws Emily classified them as strengths. If she wasn't careful she'd fall in love with her baby's father.

'Your grandmother called me at the office this morning,' Will told Emily later that day as they drove across town to accomplish his secret errand. It was his afternoon off so he intended to put the time to good use.

'She did?'

'She's really worried about you. To be quite honest, so am I.'

'I'm fine. I'm sure Dr Hathaway will say the same thing when I see her.'

'We have to tell your family about the baby.'

'We will. On Saturday. After Bert leaves.'

Will turned the corner. 'I can't talk you into mentioning it sooner?'

Emily shook her head. 'No. I'm not going to chance word leaking out before then. Once my uncle is reassured that we won't affect his precious political image he'll disappear from our lives. Then I don't care who knows about us.'

He grinned as her pronoun registered. He was making progress.

'What did you say we were doing this afternoon?' she asked.

'I didn't. However, I thought if I more or less kidnapped you you'd help me buy a house.'

Her eyes widened. 'Buy a house?' she echoed.

'My lease runs out the end of the month. Since I plan on staying in Crossbow, buying a home seems like a good idea as well as a good investment.' He tried to sound repentant. 'I was afraid you'd refuse if you knew ahead of time so I decided to kidnap you instead.'

'You're right. I wouldn't have come.' Emily crossed her arms and set her jaw.

'Why not?'

'You're pushing.'

He parked the car in front of the Texas Homes Realty Association. 'Would you rather I lived in a tent on the hospital lawn?'

'Don't be ridiculous.'

'I'm not pushing.' Will considered what he was doing more in the line of planting a subliminal message. 'I need a place to live. I hate apartments and I refuse to live in a mobile home. That limits my choices to homes or caves and, believe me, cold, dark places aren't my ideal living conditions.'

'I don't know your tastes,' she protested. 'You may not appreciate the same things I do.'

'Just help me see each house from a woman's perspective. If I don't like something, I'll tell you.'

She toyed with the ends of her hair. He wanted to reach over and untangle the braid, letting each lock run across his fingers until every strand was free, but he couldn't because the time and the place weren't right.

Soon, he told himself. Patience and control were the keys to success.

'What's wrong with a mobile home?' she asked.

'I lived in one for two semesters. A storm developed one day out of nowhere. Before my roommate and I could get to the neighbor's basement the wind had done its damage.' He stroked the scar along the hairline near his temple. 'I got this when the windows shattered.'

Emily's eyes flashed with sympathy. 'OK. Let's find you a place to live.'

He squeezed her hand, before sliding out from behind the wheel. A minute later he escorted her inside to meet the Realtor, Myra Kingsbury.

The first home was a beautiful two-story building with white pillars, a set of double entrance doors and a wide oak staircase with a massive chandelier hanging down from the second floor's ceiling.

Emily felt uncomfortable surrounded by such opulence. She'd never dreamed Will would spend a fortune on a house just for himself. Then again, if he wanted to take his place in local society, he couldn't live in a hovel.

'What do you think?' Will asked her as soon as Myra discreetly left them alone in the formal dining room.

'It's beautiful,' Emily said. 'Perfect for entertaining.'

'I sense you're not fond of it.'

She hesitated, then decided to give him her opinion. After all, he'd asked for it. 'The floor plan is wonderful, but I think it's too impractical for a family. Look at the carpet. It's white.' This was the sort of showcase house Celine would have chosen, but if Emily bought a house she wanted one with a lived-in feel.

'I don't mean to question you,' she continued, 'but

isn't this house terribly large for you?' In her mind she wondered what bachelor needed five bedrooms.

'A person can't ever have too much living space,' he commented, seemingly unconcerned. 'Any other complaints?'

She shook her head.

'Let's go to the next one,' he informed Myra.

By the time Will's watch beeped the hour at five o'clock Emily was exhausted. She'd never realized how many fancy homes were available in Crossbow. Her friends lived in the same type of middle-income neighborhood as she did, and she didn't pass through the affluent part of town on her way to work or to shop.

In spite of the showcase, magazine-quality abodes she'd seen, none of them had sparked a 'must-have' interest.

These places aren't for you, she told herself as she climbed into Myra's car once again to tour the last house on her list. They were for doctors, lawyers, judges and senators, not for someone who counted every penny.

'Based on your criteria, this is the last suitable choice,' Myra said, turning in the driver's seat to address Will beside her and Emily in the back. 'It has the space you want, but it needs some work.'

Will frowned. 'What sort of work?'

'Decorating mainly. Nothing structural.'

Emily saw Will's dubious expression in profile. 'Can't hurt to check it out.'

He shrugged. 'I suppose not.'

Twenty minutes later Myra pulled into a stately drive in an old, established part of town. 'These homes were built around the turn of the century and most have been modernized.'

'I presume this one hasn't,' Will said as she parked in front of a sprawling ranch-style building.

'The owners rewired and replumbed about fifteen years ago. However, the decor needs updating—wallpaper, that sort of thing. Mr Ross died about five years ago and his wife doesn't want to deal with the maintenance. She's planning to move into a retirement village.

'As you can see,' Myra added, 'the blocks in this area only have two houses in each. When the town was founded the wealthy families lived here—bankers and so on. Now the arrangement gives you a quiet, rural feeling while you enjoy the advantages of being in the city.'

Emily zipped her coat closed as she slid out of the back seat. Rubbing at the growing ache in her lower back, she stared at the building. The ranch-style clapboard home with its large porch beckoned her.

She walked up the wide set of stairs leading to the front door, conscious of Will's hand on her waist. Myra ushered them inside.

Emily walked from room to room, falling in love with the high ceilings, the woodwork's craftsmanship, the little nooks and crannies. Her mind raced with ideas for color schemes and wallpaper patterns.

Will followed her into the kitchen and leaned against the doorframe as she ran her hands along the cream-colored Formica countertop and touched the oak cabinet doors with reverence.

'I don't have to ask if you like it,' he said with a smile.

She grinned. 'I'm obvious, aren't I?'

'It's a nice house,' he said. 'However, there are a lot of things to consider.'

'Like what?'

'Redecorating, for one. We'll have to contract someone who can—'

She dismissed him with a wave. 'Painting and wall-
papering are no big deal. Gran and I are old hands at it.
We'll help you.'

'The yard itself will take a lot of time and energy.'

'Kevin likes to work outdoors. In fact, he was wanting
to mow lawns this summer for extra money.' She
grinned. 'I'm sure he'll give you reduced rate.'

'Sounds good to me.'

Suddenly she realized she'd been making plans that
weren't hers to make. 'Don't feel obligated to hire him,
though.'

'I won't.'

She gave an all-encompassing wave. 'Do *you* like the
house?'

'Yes,' he admitted. 'I'm thrilled over not having my
neighbors close enough to hear my voice or my television set. Also, the yard will be perfect for my dog. Lots
of roaming space.'

'As you said, maintaining this home won't be easy,'
she warned. 'Maybe you should buy the first house.' She
couldn't imagine the glamorous Celine living here—it
was too old-fashioned for a person with sophisticated
tastes.

'The one with the white carpeting?' He shook his
head. 'Not a chance.'

'What about the one with the hot tub and swimming
pool?'

'I don't want to worry about anyone drowning.'

Dear heavens! She'd forgotten that her baby would
eventually spend time at Will's house. 'Good idea. Then
which one will you pick?' she asked, waiting with bated
breath for his answer.

He stepped closer to her. 'The one you liked the best.'

He wasn't playing fair—enticing her with a home she'd love to own. 'I liked them all.'

'But you have a favorite.'

She waved, as if brushing away a pesky fly. 'Don't be ridiculous.'

He grinned. 'You were enthralled with this one.'

'Oh, yeah?'

He stepped closer. 'I could tell.'

His breath whispered across her cheek and her heart leapt into her throat. 'How?'

He shrugged, taking her hands in his. 'It's hard to explain.'

She struggled to focus on the conversation instead of his touch and failed miserably. 'Try.'

He pulled her into his embrace and locked his gaze onto hers. 'I could see it in your eyes.'

Mesmerized by how his eyes darkened, she was reminded of another occasion when she'd stood in the circle of his arms. 'You could?'

Will nodded. 'They sparkled. And your face.' He ran a fingertip along her jawline.

Her skin suddenly felt as if it were too tight for her body. Every nerve ending screamed for him to continue his gentle assault. 'What about my face?' she whispered.

'It glowed. Like it is now.'

In a split second, under his intense gaze, flames licked at the center of her being. They soon built to a full-fledged blaze.

He traced the curve of her mouth. 'This was another clue.'

Her breath caught in her throat as he lowered his head and cupped the back of her neck. 'You have a beautiful smile,' he murmured, before he planted his lips against hers.

His kiss was possessive rather than platonic, his hold as secure as if sturdy cords bound them together. Surrounded by his scent, eager for his caress, her knees weakened and she melted against him.

The attraction she'd denied ever since the fateful night of the Christmas Ball broke free of the boundaries she'd set. Her resolve to seal off her affection and think of him only in a professional manner disintegrated.

He raised his head, his eyes dark with the same passion she felt burning inside her. 'That's how I know,' he said softly.

'What have you folks decided?' Myra's animated voice at the door cooled Emily's ardor as effectively as if someone had dropped an ice cube down her back.

Emily tried to break free, but Will held her close to his side. He obviously wasn't upset at the idea of being caught in a lovers' clinch. From Myra's knowing smile, the news would be all over town before long.

An equally unwelcome thought filled Emily's mind. Had Will kissed her on purpose? Had he hoped for Myra to stumble upon them and fuel the gossip he supposedly wanted to avoid at all costs?

She stiffened, but he didn't relax his hold.

'I'll need a few days to make a decision,' he said noncommittally.

Myra beamed, as if sensing a sale. 'No problem. Any one of these will make a marvelous home for a family. Just let me know which one you want and I'll start the paperwork.'

During the trip home Emily's thoughts returned to their kiss. The thrill she'd experienced in Will's arms on the night of Christmas Ball hadn't diminished over time.

She'd intended the one-night encounter to exorcise Don's ghosts and it had served its purpose. Unfortunately, she hadn't been able to casually dismiss the same encounter as she'd originally thought she could. Although she'd denied it during subsequent weeks, an invisible string had bound her to Will long before their baby ever had.

How could she continue to spend time with him without suffering the emotional consequences?

*She* wanted to live in that house with him, not imagine him in those quaint rooms with another woman. Yes, he'd suggested marriage, but for all the wrong reasons. She wanted him to propose because she completed the circle of his existence. No other excuse would do.

As soon as he parked next to the curb in front of her house she turned toward him, keeping one hand on the doorhandle. 'If you don't mind, I'll say goodnight out here. I'm really tired.'

'I'll only stay long enough to say hello to Kevin,' he promised.

True to his word, Will's visit didn't last long. She escorted him to the door, where he kissed her again. This time, however, their lips met briefly and held only a hint of the passion she'd experienced earlier.

'Sleep well, Em.'

'I will.'

He studied her. 'Are you all right?'

She smiled at his familiar question. 'I'm fine. Just tired.' She didn't mention her backache.

'OK, see you tomorrow.'

Although it was early, Emily drank a cup of hot tea and went to bed, pleading exhaustion. At midnight the combination of pain in her lower back and the churning in her stomach woke her.

She stumbled to the bathroom, feeling an ache settle in her abdomen. When her unpleasant stint had ended she sat against the wall, too spent to move.

Helen appeared in the doorway. 'Em? What's wrong?'

'Sick.' Emily couldn't remember ever feeling so miserable. She was hardly aware of her grandmother's cool hands taking her temperature.

'I'm calling Will,' Helen said.

Emily nodded. Will would know what to do. As she closed her eyes she hoped she wasn't losing the baby.

# CHAPTER SIX

WILL groped for the ringing phone with one hand and rubbed his eyes with the other. 'Yeah?'

Helen's voice parted the sleepy fog surrounding his brain like Moses dividing the Red Sea. 'Emily's sick. I don't know what's wrong with her. Can you come?'

'I'll be right there.' Instantly awake, he dove into a pair of jeans, an old Texas Rangers baseball shirt and a pair of loafers. Ignoring his whiskery shadow as he glanced in the large dresser mirror, he grabbed his keys and slid on his jacket as he rushed to his car.

Less than ten minutes later he braked to a stop in front of the Chandler home and found Kevin waiting at the door. 'Gran's in Emily's room,' the boy announced, his hair tousled and his eyes bleary from being suddenly awakened.

Will's long strides brought him to Emily's bed. Placing a hand on her forehead, he was shocked to find her skin burning to his touch.

'I heard her vomiting,' Helen reported, sounding concerned. 'When I checked on her she acted dazed and complained of pain in her back.'

He bent over Emily. 'How long have you been like this?'

'It started yesterday and gradually got worse,' she admitted.

'Show me where it hurts,' he ordered.

She rubbed an area he classified as the costal-vertebral

angle—a space near her spine in the vicinity of her rib-
cage.

'Any pain on urination?'

'A little.' She gave him a wan smile. 'Then again, I
haven't been able to keep enough fluids down to worry
about going to the bathroom.'

'I'm taking you to the ER,' he said, forming a diagnosis. 'Can you walk or should I call an ambulance?'

She licked her lips. 'I can walk.'

Will addressed Helen. 'May I use your phone?'

'It's in the kitchen.'

After telephoning Susan Hathaway and the hospital,
he returned to see Emily sitting on the edge of the bed,
clad in a T-shirt and jeans rather than her nightgown.
'You're welcome to come along, Helen.'

Helen motioned to Kevin who was standing in the
doorway. 'We'll wait here. Kevin has school tomorrow
so he should try to get some sleep.'

'I'll let you know the minute we learn something.
And, Kevin? She'll be fine.'

The worry in the boy's eyes faded and he nodded.

Will helped Emily to her feet. Noticing her unsteadi-
ness, he carried her to his car.

By the time they arrived at the hospital a staff member
was waiting with a wheelchair and immediately took
Emily to an exam room.

Will gestured for the nurse to step into the hallway.
'Has Dr Hathaway arrived yet?'

She shook her head, clearly puzzled. 'No.'

'Where's the ER doctor?'

'Dr Radcliff is with another patient right now.' The
woman's eyebrows drew together. 'Isn't she…' she motioned to Emily's cubicle '*your* patient?'

'No.'

'I see,' she said, her voice dubious.

Will took charge. 'I want a CBC, chemistry profile, urinalysis and urine culture—stat.'

'But if she isn't your patient—' the woman began.

'Just do it,' Will commanded. 'Dr Hathaway will want those results so let's save some time, shall we?'

The automatic ER doors whooshed open and Susan Hathaway strode in. The nurse froze as the physician approached.

'Go!' Will ordered in his most authoritative tone.

The nurse cast him a baleful look but obeyed.

Susan grinned at him. 'Are you bullying the staff?'

'Not at all. I just convinced her that you'd want blood work and to get the lab right on it.'

'And what will I want?'

'CBC, chemistries, UA and urine culture,' Will said.

'Sounds like you've covered all the bases.'

'Emily's pregnant,' he said baldly.

'So she's told me.'

'Emily has severe back pain at CVA, temp. is 101, nausea and vomiting. My preliminary diagnosis is pyelonephritis, complicated by dehydration.'

'Shall I examine my patient or just take your word for it?' she asked with some amusement.

He gave her a sheepish smile. 'Sorry.'

'Technically, if you're not her physician or a family member, I can't discuss her case with you,' Susan said, her gaze turning speculative.

'I'm the father.'

Susan's grin was wry. 'Why am I not surprised?' She waved him forward. 'Come on, Dr Daddy. Let's see if I concur with your diagnosis.'

Will discreetly remained at the rear of the room while Susan examined Emily and questioned her about her health over the past few weeks. Finally, she voiced her opinion. 'I don't have the lab reports to confirm this, but I believe you have a raging kidney infection,' she told Emily.

Emily's eyes closed briefly as if she was sending up a silent prayer of thanks. 'Then I can go home?'

'Ordinarily I'd say yes, but because of your nausea and vomiting my decision will depend on your electrolyte results.'

'And the baby?' Emily asked.

'Is probably fine,' Susan reassured her. She patted Emily's hand. 'I'll check with the lab and be back as soon as I have some numbers.'

Once they were alone Will moved to Emily's side. He threaded his fingers through hers and smoothed away a strand of hair from her forehead with his other hand. 'Doing OK?'

She nodded, grimacing as she shifted positions. 'Thanks for being here.'

'Why didn't you tell me you weren't feeling well?' he gently chided. 'I wouldn't have dragged you house-hunting.'

'I've felt rotten for so long, a few more symptoms didn't really register.'

'Regardless, tell me next time.'

His order brought forth a simple smile. 'Yes, master.'

He grinned. 'Hey. I like the sound of that.'

'You would.'

Susan bustled in, and although her sharp gaze landed on his obvious display of affection he didn't release Emily's hand.

'Your reports just came through, Emily. The urinalysis shows WBCs and bacteria. Although I won't have the preliminary culture results until some time tomorrow,

I'll start you on an antibiotic. Usually I'd tell my patients to drink plenty of liquids, but since first-trimester nausea is a complication I'm admitting you until we correct your electrolyte imbalance. According to your blood chemistries, you're dehydrated enough to warrant intervention.'

'How long will I stay here?' Emily asked.

'Until everything's under control. Probably several days.'

'Will it do any good to argue?' Emily asked.

'No!' Will spoke clearly and succinctly.

Susan grinned at him. 'There's your answer, my dear. I'll check on you in the morning.'

She left to deal with the paperwork. Will remained at Emily's side until she was admitted to a semiprivate room on the maternity wing.

'I called your grandmother and she'll drop by in the morning after she takes Kevin to school,' Will said.

'Thanks,' Emily murmured, her eyelids flickering as she struggled to stay awake.

He bent down and brushed a kiss across her mouth. 'Don't worry about a thing.'

'I won't.'

Reluctantly he left the room, conscious of the quizzical stares of the few night nurses on duty. He scowled at them, hoping to quell their interest in his personal activities. The two quickly redirected their attention, but he knew the gossip mill would swing into action before he left the hospital.

It was inevitable. He hoped Emily could endure the comments and speculation that were certain to follow.


'Where's my niece?'

The loud masculine voice coming from the hallway

interrupted Emily's visit with her grandmother. It was seven p.m. and Emily was amazed at how much better she felt after sleeping away nearly twenty-four hours. She remembered seeing Will at various times, but only long enough to acknowledge his presence before she'd slipped back into dreamland.

'Someone's throwing his weight around,' Gran remarked, her knitting needles clicking furiously. 'One of the nurses needs to tell him that he's in a hospital.'

Emily smiled. 'People don't realize how sound carries.' She cocked her head to listen. 'You know, he reminds me of—' She stopped herself as a horrible thought occurred to her. Her eyes grew wide. 'You don't suppose it's—'

'Surely not,' Helen said. 'I called your uncle and told him not to come this weekend because you were ill.'

'Unless he came anyway.'

Helen dropped her knitting on her lap, plainly unsettled by the possibility. She tiptoed to the door and peeked outside. When she turned back her features revealed both astonishment and horror.

'It's Bert,' she said, dazedly taking her seat.

'He must have stopped at home and Kevin told him we were here,' Emily said, aware of a knot forming in her stomach. 'OK, don't panic. Everything is under control.' She spoke more to herself than her grandparent.

Struggling to pull her thoughts together, she fluffed at her hair and hoped she looked better than she probably did. Then again, what did he expect? She was in the hospital, for heaven's sake, not on her way to the Christmas Ball.

Remembering the event, she laid a hand on her abdomen. She had to pull off her deception.

Bert Chandler strode in, his bearing authoritative. He

was a tall man, well over six feet, and wore a tailored gray business suit, white shirt, dark green tie and shoes which were polished precisely enough for a Marine dress inspection.

His hair was combed to perfection and the silver at his temples added to his distinguished air. He was clearly the picture of a successful-businessman-about-to-become-politician.

Bert glanced at Emily, before facing her grandmother. 'Helen. Good to see you.' Emily thought he sounded as insincere as usual.

'Didn't you get my message?' Helen asked. Her knitting lay on her lap in a tangled heap as if forgotten.

'I did, but I thought since I was passing through the area I'd stop anyway.' He eyed Emily. 'I didn't realize your illness was serious. I was surprised when Kevin said you were in the hospital.'

'Kidney infections can be complicated to treat,' Emily said inanely.

'I'm sure. Especially if one considers your *delicate* condition.'

Fear stirred in her heart and she pretended ignorance. 'What are you talking about?'

'I'm speaking of your pregnancy. Did you think I wouldn't question why you were given a room on the maternity floor?'

Emily decided to bluff—she had nothing to lose. 'Sick people are assigned to whatever bed is available, regardless of their diagnosis. I could be on the surgical unit.'

'Come now, Emily. I wasn't born yesterday,' Bert snapped. 'In any event, a nurse confirmed my suspicions.'

'Which nurse?' Emily demanded. The supervisor would hear about this breach of patient confidentiality.

He waved his hand. 'It really doesn't matter, does it? As soon as the volunteer gave me your room number I recognized the wing and began to wonder. When I asked at the nurses' station how you and the baby were, the young woman assured me not to worry. You were improving and you hadn't miscarried.'

Bert would do well in the political arena. He knew exactly how to manipulate people in order to ferret out the information he wanted. He should have been a private investigator.

'You had no right—' Emily began.

'I have every right,' he said. 'Especially since I learned about Kevin's recent escapade at school.'

'How?' Emily demanded, ready to pour fire and brimstone on the school officials.

He lifted one shoulder in a casual shrug. 'It doesn't matter. I am, however, worried about the quality of my nephew's upbringing. Like it or not, his actions reflect on me.'

'They shouldn't,' Emily declared. 'You're not his guardian.'

'An easily rectifiable situation,' he commented, sounding unconcerned. 'I wouldn't be doing my duty if it was within my power to bring Kevin back to the straight and narrow path and I didn't.'

Emily wanted to ask him where he'd been all Kevin's life if he was so concerned about doing his duty. Antagonizing him wouldn't serve any purpose so she gritted her teeth and forced herself to speak calmly. 'He isn't *off* the straight and narrow.'

'That's a matter of opinion. Fighting in school, insubordinate to his teachers, under suspicion of theft—'

'Theft?' Emily and Helen echoed the word.

'Theft.' Bert glared at the two. 'Which proves my

point. You two are living with him and don't know that. What else is happening under your noses while you're—' his gaze landed directly on Emily '—running around with God knows who? It's safe to say we know *what* you've been doing.'

Emily gasped and Helen visibly paled.

'What kind of example are you setting?' Bert continued.

'That's enough.' Will's commanding voice came from the doorway. 'I won't have you disturbing the patients.'

Will's imposing figure filled the doorway and relief coursed through Emily's heart.

Bert turned as Will approached. 'You must be Dr Hathaway.'

'No, I'm Dr Patton.'

'Well, Dr Patton, we're having a private family conference. If Emily finds the topic distressing she has no one to blame but herself.'

'You're wrong.' Will enunciated both words clearly.

Bert's face took on the characteristics of a thundercloud. 'What would you know about this?'

'Because I know Emily,' Will said smoothly. 'She's ill and doesn't need any stress right now.'

'I'm sorry,' Bert said, his tone suggesting otherwise, 'but her obvious lack of judgment is proof that she isn't capable of successfully guiding a young man's future. I'm going to petition for custody and, believe me, I'll win.'

Emily threw back the blankets. Ignoring the picture her hospital gown, bare legs and stocking-clad feet presented, she stood but the intravenous line tethered her to the bed like a leash.

Will blocked her path and forced her back onto the mattress. 'What are you doing?'

'I'm discharging myself.'

He didn't budge. 'Why?'

'So I can see my attorney. Now please step aside.'

Will shook his head. 'Not a chance. You're staying right here in bed. I'll deal with this.'

She stared at him, undecided. Leaving her brother's fate in Will's hands was worrisome. Will would watch out for Kevin's interests, but she didn't want or expect him to fight all her family's battles.

Will gave her an encouraging smile. 'I'll work it out.'

Her strength ebbed and a wave of light-headedness struck. 'OK,' she said, physically and emotionally weary.

'I don't know who you are, young man,' Bert blustered, 'but this doesn't concern you.'

'Emily is having *my* baby,' Will said, sounding as if his teeth were clenched. 'And what concerns her or her family concerns me.'

If she hadn't been facing a crisis Emily would have laughed at Bert's surprised, fish-faced expression.

'Now,' Will continued, 'shall we discuss this in another room?'

Bert glanced at Emily. 'Did you two elope?'

Emily shook her head as she avoided Will's gaze.

'Are you engaged?'

'No.'

Bert's bluster returned. 'Well, then, I rest my case. Just because you're having an affair with a professional man, rather than an itinerant worker, doesn't make it right.'

Will pointed to the door, hanging onto his temper by a thread. He didn't like to see Emily distraught, and the sooner he calmed Bert down the sooner Emily would relax as well. 'Outside.'

Chandler followed him into an empty room at the far end of the hallway. 'What do you have to say for yourself?' he demanded, crossing his arms.

'I don't have to explain my or Emily's actions to anyone,' Will said, standing toe to toe with the man and keeping his back to the door. 'However—'

'However, nothing,' Chandler snapped. 'I want to know what your intentions are. Do you plan on marrying my niece or are you just going to live together in sin?'

Will managed to keep his voice even. 'We're not living together and never have. I asked Emily to marry me, but she refused.'

A speculative light gleamed in Chandler's eyes. 'She won't refuse now. If she wants me to forget the whole idea of wresting Kevin's guardianship out of her grasp, she'll not disgrace the family.'

Seeing Chandler's self-centered streak, Will curled his lip in distaste. Bert was more concerned about *his* potential embarrassment than his family's well-being. If they hadn't been working toward the same end—marriage—Will wouldn't be a party to these tactics.

'I'll tell her,' Will said, wondering how she'd receive the news. He'd warned her ahead of time so the scenario shouldn't come as a complete surprise. Knowing how she felt about marriage, though, Chandler's edict would be a bitter pill to swallow.

In fact, a bad taste filled his own mouth. Will had pursued Emily with logic, citing all manner of reasons for her to agree to his proposal. In the end, however, it boiled down to Emily's choice, and Bert was taking that away from her.

'I'll tell her,' Will repeated, 'but forcing her isn't the answer.'

'She has a choice.'

Will didn't mince his words. 'Sure. Get married or lose the boy she's raised. Sounds more like an ultimatum to me.'

'Perhaps. I won't have my brother's son growing up to be a poster child for the prison system.'

'Aren't you overreacting? He was involved in a fist-fight, not selling drugs or toting weapons to school. He wasn't thrown in jail.'

'A life of crime begins somewhere,' Chandler said. 'You don't have to like my terms and neither does she. Just be sure she knows that I mean business.'

'She knows.' Will could imagine the structured existence Kevin would live if Chandler had his way. Immense satisfaction flooded his soul at the idea of saving Kevin from Chandler's narrow-minded clutches.

For a fleeting moment he wondered how different their lives would have been if he'd agreed to Emily's proposal at the Christmas Ball. They could have avoided a lot of problems, ranging from Chandler to slurs on his and Emily's characters.

Chandler folded his arms. 'Emily will drag her feet so I'll be generous. She has thirty days to get married or I'll take matters in my own hands.'

'Thirty days?' Will wondered how much time Chandler would have allowed if he *hadn't* felt charitable. 'We can't plan anything on such short notice, and I refuse to rob Emily of the type of wedding she wants.'

Knowing Emily, she wouldn't want an elaborate event. However, Chandler didn't need to know that.

The older man frowned, as if he'd realized Will had a point. 'Six weeks,' he stated. 'That's my final offer.'

Sensing that Chandler's benevolence had reached its limit, Will agreed.

'I'll keep in close contact during that period,'

Chandler warned, 'so tell Emily that the sooner you two tie the knot the sooner I'll be out of the picture.'

'All right. And now I have a stipulation for you.'

Chandler's curiosity was evident. 'Oh?'

Will's gaze didn't waver. 'Once we're married you won't interfere in Kevin's life unless he asks for your help.'

'Now, see here—'

'Ever.' Will emphasized the word.

Chandler blinked in surprise. 'Ever?'

'You can't decide a year or two down the road to meddle again,' Will warned. 'What happens in Kevin's life won't be your concern unless, as I said, he comes to you first.'

Chandler's hesitation was brief. 'If that's the way you want it.'

'It is.'

A broad smile crossed Chandler's face and he clapped Will on his back. 'To be honest, I don't envy you riding herd on Emily. You've met Helen so you can see how Em's hardheadedness runs in the female side of the family.'

After meeting Bert, Will thought the streak ran through the Chandler genes, but he refrained from comment. He'd negotiated the concessions he wanted without antagonizing Chandler and didn't want to press his luck. As for 'riding herd' on Emily, he didn't intend to try. He only hoped she'd be content with his negotiations and terms of peace.

Will stepped aside to let Chandler precede him out of the room.

'I'll be in touch,' Emily's uncle said, before he strode toward the elevators.

As Chandler walked away Will's victory felt hollow.

He wished Emily was marrying him because she *wanted* to, and not because she *had* to. Although he hadn't admitted it before, he did have feelings for her and he was selfish enough to want those reciprocated in some small way.

'Excuse me, Dr Patton.' One of the nurses approached with a patient's chart in hand. 'Mrs McGuire is fully dilated.'

'I'll be right there,' he said, intending to speak to Emily briefly.

'She wants to push,' the nurse warned.

Heaving a mental sigh, he followed her. Emily would have to wait.

'I'm sorry you had to find out about the baby this way,' Emily began, smoothing out a wrinkle in the sheet.

'I was beginning to wonder,' Helen admitted.

Emily raised her head to stare at her grandmother. 'You were?'

Helen smiled. 'I've been in the family way myself. I know the signs. I'm relieved that Will's the father rather than Don Springer.'

'Then you're not angry?'

Helen shrugged. 'Disappointed, perhaps. I had wanted you to have a beautiful June wedding before a baby came along.'

'Don't be so sure one isn't in the works,' Emily warned. 'Uncle Bert and Will are most likely working out a deal to tie Kevin's future to a marriage license right now.'

Helen picked up several dropped stitches and resumed knitting. 'Most likely,' she said.

Emily rubbed at the itchy tape on her arm. 'I can hear

Will telling Uncle Bert how I refused his proposal. Now he'll force me into accepting.'

Helen came to the end of her row and flipped the half-knitted sweater panel around to study her handiwork. 'Would it be so bad? Will is a nice, mannerly young man. He's also a much finer person than Don ever could be.'

'You think so?'

Helen's eyes sparkled. 'Absolutely.' She stopped to count a few stitches. 'Don't you agree?'

Emily sighed. Even in their short acquaintance Will had exhibited more character in his little finger than Don could claim in his entire body.

'Yes, but I'm not the woman Will wants. He's dreamed of moving in high-class social circles with a glamorous wife. I wouldn't fit in.'

'Oh, pooh.' Helen's disgust showed. 'You don't know that. You've never tried.'

The truth stung. Emily dropped her voice to just above a whisper. 'Once he realized how much he'd given up to marry me he'd leave. And I'd be devastated.'

Emily's words hung in the air before Helen spoke.

'Then you love him?'

Emily sighed. 'Will is a very special person. I don't know if what I'm feeling is love or just infatuation. With Uncle Bert getting involved, I won't have time to find out.'

For a long minute Helen didn't say a word. 'If you feel this strongly against marrying Will then, by all means, don't. Kevin will survive. For all Bert's faults I think he does care about what happens to him.'

'No.' Emily shook her head. 'I'd marry Attila the Hun before I'd let Bert take him.'

The laughter lines around Helen's eyes deepened. 'So you're placing Will in the same category as Attila?'

Emily smiled. 'No. Just making a point.'

Helen purled another row. 'You say Will wants a society wife. It's been my experience that men don't always know what they want.'

'Will does.'

Helen shrugged. 'Maybe. More often than not, we women can guide our fellows in the direction we want. The trick is in making them think it was their idea in the first place.'

'Is that what you did with Grandpa?'

Helen gave a Cheshire-cat smile. 'I wasn't one hundred per cent successful, but things usually worked out the way I wanted them. Why, I remember once, when I was expecting your mother…'

Her eyes took on a dreamy quality. 'I wanted the house painted inside and out. Of course, your grandfather was more interested in slapping a fresh coat of paint on the barn. Rather than argue, over the next few weeks I talked about the company we'd have once the baby arrived. In fact…' she giggled '…I cleaned that house within an inch of its life. For the company, of course.'

Emily smiled. 'Of course.'

'Anyway, the rooms were spotless—fresh curtains, new tablecloth, everything. A neighbor even helped me wash the walls. You name it, we did it. Then we started working on the outside. We planted flowers and rose bushes. By the time we were finished Clem had noticed a difference and remarked on how shabby the paint was looking. Next thing I knew, he'd started scraping and sanding. By the time your mother was born everything was as bright and shiny as a new penny.

'So, you see, my dear,' Helen said confidently, 'men must be guided.'

Emily considered the comment. 'So you're saying—'

'I'm saying that Will might *think* he wants a highfalutin wife, but it's up to you to convince him otherwise. Courtship is all about discovery. You must simply persuade him that *you're* the wife he needs and wants.'

Her grandmother's tactics sounded so simple.

'I don't know if I can.'

'You won't if you never try.'

Emily thought a moment. She'd like to be the wife Will wanted. Even before their encounter at the Christmas Ball she'd felt a kinship with him. Didn't she owe it to her baby to heed her grandmother's challenge?

She stiffened her spine. 'You're right. Nothing ventured, nothing gained.'

Helen stuffed her knitting into the bag near her feet. 'Good girl. Now, I'd better run home and check on Kevin. I'll stop by again later.'

'Tonight's your bridge night so don't miss it on account of me. Dr Hathaway said I could go home tomorrow.'

Helen hesitated, as if debating her decision. 'Since you are feeling better...' She smiled. 'I'm sure Will won't let you get too lonely.'

For the next forty-five minutes Emily watched the clock while she waited for Will to arrive. Surely his conference with Bert wasn't taking this long. Perhaps he'd been sidetracked with a patient.

The supper cart clanked down the hall, bringing with it a variety of aromas. When an aide delivered Emily's tray and mentioned how Dr Patton had been summoned for a delivery, Emily's anticipation took away her appetite for everything but the red gelatin. However, she forced herself to drink the consommé and nibble on the crackers as her first meal in nearly twenty-four hours.

Sixty minutes passed. Unable to stand the suspense, she tugged her chenille bathrobe over her nightgown, slid her feet into a pair of slippers, grabbed her IV pole and headed for the door.

As she rounded the corner toward the nurses' station she saw Will standing at the counter, still wearing his scrub suit. She increased her pace, careful not to bump into two well-dressed women who were scanning the room numbers in search of their destination.

'Hi, Will,' she said, dragging the portable IV stand with her.

He turned and frowned. 'Are you supposed to be up and around?'

'I'm not an invalid.'

He grinned. 'I guess not.'

One of the women she'd passed backtracked to stare at Will. 'I know you.' She wore a designer-label coat costing more than Emily's entire clothing budget for the year. Her gray hair was perfectly coiffed in a classic bouffant style, her make-up was impeccable and her nails gleamed red.

'Forgive me, but—' Will began.

'I never would have believed it if I hadn't seen it for myself. You're that Patton boy.'

His smile seemed stilted. 'Yes, I am.'

She eyed his garb, paying close attention to his name scrawled across one breast pocket. 'You're a doctor?'

'Yes.'

'Oh, dear heavens!' She turned to the woman beside her. 'I hope this man isn't responsible for my niece's care, Mary.'

Mary, a few years younger but bearing a strong resemblance to her sister, appeared as startled as Emily. She, however, didn't have the same forceful personality as her sibling. 'Nelda, don't make a scene.'

'Well!' Nelda huffed. 'I know this man's upbringing. I wouldn't let him within ten feet of *my* daughter, and you shouldn't either.'

Emily couldn't contain her righteous indignation. 'Dr Patton is one of our finest physicians.'

Nelda measured her with a glance and obviously found her wanting because she ignored her. 'You're clearly misguided, young woman. This man couldn't possibly be a doctor, even if his title *is* stitched on his shirt.'

'I assure you that I am,' Will said harshly.

'Humph.' Nelda sniffed. 'I'm not convinced. I remember the trouble you caused, burglarizing your own employer. With a juvenile record you couldn't possibly have gotten into medical school.'

'I'm not going to discuss my past with you,' Will said firmly, his eyes blazing. 'If you continue to disrupt this unit I'll call Security.'

'Disrupt?' Nelda's face turned beet-red. 'I'm merely stating the truth and warning people in the process.'

*Will had a juvenile record?* Emily had thought when he'd mentioned something about prison that he'd spoken figuratively, not literally. Even so, she didn't believe Nelda's accusations.

Feeling compelled to interrupt Will's character assassination, she stepped forward. 'I think you should weigh every word before you speak, ma'am. People can be prosecuted for slander.'

Nelda cast a disdainful glance on Emily. 'This doesn't concern you.'

'Oh, but it does,' Emily said, adding steel to her soft tone. 'You're trying to smear not only a talented physician but my fiancé's reputation. I won't stand by and let you belittle his accomplishments.'

# CHAPTER SEVEN

THE words for Will's defense flowed out of Emily like water from a broken dam. 'Dr Patton is a responsible *and* respectable member of this community. How dare you come in here and imply otherwise?'

She squared her shoulders and clutched her pole in a white-knuckled grip. 'Will is a highly trained professional. Whatever happened in his younger days is over and best forgotten. I'm sure if people start digging in your closet they'd find a few skeletons. In other words, lady, *mind your own business.*'

Nelda's mouth opened and closed, like a fish swallowing water. 'Well!' she huffed. 'I'm leaving. I won't stand here and be insulted by this…this…little upstart!'

Emily was ready to advance, but Will pulled her from behind and murmured in her ear, 'Go to your room.'

'But, Will—'

'Please.'

Hating to retreat, she turned as gracefully as she could and stormed back to her quarters. Before she entered she glanced over her back and saw Nelda bustling toward the elevators while her sister apologized profusely to Will.

Too annoyed to sit, Emily paced the floor until Will appeared in the doorway.

'Remind me never to make you angry,' he commented as he closed the door, before guiding her to the bed. 'For a minute there I was afraid I might have to render med-

108

ical aid to Nelda. I had visions of your IV pole wrapped around her neck.'

His humor helped to defuse her indignation. She grinned. 'It's what all the best-dressed loudmouths are wearing this season.'

His expression turned serious. 'Thanks for rushing to my rescue, but it wasn't necessary.'

'Yes, it was. The woman was out to destroy you and I refused to let her.'

Will sat near her on the bed and ran his fingers through his hair, as if frustrated. 'She wasn't entirely wrong.'

She laid a hand on his. 'If you'd like to tell me about it I'll listen, but whatever happened when you were a kid doesn't matter to me. What you are today is what counts.'

He stared at her, as if weighing his options. Finally, he nodded. 'As I said before, I wasn't the type of kid most parents wanted their sons to emulate. My father left us when I was five and my mother worked three jobs to pay for necessities. Naturally, I didn't have any supervision and I got into trouble at school. I even had a few run-ins with the law—nothing major, but every cop knew me by name.'

He paused. When he spoke again a spot on the far wall had captured his attention. 'My mother started cleaning house for one of the older physicians in the community, Abe Darnell. I'd come by in the evenings to help her and one night he caught me studying an anatomy and physiology textbook. Once he knew I was interested in medicine he took me under his wing. He even helped me get a job at the local greenhouse.

'The owner had hired another kid—Owen—and myself to help plant lawns, do deliveries and so on. Things went well until Mr Hogan started missing money from the cash register. Since Owen came from a middle-income family, Mr Hogan assumed I'd stolen it and called the police.'

'But you didn't do anything wrong.'

He shook his head. 'Abe defended me, but I lost my job. Eventually, my former employer caught Owen with his hands in the till and I was exonerated.'

'But the damage had been done.'

'Yeah. So now you know the sordid details of my life.'

Emily now understood more clearly his need to avoid gossip. She could also understand why he wanted to join the ranks of the people who'd scorned him—to prove his worth. Having a woman like Celine on his arm would be the icing on the cake. Now he'd have to settle for second-best.

It was a sobering thought.

Considering all this, *could* she convince him that someone as common as herself was the right woman for him? Somehow she doubted it.

'Did you mean what you said about calling me your fiancé?' He sounded cautious.

She avoided his gaze, unable to admit the truth just yet. 'It was all I could think of to say at the time,' she said. 'Aren't you going to tell me about your discussion with my uncle?'

If he'd noticed her abrupt change of subject he didn't comment. 'Bert will relinquish all claims to Kevin if we get married.'

'I thought that would be the gist of the conversation,' she said wryly.

'You aren't upset?' His tone was guarded.

'As I said, I expected as much.' She purposely refrained from mentioning her heart-to-heart conversation with her grandmother.

'Also, he won't interfere in Kevin's life again.'

She scoffed. 'For how long?'

'For ever. Or until Kevin asks for his help.'

Her heart skipped a beat. She'd hoped for the day Bert would leave them alone. 'No kidding?'

'That's what he said.' He paused briefly before he continued. 'Although he gave one stipulation.'

Emily's joy faded. She might have known. Bert would never voluntarily relinquish an advantage. He'd probably demanded an impossible-to-meet contingency. 'What is it?'

'Our wedding has to take place within six weeks.'

Emily's jaw dropped in surprise. 'That's all he wants?'

He nodded. 'Until then he plans to take an extremely active interest in your family.'

'And then he'll leave us in peace.' She repeated it for clarification, watching Will's response.

'You got it.'

Emily considered her next move. After learning how Will's dreams were inextricably linked to his past, she didn't feel comfortable without giving him an escape clause.

'Shall we agree to a time limit?' she asked.

He raised an eyebrow. 'You want out already?'

She shrugged. 'I thought you might. Eventually.'

A furrow developed on his forehead. 'Why?'

'In case you change your mind.'

'And if I don't?'

She evaded his question. 'If you recall, *you* suggested a temporary arrangement at one time.'

'I thought it would help you feel as if you had some control over your life.'

She was moved by his thoughtfulness. 'And now?'

'Both of us still have control. Regardless of whether or not we agree right now to go our separate ways on a specified date, there's only one way to end a marriage.'

Although unspoken, the word 'divorce' hung in the air.

'We should give ourselves at least a year before making any decisions,' he said. 'We're cheating ourselves, the baby and Kevin if we don't.'

A year. Three hundred and sixty-five days should be long enough to show him that he couldn't live without her, society upbringing or not. 'OK.'

Another question remained. She toyed with one edge of the tape on her hand in order to avoid his gaze. 'Are we going to have a real marriage?'

'Is there any other kind?'

She swallowed hard. 'I didn't know what you were expecting as far as a physical relationship.'

He lifted her chin to stare into her eyes. 'We're having a baby in six months. Denying ourselves doesn't serve any purpose.'

Thinking of the sparks they generated with seeming ease, she doubted if they could resist each other while living under the same roof. In truth, she didn't want to.

'Besides,' he said a trifle wryly, 'my house only has five bedrooms. One for us, Kevin, your grandmother, the baby and my office.'

As she focused on his full lips and his familiar scent and enjoyed the warmth of his hands as they enfolded hers, an anticipatory tremor ran down her spine at the thought of sharing his bed. The proverbial moment of truth had arrived.

His steady gaze turned questioning as he waited for her response.

She managed a tremulous smile. 'Then we'd better get busy and plan our wedding.'

The following weeks passed in a flurry of activity. News of her impending marriage and motherhood circulated through the hospital and Emily constantly fielded congratulations. Several women—ones who'd set their own hopes on Will as husband material—made a few pointed remarks, but in general most were genuinely happy for her.

Although Emily felt much better as her pregnancy progressed, she tired easily. After putting in hectic days at the hospital, she spent the remainder of her hours organizing the details for their quiet wedding.

Because community halls were hard to book on such short notice, Emily persuaded Will to entertain their guests at his new house. Under her supervision and limited assistance, Kevin and her grandmother applied new wallpaper to the living, sitting and dining rooms while Will helped whenever he found the time.

However, at eight o'clock each night Will would call a halt to whatever they were doing and demand she put up her feet and relaxed while he chatted to Kevin. Invariably, she'd doze off and reawaken at ten, finding herself snuggled against him.

As their wedding day drew closer the doubts Emily had managed to keep at bay grew stronger. In her dreams she would have preferred it if Will had begged her to marry him because he couldn't live without her. Reality, however, was something different.

It was one thing to make a vow to prove she was the type of wife Will wanted and quite another to see it through, but she refused to go back on her word. She'd agreed to marry Will in order to ensure Kevin's and her baby's futures and she wouldn't change her mind now.

While Emily was glad her busy schedule didn't leave much time for reflection, her fast pace was physically draining. The arrival of a new nurse raised her hopes of seeing some relief, but those soon faded as she found herself juggling her own responsibilities with those given to their latest employee.

'I thought I'd explained how important it was to follow the discharge checklist step by step,' Emily told Jacqueline Olivier.

'I did.' The young nurse, only out of training a short time, tossed her head of shoulder-length blonde hair in a carefree manner.

'Then how could you miss giving Mrs Lytle her RhoGam before you discharged her?'

'I thought you took care of her injection.'

Emily bit back a retort. As the most senior staff member on duty, it had fallen on her to oversee the unit's new nurse. 'No, I distinctly told you to run down to the blood bank and sign out the medication.'

'Well, I thought *you* were going to do it.'

'No, I wasn't.'

Jacqueline shrugged. 'Your word against mine.'

Emily gritted her teeth. Jacqueline was right. Unfortunately, Emily wasn't certain who would be held accountable in this situation. Jacqueline was a registered nurse and had officially signed off as performing all discharge procedures. Technically, though, Emily had been assigned to orient Jacqueline to the department and was responsible for her training.

The director of nursing and birthing center supervisor wouldn't take into consideration Emily's own heavy patient load when they reviewed the incident report of a medication error. Nor would they sympathize over Emily's difficulty in monitoring the latest admission in addition to all her other duties. After all, Emily had help in the form of Jacqueline.

In the past four hours Jacqueline had shown a real knack for doing as little as possible. In Emily's mind this particular episode foretold a rocky road ahead. Their new nurse seemed more interested in her manicure and in being available when the younger male doctors made rounds than in taking care of patients.

'Call Mrs Lytle and ask her to return as soon as possible,' Emily ordered. 'It's important that she receives her Rh-immune globulin before the seventy-two-hour post-delivery time frame passes. I don't need to remind you of the serious complications to her future children, not to mention the lawsuit potential.'

Jacqueline sighed. 'I suppose. What's her phone number?'

Once again Emily struggled to keep her voice even. 'Check the chart. When you've contacted her, let me know. I'll be with Mrs Sanders.'

Crossing her fingers for Jacqueline's success, Emily strode into Nina Sanders's room. 'How are you doing?'

Nina's face shone with perspiration. 'Not good,' she gasped, clutching her belly. She was six months into her first pregnancy and Emily half expected Will to order magnesium sulfate to stop her contractions, especially since her cervix hadn't dilated. Even so, something about this case didn't seem quite right.

'We're waiting for your lab results and Dr Patton is on his way,' Emily said, trying to keep the woman and her husband calm. Once again she took her patient's vital signs, noting that Nina's temperature hadn't dropped. *Hurry, Will.*

As if her wishes had conjured him up, he strode into the room. 'Tell me what's going on,' he said.

Nina nodded. 'I started having these pains, but I couldn't really time them because they're constant.'

'Are they localized or can you feel them across your whole abdomen?'

Nina rubbed her right side. 'It hurts everywhere, but more here.'

His mouth twisted as if in thought, then he glanced at the external monitor Emily had placed around the woman's waist and studied the peaks. 'Baby doesn't seem in any real distress,' he commented.

Nina closed her eyes for a brief second. 'That's good. Isn't it?'

'Absolutely,' he said firmly, pulling a pair of latex gloves out of the box Emily held and tugging them on. After performing a quick exam, he stripped off the protective gear and reached for the chart.

'Lab results?' he asked.

'I'll see if they've come through.' Emily hurried from the room, riffled through the pages on the laser printer in the nurses' station, then rushed back to the room with two documents.

She handed them to Will, but not before she'd noticed the elevated white count.

He studied them for several minutes before he spoke. 'I don't think you're in labor, Nina.'

Nina rubbed her distended abdomen. 'Then why does it hurt?'

'You may have appendicitis.'

Nina's jaw dropped. 'Appendicitis?' she echoed.

'It happens,' Will said. 'I'll arrange for a laparotomy immediately.'

Nina's lower lip quivered. 'And our baby?'

'Both you and the baby should do fine. We have an excellent anesthesiologist on hand.'

Nina's husband cut in. 'You said that you *think* she has appendicitis. Aren't you sure?'

'No,' Will said honestly. 'Appendicitis can be a tough condition to diagnose and pregnancy makes it even more so. However, the death rate from a ruptured appendix in pregnant women is high. We'd rather risk surgery.'

The man's complexion whitened and he nodded, apparently concurring with Will's decision.

The next thirty minutes passed quickly as Mrs Sanders was prepped and taken to the OR. While the surgical personnel wheeled her down the hallway, Emily hunted for Jacqueline and found her in the lounge.

'Did you locate Mrs Lytle?' she asked.

Jacqueline tossed her hair. 'She's on her way back and not very happy about it. I told her that she could talk to you when she got here.'

Emily wanted to say, Gee, thanks. However, she was too relieved to hear of Mrs Lytle's return to comment. 'Fine,' she said. 'I'll deal with her. In the meantime, please fill out the quality assurance incident report.'

'Is it necessary?' Jacqueline asked. 'I mean, the lady's coming back. She's getting her meds. Why make a big deal? No harm done.'

Emily forced her voice to remain even. 'Notifying the QA department of a medication error is standard procedure. We were fortunate to catch the mistake when we did. If our luck holds, we can correct it before any damage *is* done.'

Jacqueline rolled her eyes in disgust. 'I still don't think this is necessary.'

'It doesn't matter what you think. Just do it,' Emily ordered.

In the intervening hours Mrs Sanders returned from Recovery minus an inflamed appendix and they admitted another young mother in labor. Meanwhile, Emily's worries grew by leaps and bounds as the seventy-two-hour deadline for Mrs Lytle's medication approached.

Just as she was debating whether to make another phone call an unhappy Mr and Mrs Lytle arrived. After breathing a sigh of relief, Emily apologized profusely for the inconvenience as she ushered the couple into a room and administered the injection.

Twenty minutes later she sent them on their way home. Although she didn't relish being called to task about the slip-up, at least she'd righted the wrong in time.

Placing Molly in charge, Emily went to an infection control meeting. When she returned she found Will and Jacqueline deep in a discussion.

'Oh, there you are,' Jacqueline said, her smile suspiciously bright. 'I saw Dr Patton and thought I'd better explain the problem you had with Mrs Lytle.'

The problem *she* had? Emily frowned. 'I've given the injection and Jacqueline and I are both filing incident reports.'

Will's cold tone caught her by surprise. 'I should hope so. I don't need to remind you of how your error might have cost this woman future children.'

'No, you don't.' Emily glanced at Jacqueline for support. 'Didn't you explain what happened?'

Jacqueline wrung her hands as if she was worried, but Emily saw through her pretense. 'I'm sorry, but I had to explain how you were too busy and Mrs Lytle's shot fell through the cracks. I should have questioned the lapse since I was signing the discharge checklist, but being new...' She shrugged.

'Don't let it happen again,' he said, addressing Emily as if he considered her at fault.

Emily thrust her hands in her pocket and clenched her fists. It cost her a great deal to hold her tongue. Trying to set the record straight now would make it seem as if she was accusing Jacqueline of lying. Regardless of the extenuating circumstances, her signature made her liable. 'Don't worry. I won't.'

The instant he left, Emily confronted Jacqueline. 'Why didn't you tell him the truth?'

'I did,' she said smugly.

'I don't have time to watch every move you make but, believe me, I will,' Emily warned. 'If you can't carry your weight, you won't be here for long.'

'Don't threaten me,' Jacqueline said, her voice hard. 'My father is the hospital administrator. I'll have a job longer than you will.'

With that she strode away, leaving Emily furious at both Jacqueline and Will. When she saw him again twenty minutes later her anger hadn't ebbed. Ignoring his close proximity, she sent a new batch of patient orders to the pharmacy and lab in the coolly professional manner she'd employed during those days following the Christmas Ball.

He sat beside her and scribbled orders in a chart. 'You're angry,' he stated without preamble.

'How observant.'

'You shouldn't take correction personally,' he began.

'It felt rather personal to me.'

'I had every right to be furious,' he stated, his jaw squared. 'My patient would have suffered.'

Emily glared at him. 'I'm aware of that. I was upset myself when I discovered the error.'

'Then why are you mad at me?'

'Because you took the word of someone you've never seen before, never worked with and didn't know from Adam, over mine. The least you could have done was let me explain.'

He leaned back in his chair. 'OK. Explain.'

She readdressed the computer screen. 'I'm busy.'

Out of the corner of her eye she saw him smirk. Irritated because she didn't want him to attribute her indignation to hormones, she faced him again.

'I would, except my statement will sound petty and self-serving since Jacqueline's already told her story. I will say this, though. Yes, the whole mess was my fault. My fault for leaving Jacqueline alone while I looked after Mrs Sanders, and my fault for assuming Jacqueline was capable of working independently. But what really hurt me was your attitude. You didn't give me the benefit of the doubt.'

Her heart was beating furiously by the time she finished her speech. For a few seconds only the background noise of the unit surrounded them.

'I didn't realize,' he said slowly.

'Well, you should have.' Her chest heaved as she tried to bring her emotions under control.

'I won't do it again.'

His comment wasn't a classic apology, but she suspected it was as close to one as he could give. In her experience few men could say those two little words, 'I'm sorry'.

Will placed a hand on her shoulder and leaned close to her ear. 'Friends again?'

His pleading expression brought out her smallest smile. She nodded once.

'I'm glad,' he said simply. Because there were too many people around, she settled for a gentle pat rather than a 'making-up' kiss.

Although Emily hoped the small wound in their relationship would heal quickly, she erected a distant but polite guard around Jacqueline. She'd always enjoyed working with her colleagues in the maternity unit so she found the strained relations with a fellow nurse disconcerting. Walking to the parking lot with Molly at the end of her shift a week later, she vocalized her frustration over the circumstances.

'Just ignore her,' Molly advised. 'She's supposedly set her sights on working in a doctor's office. If she has as much pull as she claims, she'll be moving on to greener pastures before long.'

'I suppose.'

'Forget the entire episode for now and concentrate on your wedding. Is everything all set for tomorrow?'

Comforted by her friend's reassurances, Emily nodded. 'Do you think I'm doing the right thing to have such a simple ceremony and invite only our closest friends?'

'I think it's a wonderful idea. Big weddings are over-rated.'

'Yeah, although I can't help but imagine how Will's going to compare our small reception with the flashy society bash he would have had if Celine was marching down the aisle instead of me.'

'Didn't you two decide on the arrangements to-gether?'

'Yes,' Emily said slowly.

'Then I rest my case. If Will had wanted the event you described, he'd have told you.'

Emily smoothed her tunic over her abdomen. 'Maybe we should have waited until after the baby was born. I'm getting fat.'

Molly gave her a quick once-over. 'With the dress you picked out, your little tummy isn't noticeable.'

'I'm not worried about the wedding. It's what comes *after*,' Emily said glumly.

Molly giggled. 'Ah, the bedroom scene. Honestly, Em, he's not going to notice. And if he does, it's *his* baby.' She grinned. 'If your little pooch won't make him feel like a stud muffin, I don't know what will.'

Burning with embarrassment, Emily playfully punched her friend's arm. 'Oh, you!'

Molly grinned. 'You're just having last-minute jitters. Trust me, dear. Everything will work out.'

Those were the words Emily clung to the next day while she stood in the hospital chapel next to Will, dressed in a simple floor-length white gown with her hair arranged in an elaborate chignon and seeded with pearls and tiny flowers.

She clutched her bouquet of red roses and baby's breath as she recited her vows. Her life was changing and only time would tell if it was for the best.

As she gazed at the man standing straight and tall beside her, her heart skipped a beat. Decked out in a tuxedo with a red boutonniere pinned to his lapel, he presented a picture worthy of a men's fashion magazine.

'With this ring, I thee wed.' Will placed the plain gold band on her finger and her hands trembled. Gazing upon his familiar features, seeing the gentle smile on his lips and in his eyes, she thought of everything he'd done for her—from the moment he'd reaffirmed her self-worth on the night of the Christmas Ball until now.

She peeked at her grandmother and brother as they stood together. Dressed in a beautiful ice-blue dress, which complemented her silvery hair, Helen was smiling from ear to ear. Kevin wore the rented tux that Will had helped him select, beaming with pride over his adult role of giving away his sister.

She'd been afraid Kevin would take the news of her pregnancy with resentment, but Will had taken Kevin for a man-to-man talk. Neither of them had revealed the gist of the conversation on their return, but their easy rapport indicated how well Will had handled the situation.

She refocused on her groom. Her chest ached from trying to contain the happiness filling her heart. She couldn't deny her feelings or hold them back. For better or worse, she loved Will Patton.

Emily cleared her throat, then repeated the words while she placed a matching ring on Will's finger. Perhaps she should have felt trapped but, surprisingly enough, she didn't.

The chaplain smiled. 'You may kiss the bride.'

Will's head descended as she lifted hers and their lips met in a searing kiss. She'd expected a mere peck, but instead his mouth molded itself to hers as precisely as if they were interlocking puzzle pieces. Her toes curled in her white satin pumps seconds before he broke away, smiling broadly as their guests applauded.

He crooked his elbow. 'Shall we go, Mrs Patton?'

She curled her fingers around his arm. 'By all means.'

There was a flash of light and she recognized a professional photographer snapping away. 'I didn't call him,' she whispered.

'I did.'

She slowed in her tracks, trying to retain her smile while puzzling over the change. 'Why? Molly's boyfriend agreed to take our pictures.'

'Now we'll have double the memories,' he said, clearly dismissing her concerns. 'Don't fret. Your only job today is to smile and look gorgeous.'

Will guided her along the shortest route to the white stretch limousine parked outside the doctors' entrance. She stopped short, ignoring the small crowd who'd gathered in the April sunshine to see the lucky couple. 'A limo?'

'I thought it appropriate,' he said. 'Do you like it?'

'I never expected…' she began, trying not to contemplate the expense.

The uniformed driver straightened and opened the door wide. Will nudged her forward, as if aware she was over-awed by the prospect of traveling in such luxury. She took Will's hand and allowed him to help her inside. Once she was settled he stepped in and sat beside her on the white leather seat.

She ran her fingers over the surfaces, memorizing every feature.

'What do you think?' He sounded amused.

'This is marvelous. But it wasn't necessary.'

He flung one arm around her shoulder. 'If a wedding isn't an occasion to ride in style, I don't know what is.'

She clutched his hand as the driver moved away from the curb, too touched to say more than, 'Thanks.'

'You're welcome. Now, sit back and enjoy the view,' he said, softening his directive with a broad smile.

'Aren't we going home?' she asked, having noticed how they were heading toward the outskirts of the city.

'Eventually,' he said, settling her against his chest.

'We're giving our guests time to arrive at the house before we do.'

Determined to enjoy every moment, Emily alternated between sitting back as he'd ordered and twisting in her seat to explore her lavish surroundings. She examined the taped movie selection, pushed buttons on the television and VCR, peered inside the small refrigerator and gasped in surprise as she accidentally lowered the clear soundproof barrier separating them from the driver.

Will chuckled. 'Having fun?'

She giggled. 'This is great. I've heard how luxurious these are, but I never thought I'd experience it for myself. Thank you again.'

Without thinking, she leaned over and kissed him. His hand gravitated to her back, holding her close. Surrounded by his scent and reveling in his caress, an internal heat began to build inside her.

The chauffeur's modulated voice came across the intercom. 'Shall I take another turn through town?'

Emily broke away, chagrined at getting caught in a clinch.

Will's heavy-lidded eyes spoke of thwarted passion and he gave a long-suffering sigh. 'We'd better join our guests,' he said. Then he winked and added for her ears only, 'Save that thought for later.'

All too soon they arrived at Will's house—*their* house, Emily amended—and found it surrounded by parked cars. Molly and several of the other nurses had decorated the porch railings with huge white bows and white ribbon streamers.

Emily breezed up the few steps in her long gown, conscious of Will's hovering arm. 'Don't trip,' he cautioned.

Inside, guests in wedding finery milled through the

public areas, sipping punch and drinking coffee according to preference. As Emily meandered around the living room, parlor and dining room she couldn't help but take pride in her and her grandmother's efforts. A coordinator and expensive caterer couldn't have done better. More importantly, no one could classify Will's wife as a social misfit.

Although her own dreams had included a beautiful ceremony, pleasing Will was uppermost in her mind and she'd worked doubly hard to do so.

She ducked into the kitchen and saw the countertop loaded with trays of the finger sandwiches and decorated sheet cakes that Helen and Jacinta Lopez, one of Helen's cronies, had prepared. 'Any problems?'

'None,' Jacinta told Emily kindly. 'Everything's wonderful. Your grandmother just came in to ask, too. Now, go. Enjoy.' She made a shooing motion. 'Let my daughters and me worry about the refreshments.'

Emily laughed. 'I'm going, I'm going. Has anyone seen Kevin?'

Jacinta shrugged. 'He went to the back yard a few minutes ago.'

Emily's skirts rustled as she moved to peer through the window. Kevin, with his bow tie hanging around his neck and his top button undone, stood next to two boys dressed in jeans and sports shirts. Will's dog, Gold Digger—Digger, for short—danced around them in puppyish delight.

'Tell Dr Will it's time to cut the cake,' Jacinta called. 'I'll get Kevin.'

Within minutes Emily had found Will. With Kevin, Helen, Molly, Will's partners and their wives, and a host of other friends and distinguished hospital dignitaries surrounding them, Dr Moore's voice rose above the din. 'A toast to the happy couple!'

Champagne poured freely until everyone held a glass. Once again Dr Moore quieted the noise as he raised his hand. 'To our newest partner and his beautiful bride. May you have a long, happy life.'

He'd hardly finished his toast when a loud 'woof' filled the air. Before anyone could react, forty pounds of golden fluff sailed into the room and careened into the banquet table.

The punch-bowl tipped, sloshing red punch onto the pristine white lace tablecloth. Cups rattled and fell on their sides, spilling their contents.

The punch, however, didn't capture Emily's interest. Instead, she watched in horror as the top layer of her gorgeous two-tiered cake slid off and collapsed into a heap of white icing, crushed frosting roses and crumbs.

# CHAPTER EIGHT

'KEVIN!' Will broke the stunned silence.

'I didn't do it.' Kevin grabbed at Digger's leash and held onto the panting bundle of energy. 'Honest. He was outside. I tied him myself.'

'Get him out of here,' Will ordered.

Kevin tugged. 'Here, Digger. Bad dog.'

Emily stared at the plastic bride-and-groom ornament standing at a drunken angle on the crushed cake. Mortified beyond belief, she couldn't bear to look at her guests.

Helen, Molly and Jacinta stepped forward to repair the damage as best they could. 'We have plenty of cake so don't worry,' Helen said kindly. 'Good thing Jacinta and I made extra.'

Emily nodded, although she felt as if she were watching a movie. She'd worked so hard to make this day perfect and, of all things, a *dog* had ruined everything.

'Step back,' Molly said. 'We don't want you to spill punch on your dress. Now, smile. It isn't the end of the world.'

Emily faced her guests. The men appeared amused and the women wore sympathetic expressions. She wanted to sink through the cracks in the hardwood floor or allow the tears burning at the back of her eyes to gush forth, but she refused to embarrass Will.

She managed a smile. 'Weddings are supposed to be memorable. I guess none of you will forget ours.'

Her attempt at levity broke the stilted atmosphere.

One of the doctors' wives, an elegantly dressed woman in her mid-forties, came forward and hugged her. 'Oh, honey. Every ceremony I've ever attended has some little mishap. It's just the way things are.'

Somehow Emily didn't consider Will's pet demolishing their cake as a 'little' mishap. However, she was in too great a need for comfort to correct her.

Dr Moore's wife joined them. 'Absolutely. Why, I remember when Maybelle and Frank celebrated their fiftieth anniversary...'

Emily didn't follow the story as she was too relieved to hear the conversation flowing freely once again. She glanced around for Will and discovered he was missing. As she meandered through the house in search of him her guests interrupted her quest to offer words of encouragement. By the time she could break away Will had rejoined her.

'Where have you been?' she asked in a stage whisper.

'Outside.'

She stared at him. He'd left her to deal with the disaster alone? 'Outside?' she echoed.

'Yeah. Kevin and I solved the mystery of how Digger opened the door and came in.'

'You did? What happened?'

Helen hurried forward. 'I thought we should go ahead and serve the cake without all the fuss. Is that OK?'

'Fine,' Emily said, before she cast a questioning gaze upon Will.

He gave her a quick hug. 'Long story. I'll explain later.'

The afternoon passed quickly and without further incident. Shortly after the last guest had left, Emily and her family changed into comfortable clothes and began the daunting task of restoring the house to rights.

Will surveyed the stacks of dirty glass cups and trays on every available surface in the living and dining rooms. 'Why does it look like we invited more than twenty-five people?'

Emily laughed as she piled the dishes in a large tub. 'Because we did. There are fifty trays, fifty cups and at least that many forks and spoons to wash.'

'We should have used paper and plastic,' he grumbled good-naturedly.

'But it wouldn't have been as nice,' she said. Having dishpan hands was a small price to pay for the touch of class that the beautiful pieces lent to the occasion.

'Good thing I enlisted extra help,' he said, shouldering her aside to lift the tub. 'I'll get this. It's too heavy for you.'

She smiled at his solicitousness. Did he honestly believe that her condition allowed her special privileges at the hospital? Carrying a pan of dishes was nothing in comparison.

The doorbell chimed and his previous comment suddenly registered. 'What extra help?'

'That's probably them now,' he said. 'I'll be right back.'

While Will toted his load to the kitchen Emily found two boys of Kevin's age fidgeting on the porch. She greeted them in a warm but puzzled voice.

The light-haired one was bolder than his companion. 'Dr Patton told us to be here at six o'clock.'

Having just glanced at the mantel clock on her way to the door, she smiled at their promptness. 'You're right on time,' she said, opening the door wide. 'Come in.'

Before she could turn around, Will's voice drifted over her shoulder. 'Good to see you,' he said to the boys. 'We're gathering the dishes for you right now.'

Emily hoped she hadn't heard correctly. 'They're going to—?'

'Wash and pack up the dishes,' Will said firmly. 'Judd
and Eric will do a fine job, I'm sure.'

Emily's smile became forced. She didn't have Will's
level of faith, but he was already leading them to their
job so she bit back her comments until he returned a few
minutes later.

'Judd and Eric?' she asked, recognizing the names.
'How did you get those two to help you?'

'Simple. I shanghaied them.'

She stared at him in surprise. 'You what?'

He grinned, looking handsome in his well-worn jeans
and casual open-necked shirt. 'Those two untied
Digger's leash and let him inside the house. Then they
hung around to see what happened and Kevin saw them
peeking in the window. Needless to say, a scuffle started.
To make a long story short, all three of them are on KP
duty under Jacinta's supervision.'

'I hope they don't decide to take out their animosity
on those dishes,' she said, dismayed at the prospect. 'I
have to return them to the rental agency in one piece.'

He flung a comforting arm around her shoulders. 'You
will. If they break any, they'll pay for each and every
one.' He glanced around the room. 'We should have
used the hospital cafeteria. Less mess.'

'Absolutely not!' She couldn't imagine Celine hosting
*her* wedding reception in the sterile cafeteria. 'Jacinta's
husband will be here in a few minutes to load up the
extra folding chairs and return them to the church. All
we'll have to do is sweep the floors and we'll be ready
to bring the rest of our furniture on Monday.'

They'd moved Will's furnishings several days earlier,
along with Emily's coffee-tables and her mother's side-

board and china cabinet. Wanting to have enough room for their guests, they'd decided to wait for the remainder of her family's possessions until the following week.

Yesterday afternoon Emily had packed up her personal effects and arranged them in Will's dresser drawers to her satisfaction. It had felt odd to hang her clothes next to his, sit on the edge of his bed and see his shoes in neat rows on the closet floor. The idea of sleeping beside him in his queen-size bed had been equally unnerving.

'Are you sure you don't want to drive to Dallas and spend at least one night in a swanky hotel?' he asked.

Once again her thoughts flew to his four-poster bed. 'It's up to you, but if we stayed here we wouldn't have to spend so much time on the road.'

'You were cheated out of a proper courtship. I don't want to cheat you out of this too.'

'So if I ask for a week in Hawaii or some other exotic locale you'll make last-minute arrangements?' she teased.

His gaze didn't waver. 'If that's what you want.'

She couldn't imagine spending a week in a honeymooners' paradise, watching other newlyweds billing and cooing. Until Will reciprocated her love she wasn't ready to be surrounded by couples who reminded her of the lack in her own marriage. Once she'd convinced him that silk and satin were overrated and that *she* was the woman he needed and wanted, *then* she'd be more than happy to accompany him anywhere he chose.

'I appreciate your offer,' she began, 'but I really would like to have a few nights with just the two of us in the house.' Thinking of the freedom they could enjoy, heat flooded her face. 'Once Kevin and Gran move in we won't have many moments to call our own.'

'Don't be so sure,' he warned. 'Your grandmother is deathly afraid her presence will cramp our newlywed style. Why else would she have argued for weeks over moving here in the first place?'

'Thanks for convincing her how much we need her.'

'It's the truth,' he said simply. 'I also like your granny.'

'She likes you too.'

He grinned. 'Helen's a smart woman. I can reason with her.'

'Are you implying something?' she asked without rancor.

His smile grew broader. 'No. She just sees things the same way I do.'

'Well, Mr Crystal Ball,' she teased, 'all I see right now is a dirty house. If we don't get busy we'll be slaving on into the night.'

'No, we won't.'

Something in his tone evoked her curiosity. She glanced at him. 'We won't?'

He shook his head, his eyes burning with an emotion she wanted to believe was passion but was afraid to think of as such for fear she was wrong.

'What isn't done in the next couple of hours will have to wait,' he said.

She puzzled over his mysterious comment. 'Oh, really? Did you have something else planned?'

He gave her a lopsided grin and immediately she knew she'd fallen into a trap of her own making. Without a word, he planted a swift kiss on her startled mouth, then strode off to help Jacinta's husband load the chairs on his truck.

It didn't take long for the evidence of the reception to disappear. The only clues left behind were the floral arrangements scattered throughout the house and the brightly wrapped gifts piled in one corner of the living room.

Will studied her. 'You're exhausted.'

She sank onto the sofa. 'Par for the course.'

'Why don't you go and relax on the bed?'

'It's only eight o'clock,' she protested.

He grinned. 'The same time you always take an evening nap.'

'Yes, but—'

'But nothing,' he insisted. 'While you're snoozing I'll watch television.'

'Not a very exciting honeymoon,' she said wryly.

'We have all weekend,' he said. 'After what happened today with Digger I can't believe you want more excitement right now.'

She tossed her head in exasperation. 'You know what I mean.'

He grinned. 'You'll need your strength for tomorrow.'

Her interest piqued, Emily asked, 'What's happening tomorrow?'

'It's a surprise. Now, go!'

'I'm going,' she grumbled, but the instant she stepped foot in their bedroom her exhaustion vanished. She pulled out the flowers and faux pearls in her hair and began unpinning the locks her hairdresser had painstakingly arranged. She didn't stop until her hair hung around her shoulders like a cloud of curled wood shavings.

Instead of lying down, she cushioned the headboard with pillows and sat yoga-style as she clicked on the small color television.

Will strode into the room a few minutes later. 'I thought you'd be asleep by now.'

'Too wound up, I guess.' She pointed the remote toward the TV and skimmed the channels. 'The programs are all reruns or just aren't appealing.'

He kicked off his tennis shoes, then stretched out beside her. 'Try the radio.'

Before long the strains from an easy listening station filled the room. 'Much better,' he said.

Emily agreed.

He patted a spot beside him. 'Come here.'

She needed no further urging. She lay down and he positioned her head on his shoulder.

'I thought you did a nice job today,' he said. 'I had my doubts about pulling off the whole thing, especially at our house.'

'"Oh ye of little faith,"' she quoted, letting her hand rest on his rib cage. 'Did you really think I couldn't plan a formal event?'

'I knew you were capable,' he said. 'I had visions of the house being too small, but you arranged everything perfectly.'

His compliment gave her a warm inner glow. She'd set out to prove herself on a social level and had succeeded. 'Kevin and his friends seemed to get along,' she mentioned.

'Yeah. They went from simply tolerating each other to actually discussing professional baseball teams. There's hope for them yet.'

Before she could say anything a laugh reverberated through his chest, then bubbled out of his mouth.

'What's so funny?' she asked.

He grinned. 'I hope the photographer snapped a picture of our guests when Digger tore through the house like his tail was on fire.'

'Someone probably did,' she said dryly. 'Looking

back, it *was* rather funny. I know something always goes wrong with a wedding—it's tradition, I think—but never in my wildest dreams did I imagine an animal would invade my reception.'

He chuckled. 'Neither did I.'

Emily rose on one elbow. 'Speaking of dreams, tell me yours.'

Will shifted onto his side. 'Dreams or goals?'

'Either. Both. Is there a difference?'

'Of course. I dreamed of becoming an astronaut, but it was never my goal.' He grinned. 'I enjoy breathing without having to rely on a manufactured atmosphere. To me the risk seemed greater than the reward.'

She wondered if his childhood necessity to be self-sufficient had played a part in his decision. Having taken care of himself while his mother worked several jobs, she could understand how he would have a hard time placing his faith in someone or something that he couldn't control.

'So I became a doctor instead,' he said.

She toyed with a thread hanging from a button on his shirt front placket, aware of the warmth emanating from his body. 'And now that you're a physician?'

He reached out to tuck a curl behind her ear. 'First, I'd like to see the birthing center actually completed.'

'It *is* a misnomer to call our maternity wing a birthing center,' she agreed. 'Especially when we only have two birthing rooms and the rest are traditional labor rooms.'

'Exactly. There isn't any reason why our hospital isn't more up to date in the fetal-maternal field. I thought I could make a difference when I came to Crossbow, but the powers are rather slow to move.'

'Give us time,' she said. 'Money is always tight. Too bad we can't organize a fund-raiser just for our center—

something along the lines of an old-fashioned Texas barbecue with square dancing.'

'Now, that's an idea. I'll suggest it.'

'So...' She stifled a yawn. 'Other than revamping our
hospital wing, what other dreams do you have?'

'I also want to work with medical students in a pre-
ceptor program,' he said. 'Guiding a student toward the
right field for them is a challenge and so very critical to
their future.'

She smiled. Will had filled the role of mentor to Kevin
with ease—he'd shine as a physician sponsor.

'I intend to do the same with my children,' he said.

Emily took heart in his use of the plural. 'How many
kids do you want?'

'An even dozen.'

'What?'

He laughed. 'Gotcha. Two or three.'

'Boys or girls?'

'It doesn't matter. I've seen countless patients who
insisted on getting pregnant because they wanted a boy
or a girl to complete their family. I'm more concerned
about their health than their sex.'

Emily remembered a couple who'd finally conceded
defeat after their fifth girl was born.

He fingered a long lock that had fallen across her
throat, brushing her skin with his knuckles. 'What about
your dreams?'

'Obstetrics was always my favorite,' she said, splaying her hand over her abdomen, 'so I was thrilled when
I was able to move into a position on this unit. Someday
I'd like to continue my studies and become a midwife
but...' she shrugged '...that won't be for a while. Not
until Kevin and baby here are grown.'

'Do you regret having to wait?' He placed his hand over hers.

'Well, of course,' she said lightly, to hide how his touch was causing the most delightful quivery sensations. 'I'm into instant gratification just as much as the next person.'

She might regret the delay, but she didn't regret the reason behind it. Regardless of how badly her career aspirations were derailed, she desperately wanted Will's child.

He gave her a slow and lazy grin as he moved his hand over the curve of her breast. 'Instant gratification, eh?'

She drew in a deep breath, aware of his mouth hovering inches from hers. The sugar and vanilla on his breath mingled with his spicy scent.

'What if it's more slow and easy?' he asked, unbuttoning her shirt to reveal the soft skin underneath.

Emily smiled. 'Fine with me.'

He rolled out of bed to shuck his clothing. Putting aside her shyness, she wriggled out of her Lycra leggings before his side of the bed dipped under his weight.

Once again she went willingly into his outstretched arms, accepting the touch of his hands while her own explored his rugged frame.

'You're beautiful,' he whispered, running his fingers across the curve of his child nestled within her.

She stroked his chest, threading her fingers through the light dusting of dark hair and feeling the steady thump of his heart. 'You're spectacular yourself.'

Fire smoldered in the center of her being, and as his hands caressed her naked skin those embers burst into raging flames.

As she soared into the sun the truth became crystal

clear. Their actions on the seventeenth of December had been born out of need, but tonight's activities were born out of love.

Will intercepted Tina as she placed a patient's medical chart in the wall rack outside an exam room. 'I'll take that,' he said, holding out his hand.

Tina smiled and gave him the chart. 'In a hurry today?'

He grinned. 'Yeah. Emily wants to find a baby bed this afternoon.' It was her day off, and as he only had patients scheduled in the office that morning they'd decided to use their free time to start furnishing the nursery.

'So you're all settled in?' Tina asked.

'More or less.' He thought about the past week's activities and every resultant ache and pain. After their surprise trip to an overnight bed and breakfast some two hours away, they'd spent the next several days painting bedrooms and giving everything a thorough cleaning before they'd moved Kevin, Helen and the rest of their furniture. Tonight would be the first night all of them would sleep under the same roof.

'Have fun, shopping. They have such cute things for babies nowadays.' Tina turned away, then stopped short. 'Oh, by the way, Emily rang. You're supposed to call her as soon as you have a chance.'

'Will do.' He glanced at his watch and decided to telephone her after he finished with the Fairchilds.

He opened the door to the exam room where Lynnette Fairchild and her husband, Wyatt, were waiting. 'How's mother and baby doing?'

'OK, I guess,' she answered.

Will scanned the information Tina had recorded. 'You only gained a few pounds this month.'

'I'm surprised,' Lynnette admitted. 'I'm constantly hungry these days.'

He grinned. Emily had complained of the same thing. In her case, she'd *needed* to eat before she'd blown away with the next windstorm.

'Just don't fill up on junk food,' he cautioned.

'I know.'

He turned to the section for lab work. 'I know you're interested in how your tests have turned out,' he began.

'I've been trying not to worry because I can't change anything, but it's been terribly hard,' she confessed.

'The good news is your blood work doesn't show any abnormalities,' Will said.

Wyatt stood beside the exam table and took his wife's hand in his. 'And the biopsy?'

The pap smear he'd taken as part of Lynnette's pre-natal exam showed severe dysplasia—a progression from the mild stage reported earlier. A biopsy had been indicated and, although she'd been at risk of losing the baby if he'd proceeded, the Fairchilds had agreed to the procedure. And so, on her last month's visit, Will had taken the tissue sample, carefully modifying his technique to minimize cervical trauma.

After applying an iodine stain to reveal the abnormal sites, he'd scooped out a shallow 'coin' of affected tissue and sent the sample to pathology. The results pertaining to the specimen he'd submitted had arrived several days ago.

Will spoke matter-of-factly. 'It's positive. The pathologist labeled it as a micro-invasive carcinoma.'

Lynnette's eyes showed fear. 'Which means?'

'Cancerous cells have penetrated the stroma below the

basement membrane.' Will drew a rough sketch of the cellular structure on a notepad. 'However, the cancer is still confined to less than three millimeters in depth and hasn't invaded any lymphatic or vascular areas. I'd like to tell you that I got it all when I biopsied the site, but I can't say that with any certainty.'

Lynnette leaned against her husband and clutched his hand in a white-knuckled grip.

'What comes next?' Wyatt asked, his voice like the rasp of sandpaper.

'Ordinarily, we'd proceed to a cone biopsy where I'd remove a triangular piece of tissue.' He added to his picture, showing how the point of the cone went deep into the stroma.

'Unfortunately,' Will continued, 'if I do that now, you'll definitely miscarry.'

'No!' Lynnette studied her husband as she shook her head. 'We'll just have to wait.'

Wyatt winced as he pleaded, 'Now, Lyn, if it's the only way to be sure—'

'I won't do it,' she said, her jaw set and her arms crossed. 'I won't lose this baby if I can help it.'

Wyatt glanced at Will, his eyes begging for answers. 'What do you think we should do?'

'It's a hard decision,' Will said. 'I can tell you the risks, but you two are the ones who'll have to live with the consequences.'

Lynnette grabbed her husband's arm. 'It's one thing to miscarry by accident, but I couldn't live with myself if I caused it to happen. Not after we've wanted this little guy for so long. Please?'

Wyatt's internal conflict was obvious. 'I don't want to lose you.'

Her smile was filled with love. 'You won't.'

Wyatt addressed Will. 'What would you do if you and your wife were in this situation?'

Will crossed his arms and gave himself a few moments to think before he answered. It wasn't too difficult since Emily's due date matched Lynnette's. Without a doubt, if Emily faced the same dilemma, or one similar, he'd put her life before the baby's. Knowing Emily, however, she also would resist doing anything to harm her infant.

'I'd probably adopt a wait-and-see attitude,' Will said. 'It's not ideal, but few things in life are.'

'Please, Wyatt. I *want* this baby,' Lynnette pleaded.

'If you choose to skip the cone biopsy,' Will continued, 'we'll repeat the pap smear in a few weeks. As I said, we may have been lucky and removed everything the first time.'

'And if not?'

'Then we'll move ahead with our treatment protocol,' Will said. 'By then the fetus could survive if we had to take him. But I'm not going to say what we'll do for certain because everything depends on the next smear results. In the meantime, we should think positive.'

Lynnette nodded. The concern didn't totally leave Wyatt's eyes, but it had lessened.

'Let's see how much bigger Junior has gotten.' Will grabbed the tape measure and took Lynnette's fundal-height measurement to assess how much the baby had grown. Then, using the Doppler stethoscope, he listened to its heartbeat, before allowing Wyatt the same opportunity.

'Fit as a fiddle,' he commented, as Lynnette pulled her stretch pants over her distended abdomen when they were finished. 'He's growing at the rate I'd expect.'

Lynnette smiled.

'I'm going to send Tina in with some pamphlets on cervical cancer for you to study,' Will said. 'There's a telephone number for a local support group if you want to talk to women who've shared your experience. I'd highly recommend you contact them.

'In the meantime, eat three meals a day, drink plenty of water, get lots of rest and call me if you notice any vaginal discharge or have abdominal pain. Otherwise, I'll see you next month.'

Wyatt and Lynnette thanked him, and he left the room to give Tina his instructions and to contact Emily.

Before the phone had completed its first ring, she answered. 'You must have been sitting by the phone,' he teased.

Emily didn't respond to his jovial comment and Will's inner warning system kicked into gear.

'Dr Hathaway wants us to drop by her office as soon as we can,' she said, her voice strained.

'Did they say why?'

'To discuss my blood work.' Emily paused. 'Something's wrong with the baby.'

# CHAPTER NINE

'I'M ON my way.' Will's words were clipped.

'I'll be ready,' Emily said, noticing how her hand shook as she replaced the receiver. Ever since Dr Hathaway had called she'd been a mass of nerves.

Talking to Will had made her feel marginally better, knowing he'd help her sort things out, but every obstetrical problem she'd studied or encountered firsthand came to her mind.

Fifteen minutes later Will's car pulled up in front of the house, but before his Oldsmobilé had rolled to a complete stop Emily was hurrying toward it.

'Tell me exactly what Susan told you,' he said, as she slid into the passenger seat and pulled the seat belt across her body.

'She didn't say much,' Emily admitted. 'Only to drop in at my earliest convenience to discuss my lab results.' The lab had drawn her blood for a triple screen shortly before the wedding so the conversation had to involve those tests.

She swallowed the knot of worry in her throat. 'Dr Hathaway wouldn't ask me to drop by if the tests were normal, would she?'

His momentary silence provided her answer. 'Until we hear what she has to say we're only guessing at the problem.'

She drew a deep breath. 'You're right. This is one time when my experience is a drawback. I know too much.'

Will reached out and squeezed her hand. 'Let's get all the facts before we jump to conclusions.'

She managed a smile. 'OK.'

Minutes later they entered the family practice clinic. Emily went to the area designated for Dr Hathaway's patients and signed the register before she sat on a chair next to Will. She tried not to notice the number of pregnant women and mothers with babies in their arms, waiting their turn.

'By the way,' Will said in a casual tone, 'do you remember when I passed along your idea to Greg Olivier about having a barbecue fund-raiser?'

Emily appreciated his effort to divert her attention. 'Yes.'

'He's been feeling people out for the past few days. After hearing positive comments, he wants to form a committee to start working on the idea,' he said proudly.

Excited by the news, Emily grabbed Will's hand. 'How wonderful!'

'It will take a while to put the details together, but I'm hoping we can organize the event to coincide with the Independence Day holiday.'

'That gives you several weeks,' she mused. 'It'll be close, but with a concentrated effort you should make it happen.'

'I think so too,' he said confidently.

'All of our moms want to use a birthing room, and with only two of them it's first come first served. So I know the younger couples will support you.'

Before Will could respond Dr Hathaway's nurse called Emily's name.

Emily rose, her heart pounding. Will slipped his hand around hers and she drew strength from his grip.

Dr Hathaway walked into the exam room shortly after

the nurse left. Her expression was solemn. 'I'm glad you're here,' she said to Will.

'What's going on?' he asked.

The fear Emily had tried to suppress ever since she'd received Dr Hathaway's phone call rolled through her with ferocity. Her gaze traveled from Will to Susan and back again as she braced herself for the worst.

'About ten days ago we did the triple screen test,' Susan began. 'The results arrived yesterday.' She glanced at Emily as she lifted her folder. 'Do you mind if he sees this?'

Emily shook her head. Susan handed him the chart and he immediately studied the contents.

'What's wrong?' Emily asked.

'Your alpha-fetoprotein is elevated,' Susan said matter-of-factly. 'It could mean—'

'I know what it means,' Emily said. High levels indicated neural-tube defects, like spina bifida, anencephaly and meningomyelocele. She'd seen babies born with those conditions and her heart had bled for the parents. It didn't seem possible that it was happening to her.

'We'll need to run a complete ultrasound for anatomy,' Susan began.

'You haven't run a sonogram before?' Will asked, his voice hard as he glanced up from reading Emily's chart.

Susan shook her head. 'Since Emily could pinpoint her date of conception so accurately I didn't see the need to perform one sooner. Now we don't have a choice.'

Will tried to speak, but Susan held up her hand to forestall him.

'Our ultrasound technician comes to my office every Friday. You can either wait a few days until then or I can send you to the hospital this afternoon.'

Emily met Will's gaze. 'I'm not very good at waiting,' she admitted.

He was decisive. 'We'll go now.'

'I'll make the arrangements. Although Emily doesn't have a history of NTDs in her family, her profession puts her at a higher risk so we should schedule an amnio.'

Emily recalled reading statistics showing how pediatric and chemotherapy nurses, as well as respiratory therapists, carried a greater risk for NTDs than the general population.

'Then you'll only have a short time to decide on whether or not you want to terminate the pregnancy,' Susan warned.

Emily hoped to avoid that particular scenario because her nursing judgment conflicted with her maternal instincts. 'Could something else cause a high test result?'

Will answered. 'A specimen contaminated with fetal blood for one, twins for another. Is there a history of multiple births in your family?'

'No.' Emily hadn't thought of carrying twins but, considering the alternative, dealing with two babies sounded easy. She didn't want to think of the other conditions also associated with high AFP levels—fetal renal disease and impending fetal death, to name but two.

'Let's deal with one thing at a time,' Susan said. She handed Will the stethoscope. 'Since you missed hearing the heartbeat last month, would you like to do the honors?'

Will clearly didn't need further urging. He poked the tips into his ears and pressed the diaphragm to Emily's growing abdominal bulge. A smile came to his lips as he located the sound and heard the familiar swish of the fetal heart.

A moment later Will handed the stethoscope back to Susan, as if reluctant to do so.

Susan smiled. 'It's different when the baby's yours, isn't it?'

He nodded.

'All righty, then,' Susan said, her tone becoming more businesslike. 'Emily? While I make a phone call, start drinking water.'

Emily nodded. The theory behind an ultrasound was to bounce sound waves off the fluid in the bladder so she had to force down as much liquid as she could.

Less than an hour later the ultrasound technician was smearing gel over her wand and running it along Emily's uterus. Emily tried to attribute the hospital's prompt response to Susan pulling a few strings and her favored status as Will's wife rather than because her condition was potentially serious.

Although she knew it was fruitless, her thoughts were on Will's disappointment if the test revealed a deformity. He'd already given up the type of wife he wanted because of her baby and if that child were handicapped... The situation didn't bode well for the success of their marriage.

Will stood beside her, holding her hand as the technician performed her job.

Emily glanced at the monitor, squinting to make out the fetal structures—head, arms, hands—while trying not to dwell on how badly she wanted to relieve the pressure on her bladder.

Will's grip tightened, his gaze glued to the grainy picture. Suddenly he leaned forward, his whole body tense.

'What are you looking for?' she asked.

'Signs of an NTD are, as you know, an open spine,'

Will answered, his voice distant as he watched the technician scan the developing fetus.

Emily observed her taking measurements of the critical areas, then move to the head.

Will's gaze never left the monitor. 'Other clues are a lemon-shaped head circumference and a banana-shaped cerebellum.'

The woman painstakingly measured the head with the computerized markers. At long last she clicked off her equipment and wiped the gel from Emily's skin. 'All done,' she said cheerfully.

'Did you find anything?' Emily asked, crossing her fingers that the woman's jovial attitude was a good sign.

'Well…' She hesitated, but at Will's glare she added, 'The measurements border the ranges established for the baby's gestational age.'

'Then he's OK?' Emily asked Will.

He winced. 'We still can't say for certain, although the news is definitely encouraging.'

'What comes next?' she asked, certain of what he would say but wanting her thoughts confirmed.

'An amniocentesis.'

'Will that give us the final diagnosis?' she asked.

He drew a deep breath. 'A normal AFP result on the amniotic fluid is a good sign. Elevated levels can confirm a neural-tube defect.'

'So if it's high we should prepare for a handicapped baby.' She waited for his reaction, but whatever he felt remained hidden.

'Not necessarily,' he said. 'There's a ten per cent false positive rate.'

Emily squared her shoulders and steeled herself for his response to her next question. 'What should we do?' Please don't suggest an abortion, she thought.

'It depends on how lucky you think you are.'

She remembered a comment he'd once made—'a person makes his own luck.' Will wasn't one to leave anything to chance.

'What do *you* want to do?' he asked cautiously.

She paused. 'Wait for the baby to be born.'

'If he or she does have a defect, it won't be easy on you,' he warned. The words 'or on the rest of us' hung in the air, unspoken.

Thinking of other parents in similar circumstances, she nodded. 'I know.'

'As long as you understand the consequences.'

'I do. I also don't want to tell Gran about this,' she said. 'I don't want her to worry.'

'We'll have to tell her something,' Will said. 'She'll wonder why we're going to Houston.'

'I'll tell her we're going on a shopping trip.'

His mouth settled into disapproving lines, but he finally agreed. As it happened, Gran took the news of their impending out-of-town weekend in her stride.

'I knew you'd regret not having a honeymoon,' Helen said, clearly unconcerned about their plans. 'Just have a good time.'

'We'll try,' Emily said, avoiding Will's gaze.

On the following Thursday as she lay on the operating table, waiting for the specialist to collect the vital samples, she wished this entire episode was behind her.

At long last the precious fluid was on its way to the lab. Will whisked her to a plush hotel, which would have been a real treat under other circumstances. Although she found it comfortable and basked in its elegance, the beautiful surroundings didn't dispel her worries.

That night Will held her tenderly. As if he'd sensed

her fragile state, he didn't spout any empty platitudes. Both of them had seen pathetic and pitiful cases in their careers and had consequently learned one sad fact—tragedy exempted no one, no matter how much they hoped otherwise.

What distressed Emily was how he pointedly refrained from mentioning the whole subject.

At the same time she wondered if his reticence hid his disappointment over how she had complicated his life. His whole plan had been ruined once he'd become involved with her. She'd been tempted in a weak moment to ask if he had any regrets, but cowardice had stopped her.

As the weekend flew by under Will's tender loving care, she pushed her misgivings to the back of her mind.

Emily returned to work on Monday, well rested and determined not to dwell on 'ifs' or 'maybes'. Luckily, the steady influx of maternity cases kept her focused on women's conditions other than her own.

In spite of her good intentions, by the week's end Jacqueline had managed to resurrect Emily's insecurities.

'Don't forget to remind Will about our meeting tonight,' the nurse said just as she, Emily and Molly prepared to go off duty.

Emily tried not to take offense at the familiar way Jacqueline referred to Will. 'If you're talking about the fund-raiser meeting, he already knows.' In fact, Will had reminded her of his schedule before she'd left for work.

'How do you know about it?' she asked, certain he hadn't said anything about Jacqueline being on the committee.

'My father thought that with my experience in organizing charitable events I should take part. I'm really excited because I enjoy working with Will so much.'

*I'll bet*, Emily thought. 'Isn't that nice?' she said in a too-sweet tone as she opened her locker and retrieved her purse. 'Who else is on the committee?'

'Someone from Dietary, Human Resources and Accounting. There are a few more, but I can't remember everyone.' Jacqueline waved her hand as if the other members were of little consequence.

'What sort of event do you have in mind?' Molly asked.

'Well,' Jacqueline began, 'Will suggested a dinner with a Texas flavor, but I convinced everyone that we should expand our horizons. If we want to attract big money then we need a black-tie affair, not something run-of-the-mill.'

'I think a Texas-motif dinner would be great,' Molly said. 'People like that sort of thing.'

Jacqueline uttered an unladylike snort.

'What constitutes a black-tie affair?' Emily asked, wondering what Jacqueline had in mind.

'Politicians and hospital benefits rake in the money with gourmet dinners, art auctions and orchestra music,' Jacqueline said. 'Barbecues and square dances are small potatoes. We need to think *big*.'

'And you convinced the committee this is the way to go,' Emily stated. Will had informed her of the change in plans, but he hadn't mentioned who had pushed for the change. It would have been nice to have heard the news from him rather than Jacqueline.

'Oh, absolutely,' Jacqueline gushed. 'I planned a number of these functions when I was married. In fact, I know the most marvelous chef. He owes me a favor so I'm *positive* he won't mind preparing the food for us.'

'Gourmet food?' Molly tapped a finger to her cheek in thought. 'You're not planning on stuff like snails, caviar and raw fish, are you?'

'It's sushi,' Jacqueline said, her nose in the air. 'Although I think those would be marvelous additions to the menu, I'm well aware of the simple tastes of the people in this area.'

Molly planted her hands on her hips. 'Yeah, well, I'm happy with a grilled steak so to each their own.'

Jacqueline tossed Molly a pitying glance before she spoke to Emily. 'In any event, don't forget to remind your husband. Eight o'clock sharp. My place.'

She turned away, then stopped short. 'You don't mind if your husband comes to my house, do you?'

It took everything in Emily's power to keep her voice even. 'Should I?'

Jacqueline tittered as if she found Emily's comment humorous. 'Of course not. We're using my home so I can show everyone my artwork and explain how the auction would work.'

She patted Emily's arm. 'Don't worry about a thing. Your hubby is safe with me, Emily. Bye, now.' She waggled her fingers and hurried out of the lounge.

Emily folded her arms and let her disgust show. 'Explain how an auction works? How dumb does she think we are? I'll bet that whatever she's showing isn't "artwork".'

Molly giggled.

'Did you hear her say we have "simple tastes"? I hope she doesn't tell too many people in Crossbow that or her gourmet chef will be preparing dinner for one. I can imagine the kind of *favor* this guy owes her.'

Emily slammed her locker shut and headed for the door.

Molly grinned. 'You know, Em, I don't think I've seen you this angry in a long time.'

'I have every right to be.' Emily halted in her tracks to mimic Jacqueline's voice. 'I'll take good care of your hubby, Emily.' She cleared her throat. 'I wonder how many marriages she wrecked before her own ended up in the divorce court.'

A furrow formed between Molly's eyebrows. 'You're not worried, are you?'

'No. Yes. Maybe. I don't know.' Emily drew a deep breath. 'All of the above, I guess.'

'You shouldn't be concerned.'

'Oh, yeah? Just look at me.' Emily stretched out her arms and pivoted. 'I totally skipped the dating game and went right to having a baby. Then my uncle got moralistic. If he'd kept his nose out of my business Will wouldn't be stuck with me.' Or a potentially handicapped child, she silently added.

'I disagree,' Molly said, shaking her head. 'I know how tenacious Will was in asking you out. He's the type who doesn't give up until he gets what he wants.'

Emily dismissed her statement with a wave. 'Will won't shirk his obligations and I'm a major one. He's dreamed of a wife who would help him achieve the respect and esteem he's always wanted. Jacqueline, with her fancy artwork, caviar, orchestras and gourmet dinners fits his requirements perfectly.'

'Everyone knows how shallow she is,' Molly said. 'Will can see it too.'

Emily didn't answer.

'Give him some credit, Em. Think of it this way.

Being around Jacqueline should make him grateful that he married you instead.'

Emily fervently hoped so.

By Emily's next appointment in May Susan Hathaway had received the results of the amniocentesis and Will had cleared his schedule to be present.

'I'd hoped the AFP level would be normal,' Susan admitted to Emily and Will as she showed them the report.

'Me too.' Emily's hand shook as she toyed with the hem of her maternity smock. Her disappointment was obvious.

'It isn't astronomically high so I'd take heart,' Susan commented. 'Considering your sonogram didn't show anything, I'd be inclined to lump you in the false positive category.'

'Unfortunately, you can't give any guarantees,' Will said, knowing he'd say the same thing if he had similar news to deliver to one of his patients.

Susan shook her head. 'We won't know for sure until the baby's born. While you need to prepare mentally for the worst-case scenario, I wouldn't dwell on it. We can run another ultrasound—'

Emily's response was quick and forceful. 'No. I'm not going to spend the next three and a half months hunting for problems. You said yourself there are no guarantees. Even if we happened to see the abnormality it's too late now to do anything about it.'

Will was startled by her vehemence. For a few minutes utter silence descended. 'If that's how you feel…'

'It is,' Emily reaffirmed.

He glanced at Susan. 'You heard her.'

Susan's eyes crinkled. 'Fair enough.' Once again she handed Will the stethoscope. 'Want to do the honors?'

He grinned. 'Yeah.' Just as he placed the chestpiece against Emily's uterus his hand moved, lifted by an unseen foot. 'Did you feel that?' he asked, unable to keep the awe and excitement out of his voice.

Emily grinned. 'He's getting stronger.'

Will listened intently, satisfied with what he heard. He'd heard hundreds of fetal heart tones, but this time was special because this baby was *his*. His and Emily's.

At the same time he couldn't dismiss his concern over Junior's potential health problems. He knew the odds and had advised several patients in similar situations, but facing the same scenario on a personal level emphasized his helplessness. He didn't like the feeling.

Finally, he relinquished the instrument to Susan and she performed her own assessment.

'You're doing great,' she told Emily. 'I'll see you in another month.' She turned to Will. 'How are the fundraiser efforts going?'

'Fairly well,' he said, slipping out of his 'daddy' role and into his professional one. 'It's definitely more time-consuming than I'd expected. Poor Emily has hardly seen me.'

He glanced at Emily, surprised to see her forced smile. 'We're selling tickets next month so have your checkbook ready.'

'I will,' Susan promised, before she disappeared into the hallway.

Will helped Emily off the exam table. 'Between my patients and planning this dinner I've been neglecting you, haven't I?'

'A little,' she said noncommittally.

'The dinner and auction will be over soon,' he promised. 'Then we'll have more time together.'

'I know.'

As he studied her small smile he realized that she
didn't seem convinced.

# CHAPTER TEN

THE weeks rolled past as Emily and her family adjusted to a new routine. To the world her life seemed idyllic, but as Will turned more of his attention toward the fundraising project her fears about their marriage grew rather than diminished.

In essence they went their separate ways, giving each other polite greetings when their paths crossed. She understood his hectic schedule—organizing such a large event was important both to him and the hospital.

Knowing that, however, didn't make her feel better. Their personal time dwindled down to a few stolen minutes here and there during the day. Nights, of course, were different, but even then she noticed how he shied away from discussing what lay heaviest on her mind—her baby.

In spite of his cordial manner, it was as if he'd emotionally detached himself from her. At first she thought her imagination was working overtime, but when Kevin commented on it, she had to accept the unpleasant truth.

'I'll sure be glad when this big party for the hospital is over,' Kevin grumbled on the last Saturday in June. 'I hardly ever see Will any more.'

'Join the club,' she said wryly. 'Look on the bright side. We only have another week to go and then the whole thing will be a memory.'

'Good,' Kevin declared. 'He said he'd take Digger, me and the guys fishing. We'll leave before sunup and stay out until sundown. It'll be cool!'

Jealousy stirred. Will had never promised her an outing. She gave him a sheepish smile, feeling ridiculous about her momentary resentment toward her little brother. 'Do I get to come?' she asked lightly.

'Nope,' Kevin said seriously. 'This is a guy thing.'

Suddenly Emily wanted a 'wife' thing—some activity where she and Will could spend time alone and actually talk about personal subjects. Once the baby came their private hours would be numbered.

While Emily could dismiss her envy toward her brother, she couldn't do the same with her attitude toward Jacqueline. The other woman managed to be the proverbial fly in Emily's ointment on a regular basis.

'Will and I make a great team,' Jacqueline commented the day before the dinner and auction.

Certain Jacqueline was only trying to irritate her, Emily smiled and pretended indifference. 'I'm sure the whole event would fall apart if the committee couldn't work together.'

'I'm going to be positively *lost* when this is over,' Jacqueline continued. 'I've focused on this for so long I just won't know what to do with myself.'

'I'm sure you'll think of another worthy cause to keep you busy,' Emily replied, tongue in cheek. 'If not, I can make a few suggestions. The United Way fund drive takes place in the fall.'

'Yes, but it wouldn't be the same. Our committee has gotten so close. We're like family.'

Emily wanted to gag, but she didn't.

'Planning something of this nature is so time-consuming,' Jacqueline gushed. 'It was much easier when I organized these things myself. I didn't have to get permission or approval from five other people.'

Emily doubted if Jacqueline sought out any committee

members' opinions other than Will's. A night didn't go by without her phoning to discuss one thing or another.

Sometimes Emily sensed Will's exasperation at being consulted on such trivial things as the color of balloons and crêpe paper, but he kept his thoughts to himself.

He'd answer whatever questions she posed, but didn't volunteer extra information. As Gran liked to say, Will played his cards close to his chest. If only she could think of a way for him to be more forthcoming. She wanted a marriage with open lines of communication, and since theirs was obviously lacking in that area she couldn't help but wonder if he was purposely distancing himself from her.

Was this the beginning of the end? The idea scared her.

'Even so, I hope we make this an annual event,' Jacqueline said. 'After people see the marvelous job we've done I just know they'll ask Will and me to be in charge again.'

Emily ground her teeth. She certainly hoped not.

Jacqueline picked up the neonatal nursing textbook Emily had laid out to study at home. 'Who left this on the counter?'

'I'm reading it,' Emily said.

'Whatever for?'

Emily refused to admit she was reviewing the care of infants with NTDs. 'We have to keep up to date, you know.'

Jacqueline huffed. 'I suppose.'

The telephone rang and Emily answered it. 'We're sending an eighteen-year-old mentally retarded female to you,' the ER nurse said. 'She's in active labor and her water just broke, but we can't hear any fetal heart sounds.'

After acknowledging the message, Emily hung up and repeated the information.

Jacqueline rose. 'I'm scheduled to leave in thirty minutes. I'm not getting tied up for hours.'

'Then find Molly and send her to help me,' Emily said wearily, rubbing away the ache in her lower abdomen. Carrying twelve extra pounds in front of her wasn't exactly a picnic. The next shift wasn't due to arrive yet, but someone had to tend their patient.

Jacqueline vanished and Molly rounded the corner a short time later. 'Jacqueline just told me about our new admission. What's the scoop?'

Emily recited the few facts she knew. 'Mentally retarded female, apparently low-functioning, no history of prenatal care. She showed up in ER, not understanding why she's having terrible cramps. Her water broke and they can't hear the heartbeat.'

'Oh, boy,' Molly breathed. 'This won't be easy.'

Emily silently agreed.

A moment later the elevator doors opened. Will and two nurses wheeled the gurney into the hallway as their young patient howled her distress.

'In here.' Emily motioned the entourage toward the closest labor room. She stepped aside to allow them entrance, noticing how their patient was dirty and unkempt as if she hadn't taken care of herself for quite some time.

While Molly and the other nurses transferred Ramona Dalton to the bed, Will pulled Emily aside. 'Check on her latest lab results. They drew the blood in ER.'

Emily speeded to a phone and returned a short time later to report a slightly lower than normal hemoglobin, an elevated white cell count and high levels of both blood and protein in the urine.

'It hurts,' Ramona cried as another contraction took

hold of her belly. 'Why won't you make it stop? Make it stop!'

'Good luck.' Bernie, one of the ER nurses, gave Emily a sympathetic glance as she headed for the door with her partner.

'Thanks. Has anyone found a family member?' Emily asked.

Bernie shook her head. 'We called the social worker and she's trying to locate the boyfriend. Hopefully he operates at a higher level than Ramona does, although I have my doubts.'

A scream from the direction of the bed, followed by Will's reply, recaptured Emily's attention and she hurried to lend her assistance. Will, however, had other ideas.

'You shouldn't be here,' he told her. 'Her baby's gone.'

Emily squared her shoulders. 'There's no one else.'

His grim countenance revealed his displeasure, but he nodded. 'Ramona,' he said, his voice patient, 'Emily is a nurse and she's going to be your buddy through this.'

Ramona turned her glazed eyes on Emily before she began wailing once again.

'Let's get an internal monitor on,' he said. Molly handed him the supplies and, while Emily encouraged Ramona, Will clipped the electrode to the baby's scalp.

All eyes focused on the monitor's grim results.

'Should we do a C-section?' Molly asked, slightly above a whisper.

He simply shook his head. 'Too late.'

A sick feeling rose in the pit of Emily's stomach. She took Ramona's free hand in hers and squeezed tightly. Until told otherwise, Emily would provide the necessary moral support while the remainder of the team focused on the medical element.

'Just relax. Pant when you feel your stomach cramp.' Emily demonstrated.

The girl stared at Emily through dull, lifeless eyes, clearly puzzled by the changes her body was enduring. To her credit, she obeyed Emily's coaching instructions until Emily mentioned the baby.

'A baby? How did a baby get in me? I didn't swallow no watermelon seeds.'

Emily glanced upwards as she pondered how to answer the girl's question. If Ramona's case hadn't been so sad, it would almost be humorous. She met Will's dark-eyed gaze and he shrugged, shaking his head with pity.

Fortunately, another contraction took hold, diverting Ramona's attention. 'Make it stop,' she cried, writhing on the bed. 'I wanna go home.'

Emily did her best to keep the girl from rising. Will raised his voice. 'Ramona, stay on the bed. We can't do anything about the pain if you don't co-operate with us.'

Ramona ignored him, her anguish giving her superhuman strength. Finally he said sharply, 'I don't care who you find—I'll settle for a housekeeper—but get another person to assist. Let's get her to a delivery room.'

Jacqueline poked her head in the room at that very moment. 'Is everything under control?' she asked sweetly.

'Good thing you're here,' Will said. 'I need you to work with Emily.'

Jacqueline's jaw dropped, as if she hadn't expected him to take up her offer, and she reluctantly came forward to help transfer Ramona to a gurney. Once again Emily wondered if Jacqueline considered working with such pathetic cases of humanity worth her quest to snag a rich doctor.

The next thirty minutes were tense. With the group now reassembled in the delivery suite, Molly and Will struggled to deliver Ramona's child while Emily and an ineffective Jacqueline fought to keep the young woman focused on the task.

As soon as the small, slippery body landed in Will's hands Emily went to assist him, leaving Jacqueline to console Ramona.

'Nothing to be done,' Will said, handing her the full-term infant. The cord was wrapped tightly around her throat, and from the fragility of the blue-tinged skin she had died several days before.

Emily wondered if the outcome might have been different if Ramona had received prenatal care. Pitting her deep sadness against the need for objectivity, she wrapped the baby girl in a blanket and wiped its face clean before she approached Ramona.

'Would you like to see her?' Emily asked.

Ramona glanced at her daughter with a disinterested gaze, making no attempt to accept the bundle. After a brief moment she turned her head away to stare at the far wall.

Emily's heart nearly broke. How sad to think that this perfect little baby's own mother wouldn't grieve for her. Tears burned in her throat and she turned away to place the beautiful infant reverently under the radiant warmer.

It struck her how this could be her child. A lump clogged her throat and tears burned at the back of her eyes.

'Emily.' Will interrupted her thoughts. 'Are you OK?'

She cleared her throat. 'Yeah, sure.'

Ramona lay quietly on the table, more co-operative now that the pain had eased.

Before long Will was finished with his tasks. Molly whispered to Emily, 'I'll go to the nursery.'

Emily knew she was referring to the bleak task awaiting her. Difficult as it was, she wanted to handle it herself. 'No. I'll take care of her.'

'At least let me take her downstairs,' Molly argued. Knowing by 'downstairs' Molly meant the morgue, she agreed.

While Molly and Jacqueline pushed Ramona to a private room, Emily took the small bundle away and bathed the tiny body with loving care.

Once she'd finished her tasks she entered the hallway, ready to hand over the infant to Molly. She saw Will at the nurses' desk, his mouth drawn and his shoulders slumped with fatigue. Before she could catch his attention Jacqueline dashed out of the lounge and grabbed his arm.

'That was just awful,' she sniffled. 'I didn't think I could bear it.'

Emily watched in stunned horror as her nemesis shed pathetic tears on Will's shoulder, wrapping herself around him like a jungle vine. He patted her back and murmured something Emily couldn't hear.

'What's going on?' Molly asked from behind.

Her friend's voice brought Emily out of her trance. Going to the morgue seemed an easier task than watching Will and Jacqueline together. 'I...I'm going downstairs.'

Molly's smile faded. 'What's wrong?'

Emily glanced in Will's direction. 'I...have to go.' With that, she turned and fled down the stairs as fast as her unwieldy form would allow.

She alternated between bouts of anger and extreme hurt. Being pregnant, she felt the pain of losing the baby more than anyone in that room yet Jacqueline had managed to gain Will's sympathy with her helpless, I-was-so-devastated act.

Emily was simply too good at hiding her emotions behind a strong and capable persona. She'd have felt foolish resorting to Jacqueline's tactics, but she was furious at Will for not seeing through the other woman's charade.

The morgue was unattended. Although she knew the routine—place the body in the specimen refrigerator—she couldn't bring herself to do so. She *wouldn't.*

She'd done what was necessary many times before but, with her own child kicking her ribs, she couldn't manage it today. Ramona's child deserved better treatment and more dignity in death than she'd received in life.

Emily paced the floor, waiting for the morgue attendant to arrive. Minutes ticked by, but she refused to abandon her post. The squeak of hinges broke into her thoughts. She glanced toward the room's entrance and saw Will standing in the doorway.

'What are you doing here?' she snapped, sounding as if she'd contracted a head cold.

'You were gone a long time,' he said calmly, crossing the threshold.

The picture of Jacqueline hanging on him was still too fresh. 'I know,' she said tartly. 'I'm waiting for Joe.'

He pointed to a sign posting the on-duty hours. 'You'll have a long wait. He's gone for the day.'

Emily stared at her bundle, unable to do what needed to be done.

'You shouldn't be here,' Will said.

His kind tone shattered her composure. 'I can't just leave her like this,' she wailed, longing for her husband to understand what was in her heart. 'I'm not shoving her in the refrigerator. Not when the one in our kitchen is just like it.' She cleared her throat to remove the lump.

Will pressed his lips together as if in thought. A moment later he said, 'I'll be right back.'

Emily waited patiently, listening to the whir of the cooler fans until the door opened again. Will walked in, carrying a bassinet complete with tiny mattress and a pink ID card. He set it on the desk, then held out his arms.

She surrendered her load and watched him lay the body on the mattress with reverence, covering it with the little pink blanket he'd obviously stolen from the nursery.

Without another word he opened an adult-size compartment, gently placed the bassinet on the tray and then carefully closed the door.

Touched by Will's sensitivity, tears ran down Emily's cheeks, dissolving her previous anger. 'Let's go home,' he said, flinging his arm around her.

She dug a tissue out of her pocket and blew her nose. 'Thank you.'

'You're welcome.' He led her to the elevator and pushed the button. 'I didn't encourage Jacqueline,' he said, as if he knew the thoughts running around in her head.

She didn't answer. She couldn't tell him it was OK because it wasn't. 'You didn't push her away.'

'She caught me off guard, Em. I was waiting for you.'

Emily didn't answer. She reached out to push the button again.

He grabbed her hand. 'I promised to be faithful. I won't go back on my word.'

She met his gaze. Will had too much integrity to do otherwise but his recent withdrawal seemed too complete to lay the blame solely on the demands of his temporary assignment.

'Do you *want* to be faithful?' she asked, and waited for his reply. Or would he rather be released from his vows now that the threat of a handicapped child hung over his head?

At first he appeared taken aback by her question. Then his eyes flashed. 'What kind of question is that?'

'An extremely important one,' she answered smartly.

Will's pager went off and he muttered an expletive under his breath as an urgent message from his office nurse echoed in the lonely hallway.

'I'll drive you home,' he said as the elevator arrived. He followed her inside. 'We have to talk.'

Emily pushed the button for the main floor and the elevator began its rapid ascent. 'Yes, we do, but I'm not leaving my car in the hospital parking lot overnight,' she told him. 'I'll need it in the morning.'

The elevator glided to a stop and she stepped out to go the opposite direction to Will.

He grabbed her elbow. 'I'll see you at the house.'

She met his gaze without flinching. 'I hope so.'

Unfortunately, reality intruded and the discussion Emily wanted was postponed. Will's emergency required his attention until early evening. He arrived home, gobbled down the plate of food Helen had saved, then hurried to the convention center to start organizing the tables and decorations for tomorrow's festivities.

Emily went to bed alone and woke early the next morning to the sound of the shower running. The indentation of Will's head in the pillow beside her was evident, but she was disappointed that he'd risen without her knowledge. Although they wouldn't have had time for a serious conversation, even a few minutes of cuddling would have gone a long way to allay her fears.

After today, however, she wouldn't rest until they'd addressed their problems. Bolstered by the thought, she greeted Will calmly when he strode into their bedroom, wearing only a pair of chinos.

'I didn't mean to wake you,' he said, toweling his dark hair dry. 'We wanted to get an early start.'

She rose and accepted his platonic good morning peck. 'My inner alarm clock is working too well. If it's OK with you, I thought I'd tag along.'

'Better hurry,' he said. 'I want to leave in an hour.'

Emily dashed into the bathroom for her turn in the shower, jumped into a pair of stretch pants and a maternity top, then hurried into the kitchen in time to hear Will's question.

'Want to help decorate? We can use a few extra hands.'

She walked to the table and saw Kevin's face light up. 'Cool. Can we bring some of the guys?' His new-found self-assurance had spilled over into his ability to make friends. Although he was far from the most popular kid in school, at least he wasn't resorting to fisticuffs as a way to resolve conflicts.

'If you won't goof around,' Will said.

'We won't.' Kevin addressed Emily. 'Are you gonna help too?'

'She's supervising,' Will replied, buttering a piece of toast. 'Just stay off the ladders,' he instructed her.

Emily patted her bulge. 'Are you implying I'm not as graceful or co-ordinated as I used to be?'

'Nah, Em,' Kevin broke in. 'He's afraid they don't have a ladder sturdy enough to hold you.' He snickered.

She rose, pretending affront. 'Just for that, *you're* helping Gran with the dishes.'

'Aw, Em,' he groaned. 'I'm the only kid in this town with dishpan hands.' He held them up and wiggled his fingers. 'I could be in one of those hand-lotion commercials.'

'Don't argue,' Will said, his smile contradicting his order. 'The sooner you're finished, the sooner we'll leave.'

They arrived at the convention center before nine, but a small crowd of hospital employees had already gathered. In the blink of an eye several people approached Will.

'We've got to make more room for tables,' a respiratory therapist said. 'There aren't enough seats to accommodate all the tickets we've sold.'

'Will,' a woman from Accounting interrupted, 'where do you want us to put up the banners?'

Emily watched with interest as Will dealt with each question thrown at him. Meanwhile, a girl from Dietary asked if Emily and Molly would mind blowing up the blue and white balloons.

While Emily operated the helium tank and Molly cut and tied curly ribbon to each one, Emily studied the hive of activity. One group decorated the tables with strips of blue crêpe paper, handfuls of tiny blue stars and a blue and white candle centerpiece, while another let the helium balloons rise to the ceiling. Others tacked various sizes of glittery blue and silver stars onto the walls in wild abandon.

'I don't see Ms Jacqueline around,' Emily said.

The dietician overheard her comment. 'She has a

beauty-shop appointment in *Dallas*. Apparently, our local hairdressers aren't good enough.'

'Sounds like trouble in Paradise,' Molly said, winking at Emily.

'If you ask me,' the dietician continued, 'she's been absolutely worthless. I'm glad she's not here. We'll finish a lot faster if we don't have her changing everything fifty times. I don't care if she *is* the administrator's daughter. Mark my words, she'll take all the credit.'

She stopped talking to scrutinize the placement of the huge 'Welcome' banner over the stage. 'To your left,' she called out, hurrying over to supervise the two men responsible.

'There you have it. Straight from the horse's mouth,' Molly said. 'It's nice to know Jacqueline is as useless at other things as she is at nursing.'

Emily remembered how she'd tearfully embraced Will. As far as she could tell, Jacqueline excelled only at flirting.

She searched for Will, seeing that he never remained in the same spot for longer than a few minutes at a time. In spite of the hubbub, she noticed his broad smile. He was truly in his element.

That fact became even more noticeable hours later when the banquet began. Will strode through the crowd, accepting congratulations and carrying on conversations with the greatest of ease. This was his moment and Emily was proud of him as she accompanied him on his rounds.

Knowing she'd be under scrutiny, she'd purchased the most elegant maternity dress she could find—a mid-calf-length, cream Empire-waisted gown with front pleats, buttons and a lace collar. Her hairdresser had arranged her tresses in the same style she'd worn for her wedding.

However, next to Jacqueline, who was in a creation designed by a man with an unpronounceable name, she felt like the ugly duckling. Jacqueline's sequined red gown glittered with an intensity rivaling the sun's. Her low neckline and raised hemline bared enough skin to attract the attention of even the most devoted husband.

It had been another blow to sit through the nine-course meal at the same table as Jacqueline and her parents. Emily could have tolerated the situation if the divorcee hadn't arranged the seating so *she* could monopolize Will's conversation.

Emily chatted with Mayor Janssen and his wife on her left and hardly sampled her food.

'Aren't you hungry?' Will leaned over to ask after the waitress had served the main part of the meal.

She stopped pushing the succulent beef around her plate. 'No.'

Jacqueline peered around Will. 'Don't you like Beef Wellington? I would have chosen something else for the menu, but I've never heard of *anyone* who didn't like it.'

Emily counted to ten, trying to keep her blood pressure from shooting off the scale. 'It's fine,' she said evenly, forcing a smile when she wanted to grit her teeth. Just then the baby kicked her and she rubbed at the spot.

As if sensing the tension, the mayor's wife broke in. 'I remember when I was expecting. Some times I couldn't eat a thing and then the next day I'd eat everything in sight. Perfectly natural.' She glared at Jacqueline and the moment passed.

Dessert arrived in the form of a slice of two-layer white cake with raspberry sauce drizzled over the top.

Mrs Janssen grinned. 'You know, this reminds me of your wedding. I'll never forget it as long as I live. You handled your little disaster far better than I would have. I was so impressed by your poise.'

'Thank you,' Emily said, encouraged by the older woman's praise. 'I couldn't laugh at the time, but now I can.'

'Oh, yes, I heard about that,' Jacqueline said. 'At least we won't have a dog running loose tonight.'

'Only cats,' Emily replied calmly.

From Jacqueline's startled expression, she evidently understood Emily's veiled meaning.

The mayor's wife coughed discreetly, then whispered in Emily's ear, 'Well done, my dear.'

Finally, the meal ended. Will and Jacqueline walked to the podium where they thanked the people who'd supported them in this endeavor.

Emily focused on Will, noticing how he seemed as comfortable in a tuxedo as he did in his scrubs. As he told several jokes as part of their rehearsed ice-breaking routine, Jacqueline clutched Will's arm in an easy, familiar manner. Jealousy rose in Emily's heart.

Watching their performance, Emily realized she'd been fooling herself. She wasn't the type of wife Will needed, no matter how much she wished it otherwise. Emily Patton belonged behind the scenes, not in the limelight. She was a worker bee, not the queen.

She'd agreed to give their marriage a year, but it was obvious to her that even if she had *ten* years, she'd never be the social butterfly Will wanted.

Oh, they could putter along in their marriage as they had these past few months, but she knew from the satisfaction written on his face that he thrived on events such as these.

She would always be a millstone, the backward wife

he'd married out of duty rather than devotion—the same wife who'd saddled him with an abnormal child as well.

He'd shown her compassion and sensitivity many times, the most recent being the occasion involving Ramona's baby. Now it was time to return the gesture. Loving him as much as she did meant she had to set him free.

The more she thought about it, the clearer her path became. Another round of applause filled the room and she scooted her chair away from the table. 'Please excuse me,' she told her dinner companions.

Grabbing her beaded clutch purse and shawl, she waddled away with as much grace as she could muster and didn't stop until she reached the exit.

To her surprise, Don was standing by the door. 'Nice crowd,' he said.

'Yes, it is. The committee worked hard.'

He motioned toward the podium with a brisk toss of his head. 'Yeah. Will and his sidekick are quite the celebrities. Looks to me like the rumors are true.'

Emily couldn't help herself from responding. 'What are you talking about?'

He glanced toward the couple who held everyone's attention. 'I hear you've been replaced.'

She held her head high and ignored the malice in his eyes. 'If you'll excuse me,' she said stiffly, marching into the foyer.

Molly intercepted her. 'What's wrong?'

Emily blinked rapidly to ease the burning behind her eyes. 'I'm leaving.'

'Are you sick? Is it the baby? Let me get Will.'

'It's not the baby and I don't want Will. May I borrow your car?'

'But, Em, you have to share Will's big moment.'

'Jacqueline's doing the honors.' Emily held out her hand. 'May I borrow your car?'

'My date brought me,' Molly began.

Emily pushed open the glass door and started down the stairs. 'Then I'll walk.'

'Omigod.' Molly wrung her hands. 'Wait a minute. I'll run in and borrow Nate's keys.'

Emily stopped.

'Don't move,' Molly ordered. 'I'll be right back.'

Emily didn't answer. Instead, she leaned against the handrail and slung her shawl over her shoulders. Molly returned in less than a minute.

'You're making a mistake,' she said.

'No, I'm fixing one.'

'What are you talking about?'

'Never mind,' Emily said tiredly. 'Let's go.'

'Where to?' Molly asked, as she steered Emily toward Nate's parked car.

'Home.'

However, as Molly directed her car toward Will's house Emily forestalled her. 'No. My old house.'

'It's empty!'

'Not completely. I need some time alone and it's the only place where I won't be bothered.'

'This isn't a good idea, Em.'

'It beats staying here and watching Jacqueline. If Will wants her then he can have her,' Emily said vehemently. 'I'm leaving him, Moll.'

Molly's eyes narrowed and she scowled. 'When I get my hands on that woman she'll wish she'd never come to town.'

Emily sighed. 'Forget it. It's not so much her as what she represents. Money, looks, breeding. I fall short in all three areas.'

Molly parked in front of the darkened house. 'Don't do this, Em. Let me take you home.'

Emily opened the door. 'Promise me something. Don't tell Will where I am.'

'But what if something happens?' Molly wailed. 'What if you get sick or the baby—?'

'I'll call 911.' She smiled. 'Now, go back to the party. I'll see you on Monday.'

Emily ambled up the walk and searched through the bushes for the hollowed-out rock that held the spare key. Finding it, she let herself inside.

The house had a musty, closed-in smell, but she didn't care. Too sick at heart to turn on the lights, she let the moonlight shining through the windows guide her path to her old and familiar bedroom. Immediately, she flung the dust cover off the bed and removed her dress and panty hose, before crawling between the cool sheets.

'Oh, baby,' she said aloud in the eerily quiet house. 'What are we going to do now?'

# CHAPTER ELEVEN

WILL watched Emily leave the table. Although she wore a smile, it seemed strained and her shoulders were definitely slumped. The question Emily had posed echoed in his mind. 'Do you want to be faithful?' He'd ignored his personal issues for too long, not realizing how badly his marital relationship had deteriorated because of it. Now he feared the damage might be irreparable.

Emily stopped to talk to Don and fierce possessiveness surged through him. He tensed until the crowd's laughter at Jacqueline's comment broke through his preoccupation.

He felt Jacqueline's grip on his upper arm. As if scales had fallen from his eyes he compared her to Emily, and felt nothing but utter contempt. It took every ounce of self-control to finish his master-of-ceremonies duties without pushing her away. The second he'd turned the program over to the auctioneer and his capable assistants he vacated the small platform and went to his table.

'Where did Em go?' he asked the mayor's wife, certain of her reply and yet afraid to hear it.

'She didn't say. I think she was upset.' She cast a disgusted look at the woman beside him.

Jacqueline threaded her arm through his. 'Oh, Will, she's probably resting in the lounge. She'll be back before long. Let's enjoy ourselves.'

Will pointedly removed her hands. 'If you do that one more time I won't be responsible for my actions,' he said coldly, not caring who, including Jacqueline's father, overheard.

Jacqueline bristled at his rebuff. 'Well…'

'Well, nothing,' he returned. 'I've endured all I'm going to endure, and I expect you to apologize to Emily when you see her again.'

He turned toward Mr Olivier. 'You can make my life miserable, revoke my hospital privileges—whatever—but I don't care. I've given my heart and soul to making this event a success, but enough is enough. I've sacrificed my wife's happiness to pander to your daughter's ego, but no more.'

He squared his shoulders. 'My job here is finished. Now I need to spend the rest of my evening repairing the damage I've done to my marriage. Good night.'

The three Oliviers were astonished. Mayor Janssen blinked in surprise while his wife smiled and gave Will a thumbs-up sign.

He pivoted on one heel and began searching for Emily. No one had seen her. The news of Don's disappearance was equally distressing.

Molly's date gave him his first clue—Molly had borrowed his car. Hoping she'd taken Emily home and not to the hospital, Will telephoned to check.

'She's not here,' Helen said, clearly puzzled. 'Isn't she with you?'

'She and Molly probably stepped out for some fresh air,' he prevaricated, his worry growing. 'I'm sure I'll see her shortly.'

As he was phoning the hospital he saw Molly return. Without wasting a moment, he made a beeline toward her and grabbed her elbow.

'Where's Emily?' he asked, as he forced Molly to retrace her steps.

'Emily who?'

'Don't play dumb with me,' he snapped. 'You two left together and you've come back alone. I checked with Helen and Emily isn't there. Is she at the hospital?'

Molly shook her arm free. 'No. She wanted some time to herself. To think.' She glared at him. 'You certainly have a nerve, acting concerned about Em after letting that…that *tramp* hang all over you when Emily worships the ground you walk on.'

Guilt made him fall silent. 'She's never said.'

'Of course not, you idiot. If you were afraid you didn't measure up to someone's expectations, would you hand them your heart to break?'

Will raked the fingers of one hand through his hair. The thought of Emily leaving him sent a cold shiver across his shoulders. How had he been such a blind fool?

And yet he knew. He'd been too busy with his own agenda. Even after she'd asked him that ridiculous question in the hospital morgue he'd allowed himself to be sidetracked.

He squared his shoulders. 'Where is she?'

'I'm not telling you.'

'Does her grandmother know? If I come home without Em, Helen will be frantic. Do you want that on your conscience?'

Molly chewed on her bottom lip.

'Is she at a place where she at least has a phone?'

'I…I think so.'

Will saw her uncertainty. 'What if she needs someone?' he pressed. 'She's seven months pregnant. Anything could happen.'

'I know,' Molly said crossly. 'I told her the same thing, but she didn't listen.'

Will placed both hands on Molly's shoulders. 'I know

you're following her wishes, but I love her, Molly, so help me. Not just for my sake, but for everyone's.' He paused. 'Please.'

Indecision flickered in her eyes. 'If I do, she won't speak to me again.'

'She will,' he said confidently. 'She won't hold a grudge.'

'I don't know.' Molly hesitated. 'You'd better do some fancy talking. In fact, I'd learn to grovel if I were you.'

Will drew a deep breath, frustrated by Molly's reticence. 'Fine. Just tell me where she went.'

'If you hurt her—'

'I'm trying to fix things. Not make them worse.'

Molly chewed on her upper lip. 'If you don't, I'll do whatever I can to make your life miserable.'

'Nothing you could possibly do would compare to life without Emily.'

'All right. I give up. She's at her old house.'

Will flashed her a huge smile, kissed her cheek and set her aside. 'Thank you.' Without wasting a second, he rushed from the building.

During the short drive to Emily's old home he focused on the battle awaiting him. He'd seen his wife's determined streak before, but he held the market on persistence.

He parked his car, noticing the darkened windows of the house. Emily was probably asleep since they hadn't arranged for the power company to discontinue service. As he strode up the walk he realized that without a key, he couldn't do much more than create a racket and hope she'd let him inside before the police arrested him for disturbing the peace.

He knocked but, as expected, didn't get an answer.

Frustrated, he turned the knob. To his surprise and dismay the door opened.

He stepped inside, then listened. All was quiet. He clicked on the hallway light and went straight to the bedroom.

Will had just cleared the threshold when a sharp blow to his midsection took his breath away and he doubled over. Before he could recover, blows rained down on his head and he raised one hand to wrest the weapon from his assailant's hand.

Flinging the umbrella aside, he grabbed the flailing arms. He bumped against the person's body and immediately recognized his attacker. 'Emily, it's me.'

'Will?' She sounded incredulous. Then her voice hardened. 'What are you doing here?'

He clicked on the bedroom light. 'I might ask you the same thing.'

'I came for peace and quiet.'

'*I* came because I was worried about you,' he retorted. 'What's the idea of not locking the place? I walked right in.'

Emily folded her arms above the mound of her stomach. 'And I heard you. How else do you think I had time to find my umbrella?'

'Which I took away from you as easily as candy from a baby.'

She wordlessly raised her hand to point toward the door. With her hair tumbling over her shoulders, the fire in her eyes and clad in her white slip, she resembled his mental image of an avenging angel.

He waved his hands. 'Stop.' Shooting her a rueful grin, he rubbed the sore spot on the bottom of his ribs. 'You pack quite a punch.'

'Sorry.'

'Somehow I didn't envision our meeting quite like this.'

Emily sank on the edge of the bed, her spirits low. 'I didn't either.' She'd intended to think things through, then drive home in the morning ready to deliver her rehearsed speech. Since he was here she might as well break the news now.

'I want a divorce,' she said.

He sat beside her. 'Our year isn't over.'

'I'm not the wife you want.'

'Says who?'

She rubbed her forehead, exasperated by his contrariness. 'We're not suited.'

'I disagree.'

Fueled by her emotions, Emily jumped up to pace. 'Don't be ridiculous! You want someone like Jacqueline—a hot-house flower. Well, I'm not. I'm a common old…' Her mind went blank as she tried to think of a perennial.

'I'm glad,' he said.

'I'll never be silk and satin,' she mourned. 'I want to be and I even tried to be, but that's for people like—'

His comment finally penetrated. She blinked in confusion. 'What did you say?'

'I'm glad you're not like Jacqueline,' he said simply.

She narrowed her eyes. 'Oh, yeah? Why?'

'Because she's extremely self-centered. She doesn't give unless she stands to gain something in return. Exotic flowers like Jacqueline and Celine require constant attention. To be honest, they're a royal pain.'

Emily stared at him, hardly believing her ears.

'You, on the other hand,' he said, 'are kind and generous. You also make life interesting. More importantly, you make *my* life worth living.'

She fell silent.

He met her gaze, his hands resting on his thighs. 'I didn't realize until just recently how much I admire those traits.'

An image of him smiling down on Jacqueline came to mind and she stiffened. 'You were enjoying your exotic little flower tonight.'

'I did what I thought I had to do. After you walked out nothing mattered. You see, the one person I really wanted to impress had left. Jacqueline has been impossible to work with, but I was caught up in the notion of proving myself and so I tolerated her poor behavior. I hurt you in the process, and I'm sorry.'

Emily heard his sincerity and knew how difficult it was for him to apologize, but she wasn't ready to throw caution to the wind. 'It's easy to say these things now that the fund-raiser is over. What happens the next time?'

His smile was wry. 'I doubt if there will ever be a next time. In fact, I may be a doctor without hospital privileges.'

'What are you talking about?'

'I told Jacqueline to straighten out her act.'

'I'm sure that made a big impression,' she said in a dry tone. 'If Jacqueline wants something she doesn't take no for an answer.'

'I did it in front of her parents.'

Emily covered her mouth with her hands, then sank beside him as surprise weakened her knees. 'You didn't!'

He nodded. 'I did. If you don't believe me, ask the Janssens. They heard the whole thing.'

'The mayor and his wife? Oh, Will. Why did you do

something so foolish? The Oliviers won't ever forgive or forget.'

He took her hands. 'I did it because you mean more to me than fame and fortune. You see, I wanted all that at one time, but after you walked into my life everything changed. You operated with your emotions and I didn't so it took me a while to get used to your way of dealing with things.

'When you left tonight I finally realized how badly I want you in my life, not Jacqueline or Celine. Just you.'

Tears clogged Emily's throat. She didn't doubt him one bit. Since he was prone to analyzing his alternatives before deciding his course of action, his spontaneous rebuff in front of influential witnesses revealed more than words could describe.

'Oh, Will.'

'I love you, Em.'

She sniffled. 'You've never said. I thought…'

'I've always been a private person,' he said. 'It's hard for me to discuss the things that mean a lot to me.'

'You have to, Will. Without communication a relationship can't survive.'

'I know,' he said. 'Now you know why I couldn't talk about the baby even though he's always been on my mind. I couldn't change the outcome—Lady Luck hasn't smiled on me very often—so I funneled my time and energy into this fund-raiser. It became my hiding place.'

Emily fell silent. 'I was afraid you regretted taking on me and my family,' she finally admitted. 'And with the possibility of a handicapped child… Children with chronic medical conditions can strain even the best relationships.

'I knew you'd compare the life you had with the life you'd wanted and find ours—*me*—lacking. I couldn't stand it.' She studied her hands resting in her nearly non-existent lap.

Will lifted her chin. 'Absolutely not. I hated it when your uncle pushed you into marriage. It was the logical solution to me, but I wanted you to say yes by choice, not command.'

She smiled. 'I wasn't forced. If you recall, I made my decision before I heard Bert's ultimatum. I loved you even then.'

'Then why did you mention a divorce after a year?'

'I didn't want you to be miserable,' she said simply. 'I knew you wouldn't sneak around with another woman, but I didn't want you to feel trapped. If you wanted to leave I was willing to set you free.'

He drew her close. 'Sorry, lady. I'm yours for the next fifty or so years.'

'Our life won't run according to plan or schedule,' she warned.

'I know,' he said wryly. 'Nothing about our relationship has, even from the beginning. I'll always make plans, but I can live with unpredictability if you can.' He grinned. 'In fact, I don't think I've ever felt as alive as I have since I met you.'

'And your dreams of silk and satin?' she asked, needing his reassurances one last time.

'You fit that description more than you know.' He ran his fingers along her cheek. 'With a touch of steel backbone thrown in for good measure.'

The baby kicked, poking Will in his side. He flashed a lopsided grin. 'See? Our baby agrees.'

She smiled. 'Then tell him not to be so forceful,' she said, rubbing the spot. 'And while you're laying down the rules you can tell him it's bedtime.'

Will drew her close. 'I know just how to lull him to

sleep,' he said, caressing her skin. 'All it takes is the right touch.'

To Emily's total satisfaction he was right.

'We can't wait any longer,' Susan Hathaway told Emily one sunny day at the end of August.

Emily lay on the birthing bed, pain gripping her midsection. 'We have to,' she said through gritted teeth. 'Will isn't here.'

Susan motioned to Lana, the nurse who'd replaced Jacqueline in recent weeks. 'Tell Dr Patton that if he wants to witness his baby's birth he'd better get his tail in here—pronto.'

Another contraction tore through Emily and she panted.

Suddenly Will appeared, pulling on a fresh gown over his scrubs. 'Remind me to scold you about your poor timing,' he said, his eyes crinkling above the mask.

'Tell…Junior. How's the…other…new mom?' she asked.

'Mrs Fairchild is doing great and so's her bouncing baby boy.'

'OK, Daddy, make yourself useful,' Susan demanded. 'It's time to push.'

Emily bore down with her next contraction while Will held her hand and coaxed her to continue.

'The head's out,' Susan said. Another push later she held the tiny body in both hands. 'Well, look at this,' she said, her tone soft. 'It goes to show that an obstetrician can be wrong. Come and hold your daughter, Will.'

He took the baby and headed for the infant warming bed. 'Hello, pumpkin,' he crooned.

Emily couldn't stand the suspense. 'How is she?'

Emotion choked Will's voice. 'She's fine, Em. She's absolutely perfect from head to toe.'

'Are you sure?'

Will's smile stretched from ear to ear as he returned to her side, carrying his daughter. 'Don't you believe me?'

She'd waited too long to take anyone's word for something so crucial, even her husband's. 'I want to see for myself.'

'Bossy, aren't we?' he teased, unwrapping the baby inch by inch.

Emily's vision blurred with her unshed tears of relief and happiness. 'Oh, Will. She *is* perfect.'

He deftly rewrapped her. 'And you doubted me.' He shook his head. 'Hear that, Susan? I don't get any respect.'

Susan laughed. 'Get used to it, Dad.' She stood up to peer at the baby's serene face. 'What a little sweetheart. Do you have a name picked out?'

'Angela Marie,' Emily replied, combining their mothers' names. Will's smile revealed his appreciation.

'Mark my words,' Susan said, 'Your little Angel will tie her daddy around her little finger.'

Will placed the baby in the crook of Emily's impatient arm. 'Just like her mother.'

Emily stared down at Angela. She had a faithful, loving husband and a healthy daughter, not to mention two doting relatives waiting outside for an introduction. Contrary to Will's thinking, Lady Luck had indeed smiled on them.

# MILLS & BOON®

*Makes*
**any time**
*special*

**Enjoy a romantic novel from**
**Mills & Boon®**

*Presents™* *Enchanted™* *Temptation*

*Historical Romance™* *Medical Romance™*

MILLS & BOON®

*Medical Romance*™

# COMING NEXT MONTH

## MORE THAN A MISTRESS by Alison Roberts

Anna's first House Officer job was in surgeon Michael Smith's hospital. She couldn't believe this was the same man she'd met on holiday, and parted from so badly. And Michael was no happier to see her!

## A SURGEON FOR SUSAN by Helen Shelton

Susan was appalled when her sister set her up with a blind date! But Adam had been equally set up, by *his* sister. He was *so* gorgeous, why would anyone think he needed help finding a woman?

## HOME AT LAST by Jennifer Taylor
*A Country Practice*—the third of four books.

After a year away Holly Ross felt able to come home. Many changes awaited her, not least a new stepmother. But the biggest change of all was her growing feelings for Dr Sam O'Neill, the partnership locum.

## HEART-THROB by Meredith Webber
*Bachelor Doctors*

Peter's photo was plastered on *Hospital Heart-throb of the month* posters, embarrassing him when Anna came to work with him in A&E. She was intriguing and mysterious, and Peter couldn't help being fascinated. But he'd managed to stay a bachelor this far...

## Available from 2nd July 1999

*Available at most branches of WH Smith, Tesco, Asda,
Martins, Borders, Easons, Volume One/James Thin
and most good paperback bookshops*

# FREE
## 2 BOOKS
### AND A SURPRISE GIFT!

We would like to take this opportunity to thank you for reading this Mills & Boon® book by offering you the chance to take TWO more specially selected titles from the Medical Romance™ series absolutely FREE! We're also making this offer to introduce you to the benefits of the Reader Service™ —

- ★ FREE home delivery
- ★ FREE monthly Newsletter
- ★ FREE gifts and competitions
- ★ Exclusive Reader Service discounts
- ★ Books available before they're in the shops

Accepting these FREE books and gift places you under no obligation to buy; you may cancel at any time, even after receiving your free shipment. Simply complete your details below and return the entire page to the address below. *You don't even need a stamp!*

**YES!** Please send me 2 free Medical Romance books and a surprise gift. I understand that unless you hear from me, I will receive 4 superb new titles every month for just £2.40 each, postage and packing free. I am under no obligation to purchase any books and may cancel my subscription at any time. The free books and gift will be mine to keep in any case.

M9EC

Ms/Mrs/Miss/Mr ......................................................Initials .............................................
BLOCK CAPITALS PLEASE

Surname.....................................................................................................................

Address...................................................................................................................

...............................................................................................................................

.......................................................Postcode ...................................................

**Send this whole page to:**
THE READER SERVICE, FREEPOST CN81, CROYDON, CR9 3WZ
(Eire readers please send coupon to: P.O. BOX 4546, DUBLIN 24.)

## THE Regency COLLECTION

*Where rogues find romance*

Look out for the third volume in this limited
collection of Regency Romances from
Mills & Boon® in July.

Featuring:

*Dear Lady Disdain*
**by Paula Marshall**

and

*An Angel's Touch*
**by Elizabeth Bailey**

**Still only £4.99**

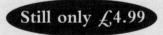

**MILLS & BOON®**

*Makes any time special™*

*Available at most branches of WH Smith, Tesco, Martins,*
*Borders, Easons, Volume One/James Thin*
*and most good paperback bookshops*

# EXQUISITE ACQUISITIONS

## BY
## CHARLENE SANDS

MILLS &
BOON

First published in Great Britain 2013
by Mills & Boon, an imprint of Harlequin (UK) Limited.
Harlequin (UK) Limited, Eton House, 18-24 Paradise Road,
Richmond, Surrey TW9 1SR

© Harlequin Books S.A. 2012

Special thanks and acknowledgment to Charlene Sands for her contribution to *The Highest Bidder* miniseries.

ISBN: 978 0 263 90037 8

Harlequin (UK) policy is to use papers that are natural, renewable and recyclable products and made from wood grown in sustainable forests. The logging and manufacturing process conform to the legal environmental regulations of the country of origin.

Printed and bound in Spain
by Blackprint CPI, Barcelona

Award-winning author **Charlene Sands** writes bold, passionate, heart-stopping heroes and always… really good men! She's a lover of all things romantic, having married her high school sweetheart, Don. She is the proud recipient of a Readers' Choice Award, and double recipient of a Booksellers' Best Award, having written twenty-eight romances to date, both contemporary and historical Western. Charlene is a member of Romance Writers of America and belongs to the Orange County and Los Angeles chapters of RWA, where she volunteers as the Published Authors' Liaison.

When not writing, she loves movie dates with her hubby, playing cards with her children, reading romance, great coffee, Pacific beaches, country music and anything chocolate. She also loves to hear from her readers. You can reach Charlene for fun stuff, contests and more at www.charlenesands.com or write to her at PO Box 4883, West Hills, CA 91308, USA. You can find her on the Harlequin Authors Blog, and on Facebook, too.

**Recent titles by the same author:**

SUNSET SURRENDER
WORTH THE RISK
EXQUISITE REVENGE

**Did you know these are also available as eBooks?
Visit www.millsandboon.co.uk**

In memory and honor of Sandra Hyatt,
a friend and fellow Desire author.

I will always remember your sweet, friendly smile
and your kind heart.

# Prologue

*Wild River Ranch, Texas*

He struck a match on his boot heel and guided the flame toward the cigarette clenched between his lips. With one long pull of breath, the tip blazed to life. Carter McCay closed his eyes as images of the fallen soldiers who'd fought alongside him flashed in his mind. He took one drag…one honorary inhalation. The ritual was agreed upon by those lucky enough to have come home, all those years ago. On the first day of every month, each one of his comrades did the same. Somewhere out there, twenty-three former marines were lighting up and remembering Afghanistan.

The subtle rush of the river pulled him out of those thoughts. He leaned a shoulder against an ancient oak and nestled into the tree's grooved bark, watching the rhythmic, nearly perfect ripples of Wild River. The water wasn't as wild as its namesake today, Carter mused. It was quiet and peaceful here, shaded from the hot Texas sun.

The dog plopped down at his feet and whimpered long and loud as the trail of smoke met his upturned wet nose.

Carter pushed his Stetson higher on his forehead and looked into questioning, soulful eyes. He couldn't blame the dog for being wary of smoke. The dog saw too much, knew too much. "You followed me up here, pal."

Carter tossed the cigarette and crushed it into the ground with his boot, then lowered to a crouch beside the golden retriever. He gave him a pat on the head. The dog sandwiched his head between his front paws and gave a big sigh.

"Yeah, I know, boy. You've had it tough." Carter ruffled Rocky's furry neck, damn glad he'd rescued the hound from his father's place. The home where Carter had grown up wasn't fit for a dog.

His cell phone pinged. Carter pulled his iPhone from his back pocket and gave a quick look. A text message from Roark Waverly appeared on the front screen. He hadn't heard from his former marine buddy in months. But he wasn't surprised that he'd leave a message today of all days. "Probably just lit one up, too," he muttered, glad to hear from his friend. But as he read on, Roark had something entirely different to say. Something Carter had to read twice.

C. Ran into some trouble. In hiding. Get word to Ann Richardson at Waverly's. The Gold Heart statue is not stolen. I can't trust Waverly's networks. R.B.

Carter frowned. What the hell what that all about?

After his tour of duty, Roark had gotten heavily involved in running around seven continents procuring valuable artifacts to sell at Waverly's auction house based out of New York. Roark had been in some tough binds through the years, and normally the marine could take care of himself just fine. Carter had been on the receiving end of his friend's quick thinking when they'd been on street patrol in a small settlement in Afghanistan. Roark had discovered that the car Carter was about to inspect was booby trapped. He'd shoved Carter out of the way before his hand met with the door handle, and Carter knew then that he owed Roark his life.

"C'mon, Rocky," he said, heading toward his Jeep without a glance back. He knew his father's dog would follow. He was as loyal as they come. "I've got some investigating to do."

Two hours later, his cousin Brady knocked on his front door and Carter led him into the great room. The room meant for entertaining was one of many improvements he'd made to the house after he'd inherited Wild River Ranch from his uncle Dale. Over the years and after a little luck and a lot of hard work, Carter had turned his uncle's small working ranch into a stellar operation that competed equally with elite Texas cattle barons.

He handed Brady a shot glass of whiskey. "Here you go, cuz."

Brady grinned. "I know it's five o'clock somewhere, but tell me, why are we drinking this early in the afternoon?"

"Because thanks to you, I'm heading to New York tomorrow."

"Me? What do Brady McCay and New York have in common?"

Carter couldn't tell him about Roark's cryptic text message. That message wasn't meant to be discussed, not even with someone Carter trusted. But he could tell Brady the other reason for his trip. As he'd researched the New York auction house Roark worked for, he'd found that Hollywood screen legend Tina Tarlington's diamond rings were being auctioned off this weekend. The famed Tarlington diamond had been in the press ever since Tina Tarlington's first marriage, decades ago. Now, there was even more buzz about all three of her diamonds since the Queen of Cinema had passed away a few months ago. Carter planned to get his hands on one of those diamonds and, at the same time, deliver Roark's message to the CEO of Waverly's.

"You're the one who introduced me to Jocelyn, right?" Carter asked.

"I can't deny that. I sure did."

"She's in New York right now, visiting a friend."

His cousin's eyebrows narrowed. "I'm not following."

"I intend to join her there and ask her to marry me."

Brady blinked and jerked back in surprise. "You intend to marry Jocelyn Grayson? I didn't realize things were that serious between you two."

"Damn straight they are. I've been hunting for the right engagement ring for weeks now. If all goes as planned, she'll be my fiancée very soon."

"You're really in love with Jocelyn?" There was a note of disbelief in Brady's voice.

Carter had to admit he was moving a little fast. But from the day he'd been introduced to the granddaughter of Brady's neighbor, Carter had been smitten. Now, less than a year later, Carter was ready to make a commitment. Putting a Tarlington ring on Jocelyn's finger would be impressive, even to an oil heiress who came from old Dallas money. She'd know, without a doubt, how much she meant to him. "She's the one for me, Brady."

"Well, then. Congratulations," Brady offered.

Carter lifted his shot glass. Now that he'd made up his mind, he couldn't wait to see Jocelyn's expression when he proposed to her with a Tarlington diamond. "To Jocelyn."

Brady hesitated for a second and stared into Carter's eyes before lifting his glass, as well. "To Jocelyn."

And after they downed the liquor, the smile Carter expected to see on his cousin's face never really emerged.

# One

Macy Tarlington never knew whether her attempt at disguise would work or not. Today, the beige scarf covering her ink-black curls and dark sunglasses hiding her violet-blue eyes seemed to do the trick. She hadn't been followed. Thank goodness. She looked a little too much like her mother, which wasn't overall a bad thing. Her mother had been known for her beauty, but resembling Hollywood's beloved Queen of Cinema had drawn paparazzi to Macy like bees to honey. They believed her DNA alone gave them the right to trample on her privacy, especially during her time of mourning.

Tina Tarlington might have been world famous and her fans might have believed they knew everything about her, from her award-winning movie roles and her three doomed marriages to her celebrity status, but they hadn't really known her. Not the way Macy had.

Walking into New York's opulent Madison Avenue auction house made her twitch with anxiety. She bumped shoulders with her good friend, Avery Cullen, as they approached the Waverly salesroom. Avery was the least likely sort of American heiress, very unassuming and certainly not a spoiled cliché. "Sorry if I'm crowding you," she whispered. "I can't seem to help it."

Avery's warm smile reassured her as she took Macy's arm. Her friend's steady touch soothed her jumpy nerves. "I don't mind, Macy. That's why I'm here, for support."

With eyes well hidden beneath sunglasses, Macy was free to dart glances all around, scoping out the large, elegantly appointed room where Tina Tarlington's prized possessions would be auctioned off. Beautifully tufted, rounded high-back chairs were lined up in a dozen rows, split in the center by an aisle. The surrounding walls were easy-on-the-eye tones of beiges and light peach. Wide white wainscoting centered the walls and wrapped around the perimeter of the room. Multifaceted crystal chandeliers twinkled and provided abundant light overhead.

"I can't thank you enough for enduring this with me." Avery had made a quick trip from her home in London to be with her today.

"I know how hard this is for you."

"Hard and necessary, unfortunately. Having my mother's things on display like this gives me a stomachache. Oh, I am *so* not looking forward to this."

Avery gave Macy's hand a squeeze as they pressed farther into the room. "Those two seats on the aisle in the back are ours," Macy whispered. "I made arrangements beforehand for us."

And as they headed to those seats, Macy noticed that every other chair in the room was taken. Even in death, Tina Tarlington drew large crowds.

An attendant came by immediately to hand them a catalogue listing the items being auctioned off, and after a brief conversation Macy nodded her thanks to the woman standing at the head of the room. Ann Richardson, the CEO of Waverly's, who had secured the estate sale from Macy, gave her a silent greeting in return before turning to shake hands with the patrons in the front row. It was important to Ms. Richardson that the Tarlington auction go off without a hitch. Waverly's stood to make a hefty commission.

Macy opened the catalogue and flipped through the pages,

noting item after item from her mother's estate. The descriptions were listed as lot numbers along with an estimate as to their value. The first item stopped her cold as memories flooded in and tears formed in her eyes.

On Macy's tenth birthday, just as the celebration was about to begin, Tina had rushed into the Magic Castle Mansion, an exclusive club showcasing musicians from around the world, dressed as Eleanor Neal, the role which had garnered her an Academy Award nomination. She'd come straight from the set, the shoot going longer than anticipated. Macy hadn't cared that her mother was late for her party or that she'd come in her professional makeup and wardrobe. She'd flown into her mother's arms and hugged her so tight that Tina laughed until her mascara had run down her face. It was *magic* and one of the best birthdays of Macy's life.

Now, the pink silk and sequin dress her mother had worn that day was described as "Worn by Tina Tarlington in the acclaimed film *Quest for Vengeance,* 1996."

Her mother's entire life seemed to have been whittled down to one-sentence blurbs and numbers. The ache in Macy's stomach intensified.

Discreetly, she closed the catalogue booklet and took a deep breath. She couldn't fall apart. Not now. She had to go through with this auction. She gave herself a little pep talk, reciting in her head all the practical reasons why selling her mother's treasures and jewels were necessary.

As she surveyed the room, people-watching, waiting for the auction to begin, she found the distraction she needed in a Stetson-wearing hunk of a man sitting across the aisle from her and one row up. His head was down, concentrating on the catalogue. The cowboy wore a crisp white shirt underneath a stylish Western suit coat that accentuated the solid breadth of his shoulders. The glint of silver from his bolo tie twinkled under the chandeliers. His profile was strong, grooved with a razor-sharp cheekbone and an angular jaw. He swung his head around and glanced at her for a split second, as if he suspected her of watching him. She panicked for an instant and held her breath. Luckily, he hadn't lingered but went on to scan the rest of the room.

But oh my! When he'd turned, she'd gotten the full impact of his gaze and found him even more appealing than she'd originally thought. A crazy jolt of warmth surged through her body. The powerful sensation was new to Macy.

Butterflies replaced the turmoil in her stomach.

How strange.

She continued to grab eyefuls, shifting her gaze away occasionally to avoid being caught. She was grateful for her little disguise. It provided her freedom to peruse something more exciting than the auction.

The cowboy glanced over the seated bidders and up toward the podium time and again. He appeared anxious and impatient for the auction to begin.

A minute later, Ann Richardson took the podium with a welcome to everyone at the auction. After a cordial greeting, the CEO turned the microphone over to the auctioneer and he stepped up to the podium. The auction began and Macy watched as, one by one, bidders raised their paddles when the first gown was offered up.

Dear, sweet Avery sat vigilantly beside her, a pillar of quiet strength. When the auctioneer's hammer fell, finalizing the winning bid, Avery squeezed her hand and whispered into her ear. "Just remember, your mother would want you to do this."

Macy nodded and slid her eyes closed briefly. It was true. Her mother had loved her possessions, and heaven knew, she had *not* been good with money. But her mother had made a point of always making sure Macy had known that *she,* not her profession or her jewels, was the most important, most beloved thing in her life. Misguided as her mother's life might have been, Macy knew she'd been loved. When her father, Clyde Tarlington, had died ten years ago, Tina might have given up, but she'd shown Macy what it was to be a survivor. To press on, even under adversity.

Once again, Macy glanced at her handsome cowboy, sitting patiently across the aisle. He'd taken off his hat, out of consideration to the people seated behind him, she presumed, as soon as

the bidding had begun. His dark blond hair was well-groomed,
thick and curling at the edge of his collar. The Stetson rested on
his outstretched leg and Macy reeled in her wayward thoughts,
thinking if she could only trade places with that hat.

The corners of her lips lifted at the idea. And Macy's foolish
heart skipped a beat.

His face was becoming familiar to her. He was a good diver-
sion, a distraction that she couldn't seem to shake. She was drawn
to him, and she couldn't figure out why. She lived in Hollywood,
where gorgeous men were a dime a dozen. She'd acted in small
movie roles opposite men more beautiful than any female starlet.

No, it wasn't his looks that drew her to him. It was something
else. He held himself with an air of confidence that belied his obvious discomfort seated in a venerable New York auction house.

She liked that about him.

For all she knew, he'd be more comfortable bidding on longhorn steers.

She liked that about him, too.

Another mental chuckle emerged. She had to stop fantasizing
about him. Macy returned her attention to the auction, grateful
to the cowboy for giving her something thrilling to admire while
her mother's life was being bartered away.

Soon the diamond rings would be up for sale.

Macy cringed and slithered down in her seat. She actually felt
sorry for the people who wound up with them.

Three diamond rings. Three doomed marriages.

"The rings are cursed," she whispered to Avery.

Her friend nodded ever so slightly. "Then you should be glad
to get rid of them."

Oh, she was. She was extremely glad. Those rings represented
pain and heartache to anyone in their possession. The love surrounding those rings would never survive. Her mother's three
failed marriages were testimony enough. Each one of her marriages had been horrific in their own way, and Macy had begun
thinking of the diamond rings as the Love Curse Diamonds. Of
course, it wasn't a good idea to tell that to the press. She needed
the money too badly to risk lowering their value. But there were

stories behind those diamonds and, unfortunately, Macy knew them all too well.

The bidding was to begin on the three-carat diamond that Clyde Tarlington had given to her mother. The setting was unique, a one of a kind. The nearly perfect gem had been placed in such a way that it formed a T with surrounding smaller diamonds nestled beside it to finish forming the letter. It was by far the most exquisite ring of the trio.

Avery nudged her shoulder and Macy, deep in thought, slid her friend a sideways glance. "Take a look." She gestured across the aisle. "That gorgeous cowboy you've been eyeing all afternoon is getting ready. I bet he bids on the Tarlington diamond."

Carter wanted that Tarlington diamond so bad he could taste it. He'd spend a small fortune on it, if it boiled down to that. He groaned with impatience.

The stately woman sitting next to him, her nose in the air, reacted to the sound he made with a high and mighty puff. Then her gaze shifted to the felt hat sitting on his lap. She gave him another sniff of disapproval.

Well, hell. He'd offended her.

Because he was in a good mood, being nearly engaged and all, he sent her a smile of apology.

The woman gripped her purse with thin wiry fingers and inched away from him without returning his smile. She didn't bother to disguise her feelings. He didn't fit in. She didn't approve of him being here.

He couldn't fault her for that thinking. He *didn't* fit in here. He didn't like crowds, tight spaces or the irritating roar of New York traffic. But he had two darn good reasons for attending the auction.

The engagement ring he was determined to buy and the friend he was determined to help.

Both were important and could be life altering.

An article he'd read in the *New York Times* this morning about possible collusion between Waverly's and their rival auction house, Rothchild's, flashed into his mind. The piece had put the Waverly establishment in a bad light.

Doubt as to whether he should sink any money into the auction at all had crossed his mind and old survival instincts had clicked in. Carter was known for making sound financial decisions, and if it were anyone else, he would've walked away from the auction. But his friend Roark was a straight shooter. If Roark trusted Ann Richardson and Waverly's, that was good enough for Carter. It was as simple as that.

The CEO sat up front but off to the side, overseeing the auction. He'd kept a keen eye on her since the auction began and wouldn't let her out of his sight. He couldn't get near her before, but he wasn't leaving until he'd delivered the message from Roark.

Before the auction began, Ann Richardson had given a tidy welcome speech to the patrons, reminding them about Waverly's honest and reputable dealings for over one hundred and fifty years. Her way of dispelling the rumors tarnishing today's auction. Anticipation stirred in his gut, and the reality of what he was about to do struck him. After thirty-one years of bachelorhood, he was ready to propose marriage and settle down with a woman.

Finally, the auctioneer announced the famous gem. "The Tarlington emerald-cut diamond ring is three carats in weight, with VS1 clarity and D color with six surrounding baquette diamonds weighing a total of one point four carats. We'll start the bidding at fifty thousand dollars."

Carter raised his paddle and made the first bid.

Three other paddles went up after his.

And by the time he lifted his paddle again, the bid had increased to seventy thousand dollars. The room got extremely quiet. Only the slight rustle of clothes and an intermittent cough echoed in the large room. As far as he could tell, there were four bidders, and all of them were actively bidding as the price of the Tarlington diamond doubled.

He lifted his paddle again.

Two of the other bidders dropped off and Carter found himself in a one-on-one duel.

It was between him and someone he couldn't quite make out from a row closer to the front of the room. The mysterious bidder wasn't giving up.

When the bid doubled again, Carter retired his paddle. It was clear that his opponent had unlimited means and wanted that diamond ring no matter the cost. Carter had too much business sense to pay more than twice what the darn thing was actually worth. He'd already overbid. When the hammer fell and the bid was won, he lifted up a fraction from his chair and craned his neck to find out who had outbid him. A young woman wearing an austere business suit and a satisfied smile had nodded to the auctioneer.

Carter frowned. He hated losing.

The next diamond presented was a ring of less iconic value than the Tarlington diamond, but with two nearly perfect carats of dazzle in a platinum setting, given to the legendary star by her third husband, Joseph Madigan. Carter wouldn't be outbid again.

"Going once. Going twice. Fair warning, this lot is about to be sold." A second ticked by in silence. Then the gavel hit the podium. "Sold!"

Satisfaction curled in Carter's belly. The diamond ring was his. He'd flown across the continent for an engagement ring to impress Jocelyn, and tomorrow night he'd be dishing it up on a silver platter.

Once the auction concluded, Carter made fast work of securing the diamond ring, along with the certificate of sale. He caught Ann Richardson as she was leaving the salesroom. "Ms. Richardson?"

The tall willowy blonde turned and surprised Carter at how young she appeared up close. She blinked. "Yes?"

"Pardon me, ma'am. But I need to speak to you privately."

"Is there a problem with the sale? You won the bid on a stunning ring."

"No, I'm happy with the ring."

"I'm glad. I hope it brings you enjoyment." She eyed him carefully.

"It will." Carter smiled. "I plan on proposing marriage to my girl tomorrow."

The caution in her expression softened. "Oh, well, congratulations, Mr.?"

"Carter McCay."

She put out her hand and Carter gave a light shake. "I have no connection to the press, if that's what you're wondering."

Her eyes widened. Then a guilty smile emerged as if she'd been caught red-handed. "I won't deny it crossed my mind," she muttered with a sigh. She glanced around, noting the patrons filing out of the room. She lowered her voice. "They can be brutal."

Carter nodded. "Is there someplace we can talk privately? It's about Roark Black."

Ann's perfect brows lifted as if that was the last thing she'd expected to hear. Concern mixed with curiosity, and she immediately began walking toward a private exit. "Follow me."

Her shiny black heels tapped across a stone hallway. Carter fell in step beside her, and it wasn't long before she ducked into a small office marked Private. She waited until he entered before closing the door. The room was windowless and dark. She flipped a switch and overhead fluorescents brought light into the office. She leaned against a large glass desk and folded her arms. "What about Roark? Is he all right?"

"I hope so. He's a friend. We go way back. I met him while on duty in Afghanistan. A couple days ago, I got a text from him with your name on it."

"*My* name?" She leaned toward him, surprised. She pushed shoulder-length hair behind her ears and took a breath. "Where's the message?"

Carter pulled out his phone and tapped the screen a few times until the cryptic message appeared. He moved beside her and handed her the phone. She stood there for a second, reading the passage a few times. "He says he doesn't trust anyone with this information but me. And he's in hiding somewhere." She looked into his eyes. "What's he gotten himself into?"

"I have no idea. He mentioned a statue. Do you know what that's about?"

She nodded slowly, rereading the message. "It's the Gold Heart statue. There are only three in existence. He might have stumbled upon something he shouldn't have." Ann turned to him again. "He could be in real danger."

Carter held her stare a moment. "He could be."

Troubled, she sighed quietly and handed back the phone. "He's a good man."

Carter nodded. "Listen, I know Roark. He's gotten himself into some really tight spots before, and he's always gotten out."

Her voice was a mere whisper. "Are you telling me not to worry?"

Carter was concerned his friend was in trouble, but he couldn't do a damn thing about it until he heard from him again. "No sense in worrying. I have faith in him. Roark knows what he's doing. But whatever it is, he sure as hell wanted me to get this message to you without going through the normal channels. He's not sure who he can trust."

"I understand. Thank you for going through the trouble. Will you promise to let me know if you hear anything more from him?"

"I can do that," Carter said.

"Thank you." She walked him to the door. "And congratulations on your engagement. I think any woman would love to have a Tarlington ring on her finger."

Carter grinned. "That's the plan."

She gave him a full-out dimple-inducing smile, and Carter figured she didn't offer those up too often. "I think your soon-to-be fiancée is a lucky woman."

Carter thanked her and left Waverly's with a diamond ring in his pocket and a hum in his heart. He'd accomplished his two goals today.

Tomorrow his life would change forever.

Pajama-clad, Macy stared at her reflection in the hotel mirror, the phone to her ear and her legs stretched out on the massive bed. She never liked reserving a room with a king bed. With her slight frame, too much of the mattress went to waste. But then, getting two doubles made her feel lonely, as if there was someone missing who should be sleeping in the other bed. Macy had offered to share her hotel room with Avery, but her friend had booked with a smaller, more secluded hotel. Macy had respected her privacy.

"Are you still thinking about that cowboy from the auction today?" Avery asked.

She smiled into the phone. The cowboy? Now, *he* would take up a good portion of her bed and nothing would go to waste. "Guilty as charged. But you can't blame me, can you? My love life isn't all it's cracked up to be. If I only had one-tenth of the lovers MovieMash.com claimed I had, it would be a miracle. I haven't been on a date for eight months. That qualifies me for that new reality show, *Dating Dilemma*."

"Oh, Macy. It only means you've been dealing with your mother's illness and grieving. You'll know when the time is right."

Avery, too, had recently lost a parent, a father she'd hardly known, so she could relate to the heartache Macy felt. Avery had been such a dear friend when Tina died. They'd shared the bond of loss together.

"You had the hots for the cowboy. That's a start," Avery encouraged.

With a sigh, Macy glanced in the mirror again and shook her head at the simple yellow-and-white flowered nightgown she wore. She made a mental note to buy sexy lingerie. "That's true."

There was something about the cowboy that called to Macy. She'd been smitten from the moment she'd spotted him. *Smitten.* Such a perfect word to describe her feelings for a mystery man who'd helped her get through a tough time today. Not that he'd ever know he'd helped her, but still, Macy had warm feelings for him that went beyond the physical.

"The poor guy," she said quietly. "He bought the cursed diamond. I overheard him saying he was getting engaged tomorrow."

"How did you hear that?"

"I have eagle ears, remember? Just as we were walking out of the auction, I heard him tell Ms. Richardson why he bought the ring. I was crushed."

Avery giggled. She thought Macy was kidding, and why

wouldn't she? Any normal person wouldn't develop strong feelings for a man she'd just laid eyes on. But Macy couldn't really share the truth, that as soon as the cowboy announced he was getting engaged, her heart sank and her stomach clenched. The disappointment overwhelmed her. It had hurt Macy to think that her fantasy cowboy was already taken, and now hours later she still couldn't wrap her head around it. "He hasn't proposed yet and his marriage is already doomed."

"You don't know that for sure," her friend said. "Wouldn't you like to think it's not the diamond rings but really some odd quirk of nature, an imbalance of romance or simply a weird coincidence that those three marriages ended with heartbreak?"

"I don't know, Av. Maybe you're right. Maybe it's not the rings. Maybe I just don't believe in love anymore. I mean, my mother and all of her close friends have had their hearts broken from love affairs. You know how much my mother loved my father. When he died in that crash, she'd been so angry with him for leaving her alone."

Clyde Tarlington had been a talented actor in his own right and a loving father to Macy, but gambling and liquor were his true loves. He'd been addicted to both. When he won big, he'd buy rounds of drinks for everyone, and unfortunately one night ten years ago, his big win meant losing the most important gamble of his life. He'd gotten behind the wheel of his car and plowed the front end of his Lamborghini into a tree just three blocks away from their home. His blood alcohol level had been double the legal limit. That night, his luck had run out.

"I know that was heartbreaking for her," Avery said.

"But she picked herself up and married husband number two and then husband number three. And you know how well those marriages worked out." Macy's throat tightened with remorse. "That cowboy bought loser number three's ring."

Avery's voice softened. "Macy, are you going to be okay? I can come over."

"No, don't be silly. It's after midnight. I'm fine," she fibbed.

Macy had financial woes that made her dizzy with dismay. Avery knew most of it, so there was no sense rehashing her legal problems. She was being sued for refusing to back down on her principles. And now she was paying the consequences, literally, with her mother's estate. She had an appointment with her New York attorney tomorrow that she wasn't looking forward to. "I appreciate you being my rock today. I leaned on you and you came through." She faked a yawn and made it noisy enough for Avery to hear. "I'm pooped. I'm going to climb into this big bed and get some sleep."

"Okay…if you're sure."

"I'm sure. I'll see you for dinner tomorrow before your flight. Have a good night."

"Same to you, Macy. Sleep tight."

"I intend to," she fibbed again.

She wouldn't get much sleep. Her troubles would follow her into the night.

Carter sat across the table from Jocelyn in a cozy corner in the Russian Tea Room, the muscles around his lips pulling tight. He stared at her with unblinking eyes. The setting, the diamond, everything was perfect. Except her answer. "No?"

"That's right," she whispered. "No, I won't marry you."

With a shake of his head, he leaned back in his seat in disbelief.

Jocelyn flipped her blond hair to one side, a habit he'd noticed her doing when she was annoyed. The long strands fell over the thin strap of her glimmering gold dress. Her full lips, glossed in cherry red, formed a pout. Then she sighed dramatically, as if the weight of the world was crushing her shoulders. "I thought you knew this thing between us wasn't serious."

He kept his tone level. "How was I to know that?"

"We've never spoken of the future," she said. Her eyes flashed to the opened velvet box he'd laid near the edge of the table. "Not in specific terms."

Carter's voice elevated. "You mean, when we were lying in bed at night and you'd say how much you wanted a family one day. Three kids, exactly. And when you said you wanted a second home in the Hamptons, those were just random ramblings?"

He had trouble believing her rejection and searched his memory for clues. How had he missed her signals? He thought they wanted the same things in life.

She ignored the question, speaking in a tight voice, "We haven't known each other long, Carter."

"A year isn't long enough?"

"Not with you living in Wild River and me living in Dallas. We haven't seen that much of each other."

Raw, ego-deflating pain gutted his insides. The flat-out rejection worked a number on his pride and made him look at Jocelyn in a new light. One that wasn't flattering. A steady tick began to eat away at his jaw.

"The ring is a stunner, really." The diamond that would never see her finger sparkled against incandescent candlelight. "But I can't accept it." She lifted a shoulder in a shrug. "I don't love you."

In one fell swoop, he gripped the plush black ring box and clicked it shut before shoving it into his pocket. He didn't want to look at the damn thing anymore. "Can't be clearer than that."

"Well, I'm…sorry."

She didn't sound all that sorry.

"Hell, your apology fixes everything. I suppose you want to be friends now?"

His ego was taking a big hit, but his heart hurt, too. He'd wrapped his future dreams around spending his life with Jocelyn. How had he gone so wrong? He'd known Jocelyn was a high-maintenance woman, but he figured he could make her happy. Now, he felt like a sap.

Her chin angled up, and when she spoke it was as if she were speaking to a dog that should obey. "Don't be mad, Carter."

Was she kidding? Anger was only one of the emotions torpedoing his belly. "Don't tell me how to feel, Jocelyn. Even you've got to realize this is a blow to me."

"You had it wrong. You made a lot of assumptions about our relationship."

"I made…" Carter kept his anger contained. He spoke quietly, through clenched teeth. "You tempted me into a relationship, in case you're forgetting. From the first day we met, you were all over me. Remember the Wild River County Fair? You brushed your body up against mine so many times, I needed a dunk in the river to cool myself off. You came after me, as I recall. And we've been together ever since. So excuse me if I'm pissed off. Excuse me if I don't understand."

And what about all those nights she'd screamed his name and told him he was the best lover she'd ever had? Or the midnight rides they'd take on horseback at the ranch? Or the way she clung to his arm whenever they were out in public, as if he was the most important person in her life? Was it all an act?

"You don't understand. I wasn't after you."

"Like hell you weren't."

"You really don't get it. I thought I was transparent. Clear as glass." She rose from the table, clutching her small beaded purse. She shot him an unflinching gaze. "I'm in love with Brady. I was trying to make him jealous." She gestured with a swipe of her hand. "All of this was for Brady's sake."

Carter sank back into his seat, his eyebrows denting his forehead. He hadn't seen this coming. "My cousin?"

Carter had met Jocelyn one day when she was visiting her grandmother, Brady's neighbor. She'd come by Brady's place and the three of them, Brady, Carter and Jocelyn, had driven out to the county fair.

He stood abruptly and towered over her, pinning her with a glare. A bitter taste formed in his mouth. "So all this time, you were trying to make Brady jealous? How's that working out for you?"

She stiffened and her gaze narrowed to two eye-lined slits. "Shut up."

She made a move to pass by him, to escape his wrath, but he wasn't through with her yet. He took hold of her arm, garnering her full attention. "You played me for a fool."

She straightened her stance, holding her head high, like a member of royalty. "You are a fool. You're a dumb stupid hick who let me string him along."

His teeth ground together and his words came out low, from

deep in his gut. "I'll make sure to tell Brady you said that. Being as we're related, that means he's a dumb stupid hick, too. He was right about you. Yeah, the dumb stupid hick doesn't think too highly of you. And this time, I'm not disagreeing."

She flinched. His victory was small consolation, and while he knew better than to speak that way to a woman, he couldn't stop himself because *her* indiscretion had been much worse.

He released her at the same moment she yanked her arm free. "Leave."

She did. She walked away, and Carter didn't bother to watch her exit. He headed for the bar, unnerved and feeling like hell. He needed to soak his sorrows with a double shot of whiskey. Jocelyn wasn't the woman he thought she was. She'd been using him all along. Yeah, but he had to admit, she had him good and fooled.

No woman would ever fool him again, and after his liquor arrived, Carter downed the drink in celebration of escaping the hangman's noose.

Thirty minutes later and fortified with the best whiskey money could buy, Carter stepped out of the restaurant and was hit with a blast of humid August night air. It was the only thing about New York that reminded him of Texas—cloistering humidity. The heat crept up his collar and made him sweat.

All of a sudden a crowd emerged, swarming a woman who was trying to enter the restaurant. Bulbs flashed, the rush of footsteps sounded on pavement, shouted questions flew through the air. More than a dozen paparazzi crammed her as she made a feeble attempt to push her way out. Her shoulder was bumped once, twice. She swiveled right, then left, trying to break away. Questions were leveled at her like grenades. When her eyes met his, in that brief moment, Carter saw a caged animal struggling to get free. She was trapped.

Recognition struck him smack between the eyes. She was the woman he'd glimpsed at the auction yesterday.

Someone yanked at the scarf hiding her jet-black hair. Long, luxurious curls spilled down her shoulder, and she reached behind her head to put the scarf back in place. Carter had seen enough. He muscled his way through the crowd, giving a few well-placed shoves himself to get to her. When he finally faced her, he gripped both her hands in his, firm but gentle. She gazed at him with desperate, deep lavender-blue eyes. Carter had no time to dwell on her beautiful face. He blocked a cameraman's shot with his body, and the Stetson riding low on his forehead lent another measure of concealment. Use everything in your arsenal, he'd learned in the marines.

He leaned in real close. "I can get you out of here. But you have to trust me."

# Two

Fraught with panic, Macy faced the man from the auction, certain she was hallucinating. It couldn't be him. She'd dreamed about him last night, and this morning, when she should have forgotten all about him, he'd still marched into her thoughts during quiet moments.

Shouted barbs, flashbulbs snapping and body heat from tabloid junkies brought her back to the here and now.

"Got yourself a cowboy," shouted a photographer from the back of the pack.

"Are you doing nude scenes with him, Macy?" another asked.

The vultures chuckled.

It angered her that they called her by her first name, as if they were her friends, when the question itself was rude enough to warrant enemy status. Tina knew how to handle the paparazzi. Macy did not. And she paid the price for not being as charming as her famous mother had been.

Her heart pounding, her body abused and her head clouded with uncertainty, Macy glanced down to find her tightly wound fists encased in strong, protective hands. When she gazed up

into the cowboy's eyes, he reassured her with a nod. His words
had been like velvet to her ears.

*Trust me.*

She did.

Someone bumped her from behind, and the cowboy's gaze
grew fierce, giving the photographer ample warning. "Back off."

Then he met her stare again. "You coming?" His voice was a
little more insistent this time.

Macy didn't have to think twice. She was out of options. The
crowd herding her had become more curious now that the cowboy had intervened on her behalf, peppering her with questions
as to who he was.

She honestly didn't know.

But she was about to find out.

She nodded, and he gave her a fast smile. "Let's go."

The cowboy's grip was steady on her hand as they took off at
a run. Mentally she cursed the Paciotti pumps slowing her down.
She struggled to keep pace with his strides.

"Don't look back," he ordered. He guided her down an alleyway, dodging garbage cans. She ran on the pads of her feet to keep
from stumbling on three-inch heels. Her scarf flew off her head,
clinging on by the knot at her throat. The material whipped at her
shoulders. Sweat beaded on her forehead and her nerves rattled
as the cowboy led her away from the tabloid hounds dogging her.

The sound of labored breaths and footsteps shuffling from behind dropped off a little at a time as they hurried along the narrow alley. It wasn't a herd following them anymore, just several
hangers-on. Those few were persistent, and the cowboy tightened
his hold on her hand when they reached the end of the alley. He
took half a second to glance both ways on the side street before
gesturing to the right. "There."

She followed him, running quickly to a shiny black Lincoln
Town Car. "Get in and we'll be off." She glanced behind her to see
four photographers snapping pictures at the base of the alleyway.

Her savior opened the back door for her, surprising the chauffeur, who was eating a burrito in the front seat. She climbed in-

side and slid over. He joined her a second later. "Give it some gas, Larry. And be quick."

"Yes, sir." The chauffeur tossed his food down and fumbled for a second, obviously caught off guard. Then the engine revved to life. Before the paparazzi got within twenty feet, they had pulled out, Larry driving as fast as traffic allowed.

"Wow." Macy leaned back in the seat and closed her eyes. The past twenty minutes were a blur. One second she was on her way to meet Avery for dinner, and the next she was being pursued by overly zealous tabloid maniacs.

She tried to slow her breathing, but then there was the Stetson-wearing cowboy to think about. From the moment she'd laid eyes on him, he'd thrown her off balance.

She turned to face him and caught a whiff of his musky cologne. The scent was a turn-on in its own right, but on him, now *that* was really something. She'd already put him in white knight status; he didn't need any more help. "I don't usually accept rides from strangers," she offered, clearing the air.

He chuckled and deep twin dimples appeared, softening the sharp planes of his face. Okay, this was just not funny anymore.

"But you made an exception for me?"

"I knew I could trust you. I saw you yesterday at the, uh, the auction. I was there, too."

He gave her an appraising stare. "I know."

"You know me?"

"No, can't say that I do. But I noticed you. You were trying your best not to look conspicuous. Guess the designer sunglasses and scarf gave you away. It's kind of hard not to notice a beautiful woman covering herself all up. Not that I blame you for trying to disguise yourself." He gestured with a tilt of his head to the direction they'd just come from. "Does that happen to you often?"

He thought she was *beautiful,* even under the disguise. "Lately, yes…unfortunately."

They were traveling down the street, and Macy had no idea where they were headed. All she saw behind him through the window was a flash of streetlights and neon signs.

He took care with removing his hat and laid it between them. He continued to watch her. Normally she'd squirm under the heat of a stranger's stare, but oddly all she felt was excitement, as if she was living out her fantasy. She still couldn't believe she was in his car, driving toward who knows what.

Then she reined in those thoughts. He was engaged. Or going to be soon. Her fantasy was over. "I'm Macy Tarlington."

His eyes flickered with recognition. "Tarlington?"

His recognition wasn't aimed at her. He didn't know who she was. It was the Tarlington name that turned heads in every civilized country around the world. Apparently, the cowboy had never seen any of the work Macy had done on film. She wasn't a star by any rights, but most people in the know would recognize her on the street. "My mother was Tina Tarlington."

"I'll be damned." He shot her a charming smile then put out his hand. The large capable hand she'd already held. "Carter McCay. I'm from Wild River, Texas."

Of course, he was a Texan. With that charming accent, where else could he be from? "Hollyweird, California."

His lips quirked up and they sat staring at each other, their hands entwined in a slow shake.

Macy would've lost her footing if she'd been standing from the way he watched her. "I want to thank you. I don't know how I would've gotten away from them if you weren't there."

He finally released her hand, and she was momentarily at a loss. "Appeared that way to me, too."

"You saved me," she said, still awestruck.

"You needed saving."

Macy held in a sigh. His fiancée was a lucky woman. "Are you in the habit of saving women, or am I the only one?"

"I'm not in the business of saving anyone *anymore*."

"Meaning you once were?"

"Once, a long time ago." The city lights reflected in his eyes as his gaze shifted out the window. "I was a marine."

"Ah, that explains your call to duty."

His gaze snapped back to hers.

"I mean, isn't that wh-what you do?" Oh boy, she didn't want to insult the man who'd saved her. She found herself fumbling with an explanation. "The first to go in when there's a crisis."

His lips twitched as if he found her amusing. "I'm a Texan. We don't like seeing women being manhandled. Marine or not, any man worth his salt would have done the same. "

Macy decided she liked a man who used the phrase *worth his salt*. "No matter the reason, I'm appreciative."

"Why were those bozos so dang persistent anyway?"

The dreaded question.

Macy darted a glance out the window. "I suppose they think they're justified."

His lips tightened. "Nothing justifies shoving a defenseless woman and sticking cameras in her face."

"If you knew me better, you'd know I'm not exactly defenseless," Macy quipped. "I was caught off guard. Usually I'm more prepared."

"Can't imagine living like that."

"It's worse now. My mother's death put the spotlight on me." She tried to pass off her troubles with a shrug. "I'm the center of some controversy."

His gaze remained on her, searching, waiting. But Macy held back. Though her recent episodes had been all over entertainment news when she'd walked out on two separate productions, trying to explain them to a stranger would be awkward. Thankfully, her lawsuits related to those incidents, weren't public knowledge yet.

She didn't answer the question in Carter's eyes.

"So, why the auction?" he asked. "Your mother was…"

"Broke. She wasn't good with money and she loved beautiful things."

His eyes widened, as if she'd told a telling tale. "You want a drink? All I have is champagne."

The bottle of Dom was sitting in a sterling-silver bucket in the center back of the town car. He picked it up along with two crystal flutes and poured them each a glass. She accepted one and glanced out the window again, noting the city lights fading, fast becoming a distant memory.

"By the way," she whispered, taking a sip of the bubbly. "Where are you taking me?"

Wind blew her hair off her shoulders. The cool breeze refreshed her mind and rejuvenated her body. She stood on the deck of a private yacht watching the glorious Manhattan skyline. To think, if Avery hadn't canceled their dinner date right before she'd arrived at the restaurant, and if Macy hadn't gotten out of her cab to walk the two blocks to her favorite sushi place, her evening would have been a lonely night of salmon sashimi and wasabi.

The term *too good to be true* was overrated, except when it came to Carter McCay. He'd been a perfect gentleman, offering to take her back to her hotel.

"What's my other option?" she'd asked.

And now, she was sailing the Hudson River with her handsome cowboy. She'd had a million questions for him while in the limo, but she'd refrained from asking. She wanted to pretend for a little while longer that all was right with the world while trying to forget the mob scene that would have taken her wits if Carter hadn't rescued her.

She was being reckless for a change, driven by her coping mechanisms not to overanalyze everything. She was going with the flow. As her mother used to do.

Carter leaned his elbows against the railing next to her. She smiled at him. The "flow" was pretty darn great from her stance. His presence made her stomach flutter, but at the same time, she felt safe with him. She trusted him. And for a girl who'd grown up with the Hollywood scene, trust didn't come easy.

"This is nice, Carter. It's so peaceful out on the water."

He inhaled deep and nodded. "That was the plan."

"But the plan wasn't for me, of course."

"True. Did you notice what I bought at your mother's auction yesterday?"

"I noticed. You bought one of her diamond rings."

"Yeah, and like a fool, I thought a Tarlington diamond would seal the deal. I proposed to my girl tonight."

"Tonight?" Uh-oh.

He looked out to the water, focusing away from the city lights to the darkness. "Yeah. Right before I met you. She turned me down flat and pretty much made a fool out of me. Seems she was using me to get the attention of my... Of someone else."

Was that woman nuts? "Oh wow. That's pretty crappy."

"Nothing *pretty* about it."

"It's so wrong."

"Wrong," he repeated with a nod.

"Why, it's dreadful and appalling. *Depraved*."

"Hold on," he said, putting up a hand. A soft chuckle rose from his throat. "You're not making me feel any better."

Macy grinned. "But I made you smile."

He chuckled again. "Yeah, you did."

His gaze flowed over her, his eyes sparkling with appreciation. "Thanks."

Carter wasn't someone to toss away like yesterday's garbage. Macy realized that just from being with him for this short span of time.

That damn curse. She wished she'd stopped him from bidding on the ring. She wished he hadn't gotten hurt by the rejection. If she hadn't needed the money for attorney fees and to pay off her mother's debts, she would have held on to the rings so no one else would have to endure the pain and suffering those diamonds brought on. And it became obvious to her that the limousine and the private yacht, stocked with champagne and aphrodisiacs, were meant for the newly engaged couple. She should have realized it from the beginning, but being with Carter made her fuzzy-brained.

"Seriously, I'm really sorry, Carter."

He nodded and stared into her eyes. "You wanna know something? Meeting you tonight was just the dose of reality I needed. You helped me forget how gawd awful I felt walking out of that restaurant. You may have helped me just as much as I helped you."

"I doubt that, but it's nice of you to say."

"It's true, darlin'." Carter faced the water again and blew out a deep breath. "Man, I'm ready to get on home to Wild River. It's no secret I don't like the city."

"This city in particular?"

"New York especially, but I don't like any place where skyscrapers block the sunsets. Where you can't walk down a street without being crammed and bumped. I like wide open spaces. And we have a lot of that in Wild River. It's peaceful there. A man can think."

Macy closed her eyes. "Mmm. Sounds like heaven."

"Pretty close. What about you? Are you a big-city girl?"

"I kind of had to be. My mother and father were both actors. I grew up around glamour and glitz. But with that also came petty jealousy, vanity and overindulgence. So, no. I don't like big cities. For me, when I go back to Los Angeles, I'll be facing the same kind of scrutiny. Different reporters hounding me, but with the same agenda. I won't have a moment of real privacy. I dread it already."

"There's no place you can go to hide out?"

Macy shook her head. She'd authorized the money from the auction to pay off her mother's debts and to pay attorney fees to settle her lawsuits. She didn't have the money or the means to take off to an exotic port where she wouldn't be recognized. "Not really."

Carter was quiet for a few minutes as the yacht rocked gently, cruising by Ellis Island. Beams of light from the Statue of Liberty glistened along the water's surface. Carter's musky scent traveled on the breeze. Standing so close to him, Macy felt immeasurably safe and protected. The feeling wouldn't last. Soon, she'd have to face reality.

She sighed and let the wind whip at her face.

When she opened her eyes, Carter was staring at her, his expression determined. "Why not come to Wild River with me?"

"Wh-what?"

"You can hide out there for as long as you want. I have a big house and thousands of acres. Nobody'll know you're there."

"I, uh…uh…"

"You can leave with me on the red-eye. We'll be in Texas at breakfast and having lunch at Wild River before noon."

It sounded like heaven, but Macy couldn't just fly off with a stranger. Could she? She didn't know much about him, other than he was wealthy, handsome, honorable and kind.

Oh boy. She'd just answered her own question. But could she really do this? Could she really run away from her troubles for a while? With Carter? What did she have waiting for her in L.A. anyway? She'd have to figure out her future soon, but she hadn't been able to think of much else but getting through the auction. It had consumed her thoughts and sapped her spirit. Now she'd been offered a brief respite. "I don't really know y—"

"Look, up until a few hours ago, I was in love with a woman and ready to be married. This is purely an offer with no strings attached. I won't be sneaking into your room at night."

Why not? Didn't he find her appealing? A nervous laugh escaped. "Oh, I wasn't thinking you would."

His tone turned serious. "Just so you know, I'm offering you a place to stay, period. It's up to you. Soon as we're off this yacht, I'm making arrangements to get back to Wild River. The invitation is yours if you want to take it."

Because that seemed to be what Carter McCay did. He saved people. And Macy had a big decision to make. Does she go home to Hollywood and face the photographers, the disruptions to her privacy and the bellyaches, or fly off with the sexy cowboy of her dreams?

Shouldn't be such a hard decision.

But Macy wasn't like Tina Tarlington in that respect. She didn't usually do things by the seat of her pants.

Except this time.

Macy needed the peace.

She needed time to think.

She needed to get a handle on where her life was heading.

When it came right down to it, Macy didn't need any more encouragement. She turned to Carter with a brave smile. "I'll take it," she said. "You won't even know I'm there."

* * *

Macy sat in first class with Carter on a plane nearly empty of passengers. She was heading to Texas, a place she'd visited a few times when she was a young girl. What she remembered about Dallas, Houston and Austin was that everyone was polite and the men were tall, friendly and wore cowboy hats. She'd been fascinated, tagging along with her mother when she'd begun a promotional tour for *Striking Out for Texas,* a Western film that eventually tanked. Her mother hadn't been happy about it. The public had seen Tina Tarlington only as a sequin-gown-wearing glamour queen and that's where they wanted to keep her. A tomboyish, ponytailed Tina with a twang wasn't big box office. Her mother had faulted the director for the failure due to his lack of vision. Much to Macy's dismay, she'd never made another Western.

Macy's fascination with Texas cities had soon turned to disappointment. As a twelve-year-old, she'd expected to see horses roaming the range and longhorn steers grazing. The Texas she'd seen wasn't anything like Carter McCay had described to her. Now, a shot of mental adrenaline brought on a round of excitement. She couldn't wait to see the land Carter owned. She couldn't wait to see Wild River Ranch.

He sat across the aisle from her, lounging in a big leather seat, his long legs stretched out in front of him. With his eyes closed, she could take time to really admire him. His lashes were unfairly long. Brad Pitt dark-blond hair touched his collar, unruly for a military man but perfect for a rancher. His shoulders seemed to stretch a yard wide.

Carter wore a tan shirt now, tucked into slightly worn blue jeans, leather boots and a silver belt buckle with the initials W.R. She assumed the initials were for the ranch, Wild River. Macy had seen Carter only in dress clothes, but it didn't take her long to figure out he'd look good in anything he wore. The hat, now covering half his face in a downward tilt, was a constant. On Carter, it wasn't a fashion accessory—it *belonged* on top of his head.

His eyes snapped alert, and he turned his head her way. Caught staring at him, she darted a glance to the overhead compartment, refusing to look into his eyes.

"What's that I heard about a nude scene?"

Oh boy. Macy's heart pumped double time. She'd hoped he hadn't picked up on that comment from the dozens being leveled at her earlier. "It's…nothing."

Carter, apparently done with his little nap, turned his body to face her completely. The full force of his gaze was nothing to sneeze at. "That so? You gonna make me look it up online?"

Macy's mouth fell open. "You'd do that?"

Carter's eyes lit with mischief. "So, it is something."

"Nothing I want to talk about."

"I'm not a fan of computers, Macy. But I use them when I need to."

"Trust me. You don't need to know."

His lips twisted into a frown and Macy thought about how he'd come to her rescue. How, he'd offered her a place of refuge. She supposed she owed him some sort of explanation.

"Oh, all right. I was doing a movie. It wasn't a big role or anything, just this little independent film about five women stranded on an island together. I had this scene where…"

Carter leaned forward, his gaze sweeping over her in a way he'd never done before. As if he was just noticing her as a woman. A tremor quaked through her belly, making her extremely queasy.

"Go on," he said, his brows lifting expectantly.

Sure, mention five females and nudity in the same breath, and suddenly men begin actually *listening* to women. She took a swallow. "Well, there was this one scene where I was to be bathing naked in this tropical lake and, uh…"

"And?"

"Well, you get the picture, right?"

Carter swept his gaze over her again. This time, with more heat than she'd expected from a jilted man. His hazel eyes darkened. "I'm beginning to."

She'd wanted those words back the second she'd said them. Goodness, she wasn't asking him to picture her naked, yet the gleam in his eyes was enough to make her faint.

She pressed on. "Well, I chickened out. I couldn't do it. I couldn't allow millions of people to see me in my birthday suit.

The studio offered a body double, but everyone would still think it was me anyway. So…" She wished she didn't have to reveal such a humiliating experience to him. "I, uh, refused to do it. I sort of had a tantrum about it." Lessons learned from her mother. "Finally, they rewrote the scene without the nudity. Needless to say, I made a lot of people unhappy."

Carter leaned back in his seat and nodded, and that awkward awareness between them was gone. "You stuck to your principles."

"I should have never agreed to it in the first place."

"Yeah, well. Hindsight can be a bitch. We do things we're thinking are right at the time, only to find out later how wrong we were."

From the regret in his voice, Macy knew he was speaking about his own situation. She lowered her tone and gave him a soft smile. "I'm sorry about what happened yesterday with your—"

"Jocelyn?" He shifted his gaze to look out the window. "Yeah, I didn't see that coming. I'm not sure what happened there, but I guarantee you I won't let it happen again. I've got my guard up now."

Macy nibbled on her lower lip. "You know, you can throw me off your property anytime you want. If you regret inviting me to stay at your place and would rather be alone, I'd understand."

He faced her. "Don't worry, Macy. Like I said, I've got ten thousand acres. You won't get in my way. And I won't get in yours. I don't live with regrets. So don't you worry your head off about me. Is it a deal?"

Macy smiled, more assured now. "It's a deal."

# Three

The second Carter planted his boots down on Texas soil, he felt better. He'd been gone only a few days, but he was damn grateful to be back on his own land. Coming home to Wild River never got old.

Jocelyn had bruised him, and he couldn't quite shake the feeling. He'd never asked a woman to marry him before. He'd never had the inclination. Jocelyn had reeled him in like a sucker, and just when he thought things were going great, she'd tossed him back into the water to fish for someone else.

Macy had been bruised, too. Her circumstances were different, but when he'd spotted her outside the restaurant, he'd seen a look of pain and disbelief in her eyes. He'd felt a kinship with her that, even now, he couldn't truly define. It was the reason he'd invited her to Wild River.

He glimpsed his fifteen-room house and breathed in the earthy scent of range and cattle before he turned from the car to reach for Macy's hand. She slid her palm into his and climbed out of her seat, as graceful as a doe, to stand beside him. "You ready for a slice of heaven?"

Those violet eyes of hers swept the Wild River vista and a little sigh escaped her lips. Carter's chest puffed out some at her thunderstruck look. "Oh, it's stunning, Carter."

Carter had worked with an architect to give his home just the right mixture of down-home comfort and modern-day style. The result, much to his satisfaction, turned out to be a wood and stone structure with bay windows and skylights. Stone pilings and wrought-iron fencing surrounded the grounds. Beyond the house lay the outer buildings that made up the ranch itself, with corrals, barns and feed shacks.

"No tall skyscrapers blocking out the sunrise here." He glanced eastward toward the orange blast of light lifting from the land in midday splendor. "Every room at the back of the house has a big window facing east. Same goes for sunsets for the rooms facing west."

"And I bet you make sure you see the sun rise every day."

"I'm up at the crack of dawn."

Macy's eyes rolled at his clichéd response. "Just like a regular cowpoke."

He chuckled. Damn, but it felt good being home. "I'm a businessman, but I'm a rancher first. You gotta love the land and all that goes with it."

"I'm feeling better already. I think I'm going to like it here," she said softly, and Carter didn't doubt it. His land had everything.

A four-legged ball of fur shot out of the barn, wagging its tail around and around like a jet propeller, and raced straight for Macy. Her face lit up. "Oh, isn't he cute."

"Say hi to Rocky. He sort of runs the place."

Carter lowered down at the same time Macy did and their hands touched as they stroked the dog's blond coat.

"Hello, Rocky," Macy said with reverence.

"You like dogs?" he asked.

"What's not to like? I had a dog once." Her eyes grew distant and she sucked in a breath, shuddering. "My, uh, dad accidentally ran Queenie over. She died. It was awful."

"That's rough. Rocky here had a brush with death not too long ago."

Macy kept vigilant, stroking the top of Rocky's head and shoulders, and the darn dog was lapping it all up. "What happened?"

"There was a fire."

"Oh no!"

"Yeah, Rocky almost didn't make it."

"Oh," Macy said, intent on the dog. "Did you rescue Rocky too?"

Carter grunted and rose to his full height. "In more ways than one." But he wasn't going there today. He didn't want to ruin his good mood thinking about Riley McCay, his alcoholic father and the dog he couldn't care for. He turned to Henry, his foreman, who'd been giving Carter strange stares since he'd picked them up at the airport. Henry didn't know what to make of Macy. He'd expected to see Jocelyn standing beside Carter outside the terminal gates.

His foreman retrieved Carter's bag and Macy's flamingo-pink suitcases from the back end of the vehicle and set them down on the ground, with a shake of his head. Carter's lips pulled tight to keep from chuckling at his mystified foreman's expression. "Thanks, Henry. I'll take Macy's bags into the house myself. Appreciate the ride."

Henry nodded and shot a glance to Macy.

She looked up at the same time. "Yes, thank you, Henry."

He tipped his hat to her, got in the SUV and drove off.

"I think you've made a friend there," Carter said, heaving her suitcases.

"Henry?" she quizzed, looking up.

He pointed to the golden retriever. "I was talking about the dog."

A genuine smile lifted her lips. "I think Rocky and I are going to be good friends."

Macy rose and followed Carter toward the house, Rocky at her heels. At least his new houseguest liked dogs. Jocelyn would hoist her nose at Rocky and claim he triggered her allergies. The two hadn't been friends.

Not that Carter was comparing the women or anything.

After Macy gushed over the interior living area of his home, which managed to puff his chest again, he walked her down the hallway, offering her one of three bedrooms. She stuck her head inside all of them and then met him back in the hallway. "Where is your bedroom?"

Well, damn. That was right to the point. If he'd been gulping whiskey, he might have spit his liquor at that one. "The last room down the hall and to the right." His brows knit together. "Why?"

"I appreciate you letting me hide out here, but I don't want to invade your privacy. I'll take the one farthest from your room."

That made sense. "Fine."

He set her bags down in a room with a queen-size bed, white oak furniture and a bedspread with yellow and blue flowers. Macy walked over to the window. "Looks like I get the sunsets."

Carter sidled up next to her, and her fresh scent tickled his nose and brought memories of picking peaches on summer days. He inhaled deep and long, surprised that he hadn't noticed her scent before. Fruit-infused soap or shampoo, or whatever the hell it was, wasn't what he'd expected from a Hollywood actress with a legendary mother. "You won't be disappointed. They're mighty glorious."

Macy sighed.

Carter's stomach grumbled, and he didn't apologize. He had an enormous appetite. "Ready for lunch?"

She glanced at the bed, then at him. "I, uh, I'm fine right now. You go on. I'm going to rest a little."

"Okay, you know where the kitchen is. Henry will have made up something delicious by now. Have at it, anytime you want."

"Henry? He's the cook?"

Carter gave her a wry smile. Hers wasn't an unusual reaction. Henry often surprised people. "His wife, Mara, took ill this week. Turns out, Henry's a pretty good cook. We share duties at Wild River. But Henry doesn't do windows, or any other cleaning. Mara does that. She'll be back tomorrow to help clean up his mess. Oh, and feel free to use the pool, the sauna or the spa, anytime you want."

"Thank you, Carter."

He nodded. "Dinner's at seven. See you then."

Carter walked down the hallway to his room and tossed his suitcase down, then hightailed it outside to speak with Henry.

He found him in the office/tack room, just outside the barn. "Need a word with you, Henry."

"Sure, boss. But I got some news for you, too. I didn't want to speak in front of the lady before."

"All right, you first."

Henry began, "The inn over by the river got broken into while you were gone. A window was smashed and doesn't appear that there's any other damage. Window's already been replaced. Thought I'd tell you. It's not the first time it's happened though. Bucky reported someone snooping around over there, but they'd taken off by the time he'd driven up."

Carter rubbed at his neck. He hated the thought of anyone messing with his property. He'd been trying to decide whether to refurbish the inn or tear it down.

"I met an old guy in town the other day. He was pretty sharp and looking for work. Thought maybe he'd make a good ground-skeeper. You know, someone to check the property and make sure nothing's disturbed."

Carter mulled it over for a second. With Macy Tarlington staying at Wild River, a little extra security wouldn't hurt. "It's not a bad idea, Henry. Why don't you give him an interview and get back to me."

"Will do. Now, what can I do for you?"

"That woman I brought here today—do you recognize her?"

Henry jerked back a bit, surprised. "Should I?"

Relieved, Carter gave a shake of the head. "Maybe not. It's good that you don't, actually. But Mara might."

And Carter spent the next ten minutes explaining to his foreman about Macy and how important it was to keep her identity a secret. Carter didn't think any of the ranch hands would recognize the daughter of a Hollywood legend since Macy had kept herself under the radar until recently, but their wives and girl-friends might. It was a chance they'd have to take. For the most part, folks kept to themselves, and for as long as he could, he'd make sure Macy got some privacy on his ranch.

Macy glanced around the room that would be her sanctuary and shook her head. "You are plum crazy, girl," she muttered, picking up Carter's Texas drawl. "Coming to live with the tall, tan, too-good-to-be-true Texan."

She flopped onto the bed and grabbed a pillow, hugging it to her chest. She'd been lured to Wild River by her own curiosity and a brand-new sense of adventure. But while that was all true, she hadn't been completely honest with Carter about the diamond ring he'd bought at auction, and as a result he'd become the diamond's latest victim. She couldn't blame him for being bitter and cautious now about relationships. Macy felt the same way. She'd seen her mother fall in love three times, and all three times had been a disaster.

She no longer believed in love or happily-ever-afters. She didn't know too many couples who'd sustained their marriages more than a decade. And living in Hollywood, she'd known the truth about the few long-term marriages, too. It seemed that no one was happy for long. Very few of those marriages had held firm to their commitment.

Sad but true.

Giving in to fatigue, Macy relaxed back on the bed and closed her eyes. To hell with unpacking. She wasn't going to be prag-matic now. She was taking a break from reality. No lawyers right now. No tabloids. No worry about saying the wrong thing. No one hounding her.

A sudden movement on her bed startled her, and the scent of rawhide followed. She snapped her eyes open. She'd been wrong. She was being hounded, but she didn't mind the nuzzling. She could get used to this. "Hello, Rocky."

The dog curled his body next to hers and laid his head down. She looked into his big caramel eyes and smiled. Carter had been right. His ranch had everything.

An hour later, refreshed from her nap, Macy showered and changed into fresh clothes, a pair of white jeans and an indigo tank top. Her hair was still wet when she drew it back into a ponytail. Five minutes in the Texas heat would dry it.

She thought better about stepping into flip-flops and opted for her Nikes. Carter had given her half an hour to pack before the car had come for her at the hotel. As it was, she'd packed only enough clothes to last her through a short stay in New York, and not too much was suitable for ranch living.

"Guess I'm going to do some shopping while I'm here," she muttered to Rocky.

The dog wagged his tail at the sound of her voice. He hadn't left her side since he'd plopped onto the bed. They'd enjoyed the nap together, and he'd sat outside the shower door while she was cleaning up.

Macy grinned at him. "You want to show me around after lunch?"

Another tail wag.

Macy found the kitchen easily. It wasn't hard to miss, and it was definitely Texas-size with wood beamed ceilings, homey tiled counters and a table big enough for a small army. She rummaged through the double-door refrigerator, coming up with brisket and swiss cheese. She was too hungry to go to any more trouble than throwing a sandwich together. She slapped mustard on sourdough bread and made quick work of eating her lunch. Every so often, she'd pull off a piece of beef and toss it to Rocky.

He gobbled it without chewing.

"No doubt he'll be your friend for life."

She spun around so fast, her ponytail whipped her cheek. She found Carter leaning against the kitchen doorway, staring at her. He flicked his gaze over her in one sweep and then focused on Rocky, but it was enough to freeze all movement in her chest. She cleared her throat and wondered when she'd stop reacting to him this way. "Oh, I'm sorry. Maybe I shouldn't be feeding him this, uh—"

Carter sauntered into the kitchen. "He eats anything." He grabbed a beer out of the refrigerator and offered her one.

"No, thanks."

"And refuses nothing. At least, I've never seen my father's dog deny himself a meal of any kind."

"Good to note."

"Out of necessity," he added. "He wasn't always fed."

"Oh." The dog used to belong to Carter's father. Macy connected the dots. They stood facing each other and she watched Carter's throat work, swallowing a gulp of beer. "I'll just clean up my mess and get out of here."

Carter had the beer to his lips again and stopped from sipping to eye her over the bottle. "You know, we're bound to bump into each other. You don't have to run off. The kitchen is big enough for both of us."

Not from where she was standing. Whenever Carter entered a room, he commanded all the space and Macy saw nothing else. "Gotcha."

"Where are you going anyway?"

"Just exploring. I thought I'd stretch my legs and take a walk."

He blinked and a look of concern crossed his features. "I should probably go with you the first time." He gulped down the rest of his beer.

"You think I'll get lost?"

"It's a big ranch."

"I'm a big girl." She pulled out her phone. "I've got GPS."

He clearly didn't find her amusing. "Come with me," he said. Thankfully, he didn't take her hand. It was one thing to hold his hand when they were running down an alley to safety, and another altogether while alone in his big, gorgeous house. She followed him to his bedroom and waited at the doorway while he searched through a walk-in closet. He pulled a red plaid shirt off a hanger and she noted how he scrutinized it for a long few seconds. Macy noticed a few other female things hanging in his closet before he turned to her. "Here you go."

She balked at wearing Jocelyn's clothes and shook her head. "No, thanks."

"You don't want to wear it?" Carter's voice rose in question.

"Not my style." She didn't want anything to remind him of the woman who'd jilted him. Why add insult to injury?

His gaze touched on the small cleavage exposed by her tank top, and silently she drew a breath. "Fair enough. Soon as I can, I'm gonna give this stuff to charity anyway. You got anything to wear besides white jeans?" He focused on her pants, and Macy's throat nearly constricted. "Those will stick out like a sore thumb around here."

"I wasn't planning on ranch living when I packed for New York."

"I'll take you into town to get some clothes tomorrow. Maybe some boots, too."

He reached into his closet again and came up with a tan-colored felt hat. He set it onto her head. "This is one of mine," he said, giving her a solid look. "Pretty good disguise, too. Those long curls of yours are bound to cause attention."

Macy tucked her hair under the hat.

He gave her a look of approval. "Put on your shades, and we're good to go."

Macy stood in the center of a broken-down gazebo and swirled around with her arms outstretched. A joyous smile lifted her lips. If she flung her hat into the air, it would be reminiscent of Mary Tyler Moore's famous opening scene, and Macy would do it if Carter wasn't standing a short distance away, watching her every move.

Yes, the gazebo was broken down, the pristine white paint chipped from age and neglect, with much of the structure unsupported. But the floor would make a good-size stage, and the grounds themselves could be amazing with a little tender loving care.

Right now, the actress in her envisioned young children sitting on the gazebo's wooden steps, cold reading, learning techniques to perform upon the stage.

Rocky sat on dry grass, watching her, too. "It's perfect," she whispered, reluctant to leave, her mind spinning with possibilities. Carter waited at the back door of the inn. He'd taken her here to show her the seventy-year-old structure that was also abused by neglect. The relic sat one mile into McCay property, and before they'd gotten inside, Macy had spotted the gazebo that drew her like a magnet.

She glanced at Carter, who was waiting and watching her. "Okay, Rock. Looks like we have to go."

When she reached Carter, he gestured toward the gazebo. "I'm thinking about tearing it down."

"No! You can't do that."

Carter's brows furrowed at her outburst. "Why not?"

"It's wonderful, that's why not. It could be grand again with a little work."

"It's dangerous. It won't hold in a storm."

"Can it be braced?"

Carter scoffed at that, and Macy thought he was being unreasonable. But what did it matter anyway? She wouldn't be teaching here, or anyplace else for that matter.

Carter showed her around the six-bedroom inn that had come with the land he'd purchased as an expansion of his uncle's original property. Macy had to give him credit for being a self-made man. He'd taken an old run-down ranch and built an empire.

Already, in the half day she'd been here, she had seen how different his life was than the flaky phoniness of Hollywood. They were worlds apart.

Carter showed her the dilapidated upstairs bedrooms. Five of the rooms were dusty, the walls a mess of stained old wallpaper and filthy warped floors. Just as he was about to lead her down the staircase again, Macy pointed to one room at the end of the hallway. "Wait, Carter. What's in there?"

Carter hesitated, his expression closed off. Before he could answer, Macy, too curious for her own good, walked toward the door and pushed it open. She poked her head inside. "Oh wow. This is...amazing." She turned to him in surprise. "It's completely refurbished."

He frowned. "I know. It's just one room."

Macy glanced at the freshly painted walls, the king-size bed decorated with a brown silk comforter and the polished wood floors. "It's a picture of what the whole house could look like."

Carter's mouth twisted again, as if he'd bitten into a sour lemon. "Yeah, well, we'll see."

He turned and started for the stairs.

Macy closed the door softly and followed him downstairs, a dozen questions filling her mind.

They wound up in the kitchen. Cobwebs in the corner of the ceilings made her arms itch. Carter stood by a bay window, looking out. "Do you think it's worth fixing up?"

"Yes, of course. It's full of charm."

He shrugged. "For some, it's charming. For others, it's old and run-down, just like a lot of places around here."

Panic rose in her throat. "You're not seriously thinking about destroying this place?"

"It's an eyesore on the property."

Macy doubted that. The house wasn't set on the highway, but deep into Carter's land. No one could find the place, much less *see* it, unless they were searching for it. "With a little time and effort, the house could really shine. You could open it to the public and rent out rooms or use it as a guesthouse."

He contemplated for a few moments, then gave her a nod, as if her opinion mattered. "I'll think about it."

They left the inn and walked along the river's edge. Macy let the peace and calm settle into her bones. The quiet surge of the water glistening under the Texas sun soothed and filled her with ease.

"This is exactly what I needed," she whispered.

"Wild River does that." It was a statement of fact, one that wasn't up for interpretation. Carter truly loved this place.

Cottonwoods shaded them as they strolled on, Rocky at Carter's heels. She felt safe here, out in the middle of nowhere, living with a stranger. Carter had hardly known her before offering up his home, and with him by her side, Macy felt protected.

"I'm glad you invited me here," she said, holding back another round of thanks. She didn't want to sound like a broken record.

He looked toward the river, his eyes squinting against the rays of sunlight. "Stay as long as you need, Hollywood."

She chuckled at the nickname, not sure she liked it yet. She wasn't the clichéd Hollywood type, but then, as she gazed at herself in the water's reflection, she could see his point. Everything about her spoke of disguise and fraud.

In her heart, Macy knew who she really was, but she hadn't been allowed to follow her own dreams, not when she was busy living her mother's.

Now, she was at a crossroads, unsure where to turn.

She vowed she wouldn't let it get her down.

Not while she was living at Wild River.

She was on vacation... *from life.*

After dinner, Carter left Macy to her own devices, needing to get something off his chest. Or at least, get an explanation from his cousin. At Brady's house on the outskirts of town he climbed out of his Jeep, slamming the door closed. He glanced at the front entrance and drew a deep breath. Having to admit being rejected wasn't easy, but under these circumstances, it really burned.

No one answered his knocking. But the scent of a fired-up grill drew him to the backyard. He found Brady on his deck cooking a steak. Smoke ruffled the heavy air as he met his cousin's inquisitive stare.

"Hey, Carter. Didn't expect to see you so soon. Thought maybe you'd be out making wedding plans." He poked at his steak with a long-pronged fork and turned it over.

Carter's mouth twisted. "That's not happening. She turned me down."

Brady set his barbecue fork onto the side of the grill and snapped up his head. "She did?"

Carter leveled him a direct look. "Thought maybe you'd know why."

Brady's brows gathered tight. "Me? How should I know? Didn't she give you a reason?"

Carter paced behind Brady, carefully choosing his words. He'd always been close to Brady, and he trusted him. The man had scruples and had brought himself up from poverty to become quite successful in commercial real estate. Carter wasn't accusing him of anything, but a man had a right to know what end was up. "She did. But I'd like to know what you've got to say about it."

His cousin moved his steak to the side of the grill, taking it away from the heat, and turned to him. "You have dinner yet?"

"I have. And I'll leave you in peace to eat yours once we talk about this."

"Hey, I'm sorry Jocelyn turned you down, but I gotta say…"

Brady hesitated and Carter pressed him. "Say what?"

"Fine, I'll tell you, since you're intent on knowing the truth. I don't care for the woman, but I kept my mouth shut after you two started dating. She visited Regina time and again and was always bad-mouthing the old lady. Like her grandmother was a burden or something. Regina loves that girl something fierce, and it pained me to see it. Don't get me wrong—Jocelyn's pretty and all, and I suppose she has some nice qualities. Obviously, you thought so. I believed it was just me thinking she was uppity. She was forever coming over here, asking me to help her with Regina. Not that I minded helping the old lady, but Jocelyn had a way about her that put me off."

Relieved, Carter took it all in. "You didn't tell me any of this."

"I didn't think it was getting serious between you. I mean, Jocelyn made it seem—"

"What?"

With a shake of his head, Brady refused him an answer. "Nothing. She doesn't matter. How're you doing with all this? You were fixed on marrying her and settling down. Man, I hate to say this, but you're probably better off."

Carter glared at him, hating to hear the truth.

"I'm sorry. But you asked." Brady went inside the house and returned with two beers in his hands. "Here you go. Drown your sorrows."

Carter's mouth twisted. He grabbed the bottle. "According to you, I should be celebrating."

Brady took a swig and nodded. "We've always been honest with each other."

Carter lifted the bottle to his mouth, tilted his head way back and guzzled half of the beer in one huge gulp. "True. Man, this is tough, but I got to tell you why she broke it off with me."

Brady began shaking his head. "No, you don't. Not if it's personal, you don't."

"It involves you, Brady. I have to so you and I will be square. I don't want anything coming between us. Hell, you're all the family I got."

"Not true. You have Riley."

Carter blew that notion off, swearing an oath.

"He's your father," Brady said.

"As I said, you're all the family I got. Getting back to Jocelyn, it seems the whole time she was lying with me at night, she was thinking about you."

A sharp intake of breath pulled Brady's chest in. His voice elevated. "What?"

"She claims she's in love with you."

Brady began shaking his head. "That's not possible."

"It's the reason she gave me, and she made no bones about it. She was clear as day. She was trying to make you jealous." Carter waited a beat. "Were you?"

Brady set his beer down and looked him in the eye. "No. Never even occurred to me. I thought you were making a mistake, but if you two were happy, I was staying out of it."

"Okay. I gotcha. Just had to know."

"Man, I'm sorry."

Carter finished the rest of his beer and cocked him a crooked smile. "For being irresistible?"

"For you getting hurt."

He couldn't deny he wasn't feeling hurt, angry, betrayed and a mess of other emotions, but he'd learned his lesson. "It won't happen again. I'm off the market for marriage now."

Brady lowered his voice. "She really did a number on you."

Carter's lips twisted again. "I'll get over it."

It wasn't just Jocelyn that he'd lost, but the possibility of a wife and family that, now, he wouldn't allow to remotely enter his mind. He was through. Finished. Done. It was liberating, even through the pain.

"You can eat your supper."

"Thanks, now that you've ruined my appetite."

"Right," Carter said without a hint of remorse. Brady's appetite rivaled his own. That was at least a fourteen-ounce steak he was grilling up. Carter knew beef like nobody's business.

He shook his cousin's hand. "Stop by the house soon. I brought home a houseguest. I'd like you to meet her."

Brady's brows flew to his hairline. "*Her?* You brought a woman home from New York? Man, you don't waste any time."

Laughter rose up from his throat. "It's not like that. Macy is—"

"Macy? Is she old? Fat? Ugly?"

Carter didn't have to think twice. "Pretty, bordering on beautiful. Around twenty-six years old and shaped like a goddess— well, a *slender* goddess."

"You're kidding me, right?" Brady's expression changed to disbelief. "This is a joke."

"It's no joke, but it's not what it seems."

Carter took the next few minutes explaining to his cousin about how he met Macy right after being dumped and the odd sort of kinship he felt toward her after seeing her being attacked by the paparazzi. She needed someone's protection, and he'd been there. She'd been a vital distraction to his heartache, too, and he wasn't sorry he'd asked her to stay at Wild River.

Brady scratched his head. "Okay, I'll stop by sometime."

"Good. Your steak's getting cold. Eat. I'm outta here."

Carter was almost out of Brady's backyard when his cousin's wry voice stopped him cold. "Wonder what Jocelyn would say if she found out you have a gorgeous female houseguest?"

Carter pivoted on his heels to face Brady. "Now, how would she find out something like that?"

"Maybe I'll just mention it to Regina tomorrow when I'm fixing her shelves."

He shrugged. Jocelyn wasn't his concern anymore. But payback was a bitch. "Whatever floats your boat, cuz. Just don't mention Macy's name."

Brady nodded with a wicked smile.

And then Carter was off.

## FOUR

# Four

Soft, inky locks of hair curled at the base of Macy's neck in damp wisps. Her attempt at piling those strands on top of her head wasn't working too well, and the whole picture she made sitting on the lounge chair at the pool captured Carter's attention from the kitchen doorway. Her soft shoulders were exposed and glowing golden, as was every inch of her skin but for the strip of snow-white material covering her curves in a two-piece swimsuit. His mouth had nearly dropped to the ground when she'd found that bikini at the River Rags clothing store in town a few days back.

Carter had tried to talk her out of buying the damn bikini. The point of shopping for clothes was to make her look less conspicuous, not draw any unwanted attention. But her argument had made sense. "No one will see me in it. And I love getting a good tan."

Apparently, she hadn't thought he'd counted.

Because he saw her wearing it, and the image wasn't one he'd likely forget.

She looked rested, which was the plan, and she had stayed

out of his hair, just as she'd promised. Trouble was, Carter had seen glimpses of her quiet pool time for three days straight and had wanted to join her.

She came from a different world, he told himself. And he'd already been burned.

Good sense had him turning away from the kitchen sliding glass door, but her inquisitive voice carried to his ears. "Is that you, Carter?"

"Uh-huh. It's me. But don't let me disturb you."

"I can use some disturbing." Her voice held a gentle ring of frustration. She closed the book and turned her pretty violet eyes on him.

He strolled outside and sat down in a wrought-iron chair in the shade three feet away from her.

"Chicken," she said with laughter in her voice.

He unfastened the top two buttons on his shirt. "Must be ninety degrees out here. I do enough baking out on the range."

She tilted her head to the side and then shot a glance over the deep blue waters of his massive pool and the beautiful garden surrounding it. "You could actually use your own pool, you know."

"And ruin my cowboy image?"

A bubble of laughter escaped her throat. He laughed, too, but his focus drifted from her pretty face to honeyed California skin bathed in sunlight. Her legs were long and sleek and perfectly shaped. Her stomach flat and her breasts… Carter lifted his gaze to meet her eyes.

She flushed pink. Damn, did she expect him not to notice her killer body? His voice grew husky. "Just what kind of disturbing did you want me to do?"

"I, uh…" She gazed past the pool area and garden to the vast open spaces beyond. "I'm bored. I know it's not your problem, and I don't want to seem ungrateful, but besides Henry and Mara and you, I've had no human contact for three full days. Well, there was the shopping trip to town, but that was a quick outing and I didn't exactly make any friends along the way, with my disguise and all. Speaking of that, I don't think anyone around here would know me—"

"Do you know how to ride?"

Her brows gathered together. "Horses?"

He nodded slowly.

"Of course. I practically grew up riding. My father did a motion picture in Spain and we stayed at this magnificent hacienda. I was six then and I've been riding ever since."

"We'll go after dinner. At sunset."

"Really?"

Carter scratched his head. He hadn't been a good host. The hope in Macy's voice was proof positive. "Just be sure to wear those cowboy duds you bought. And a hat."

"It'll be dark. I don't think I'll need a disguise."

"It's not for purposes of disguise." His gaze flashed over her body in an unconcealed sweep that brought his message home.

She blinked and whispered, "Oh?"

She had to know how tempting she looked to him right now. If she hadn't caught him watching her at the door, he would've marched back into his office and tried to forget the sexual awareness that had been niggling at him all week. He was still shell-shocked from Jocelyn's deception. And Macy was a distraction to his bruised ego, but lusting after her wasn't in the cards.

But neither of them needed any complications in their lives right now.

"Excuse me, Carter, Miss Tarlington." Mara stood at the back doorway.

Carter was grateful for the interruption. Things were getting a little hot out here. "Hey, Mara. What can I do for you?"

"Henry's finished with his interview. He's impressed and would like you to meet with Mr. Fargo, if you've got the time today."

"Sure, have Henry bring him into the office."

"I plan to go home with Henry afterward, if that's all right. Supper's ready and keeping warm."

"That's fine. Thanks, Mara."

"Okay then. I'll be saying goodbye to both of you."

Macy sat farther up in her chair, poking her head around him. "Bye, Mara, and remember to call me Macy."

Mara nodded and then was gone.

Carter rose from the patio chair and glanced at Macy tying up the straps of her bathing suit top. As she tightened the drawstring, her breasts pushed together. He drew a breath quietly and excused himself.

"See you at supper, Carter," she said.

"Right," he muttered. He wasn't sure which was worse, inviting Macy Tarlington to Wild River Ranch or enjoying her being here even more.

Carter sat behind his large walnut desk in an office situated on the opposite end of the living area of the house. As often as he could, he conducted business from here, rather than driving into Dallas, where he held six thousand square feet of office space for McCay's Cattle Company. His work included more than cattle buying and selling lately. He'd diversified and had his hands in other ventures as well, but his bread and butter would always be ranching. It was his first love.

Carter met his prospective employee with a cordial smile. He believed that nothing told more about a man than the sincerity in his eyes. "I see from your résumé, Mr. Fargo, you've got an extensive amount of experience."

"I've been around the block a few times," he said with a twinkle in his eye.

Carter nodded, continuing to sift through his papers. "You've done construction, government work and teaching, among other things. What did you teach?"

Bill Fargo leaned over and looked at his paperwork upside down on Carter's desk. He pointed to the middle of a page. "Says right on there, American history. I coached football for a few years, too."

Carter leaned back in his seat, perusing the gray-haired man. He was well-groomed, nice looking and in his sixties. Carter liked his confidence. "I played in high school. Running back."

Bill Fargo gave him a quick once-over. "You hold some long-term records."

"I do." Texas and football was like chips and dip. One's just not good without the other. "It was a while back."

"Nineteen hundred yards in a single season. You ran for thirteen touchdowns."

Carter chuckled. "You did your homework."

"I would take credit for that, but the truth is, I noseyed around town and asked about you. Seems Wild River residents don't forget football records."

Carter knew that for fact. "I'm curious. What else did you learn about me?"

"Ex-military. Father's a drunk. You're fair in your dealings and run a tight ship."

The side of his jaw itched. Carter pressed his fingers there, scratching it and staring at the older man. He'd never had his life summed up so succinctly before. The man could have added "recently jilted by your girlfriend" to the list. "The job is for a groundskeeper. To keep watch over the land and an old structure I'm thinking about renovating. You don't have experience in that."

Bill Fargo crossed his arms over his slender frame and sat back in his seat. "I kept twenty boys and girls interested in history every semester. Kept a forty-man football team of teenagers from fighting, drinking and bad-mouthing authority. If I'm given a job, I do it. I've got some experience with firearms, too."

Carter's brows lifted. "I don't doubt that." He studied his résumé under *Hobbies*. "You're a hunter."

"That's right."

"Why do you want to work here?" Carter asked.

"I need work and Wild River's a nice enough place to live."

Carter liked the old guy. He believed he'd get an honest day's work out of him. "Fair enough." Carter took a second to go over his résumé once more. Henry liked him enough to recommend him, and he'd made a good impression. "Everything looks good. If you're in agreement with the terms, you're hired."

Carter extended his hand and Fargo's grip was solid and steady as they shook on it. Then they rose from their seats. "See Henry tomorrow and he'll go over your duties. Is there anything else I can answer for you?"

"Can't think of a thing," Fargo said.

"Great. Then thank you for the interview."

They said their farewells and Carter watched the older man walk out. He debated about telling him that Macy Tarlington, daughter to the legendary actress, was staying on the property. His trust went only so far, and Carter found himself protective of his new houseguest. He'd wait to see how well Bill Fargo worked out on the ranch before divulging to him Macy's real identity.

"Thought you should know, I hired someone to keep an eye on the inn at night."

Startled, Macy glanced up from arranging dinner plates on the kitchen table. She'd been deep in thought and hadn't heard Carter come in.

"He's an older man, but capable. You might see him around the ranch."

Carter walked into the room, his deep Texas drawl drifting over her. He moved with lazy grace, his boots clicking on the stone floor until he was right beside her.

"I, uh, I thought it was safe here."

"Usually it is. Nothing like this has happened before. Must've been some kids looking to get into mischief. A window was broken. Not a big deal. But being that you're here now, couldn't hurt to have some extra security."

"Extra? What else do you have besides the fences and gates?"

She gazed into his clear hazel eyes. He smelled good, like raw earth and musk. He gave her a sly smile. "My men. Most of them carry handguns."

Macy swallowed hard. She came from a place where owning guns was practically politically incorrect. "Why?"

"Rattlesnakes and rustlers."

"You're joking?"

Carter brushed her shoulder softly when he turned to get the pitcher of iced tea out of the refrigerator. He brought it over to the table. "You wouldn't say that if you were staring into the beady eyes of a diamondback."

She gasped. "Have you?"

He poured iced tea into two glasses. He set one by each of their plates. "At least a dozen times."

She rubbed the shiver out of her arms. "I hate snakes."

"They probably don't like us too much, either. Hazards of ranching."

"But this place is like a resort. I mean, you've got lovely grounds, gardens and pools. And a tennis court."

Carter sipped his tea. "It's all a facade."

"Now you *are* joking." Macy nibbled on her lower lip. She'd never thought, for one moment, that she wouldn't be safe on the ranch. "You didn't say anything about snakes when you showed me around the grounds the other day."

"I was watching, don't you worry."

She thought back to how carefree she'd felt on that walk. "But you didn't have a gun on you." She paused and blinked. "Did you?"

"I had a knife." Carter smiled and walked over to the stove top. "You're not backing out on the ride, are you?"

"Oh, uh…" The thought had crossed her mind, but Macy rarely wimped out on anything, nude scenes excluded. "No. Don't be silly. I still want to go." A little tremor ran through her. "You'll be armed, right?"

He laughed. "Yeah. But just so you know, it's kinda hard getting bit by a snake atop a horse anyway."

She remembered the movie *Snakes on a Plane*. If they could get on a plane…

Carter lifted the lid on the roasting pan. Mara had left them pot roast, potatoes and steamed vegetables. He took a whiff and made a sound of satisfaction. "Mmm. You ready to eat? I'm hungry."

"It does smell good."

Macy redirected her focus. She couldn't think about guns and rattlesnakes over dinner. Her mind flashed to a few hours ago when Carter had joined her at the pool. Had she mistaken his innuendo? She didn't think so.

Surely, he was still in love with Jocelyn. Even though she'd betrayed him, losing the person you wanted to spend your entire life with had to stay with you awhile.

Her mother had never gotten over her father's death. She'd blamed him and had been angry at him for throwing all three of their lives away so easily. There were times Macy was sure her mother hated Clyde Tarlington.

With Carter lending a helping hand, the food was dished up and they ate quietly. He didn't talk, fuss or drink while he was dining. He gobbled up his meal quickly, as if it was his last one. She'd once heard a friend who'd come from poverty say that eating quickly was a survival habit from childhood. Food had been a luxury, and she'd never known when or *if* she'd get the next meal.

Macy smiled at Carter. His plate was clean, while she still had half her meal remaining. "Did you always live at the ranch?" she asked.

He leaned back in his seat and folded his arms over his middle. "No. This was my uncle's place. I lived with him on and off, until I was twelve. Then my uncle took me in permanently and I spent my teen years here. I learned ranching from him. Back then, the house was just three bedrooms and one bath and the herd was small but sturdy. My uncle did okay. He was a good man."

"What happened to your mom and dad?"

Carter stared at her and shook his head. For a second she didn't think he would answer. His face filled with pain he'd tried to cover up, but she saw through it. Maybe because she'd recognized the gesture—she'd been known to conceal her own pain at times.

She was sorry she'd asked about his parents, but before she could apologize for her curiosity, Carter gave her this much. "My mom died when I was eight. I remember her fighting with my dad almost every night. She'd be crying in her bed, and I would cry, too. Riley's selfish and weak and drove my mother to an early grave." Carter scrubbed his jaw, thinking and staring out the window. "He's a drunk. Has always been a drunk."

Those words hit home. She'd heard them spoken too often when her father was alive. The sick feeling she'd had as a kid invaded Macy's stomach now. She wondered if Carter had had those very same feelings as a boy. She'd gathered he and his dad weren't close. But she'd never guessed that she and Carter would have so much in common. "I get it."

Carter shook his head hard. "Doubtful, Hollywood."

"No, I mean I *really* get it. My father drove his car into a tree ten years ago. He was drunk out of his mind. He'd won big at the off-track betting venue and was celebrating hard. He was a drinker and a gambler. Back then, Clyde Tarlington's death was big news. Surely, you've heard about it."

Carter shrugged and shook his head. "I was overseas at the time. Was it hard on you?"

She nodded. "The worst. My mother went into a deep depression and couldn't really deal with me. I was sixteen at the time."

"That's a tough age."

"Tell me about it."

Carter's chair scraped stone as he pushed back and rose from his seat. Clearly, he was done with this conversation. "Hey, Duke and Honey are waiting for us. And they need the exercise as much as we need to clear our heads. You ready?"

"I've got my boots on, don't I?" She kicked up one foot to show it off.

Carter glanced at the boots she'd bought in town the other day. Then he skimmed his eyes over blue jeans and the plain white shirt she wore and gave a nod of approval. "Let's ride."

# Five

Her butt was sore, but she wouldn't complain just yet. Honey was a true honey of a horse, a palomino that stood fifteen hands high, golden blond in color and tempered with a sweet nature. Carter had picked the right horse for her.

He did everything really well, it seemed, and it was beginning to grate on her nerves. How could a man be so perfect? He had to have some flaws. Please, dear heaven, let him have some flaws.

Because from where she sat right now, with Carter in the lead, leaning back in the saddle, comfortable and relaxed on Duke, the black stallion that Carter had broken himself, and a tan Stetson riding low on his forehead, she didn't see one darn flaw.

Macy had dated some good-looking men over the years. Some of them were actually nice and some had treated her fairly well. But none of them had panned out. Ultimately, it wasn't their flaws that had turned her off. What it always seemed to boil down to was Macy's world-famous mother. They'd been more interested in dating Tina Tarlington's *daughter* than getting to know Macy as an individual. Dating a Tarlington had been their key motivation, and as soon as Macy had figured it out, she dumped them.

She wanted a man who saw her for herself, not someone more impressed by who had signed her birth certificate.

Was that too much to ask?

Duke took off at a trot and Honey followed. Macy tried to seat herself firmly on the saddle for the ride, but her butt bumped hard leather so often, she winced in pain, gritting her teeth. She had a death grip on the reins, and luckily Carter didn't look back to see her ridiculous attempt at riding. After a few minutes, Carter brought his horse to an even gait, and Honey slowed, too. Macy finally caught her breath. She was sure her rear end would never be the same. She called out, "Can we stop soon?"

Carter turned around to look at her.

"I, uh, I wanted to see that part of the river." She pointed to a nondescript piece of land along the bank.

She heard a slight chuckle rise up from his throat. "It's no different than any other part of the river, but sure. If you need to stop, we will."

"I don't need to stop. I want to."

"Right."

Carter led the way, guided by a descending blaze of sunshine. The rays lent a pinkish hue to the land and gleamed over the water. The air was heavy but the water invited. Macy's horse automatically followed Duke, and within minutes—and Macy *was* counting—they reined in their horses. Carter swung his leg over the stallion and dismounted, gaining his footing easily in one fluid motion. He gave his horse a pat on the back then strolled over to her. Macy tried to duplicate his dismount, but her boot connected with the horse's rump and Honey jostled slightly. Macy lost her balance, kicked the horse's rump again and hung on to the saddle horn for dear life.

Carter was there to grab her before she fell to the ground. "Whoa, hang on." His velvet voice slid over her.

Macy found herself in Carter's arms, pressed against the hard planes of his chest as he lowered her. The toes of her boots touched the ground first, and she was sandwiched between Honey and the hunky cowboy. Her heart skidded to a stop. And it pissed her off. Darn him. He'd rescued her again. She stared into his eyes. It was a mistake. Instead of finding desire, she saw amusement twinkle in his eyes.

"Maybe you're not as good with horses as you think you are."

She removed her arms from his neck and gave him a little shove. "I am. I've been riding a long time."

"When was the last time?" he asked, unfazed by her push.

"Oh, um. Let's see." She pondered a moment and then remembered. "It was three or four years ago."

Carter pushed his hat farther up on his forehead and stared.

"Maybe five or six years ago."

He held her gaze.

"Okay, it's been about eight years ago, at least."

Carter's voice was smooth as silk. "Seems like I've forgotten more than you know about horses."

She was still smarting from being held tightly in his arms. "Not true. I'm just rusty."

Carter turned his back on her and she immediately rubbed her rump, trying to press out the knots and ease the sore spots. She was sure her bottom was raw.

"Remind me to give you a balm I've got back at the house. It'll fix your pretty little *butt* all up."

He whipped his head around and caught her just as she was removing her hand from her behind. He laughed.

"You're enjoying this too much, Carter McCay."

"I can honestly tell you, I am."

He moved to the riverbank and bent to pick up a pebble. She saw him toss it far, skipping over water that was motionless. Ripples interrupted the calm and swept out in a large circle. It was soothing to watch.

"Doesn't look like a wild river to me."

"Not tonight it's not. But it can be. Sometimes, the river fools you. It can become deadly when you least expect it."

The sun faded on the horizon. Dusk was Macy's favorite time of day, and they stood there quietly for a while as the light finally ebbed entirely.

"I like it here," she said aloud.

Carter swiveled his head and their gazes met. "I knew you would."

"But I can't face another day of lounging around. I'm learning something about myself."

"What's that?"

"I don't relax well. I need something to do." The idea had come to her today when she'd been bored out of her mind. She'd been mulling it over ever since. She couldn't expect Carter to entertain her every day. He had a business to run. And she promised him she wouldn't be a burden. The solution would benefit them both. "Carter, you can tell me no, and I wouldn't blame you at all, but I'd like to help you fix up the inn. I could use a project. And my services come cheap. I'm...free."

Carter didn't hesitate to answer. "No."

"Why not?"

"I haven't decided about the inn yet."

"But, it's perfect. You can't still be thinking of tearing it down? Tell me you changed your mind about that."

"I can't tell you that. I'm not ready to make that decision."

Macy crossed her arms so hard they jammed into her ribs. She eyed him carefully. "So that's it."

"I didn't say that."

It wasn't what she'd meant. He was stubborn. That was his flaw. Lord have mercy. She almost did a happy dance, right there on the riverbank, under the moonlight. Carter was a stubborn mule.

She laughed and he sent her a look of astonishment. "Why are you laughing?"

She lifted a shoulder. "No reason," she fibbed. Now she had a valid reason to hold on to when his image flashed through her mind at night right before she dozed off to sleep.

The cowboy wasn't perfect.

What a relief.

He leaned close, skeptical. "You're not going to argue with me about it?"

"Oh, I definitely will. I'm pretty relentless when I think I'm right."

He frowned. "Which is most of the time, I take it."

She smiled wide. "Of course."

"Bye, Mara, and thanks again for lunch earlier," Macy called out by the front doorway.

"You're very welcome," Mara answered from the kitchen.

Macy exited the house, looking like a country girl in Carter's felt hat and a new pair of blue jeans. Late-afternoon sunshine made her squint, and she immediately plopped sunglasses onto the bridge of her nose. Marching past the corrals, she saw Henry speaking with one of the men. She waved to him and he tipped his hat then she turned her attention to the road leading to the inn.

Macy had met a few of the ranch hands over the past few days, and no one seemed to recognize her or make her feel out of place. They'd greet her with a smile or wave and then go about their business. Wild River seemed so remote and out of touch with the world she'd known that Macy felt completely at ease here.

Too much at ease. The walk would do her good. She was getting cabin fever, and her restlessness couldn't be bottled up for much longer. With Carter gone all day on business in Dallas, there was only so much reading and sunbathing a girl could do.

Rocky raced out of the stables and caught up to her, his tongue hanging out of his mouth in a dog smile. "Hey, Rock. You'll keep me safe from the snakes, right?"

He fell in step beside her. She didn't know what she'd do without her trusty companion. He was good company for a lonely heart.

She walked briskly, hoping to burn calories, and hugged the path along the river as much as she could. She hadn't forgotten about the snakes, but Macy wouldn't let that stop her from taking a walk. She would tread cautiously and out in the open, avoiding brush and scrubs, keeping her eyes peeled. Mara had told her today most of the snakes on the property were harmless garden snakes. She'd lived in Wild River all of her life and had never encountered a diamondback. After that, Macy's mind had been made up.

Carter's longhorns were scattered on grazing land, and she

could make out their horns even from this distance away. As she headed in the opposite direction of the herd, toward the inn, the powerful scent of cattle hide and dung faded.

"Your master is being stubborn, letting that wonderful house go to waste."

She was drawn to the inn and hadn't stopped thinking about it since Carter had shown it to her days ago. She'd hounded him every day about letting her refurbish it, but he wouldn't relent. Something was holding him back, and he wasn't talking.

She reached the inn unscathed and thanked Mara again for giving her encouragement. Rocky followed her inside and she walked around the dusty downstairs rooms again, envisioning the place in its heyday, when guests had stayed here. The parlor would have been lush, with velvet drapes and tufted chairs, the carpets woven in intricate patterns. Sidebars would have held the finest china and cut crystal. The place would have resembled a Texas palace. "It's such a shame," she whispered, her shoulders slumping.

Macy walked outside and found herself on the gazebo again, in the center of her would-be stage. With the river just yards away and giant oak trees lending shade to the area, creativity could blossom here. It was a place of inspiration.

A noise behind the trees startled her. Something was shuffling around. Rocky barked and fear froze her. The dog nestled between her legs, protecting her, his bark higher pitched now and more emphatic. Images of a big, eight-foot-long snake creeping its way through the hedges flashed in her mind.

She sunk down to her knees, holding on to Rocky, madly searching for the creature to appear. Her heart in her throat, she asked, "Who's th-there?"

A man stepped out from behind a cropping of trees. "Sorry, ma'am. I didn't mean to scare you." The man shot Rocky a smile and the dog quieted.

He approached slowly, speaking with a kind voice. "I'm Bill Fargo. Mr. McCay hired me to look after the grounds."

Macy breathed a sigh of relief and rose from her crouched position. The man wore a shirt and trousers the same hue as his thick gray hair. It wasn't exactly a uniform, but it came close enough. "Oh."

"Who are you?" he asked.

Macy stared at him.

"Sorry, ma'am." He softened his tone. "I'm just doing my job." He really did appear apologetic.

"My name is Macy. I'm Mr. McCay's houseguest. I thought Carter said you were to be working at night?"

He turned his wrist and glanced at his watch. "From four in the afternoon until midnight."

"Did you follow me here?"

He shook his head. "No. Just happened along at the same time. Is that your dog?"

"No, Rocky is Mr. McCay's dog."

Bending to Rocky's level, Fargo put out his hand. Rocky crept over to him and carefully sniffed his fingers. "He's a good watchdog."

The dog stopped sniffing, tilted his head and licked the man's hand. Macy sighed. So much for Rocky protecting her. "He's a pussycat."

Bill Fargo chuckled. "In Rocky's defense, he knows I'm not a threat." The man rose to meet her level gaze. He stood a head taller and looked quite fit but for a slight belly bulge. "It's a great place. I've been exploring."

"I agree. I'm sort of drawn to this place."

"Well, nice to meet you, Macy. I guess I'll be seeing you around. Next time, I hope I won't frighten you."

"And next time I won't picture a reptile crawling through the bushes, ready to have me for a snack."

The man walked off smiling, and Macy entered the house again. She climbed the stairs and went straight into the one bedroom that had been completed. The last time she was here, Carter had rushed her out of it, but now she had time to look around. She wondered if Jocelyn had a hand in decorating this room. Had it been her project? Had she convinced Carter to let her fix it up right before she'd dumped him?

From the window, she noted oak and cottonwood trees forming a backdrop that defined the perimeter of the backyard. Sunlight danced through the branches, casting a feathery glow of light and shadows over the grounds. The gazebo in the center of the property appeared like a valiant injured soldier trying to stand at attention.

Macy sighed.

She heard an engine's roar and searched in the direction of the sound. It grew louder. Then a Jeep came into view, the driver a dark blond cowboy wearing a black hat.

She lost sight of him as he drove toward the front of the house. Her nerves jumped and she fumbled with a single bud vase she'd picked up. Almost dropping it, she set it back onto the nightstand with care.

Carter was here.

She reminded herself for the umpteenth time that he wasn't on the auction block. She couldn't bid on him and hope to win. He was off-limits for half a dozen reasons.

"Macy?" he called from downstairs, his deep rich voice curling her toes. "You in here, Hollywood?"

Rocky left her side once he heard Carter and flew down the stairs.

Macy popped her face out of the doorway. "I'm up here."

She lowered down on the bed, her heart beating fast at the sound of Carter's boots hitting the stairs. When he entered the room, the scent of lime and musk followed, and Macy glanced up to greet him. "Hi."

He sat down on the bed next to her. He spoke quietly. "Hi."

"Were you looking for me?" She didn't know why he would be. She was making conversation.

He surprised her and nodded. "I was."

"Why?"

He shrugged with a quizzical look. "I don't know. Mara told me you'd gone for a walk. I figured you'd end up here."

"You figured right. I met Bill Fargo."

"I know. I saw him on the road. He said he nearly scared the stuffing out of you. I haven't told him who you were, exactly. I figured it's best to keep it quiet for now."

"I thought he was a snake." She sent him a withering look. "I know, I'm pathetic."

Carter shook his head with laughter. "No, you're not. I might have exaggerated a little about the snake problem here. Just wanted to keep you on guard, in case you might come across one."

"Well, it's not as if I'd go up to a snake and try to make friends."

He rubbed his chin and held back a grin. "Then my strategy worked."

She wanted to slug him.

He took off his hat and set it between them, then ran a hand through his hair. The ends curled up and relaxed down against his collar. Macy's mouth went dry. The simplest gesture from him got her wheels spinning. With Carter around, her balance was always being tested. Then she remembered how stubborn he was, and the question that had been on her mind poured out. "Did Jocelyn fix up this room?"

Carter jerked back. His eyes blinked rapidly. "What?"

"I was wondering if your fiancée started work on this house?"

His mouth twisted and he rose from the bed. He strode to the window and looked out. "She was never my fiancée."

"Oh right," she whispered. "Sorry."

Silence filled the room.

Macy rose and went to him. "I didn't mean to pry."

He turned to her, his eyes blazing. "Didn't you?"

"No, I, uh," she began, retreating a step. "If you don't want to tell me, it's fine."

Carter closed his eyes and drew air into his lungs. He didn't owe her any explanation, yet she wanted desperately to know. And it wasn't just about getting a chance to work on the inn. She'd been here a short time and they were still strangers, but not really. For some odd reason, they jelled. They sort of fell in step with each other, and though he made her heart do silly things, she felt something akin to friendship with him. He mattered to her.

His fingers went to his forehead and he rubbed there, squeezing the skin together. "Jocelyn didn't even like this place. She thought I should tear it down."

"Oh." That was a shocker. She watched Carter's hazel eyes turn a deeper shade.

"I've been considering it, but not because of her."

Macy didn't get it. "Then why?"

Carter spoke through tight lips. "It has to do with my father."

Macy waited, curious and dying to know, but she held her tongue. It was obvious this was a sore subject. He gazed at her, searching for trust. Something he saw in her eyes must have convinced him. He spoke in a detached tone. "After his last rehab, we'd agreed he'd be the groundskeeper here and work with the decorators. You know, let them inside and make sure they had everything they needed. It was a test, and he promised me he'd cleaned up his act. He was going to live here when it was all done and run the place." Carter scoffed with disgust. "That lasted about two weeks. The decorator came to me one day when he didn't show. I went looking for him and found him passed out on his backyard cot. His house was on fire. Apparently dear old dad left a burner on at the stove. Smoke was everywhere, but he was too damn drunk to wake up and save his own life. Then I heard Rocky whimpering. He was trapped inside the house."

"Oh no! How awful."

"I got him out of there and took him home with me."

"What about your father?"

"Had a bout of smoke inhalation, but nothing gets Riley McCay down. He's fine to drink another day. Boarded up the walls, from what I hear, and is living out of two rooms in that old house."

"It's a good thing you showed up when you did, Carter. Or neither of them might have survived." Images of her own father flashed in her mind. How she'd wished she could have gotten through to him before he'd gone down the path of self-destruction.

There was silence. Carter took a breath and blew it out, clearly bitter about his father. "So now you know."

"But—"

He put two fingers to her mouth, stopping her from speaking.

His touch, finger pads to her soft lips, caused commotion in her belly and she gazed into his gorgeous hazel eyes. "*But,* I've had a change of heart. You made me see value in this house. I can't let it sit anymore. So, if you're still willing, you can fix it up. I spoke with my accountant today and—"

"Really?" Macy blurted between his fingers, overwhelmed with joy. She hadn't heard much else other than he had changed his mind. "I can decorate the inn?"

He removed his fingers from her mouth and nodded.

"Oh, thank you." She threw her arms around his neck and lifted up to kiss him solidly on the lips. "You won't be sorry."

# Six

Carter was already sorry.

He held Macy in his arms, splaying his hands on her tiny waist. She was pressed close, her breasts crushed to his chest. His pulse quickened as he looked down at her mouth. Her lips were full and soft and generous. Her expressive violet eyes were closed, but Carter had seen the look of sheer joy on her face, and it was impossible not to feel the same way.

His body grew tight and hard. Awareness coursed through his veins. Her eyes fluttered open after that one teasing kiss, and she stared at him. He held his own, until her mouth parted and her subtle female scent drifted up to his nostrils. A man could take only so much before he caved.

He bent his head farther and nipped at her lips. A little whimper rose from her throat, a plea asking for more. Carter wasn't going to deny her. He brought his mouth to hers and kissed her fully. She fell into his arms, as if she wanted to be there all along, as if she belonged there.

A shudder ran through his system. She didn't belong in his

arms, but her kisses were too damn tempting, her mouth too appealing and the taste of her too damn good.

Was it an ego stroke, or real passion? Carter didn't want to know. Both of them were in lonely places right now, and if they could bring each other a little pleasure, why not? He pulled her closer and took her in another kiss. This time, he got real serious.

She grew bold and brought her hands to his chest, then stroked up his shirt to toy with his neck. He liked a woman who went after what she wanted. He liked her hands on him. He wove his hand into her hair and pulled her ponytail loose. The silky blanket of curls fell down her back. His fingers threaded through the thick locks. "Open for me, darlin'."

Her lips immediately obeyed and he drove his tongue into her mouth. He kissed her again and again, their mouths caught up in a frenzy of lust.

Macy whispered his name softly, reverently between kisses. "Carter."

He wanted her then and was fully aware they were standing in the only room that housed a big, welcoming bed. No strings attached, he'd told her when he'd invited her here. He'd promised her that, and he was about to make that clear a second time. He pulled away from her slightly and met with eyes filled with desire. "There's—"

Something flashed outside the window, and out of the corner of his eye he saw Henry's truck coming up the road. "Crap."

Carter put his head down, bunched up his face for a second and then stepped away from Macy. "Henry just pulled up. He must be looking for me. It'll be only a minute before he comes up here."

Macy gasped and pulled herself together quickly. It wasn't as if she'd been naked or anything, but she looked flustered.

"I'll go down and see what he wants."

Carter grabbed his hat, set it on his head and gave Macy one last look before leaving the room. Regret battled with good sense as he went down the stairs. It was a good thing Henry interrupted what might have happened, he told himself. He wished to hell he believed that. He hadn't quite recovered, but he put on a good show for Henry when he met him out front. He was sitting in his truck, and Carter leaned against the passenger window. "Hey, what's up?"

"Looks like Belle is ready to foal. You said you wanted to be there."

"Yeah, I do. How's she doing?"

"Being it's her first time, she's a trouper. I've gotta get back to the barn."

"I'll come relieve you in a few minutes."

Macy appeared in the doorway, her hair back in a ponytail, her hat sitting pretty atop her head. Henry tipped his hat and didn't voice the question Carter noticed in his eyes. Henry knew how to be discreet when he had to be. "Miss Tarlington."

"Hi, Henry. Anything wrong?"

"Not a thing. It's good news."

Carter turned to her. "You ever see a mare give birth?"

She shook her head. "No."

"You want to?" he asked.

Macy glanced at Henry first then looked at Carter. With a broad smile, she nodded. "I'd love to."

"Well then, I'll be going. I'll see you both at the ranch," Henry said, revving the engine.

Carter stood in front of the house, watching the Ford truck make its way down the road. When the vehicle was out of sight, he turned around and gave Macy a direct look. Her eyes, when unconcealed, were like a bouquet of blue violets, shocking in their intensity. He glanced at her mouth, tenderly swollen from his kisses. He set his hands in the back pockets of his jeans and leaned back on his boot heels. "Listen, when I invited you here, I said there were no strings attached, and I meant it. You don't owe me anything, and you shouldn't feel obligated because—"

"Don't you dare!" Macy's lips pursed tight together. They were ready to turn a shade of purple.

He jerked back and blinked at her tone.

"You think I kissed you because I feel I owe you something? Man, that's rich, Carter."

Carter's voice rose. "Why are you so riled?"

Her voice elevated a notch higher. "I'm not riled."

Fumes were practically coming out of her ears. "Then why the hell are you barking at me?"

"I. Am. Not. Barking. But if you think I kissed you for any other reason than because I wanted to, then you don't know me very well."

"Well, that's right. I *don't* know you very well."

"At this rate, you're never going to find out."

"Maybe it's best if I don't." The last thing he needed was to get complicated with Macy Tarlington. He'd been a fool once with a woman, and he wasn't about to repeat his mistake. No matter how good that kiss had been. No matter how much Macy tempted him with pretty hair, gorgeous eyes and a killer body. "Besides, *I* kissed you. That peck you gave me wasn't all that inspiring and hardly rated as a kiss at all."

"I was thanking you, Carter." She spoke as if he should've realized that. As if he was a moron. "If my kisses were so bad, then why in heaven did you react that way?" Her voice lowered as she glanced at the zipper of his jeans.

She'd turned him on. It wasn't a crime and he wasn't going to apologize for it. He met her challenge. His voice a thick rasp, he answered, "Don't go analyzing my reaction to you. You're a beautiful woman and we got caught up in something a second ago. That's all it was." He pushed the brim of his hat lower onto his forehead. "I've gotta get going. You want to come and see Belle give birth, hop into the Jeep."

He strode over to his Jeep and climbed into the driver's side. Rocky followed, racing into the front seat next to him, taking up all the space. The dog turned big eager eyes to Macy, and Carter half hoped she'd changed her mind. But sure as shooting, she marched over to the vehicle and got into the back. Before she could get her butt planted firmly onto the seat, Carter gunned the gas pedal and took off.

Seeing the colt's birth might have been the most fascinating thing that happened to Macy this year, if Carter hadn't kissed her. *That* ranked one notch higher in her Top Ten List of All-Time

Thrills. Macy couldn't shake off the feeling of his arms around her, their bodies melding or the heat of his breath as he laid claim to her mouth. Her lips still stung a little, in a good way. Macy had let go of all her doubts and inhibitions up in that bedroom and simply gave in to what she was feeling.

Carter had turned on the heat.

But after the interruption, he'd shut down cold.

Macy wasn't looking for love, hardly believed in it herself, and she knew Carter wasn't in the market for another girlfriend. He'd had his heart broken and his faith shattered. And, she couldn't forget, he was the bearer of the cursed diamond ring.

Yet still, Macy tingled in places she'd forgotten *could* tingle. Her nerves jangled at the memory of that kiss and what might have happened if Henry hadn't driven up when he had.

If she was ever to take a leap of faith with a man, it would be with Carter. No doubt about it.

Macy leaned on the corral fence. The air was warm and sticky, the sun taking its last dip before setting on the horizon. To think, it was just an hour ago that the foal had been born, a colt. Macy had watched in awe and slight horror, seeing the mare strain and stretch to deliver her little babe. As soon as the foal was born, covered in a layer of stable straw, Carter checked under Belle's neck for a pulse and then patted her lovingly on her flank. She'd rebounded from the delivery and lifted up to stand tall in the barn's stall. Mama and foal were healthy, Carter had reported.

Now, Carter led the mare and the spindle-legged foal into the empty corral. The colt followed close to its mama, and Macy's heart tripped over itself. Mother and son were beautiful in their awkward grace. As the colt nursed, Belle stood still, swiveling her head to catch a sideways glance of her newborn. They were dark brown in coloring with black manes, their coats like gloss under the setting sun.

Carter left them in the center of the corral and came to lean his back on the fence next to her. He was inside, she outside. He didn't look at her when he spoke, instead focusing on the two horses. "He's a fine-looking colt, isn't he?"

"He's amazing. It's hard to believe he's walking already."

"It's in his nature. He's a prey animal. His instincts tell him to get up and go, avoid predators at all costs. Foals have to be quick on their feet. He'll be trotting before bedtime, and in the morning he'll be able to gallop."

"Seriously, on those legs?"

Carter grinned. In the olden days, she'd be called a greenhorn for being naive. "Those legs are about ninety percent of his mama's in height. Tomorrow they'll even be stronger and will easily hold his weight. You watch and see."

"I'll do that," Macy said good-naturedly. The mood between them had eased some after the colt's birth. It seemed neither one of them could hold on to tense feelings after witnessing something so wondrous.

Macy always thought birth was a miracle in itself, but to witness the colt's progress an hour after his delivery was truly inspiring.

In the distance, cattle bellowed, their sound almost familiar to her now. This ranch was massive, with so many things going on all at once. The air was damp and uncomfortable and the stubborn man beside her way too good-looking for her equilibrium, yet Macy felt at peace. It settled into her bones now, and a sense of wonder and joy filled her. Tears welled in her eyes, and she fought them hard. She didn't want Carter to see her cry. She turned her head and pretended to gaze at the crescent moon. Even the sky was perfect right now.

"What's wrong, Hollywood?" Carter asked. He wasn't looking at her. He had a sixth sense about things. He seemed to see what she didn't want him to see.

"I got something in my eye. I think it's dust."

"It's not dust."

"How do you know?" She whipped her head around to stare at his profile.

He shrugged. "I just know. If it's about what happened back at the inn…"

"It's not. I assure you it isn't." She spoke adamantly, perhaps too much so, because he finally looked into her eyes. She squared her shoulders. "Maybe it's seeing...I don't know...a miracle, right before my eyes."

"Okay," he said softly. Her knees nearly buckled from his sweet tone. "Just making sure."

They stared at each other a long time. Only the shuffling of the mare's hooves and the distant hoot of an owl sounded in the silence.

A change of subject was needed. "I'd like to start work on the inn tomorrow."

"I figured as much. I'll have Henry make sure the locks on the inn are changed."

"You've never locked it up before...at least not since I've been here."

"There was no need to before."

Meaning, before this, he didn't care what happened to the inn. His bitterness toward his father translated into disregard for the inn. At least now, he was willing to protect it, the same way he protected most other things in his life.

*The way he'd protected you.*

"I'll have Henry give you the new keys in the morning."

"That's great. Thank you."

"We'll have to talk about your budget."

"Sounds good. I've learned to live on a shoestring. I can be thrifty."

Carter nodded. "I've had to do the same. But, if we're doing this, I don't want to pinch pennies. You'll have all you need to make the place shine. I only have one condition."

Carter sent her a serious look and Macy blinked. "I'm holding my breath. What is it? You want the walls purple or retro furniture or something?"

"Very funny. I'm asking you to use local vendors for most of the work."

"Oh?"

"Texans stick together. Folks around here like to keep the neighbors employed."

"That's very upstanding of you."

"I know." He sent her a bone-melting smile. "I'm that kind of guy."

It wasn't easy, but she ignored his down-home charm. "Of course, I'll hire locals for the work." Her mind was spinning. She was determined to do a good job with the inn. It was a project she could sink her teeth into.

"Good."

Macy's heart raced and her exuberance spilled out. "Carter, I can't tell you how excited I am about this."

He glanced at her lips as she spoke and then pierced her with a solid, no-fooling look. "I got that already."

Heat flushed her cheeks. She didn't often blush, but Carter had a way of awakening emotions that didn't usually surface.

His gaze drifted to the mare and her colt. "How about Midnight?"

"Midnight?" She swallowed. "For what?" Was he making a date with her? Surely, he didn't want to talk budgets in the middle of the night. After the way he'd kissed her, the direction her mind traveled was X-rated. Then it dawned on her. "Oh, you mean as a name for the colt?"

He grinned. "What else?"

He was a tease, a heartthrob and a gorgeous hunk of man. "I like Midnight. It's sort of…perfect."

"Midnight it is." He tipped his hat and left the corral fence, ushering the horses into the barn for the night.

When he disappeared through the double-wide doors, she strode into the house. She had an inn to refurbish. She would focus all of her energy on the task and not give Carter McCay more thought than absolutely necessary.

She clung to that notion for dear life.

Two nights later, Macy sat at a bridge table in the parlor of the inn going over her decorating plans when a knock sounded at the door. She'd locked herself in, as Carter had instructed when the new dead bolts were installed. Glancing at her watch, she noted the time. It was after seven. She'd gotten carried away with paint

and floor samples and didn't realize the late hour. She'd missed
dinner at the house with Carter.

"Miss Tarlington? Are you all right in there?"

She recognized the man's raspy voice. She piled her notes and
samples in a stack then stepped away from the table and opened
the door to face Bill Fargo.

"Sorry to bother you, miss. I'm doing my rounds, checking
on things. And well…"

"Let me guess. You have orders to check on me."

Contrite, he answered her with a quick smile. "Just doing
my job."

"I'm fine in here. But, wow…I didn't realize how late it was.
Do you have time to come in for a minute? I'll take a break."

He wore a cowboy hat, not the same as Carter's, but it suited
him in slate gray to match the rest of his attire. He looked as if he
fit in around here already, though he'd been on the job less time
than Macy had been at Wild River. He was the newbie.

"I have a few minutes." He stepped inside and took off his hat.

"I'm working on plans for the house." He followed her into the
parlor just off the entranceway. "Please, have a seat."

On a nod, he pulled out one of the four folding chairs around
the table and waited for her to sit before he took his seat.

Gentlemanly charm got to her every time. "Thank you."

"You're welcome."

"Would you like some iced tea? I have a thermos and an extra
cup."

"That'd be nice. I'm a little thirsty."

Macy poured iced tea into two foam cups and handed him
one. "So, you know my last name."

He nodded. "Yes, I do. I know who you are."

"Did Carter tell you?"

He shook his head. "He told me your first name. I figured out
the rest. I'm a drifter, but I'm not a recluse. I guess you could say,
I enjoyed your mother's work. She was a fine actress."

Macy had heard that compliment a thousand times. Her
mother moved people with her acting ability, but it was her life-

style and celebrity status that had kept her name in the limelight. "She was a wonderful mother."

"I'm sure you miss her."

"I do. The heart condition that claimed her life moved fast. One day she was healthy and vital, and it seemed the next she was frail and ill. But it was a blessing that she didn't linger. I know that in my head, but I wanted more time with her."

"That's understandable." He sipped his drink and gave her a smile that reached his eyes. They were perceptive eyes, ones that had seen a lot of life. "Mr. McCay said you're at the ranch for some solitude. I won't breach that confidence. I keep to myself, too."

"Then you do understand." Macy returned his smile before sipping her iced and then glanced at the paint chips on the table. "I could use a second opinion. I can't quite decide. Would you mind?"

"I can't say I have decorating sense, but I know what I like."

Macy pulled out a string of paint samples that were attached to a metal ring. "I'm leaning toward Stone Mountain. There's a hint of lavender in the grayish hue. I also like Chocolate Milk and Brown Sugar for the upstairs bedrooms. I can't decide. I like them all."

Bill Fargo took a long time to look them over, his eyes assessing and his gaze thoughtful. "Can you choose more than one?"

"I could. I was thinking of doing each room differently. Giving them their own personality."

"Then I think you've made wise choices." He picked up a sample of Sage. "This one reminds me of the kitchen in the house I grew up in. It's warm and friendly."

Macy grinned. "Really? I think so, too. That was my exact choice for the kitchen." She leaned her elbows on the table and tilted her head toward him. "Where did you grow up?"

Fargo's face tightened a fraction and Macy immediately wished she hadn't asked. Here she was, trying to keep her own background hidden only to pry into someone else's life.

"Oh, I grew up on the East Coast, but I've lived all over the country. I can't say that my life was dull, that's for sure."

There was no ring on his finger, but she wondered if Fargo had been married at one time.

She commiserated. "Mine sure wasn't."

Fargo's mouth spread into a smile. "I'll bet we both have stories to tell."

"I'd love to hear yours one day."

He rose from the table. "Maybe one day. But right now, I'd better get back to work. Can I give you a lift back to the house?"

She peered out a slice of window the frayed curtains didn't cover. "It's getting dark. Rocky usually leads the way home, but Mara took the poor baby into town today to get his yearly vaccinations. Yes, I'd love a ride home."

Macy gathered her belongings, making sure to take the paint samples. Hopefully tomorrow the local painters she'd hired would start work upstairs. Macy didn't know how long she'd be here at Wild River, but indefinitely wasn't in the cards. She had a life to return to, but while she was here she wanted to accomplish as much as possible.

Later that night Macy sat up on her bed, tired of tossing and turning. Plaguing thoughts kept her from sleep, and she'd learned not to fight it. She rose from the bed and put on her silk robe. She felt stifled in her room, but it wasn't the place or the heat that really bothered her. Her future loomed large in her mind tonight.

She left Rocky soundly sleeping at the foot of her bed and envied his ability to sleep like the dead. What a watchdog. The door creaked as Macy opened it and tiptoed out of the room. The hallway, devoid of windows, was black as pitch. She padded her way down the corridor, feeling her way. Her shoulder bumped the wall with a soft thump. She quickly righted herself and continued, moving with more confidence now.

She stepped on something. Sharp pain shot through her foot. Her toes curled. Caught off guard, she went down with a loud bang, her body hitting the hard tiled floor. "Ow! Oh, ow! Ow!" Her voice boomed through the hallway.

Her body folded like an accordion. She grabbed her foot.

"Macy?"

Suddenly, Carter was there, bending over her. He came down on one knee and looked her over, searching her eyes first. The hallway was no longer dark as death. Carter was backlit with light coming from the living room. Water droplets covered his chest. He was wet. All over. Only a towel covered him from waist to thigh. Her heart in her throat, the pain in her foot dulled. She stared at him.

"Are you hurt?"

"I...I stepped on something."

Carter reached behind her and came up with Rocky's rawhide bone. One end was gnawed to an arrowhead point. "Yep, that looks painful," he said.

Macy stared at his bare chest. Underneath those cotton shirts he wore lay a plank of hard abs and brawn fit enough for *Muscle-Mag*. She'd known he was mouthwatering, but seeing him in the raw was a whole lot better than her imagination had conjured up.

"Let me take a look." He lifted her leg and examined her foot. His hazel eyes scoured her from heel to toe as his fingers lightly caressed the pad of her foot. A tremble coursed the length of her leg where he held her firm. As she leaned back to allow his perusal, her robe slipped off her shoulders, trapping her arms. "Looks okay. No blood." He lowered her foot down carefully.

"Th-that's good."

He leaned closer and used one finger to wipe away a droplet of water at the base of her throat. His slight touch heated her skin. "Didn't mean to drip on you."

*Drip all you want.* Macy swallowed and forced a glance into his eyes. "It's okay."

On bent knee, his gaze flowed over her like a rapidly moving river, taking all of her in. She was wearing a soft pink nightie that barely covered her thighs. He went there and then farther up to view the cleavage between her breasts. "Macy," he said, eyes blazing. "Where were you going?"

"I, uh, couldn't sleep. I was going to stretch my legs. Maybe get a drink of water." Thankfully, she was heading in the opposite direction of his bedroom, so he wouldn't think she was desperate for something erotic and sinful.

A lock of moist hair fell onto his forehead. A few beads of water ran down his face, and he dripped on her again. Oh wow. On second thought, yes, definitely something sinful. She peered at his chest again. It was hard not to. "What were you doing?"

"I couldn't sleep, either. Took a swim."

"I gathered. You, uh, you do have swim trunks on under that towel, right?"

His eyes gleamed. "What if I said no?"

Macy took a big swallow. "Then I'd know you like to go skinny-dipping in the moonlight."

"Nah," he said, sending her a crooked smile. "Sorry to disappoint you. It's not fun to skinny-dip without a partner. Ready?"

Her eyes widened. "For a skinny-dip?"

Carter winked. "Maybe one day, Hollywood. Are you ready to get up?"

"Oh, um." She nibbled on her lower lip, feeling foolish. She had to learn not to make assumptions. "Yeah, I should be okay to stand."

Without hesitation, he gripped her hand and put his other arm around her waist. "Easy now." He bore the brunt of her weight as he set her onto her feet with care. He held her steady, but another spike of pain ran up her limb from the pressure of standing.

"Oh!"

Lowering his head to her level, Carter caught her attention. "You okay?"

She was in his arms again. How could she not be okay? "It's just a little sore."

"Hang on," he said, then she was lifted up, and immediately her arm wound around his neck. He carried her caveman style to her bedroom. With care, he lowered her onto her bed. She clung to his neck a moment too long.

It was dark and intimate and they were barely dressed.

"Macy." He held warning in his tone. He was half on, half off her bed, and she lay underneath him.

He hesitated, glanced at her mouth, and she held her breath. Something flashed in his eyes and her desire escalated. What had gotten into her? She wanted to make love with a man she'd known only a few days.

Carter blinked and took a deep breath before bringing his mouth down to lay claim to her lips. It was sheer heaven, having him kiss her again. Her heart pounded against her chest. His mouth was hot and demanding, but the kiss lasted only a few seconds before he pulled away. Carter rose to full height and stood over her bed. He spoke with a low rasp. "Get some rest, Macy. I'll see you in the morning."

She waited for him to walk out and shut the door before she slammed her head into the feather down pillow. Her foot ached, her ego was bruised and now she had nothing but counting ceiling tiles to look forward to tonight. She mumbled, "Yeah right, Carter. *As if* I could get any sleep now."

# Seven

The painters were in and out in three days and Macy was pleased at how the interior of the house was shaping up. It was amazing how much better the inn looked with a fresh coat of paint. The colors she'd chosen were soothing and subtle but with enough character to add charm and a sense of home. It was like putting the first brushstroke on an artist's canvas. The rest of the picture was hers to create.

With workmen making repairs, the place was shaping up nicely. Macy was proud of what she'd accomplished in such a short time. By the middle of her second week at Wild River, she had everything under control.

"How do you like it, Rock?" she asked of her furry blond companion. They stood facing the front of the inn.

Rocky turned his eyes toward the house and gave a quick little bark. There were times Macy wondered if the dog was half human. He seemed to know what she was saying most of the time.

"Yeah, pretty great. I think so, too."

A team of landscapers were working diligently to tear up the weeds, retill the soil and ready the ground for the white iceberg roses she'd ordered to line the path leading up the house. Masons had already inlaid cobblestones in various areas of the garden.

Things were moving fast.

If she wasn't careful, she'd be through here before she was ready to head home to Hollywood. She was almost broke and the thought of what she faced when she returned—life without her mother and without a plan of action, and the relentless paparazzi—was something she didn't want to dwell on. Not when she found it easier and easier to sink into life at Wild River.

She strode to the old gazebo. Her heart warmed every time she looked at it. The eternal optimist in her saw this gazebo restored to its one-time elegance. And as long as she was being hopeful, she imagined it as a glorious outdoor stage for a summer playhouse theater with her at the helm. Wouldn't that be the icing on the cake?

Bill Fargo stepped up. He'd been meeting her at the house every afternoon since that time when they'd shared a glass of iced tea. It had gotten to be such a routine that when Macy packed her small cooler, she always brought enough lemonade, cookies or fruit for two.

"Ready for a break, Bill?"

"I am."

"I brought Mara's lemon cookies today."

"My stomach's grumbling already."

Macy retrieved the cooler from the house, and they sat on the gazebo's steps this time. Rocky nuzzled Bill's knee, and he began stroking the dog's coat. Rocky liked Bill and so did Macy, though she didn't know very much about him.

"Did I ever tell you how I met the woman of my dreams and told her flat out, on that first night, we were destined for each other?"

Macy shook her head, the whole time smiling. Bill told the best stories. "No, but it sounds romantic."

"It was back then. We were both in our twenties. We didn't know each other at all. I saw her laughing in a group of my friends. I walked right up to her and we were introduced. It was 1972 and I was just out of college. Oh, her laugh was wonderful.

I knew then, I was going to marry her. I told her that night. She thought I was crazy." Bill got a distant look on his face, as if reliving the moment. "When you know, you know."

Macy's encounters with love were nowhere close to that. She'd probably never been truly in love before. She didn't have a good track record with the few men whom she'd thought she'd loved. She'd forgotten them pretty easily. And her mother? She'd had disastrous results in the love department, so Macy was curious at what Bill Fargo had meant.

"But *how* do you know? For sure, I mean?"

But his answer was interrupted when Carter pulled up to the inn and bounded out of the Jeep. Rocky took off, racing toward him, and the cowboy bent to give the dog several loving pats on the head. Then he strode over to them. The sight of him got Macy's heart pumping hard.

"Hey there," he said to them both.

They returned the greeting and Carter took a seat to the right of Macy, sandwiching her in between the two men. "Thought I'd stop by and see the progress."

"It's coming along," Macy said.

"Macy's doing a fine job. I've been checking on the house every day, and the transformation is outstanding," Bill added.

Carter nodded, then glanced at the opened cooler. "Those cookies for anyone in particular?"

"Mara made them. Want one?"

Carter grinned. "Does the sun shine?"

Macy handed him a cookie. "The rooms are all painted, and I think you'll like what you see in there."

"Okay." He didn't seem all that interested. "Glad you used the McManus brothers?"

"Yes. They're very good painters. Thanks for the recommendation."

"You'll find that true of most the workmen in Wild River. They need the jobs. It means putting food on the table and keeping their kids clothed. They take pride in their work."

After a few minutes of jawing, as Carter would say, Bill rose and thanked Macy for the cookies then excused himself to get back to his rounds.

Carter finally bit into his cookie, and his face lit up. "These are better than I remembered." He finished one and then took another from the batch. Then matter-of-factly, he asked, "You coming to dinner tonight?"

"Oh, I uh…" With the back of her hand, she brushed curls away from her forehead, buying time to think. She'd deliberately kept her distance from Carter, working late and missing meals with him. Humiliation was a hard thing to recover from, and after nearly throwing herself at him, she'd wanted to dig herself a hole and jump in. But she'd also been a little miffed at him, too. He wasn't interested in her, and he'd made that abundantly clear. "Why do you ask?"

His shoulder went up in a shrug. Could it be he missed having dinner with her? "I have a craving for barbecue pork ribs. I thought maybe you'd like to try them. There's this little place outside of town… They make ribs you'd sell your grandmother's soul for."

His devotion to food made her chuckle. "Really?"

He sent her a sincere smile. "I wouldn't lie to you."

Except for a few quick trips into town for clothes and supplies, Macy hadn't ventured off the ranch. The idea excited her. "Sure, I'd love to go. But I'll need an hour to shower and change."

He nodded. "You might want to disguise yourself a little. The Bear Pit has a crowd every night."

Macy had a surefire way to keep people from recognizing her in a small Texas town. "Don't worry. I have the best disguise ever. I'll use it tonight."

Carter had showered and dressed in twenty minutes, then spent the rest of the time waiting for Macy in his office while going over the payroll accounts. He checked his watch just as his stomach complained. Macy was taking longer than the hour she'd asked for and patience wasn't his best virtue, especially when he was hungry.

Carter got to thinking about his marine buddy, Roark Black,

and wondered what the hell kind of trouble he was in. He hadn't received another text from him yet, so yesterday Carter decided to text him to let him know he'd contacted Ann Richardson about the Gold Heart Statue. He'd kept his message vague, but it was enough to let Roark know he'd done what he'd asked. Whatever his friend was caught up in, he hoped to high heaven Roark would find his way out safely.

When Carter heard voices in the parlor, he rose from his desk abruptly. "Finally."

He strode out of his office, his mind now on Pit's Blue Plate Special, a slab of ribs coated with whiskey sauce, mashed potatoes and creamed corn along with the best darn buttermilk biscuits in the whole county. He could almost taste it already. When he reached the door to the great room, he stopped up short.

A woman dressed in a soft paisley blouse tucked into a tan skirt and tall leather boots stood speaking with his cousin Brady. The woman's back was to him, but her long hair hung down her back straight and smooth, parted down the middle. The two were laughing, and Carter thought for a moment that he'd interrupted a private conversation.

What was Brady doing here?

His cousin hadn't noticed him. His attention was focused solely on the woman.

Then Carter realized his mistake. That wasn't just some woman. It was Macy. And she was having a grand time with Brady. The devil of it was that Brady was enjoying her attention, *too much*.

Carter's gut clenched and emotion poured over him like hot oil. When Macy turned his way, she tilted her head slightly, acknowledging him. "Here's Carter now."

He blinked and shook his head. He couldn't believe the transformation. Macy looked like an entirely different woman with stick-straight hair. Every curl was gone, replaced by a plank of black hair tied loosely with a band at her nape. She'd done something to her face, too, drowning out her natural color with makeup or something.

Brady shot him a grin, and Carter wasn't proud of the jealousy bouncing around inside. He couldn't forget the reason for Jocelyn's rejection: she'd loved Brady and not him. And now, seeing Brady and Macy smiling together was like a shot through his heart. Shouldn't be so. He didn't have feelings for Macy.

But he'd be lying if he said he wasn't attracted to her.

Kissing her had convinced him of that.

But jealousy?

"Brady, what are you doing here?"

Macy's eyes went wide from his directness, but Brady took it in stride. "I'm on my way out of town. Thought I'd stop by to meet your houseguest. As you can see, Macy and I have already met."

"Yeah, I can see that." Carter stepped farther into the room. "You had me fooled for a second," he said to Macy. "I almost didn't recognize you."

She touched the hair at the base of her neck. "It's my secret weapon. I can't straighten my hair too often. People will catch on. But now seemed like the perfect time."

She reached into her handbag and slipped on eyeglasses. "They're magnifiers, so items might appear larger," she said, darting a glance at both men, keeping her eyes above their waists, but the innuendo was there. Carter wasn't sure if Macy was teasing or flirting. Or had it been an innocent comment?

Brady chuckled. "Wow, Macy. You're a trip."

Macy laughed with him. "I'm told."

Carter's lips tightened.

"Come on, Carter. You have to admit, no one will know it's me."

Carter stepped closer and took her arm gently. "I'm starving. Are you ready? Or do you have anything else to add to your disguise?"

"Not a one. I think this will do."

"You two have fun." Brady walked outside with them and bid them goodbye.

Carter silently cursed at himself for being a jerk to his cousin, but he couldn't deny he had a protective streak when it came to Macy. But he was fighting other emotions, as well. He felt possessive of her, and seeing her with Brady just now nearly unraveled his good sense.

"He's nice," Macy said on the drive to the Bear Pit.

Carter turned to her. "He has his moments." He didn't want to spend the evening speaking about Brady's virtues. He still couldn't get over the way Macy looked. "It's hard to believe you're the same woman. You look like an Indian princess or something."

"It's the MAC makeup. It's what actors use. I put a dull matte finish on my face, but the only problem I have is with my eyes."

Carter couldn't help admiring them. "Nothing wrong there. They are the damnedest shade of violet I've ever seen."

"That's the problem. They're so unique, they can be a dead giveaway."

"The eyeglasses help."

"Let's hope. I'm hungry for some ribs." She rubbed her stomach, and Carter's gaze drifted to her clothes. In those boots and Western gear, she would fit right in at the Bear Pit.

For some reason, that made Carter extremely happy.

The place was a honky-tonk to the tenth degree and Macy loved it, right down to the sawdust on the floor. A live band played George Strait, Tim McGraw and Trace Adkins songs on a small stage at the opposite end of the large restaurant. She sat in a red vinyl booth facing Carter and tapped her boots to the beat. She ate barbecue ribs with gusto, chucking aside rules of etiquette and femininity.

"I told you, didn't I?" Carter said, wearing a satisfied grin. He was about as handsome as handsome gets, especially when those dimples appeared. *Especially* when his stomach was full of the Blue Plate Special and he was crowing about it.

"It's delicious. Just like you said." Macy finished half of her ribs and about the same of her mashed potatoes. She'd eaten one biscuit she swore was the size of a baseball. "I'm so full, I couldn't—"

The waitress slid a seven-layer chocolate cake in the middle of the table. "Bear's Bake, just as you ordered, Carter."

It was the biggest slice of cake Macy had ever seen.

Carter sent the waitress a smile and a wink. "Thanks, Jody."

The blonde woman's gaze stayed glued to him. She ignored Macy as if she wasn't sitting across from him. Normally, she would be relieved to go unnoticed, but her behavior bordered on insulting. "Haven't seen you here in a long while."

"Too long," Carter said. "I won't let that happen again."

"See that you don't." Finally, she gave Macy a cursory glance, then shot Carter a sweet look. "This one doesn't mind getting her hands dirty. Or her clothes. I like that."

Carter had a belly laugh over that, and the waitress took off.

"What?" Macy didn't like being the butt of a private joke.

Carter didn't say a word, but a quick glimpse to her chest had her looking down.

A loud gasp escaped when she spotted a big round barbecue stain on her paisley blouse. "Oh no!" Some of the greasy sauce had also dripped onto her chest, right between her breasts.

"Just sit tight," Carter said. He moistened a napkin and leaned way over the table to dab at her blouse. He was close, taking his time with the scrubbing. His face came inches from hers, and she breathed in his lime aftershave. It was intimate, how he was touching her, and goose bumps erupted on her arms. Then he moved his attention to her chest, and her skin prickled underneath the napkin as he gently stroked her. She drew a deep breath, which managed to fill out her chest. He stared at the stain for a moment then lifted his face a fraction, his eyes blazing hot as he looked at her. He took a hard swallow. There was a flash of awareness, a hunger that had nothing to do with food. They stared at each other a long moment.

"Can't get it all off," he said quietly.

"Not for lack of trying," she whispered.

His eyes roved over her breasts with unabashed admiration. "It wasn't a hardship."

Her words slipped out, countering his attention. "For me, either."

The band played a slow ballad, and Carter rose from his seat.

He came to stand beside her at the table, and she faced his out-stretched hand. "Dance with me?"

She was a mess of whiskey-sauce stains, but it wasn't enough to stop her from dancing with Carter McCay. She slipped her hand in his and followed him toward the music. Once on the saw-dusted wooden dance floor, he turned to face her, his eyes heavy lidded as he drew her against him. He curved his arms around her waist and she clung to his neck.

They began moving, gently rocking to the rhythm. There were ten other couples slow dancing. "I like this song," Carter whispered in her ear.

Macy laid her head on his chest. "Hmm. I think it's my favorite, too." It wasn't a lie. It was *going* to be her favorite from now on.

Carter moved with grace, swaying back and forth in tune to the rhythm of the music, and Macy followed easily, her boots gliding across the floor. She wished she could bottle this moment and pretend they were in a cocoon of time, where nothing and no one could interrupt them. She would get lost, never wanting to be found.

"Truth is, Hollywood," he said in a low rasp, his breath warm against her throat, "I don't dance much."

"You're doing fine."

"Maybe I just wanted to hold you."

"I won't complain."

"You're easy to be with."

"I can be a pain."

He chuckled, and she felt the vibration of it rumble through his chest. "I'm not touching that comment."

"It's good that you don't. What did the waitress mean, 'This one doesn't mind getting her hands dirty'?"

Carter spoke close to her ear. "Jody has a big mouth sometimes. It's not important."

Macy pulled back to look into his hazel eyes. "I'd like to know. I mean, the woman insulted me."

"Trust me. She really didn't mean anything by it. It's just Jody."

"You're not going to tell me?" She should just be quiet and enjoy the dance.

His lips quirked. "Is this you…being a pain?"

She lowered her head and looked over the top of her fake eyeglasses. "I'm not even trying."

Carter grinned, and those deep dimples came out. They were *his* secret weapon, whether he knew it or not.

Her lips formed a pout. She couldn't help it. Her curiosity was killing her despite Carter's charm.

He regarded her with a closed-off expression, then finally said, "It was about Jocelyn. She didn't like it here. The last time we came, she sort of kicked up a fuss about the food and the service."

"Whoops. Sorry I asked." Macy really put her foot in it. Jocelyn was a sore subject with Carter.

He pulled Macy close and crushed her breasts, sauce stains and all, into his chest. It was absolutely the place she wanted to be. His lips formed words against her throat. "I don't want to talk about her anymore."

Her breath caught. She managed a throaty, "O-kay."

"Fact is, darlin', I'd rather not talk at all."

She couldn't argue with that or anything else. Her bones were melting.

He lifted her chin with his thumb, looked into her eyes and shut her up for good with a slow, sensual, heart-stopping kiss.

When the dance was over, Macy guiltily looked around to see if she was being gawked at. Carter had kissed her as if he meant business, right there on the dance floor. But the people at the Bear Pit didn't seem to take notice. Not one bit. If was as if bone-melting kisses were an everyday occurrence or something. Maybe they were.

But not for Macy.

Carter took her hand when the band started playing a rockabilly tune and led her off the dance floor to the table. They stood by their booth and stared at the huge slice of chocolate cake sitting front and center, like a creamy edible centerpiece. "You want cake?"

"No thanks. I've already had my dessert." She glimpsed his mouth.

He blinked.

"If you want some, go ahead. Please," she said.

He picked up his hat from the booth's seat and flicked his fingers over the brim, brushing it off. And then he shifted his attention to her, his eyes a dark, daring blaze. "Cake isn't what I want right now."

Macy took a gulp of oxygen, her nerves a mass of tingles, and asked softly, "What do you want, Carter?"

Music blared in the background. The floor got rowdy with foot-stomping Texans and their girls. She wasn't Carter's girl, but for a moment back there on the dance floor, it sure felt as if she was. She waited for his answer. He wasn't a man she could deny. If he wanted her, she would go willingly.

A tick worked his jaw and he ran a hand through his hair, making the ends curl up at his collar. He did that, she noticed, when he was trying to make a decision. He drew a breath and regret singed his eyes. Then he tossed his hat back onto the booth's bench and sat down. "On second thought, maybe I will have some cake." He gestured for her to sit down. "C'mon, try it. It's like nothing you've ever tasted before in your life."

*Wanna bet?* Disappointed, Macy lowered herself into the booth. She wouldn't press Carter. He needed space and freedom. He'd kissed her like a man who hadn't been heavily involved with a woman just weeks ago, but that was the point, wasn't it? That kiss was more about forgetting Jocelyn than it was about his desire for Macy.

Her heart ached. Carter was an amazing man, and she wanted him more and more every day. She knew nothing would come of it in the long run. Macy had a life in Los Angeles, or rather a home, but she didn't have direction. She needed that more than anything else. Now that her debts were paid, her hope was that her absence in Hollywood would cause the buzz about her to die down. When she returned, she'd like some peace of mind to find her place. She needed to carve out a future, somehow.

But she had time. She'd promised herself she wouldn't worry

about *later* when she could be living in the *now*. That's why she came to Wild River in the first place.

Well, that and because she couldn't imagine refusing the gorgeous Texan his offer.

"Okay, Carter. Lay it on me. I'll bite."

His brows rose and he laughed as he cut her a ginormous piece of chocolate cake. He slid it over to her. "It's heaven on a plate."

She picked up her fork and dug in. The cake went down creamy and silky smooth. It was the second-best thing she'd tasted tonight. She let out a contented sigh and sent him a smile. "Mmm...you're wrong. It's heaven in *Texas*."

Carter leaned back in his seat and folded his arms across his middle, giving her a smug, satisfied look. "You got that right."

She did. Only, Macy wasn't speaking about chocolate cake.

After last night with Carter, Macy had a ton of nervous energy. She'd rationalized in that his backing off from her was for the best, but her heart said other things. So today, Macy poured herself into her work at the inn, and it was doing the trick. She thought about Carter only every hour or so.

"You are pathetic, Macy," she muttered as she walked the upstairs hallway.

She poked her head inside the bedroom she was planning on decorating next. This one needed furniture, an armoire and a headboard, at the very least. She'd flipped through catalogs, but nothing jumped out at her. She wanted something special and authentic, antiques from the area, to finish off the room.

The room dimmed and Macy stole a glance out the window. Threatening gray clouds moved in and filled the sky. The air cooled down. She crossed her arms and rubbed away a slight shiver. "Better pack up," she said. She'd been warned about fast-moving Texas storms.

Rocky, the traitor, had already left. Seemed the dog loved her to pieces, until dinnertime. He'd trotted back to the main house an hour ago, led by his tremendous appetite. She'd already had break time with Bill Fargo. He'd told her a funny story about his youth while they munched on cheese and crackers.

Darkness was descending quickly. A loud clap of thunder made her jump. "Oh!"

There was a sudden flash. Then the power went out.

Macy stood alone in the dark. She shivered again then attempted to make her way out of the bedroom. There was no light, and she knocked her shoulder into the doorjamb. "Ouch!"

She rubbed away the pain on her shoulder, trying to get her bearings, waiting for her eyes to adjust to the dark.

Another clap of thunder struck, louder this time.

A noise from downstairs jerked her to attention. She froze, listening. She heard rustling and hoped it was a tree brushing the window. Glass broke. The sound rang out in her ears. Another bang erupted and glass splintered again.

It was raining and the wind wheezed slightly, but it wasn't strong enough to break a window.

Someone was out there. Trying to break in.

Macy stood paralyzed with fear, defenseless.

This wasn't happening, her mind screamed.

She heard a man's voice, raspy and old, cursing. Someone was really downstairs.

Macy's entire body shook now. She couldn't stop it, but she knew she had to do something. She took a step back into the room, felt for the door, her arms flailing out, searching. Finally, once she made contact, she closed the door as quiet as a mouse and leaned against it, sending up silent prayers.

Footsteps on the stairs brought more fear. She held her breath, panicked. What could she do? She had no weapon.

"Macy? Macy, are you up here?"

His voice broke through her fear, and her knees buckled with relief. "Carter! Oh, my God, Carter!"

A thin stream of light beamed under the doorway and then he was there, opening the door. Light poured in from the flashlight he held. She squinted and saw a look of genuine concern on his face. He dropped the flashlight to the ground and grabbed her waist, folding her into his arms. "Macy, darlin', are you okay?"

She shook uncontrollably and he tightened his hold on her. "I...d-don't kn-know."

"It's okay. It's okay," he repeated, kissing her forehead, her hair. "I'm here now. No one's going to hurt you."

Tears spilled down her cheeks. She couldn't stop shaking. "I w-was so scared."

"I know. I know." His voice was velvet, soft and warm and smooth. "Calm down, sweetheart. Calm down."

He freed one hand and used his fingers to pry something out of her hand. He brought it into the light. "A candlestick?" Admiration touched his voice. "I'm glad you didn't use it on me. Looks painful."

She couldn't laugh. She couldn't smile. She had grabbed the tall bronze weapon out of sheer panic at the last second. "D-don't let me go, Carter. Don't."

His lips came to that sensitive spot behind her ear. He murmured softly, his breath whispering over her skin. "Wasn't going to."

She didn't want to think about anything other than being with Carter, but she had to ask. She spoke in a hushed tone. "What happened out there? Does someone know I'm here?"

"It's not that, trust me."

"But how do you know?"

"I got a glimpse of him running away. Must've scared him off when I pulled up."

"I heard him cussing. He sounded...older," she said.

Carter searched her eyes and nodded. His voice was gruff yet reassuring at the same time. "It wasn't you he was after, Macy. Don't worry. He probably just wanted to get out of the rain. Fargo and Henry are out looking for him now. I have an idea who it was, and I've sent them in search. They'll report back to me later."

"Carter?"

"Shush, darlin'. It's all right."

"Shouldn't we call the police or sheriff or someone?"

Carter shook his head. "Not tonight. I'll take care of it in the morning."

He ran his hands down the sides of her body, his fingers splayed wide as he caressed her. Macy focused her attention on how good he made her feel. With him holding her, his strong

body acting like a shield to protect her, Macy could forget her
fear and concentrate solely on him. He murmured, soft and low
"You have no idea how much I want you right now."

Macy's body shook again, this time from the impact of his
sensual words. "I want you, too."

His eyes darkened and he reached up to pull the band out of
her hair. Then he dug his fingers into her long, natural curls and
spread her hair out, letting it fall past her shoulders. Her body
reacted to his touch and the pure lust she saw in his eyes as he
let the tresses flow through his hands. Her shaking stopped, re
placed by a surge of desire so strong, Macy couldn't speak the
words forming in her mind. She was overwhelmed with emo
tion and needed Carter more than she needed her next breath.

She stepped out of his arms a moment and he followed her
movements with intense interest. She untied the straps of her hal
ter top and let the material fall away. Her breasts were bared, and
the cool, damp air touched them. Carter's gaze was hot enough
to heat the entire house. Appreciation shone in his eyes, which
made her feel beautiful. She reached for his hand and brought
it to her mouth. She kissed his palm then stepped closer to him.
He didn't need any more encouragement.

He cupped her breast with one hand and filled his palm. He
looked at her as he stroked his thumb over the extended tip. She
closed her eyes. She was truly in heaven.

Then he brought his mouth down over her other breast, and
she let go a tiny sigh. He moistened her nipple and made it peak,
his tongue circling until she ached from dire need. Her body
flamed, the heat spiraling down below her waist. She tossed her
head back, lengthening her frame. He kissed her again and again,
finding her shoulder, first one then the other. He moved his lips
to her throat, planting tiny moist kisses there, working his way
up her chin, until he finally took her in a long, sensual tongue
to-tongue kiss that brought with it only one inevitable finale.

"Take me, Carter," she breathed between his kisses.

"Planning to, darlin'," he murmured, his breathing heavy.
The palm of his hand flattened on her breast, applying sweet
exquisite pressure.

She had to touch him, to bare his body to hers. She needed him, desperately. There was no holding back, no time for modesty or coyness. She straightened and began unfastening the snaps to his shirt. It was easy pulling them apart. He helped her get his shirt off and then…then she laid her hands flat on the solid, powerful wall of his chest. Muscles bunched underneath her fingers. He was ripped, perfectly sculpted with definition, and damp from his jaunt in the rain. To save her.

A powerful shudder racked her body.

"Wow," she whispered.

"Give me a few minutes before you say that." A rumble of laughter rose up his chest and quaked under her palms. Carter found her amusing, but she found him nothing but stunning.

He reached for the zipper of her jeans and made fast work of undressing her. Once she was clear of pants and panties, Carter drew her up against him again and pressed his hand between her legs. Electric jolts shot through her as he stroked her most sensitive area. She brought her mouth to his chest and kissed him, wanting to bring him pleasure, too, but his forceful, demanding touch was no match for her mere kisses.

She squeezed her eyes closed and rode the building wave.

He grabbed the back of her head, brought her mouth to his and filled her with a lusty kiss. He whispered over her lips, "Let go, sweetheart."

She moved with him now, standing beside the bed, the rain ravaging outside and Carter doing the same to her inside. Her breaths came up short, her gasps closer together. She couldn't take another second of the toe-curling, heat-inducing spasms.

She broke apart, her body releasing in sharp, shattering tremors. Carter held her tight while she exploded with pleasure in his arms.

It took a minute to come down from the precipice. Everything felt better, clearer, fresher, and she'd never been happier.

Carter kissed her cheek and spoke into her ear. "*Now* you can say it."

She smiled wide and said softly on a sigh, "Wow."

He grinned and picked her up. She wrapped her arms about

his neck, and he carried her a few steps to the new bed that had been delivered just yesterday. "It's time to initiate this bed."

He lowered her down carefully, and her head came to rest on a pillow sham. His gaze traveled over the length of her slowly, lazily, perusing every slight curve. "You're...beautiful."

She smiled. She felt beautiful. "You have to say that. I'm naked."

"I'm not lying," he said quietly, and the solemn look in his eyes made her believe him.

She was ready for round two. She'd go ten rounds with Carter and not be sorry. She wanted him. Wanted to bring him the same pleasure he'd just given her.

"Take off your clothes, McCay."

"Those words," he said, unbuckling his belt, "are music to my ears."

She'd felt his erection through his clothes when he held her, but nothing prepared her for the sight of Carter McCay naked and aroused.

She gulped down her compliments. Her mouth went totally dry. He approached the bed, laying one knee onto the mattress. She reached for him, her hand wrapping around the silky, thick member. "May I?" she asked, though she was pretty sure of his answer.

"Darlin', you have free reign to touch me anywhere. Any *time*." He shot her a look so intense, she trembled.

"G-good to know," she said. She covered him and slid her hand up and down, felt the pulsing need and the shaft thicken even more. She watched Carter's expression change, saw the lust in his eyes as she stroked him. It was surreal. A few weeks ago, she would never have guessed she'd be making love to a strong, gorgeous cowboy hunk of man and bringing him intense pleasure.

Her stroking accelerated. Carter's eyes closed tight. She was turned on from arousing him, and her body ached now. She wanted him inside her. She wanted to be covered by him.

Carter groaned and gripped her hand. He stilled her, and she knew then he was close.

"I have protection," he said, finding his jeans and coming up with it.

Of course he did.

Thank goodness. Macy hadn't thought about it. Not once.

He was ready for her now and he joined her on the bed, kissing her mouth and fondling her body again, making sure she was ready.

She was so ready.

Carter came over her, his eyes on hers, and he nudged her between the legs. "Open again for me, sweetheart," he commanded.

"It's been a long while, Carter," she warned.

"I won't hurt you."

She knew that. It wasn't what she meant. She was out of practice.

He reassured her with a kiss and entered her body with a slow, precise thrust. She welcomed him with all she had. It was heaven all over again.

Carter made love to her like a man on a mission to please. They were in tune with each other, their bodies perfectly aligned.

His thrusts grew stronger, harder, Macy accommodating him with each movement. His release came fast and hard. She toppled over the edge, seeing him arch above her, still his body then thrust once more with an erotic groan of completion. She came with him and they filled the room with moans of intense satisfaction.

It was good...so good.

Carter lowered himself to lay atop her slightly askew to allow her breathing room. He kissed her and she wove her hands through his hair. The dark blond locks, thick and long, curled at his nape, and she relished the freedom to touch him. He was her sexy cowboy for the night.

He'd rescued her once again.

They lay quietly for a while, Macy speechless, for once. She didn't know what to say to him. She didn't know how this changed their relationship, if at all.

"Wow," Carter said. It wasn't a word he'd ever used, and she wondered if he was teasing her.

"I agree. Guess fear of death is a pretty hefty aphrodisiac."

Carter lifted up on his elbows to look into her eyes. His musky scent surrounded her. She drew it into her lungs and savored it. "I wouldn't let anything happen to you."

"How'd you know I was in danger?" she asked softly, running her hands through his hair. Once she'd gotten free reign, she couldn't get enough.

"I, uh, came to bring you home for dinner."

That surprised her. She tilted her head in question. "Why?"

"It was getting late."

"I've stayed late before and missed dinner."

"Yeah, well. That's going to change now."

He kissed her quiet and Macy got the hint.

Carter had made his decision, and the time for talking was over.

# Eight

Midnight pranced around the corral, kicking up mud leftover from the night's storm. Now, sunshine warmed the morning air and began drying the earth. Carter squinted and lowered the brim of his hat to block out the glare. He was up as early as usual, but instead of going into his office, he'd come outside to clear his head. The rain last night had washed away sweltering heat and brought freshness to the air that did him good as he inhaled deep.

He'd always liked this time of morning, just after dawn, when the world was full of peace. He could sit here and watch the new colt take instruction from his mama for hours. It was as it should be, the parent actually parenting the child.

He'd come a long way since those days growing up in the shack on the other side of town, his mama gone and the foul smell of whiskey tainting the room. His life was good now. He worked hard, used the smarts God gave him and made enough money for five lifetimes.

He should be satisfied with that and he would be, but that break-in last night rankled his good nature. He'd had to rein in his fury for Macy's sake.

She'd been scared out of her wits, and he couldn't blame her. He'd invited her here, promised to give her solitude and peace, but instead she'd been tormented by an intruder.

"Hey, McCay. Want some coffee?"

Carter smiled at the sound of her sassy voice and turned to see Macy coming out of the house with two steaming mugs in hand. Coal-black curls framed her face and fell in wild disarray down her back. Her eyes, free of makeup, looked brilliantly clear in the light. She wore a red-and-blue plaid robe and leather boots. He had to smile at that. The Hollywood starlet looked pretty at dawn and too much as if she fit in around here.

His heart did a little flip watching her glide toward him, and he passed it off as sexual contentment. Last night, they'd made love twice before he'd driven her back to the house. As they approached her room, she'd paused by her door, lifting hesitant eyes his way as if unsure of his intentions. Carter had gripped her hand tighter and led her to his room. She'd gone willingly, and she'd slept through the night curled next to him. He'd wanted her to feel safe, but it didn't end there. She'd gotten under his skin, and he wanted her in his bed for the remainder of her stay at Wild River. "Sure, wouldn't refuse coffee from a gorgeous woman."

A smile spread over her face as she sidled up next to him and carefully handed him a cup. "You're up early."

"I was about ready to come join you in bed."

She snapped her head up, her eyes wide, and then whispered in a hushed tone, "Should I go back inside?"

The sexy morning lilt of her voice did things to him.

"I wouldn't want to disappoint you," she added.

"Doubt you could do that." Carter slid his arm around her waist and pulled her close. She went willingly, coffee cup balanced in one hand. He nuzzled her neck, roving his lips over her throat and tasting her sweet skin once again. He glanced around the yard. His ranch hands hadn't begun working yet. With no one in sight, he brought his mouth to hers and took her in a long, lingering kiss.

She made a little throaty sound, a sexy moan reminding him

of the hot night they'd spent making love at the inn, and Carter cursed under his breath. He wanted her again.

Last night, when she'd been in danger, his protective instincts took hold. He'd been more concerned about Macy than catching the intruder. Afterward, he couldn't seem to let her go. He'd caved in to his lust. Macy had intrigued him from the moment he'd laid eyes on her on that New York street, and last night was the culmination of temptation and raw desire.

The mare whinnied and they both turned their attention to the horses. Carter sipped coffee. "Watch the colt. He's something." Midnight parading around the arena, strutting, sniffing and mimicking his mother, made for great entertainment.

"He's wonderful," she said, and it touched Carter how sincerely awed she was witnessing something Carter could easily take for granted.

"You sleep okay?" he asked.

She nodded. "Thanks to you. I'm not a wimp usually, but I was pretty scared last night."

Carter's gut tightened and he swore silently. "I'll see to it that never happens again."

"How?" she asked.

Carter kept his focus on the horses. This wasn't an easy thing to admit, and it took him a few seconds to force the words out. "I'm ninety-nine percent sure I know who broke into the inn last night. It was my father."

"Your father? Oh, Carter. No."

He ground his teeth. "I'm afraid so. He's got this fool notion that he should be overseeing the inn. Even though I banished him, after what happened the last time. He was probably all boozed up. I'm so damn mad that he scared you, I could spit."

Macy's expression softened. Sympathy touched her eyes. "I'm so sorry."

"Don't be. It's expected. He's never going to change."

"Don't say that. Don't give up on him."

"I'm afraid it's too late for that. Not only is he checked off my list, after how he scared you last night, he's disappeared from it. Poof. Just like that, he's gone. I'm done with him."

Macy's lips formed a tight pout. "It's heartbreaking to hear you say that. Your father needs your help."

"You want me to *help* him?" He began shaking his head. "No way."

His brain wouldn't go there. Not after what his father had put him through. Not after he'd sent his mother to an early grave and almost killed Rocky in that fire. Fathers were supposed to raise their children, not the other way around. "He doesn't deserve it, Macy."

Macy set her coffee cup down on a post, making sure it didn't teeter, before she turned to him, her voice firm. "Everyone deserves another chance."

"He's used up his quota of chances." Carter gulped coffee too fast. It burned his throat on the way down. "Damn it."

"Carter," Macy pressed, "you can't just give up on him."

"I can. I have." He didn't want to have this conversation right now. "But you should know, it's not for lack of trying. I've spent years trying to clean that man up. It's impossible."

Macy looked toward the corral. She pretended to watch the horses, but he could see her mind was a million miles away. Then softly, as if she were speaking on a breeze, she said, "Maybe if someone took my father by the scruff of his collar and shook some sense into him, he'd be alive today."

Carter glanced at her profile, the stubborn slant of her delicate chin. Macy still ached from her father's death. Maybe she was feeling guilty for not intervening with him. Or maybe she'd just wanted to make a point. But her situation was different. She'd been a young girl when her father died. Carter had put up with his father's antics for his entire life. People got hurt and lives were damaged.

"You don't know the facts, Macy. And I'm not about to spill my guts to ease your guilt. Just drop it."

She whipped around to face him, a spark of defiance in her eyes. "I'm not trying to ease my guilt. I have no guilt. Just regret. And you're being bullheaded!"

Carter kept his gaze trained on her. He wasn't going to let her get involved in this. His patience was shot to hell. He raised his voice. "I'm telling you how it's going to be. It's none of your business."

"So, you're saying butt out?"

"Bingo, you win the prize." He winced at his harsh tone, but he wouldn't back down.

She stared at him for the longest time, then grabbed the mug from his hand, lifted hers from the post and then twirled around. Marching toward the house, she held her head high and mighty as if she was right and he was the fool who couldn't see it.

Damn it. They'd just had their first argument, and it was about his *father*. If that didn't take the cake, he didn't know what did.

It sure wasn't the way Carter wanted to start the morning.

Bill Fargo was a wise old goat, clean-cut and stately and just the type of man Carter would have liked to have for a father. It still plagued him why the man wanted to work at Wild River Ranch for a modest wage, when it was obvious he could be holding down a more lucrative job. But Carter wasn't going to look a gift horse in the mouth. Whatever the reasons, he was glad to have Bill.

"I came in early to explain what happened last night," Fargo said after Carter let him into his office.

"We spoke on the phone last night. That's enough for me." Carter leaned against the edge of his desk, offering Fargo a seat, but the old guy decided to stand.

Fargo rubbed the back of his neck. "I appreciate that, but I take pride in my work and I'd feel better you hearing it from me in person."

"Okay." It was a fair plea.

Fargo's brows gathered as he recalled the incident. "I'd just checked on Macy about ten minutes before it started storming. I had driven clear across the other end of the property when the rain came down hard. Soon as it hit, I turned the truck around to get her and bring her back to the main house."

"Did you see the intruder trying to break in?"

"No. When I got there, I noticed the broken window first, and that's when you drove up. I think we spotted him at the same time.

He took off running into the brush. You told me to go after him while you checked on Macy. I lost sight of him in the darkness, and by the time I got to the truck he was gone. I searched for an hour but couldn't find him. I'd first thought it might be a youngster thinking the place was abandoned, wanting to get in out of the rain. But what I saw changed my mind. It wasn't a boy but a man, and he wasn't so much fast as he was cagey. He could have been close to my age. You said you thought you knew who it was."

Carter tensed. Every time he thought about his old man, his nerves jangled. He'd never make Father of the Year, but was staying on the right side of the law too much to ask? "Yeah, unfortunately I do. It was my father, Riley McCay. It's an old song I won't sing again, but he won't be bothering Macy or coming onto the property again. I paid him a little visit today. Not that his word is any good, but my old man has managed to stay out of jail all these years. He knows that'll change if he's spotted on my property again. Next time, he'll be hauled in by the law."

Confronting his father hadn't been pleasant, but it had been necessary. Carter cursed himself silly for feeling sorry for the guy after he'd left his father's place.

Fargo's eyes narrowed and his face slanted in a thoughtful expression. "You've had a tough childhood."

The spot-on assessment surprised him. "You think I'm bitter?"

Fargo shook his head and spoke with sincerity. "Not at all. The truth is the truth, and it's not always pretty. I've had my share of bad experiences, so let me say this, no one should judge you or what you do, because they don't know what you've gone through in your life. And I bet you've been the adult in that relationship since you were a boy."

Carter stared at Fargo and then smiled. Yep, he *was* a wise old goat. "Can't argue that point. You know the saying, what doesn't kill you makes you stronger."

Fargo laid sympathetic eyes on him. "You got strong pretty fast, I'd say."

Carter sighed and leaned back, painfully admitting, "Not fast enough."

Fargo acknowledged him with an understanding nod.

"Macy thinks I'm too hard on him," Carter confessed. It felt pretty darn good releasing his frustration and the emotions he'd bottled up inside. Just being able to say these things aloud gave him some measure of relief. He felt he could trust Fargo with his thoughts. Man, was he looking for a father figure or what?

"And Macy's opinion is important to you?"

Carter had to think about that a second. He wasn't sure what Fargo was getting at, but he knew that after making love with her, the last thing he wanted was to hurt her. He still felt it wasn't any of her business, yet it was hard for him to admit that he should have held his tongue. After all, she'd given him the best night of sex he'd had in a long while. Then he'd turned on her. He felt like a heel. "She's told you about her father, right? He died as a result of his drinking."

"And you think she's transferring that situation onto yours?"

Carter lifted away from the desk and shrugged, his impatience getting the best of him. "Hell, I don't know. Maybe."

"Seems to me that you might want to straighten things out with her."

Carter's stubborn nature wouldn't have allowed that before this conversation, but Fargo made him realize that he owed Macy an apology. Her opinion did matter. He cared what she thought about him.

An hour later, Carter strode out of his office with a plan. The air was warm, the sun still bright as he walked with purpose to the inn on foot, trying to clear his head of Jocelyn's duplicity, his father's latest antics and his feelings for Macy.

Halfway there, Rocky joined him, coming from the direction of the inn, his tail wagging and his body twisting in jubilation. "Hey, boy." Carter bent to give him a pat on the head. The dog lifted up, pawing at his thighs, begging for more attention. "I hear you there. Is Macy giving you the cold shoulder, too? Nah, she wouldn't do that to you. I'm the only dog she's mad at."

Rocky was rewarded with more attention, then fell in step with Carter as they approached the inn. It didn't take him but a second to find Macy. She was standing in the center of the gazebo, rehearsing lines. He couldn't hear what she was saying, but her gestures were fluid, sincere and emotional. Through her actions and expressions, Macy managed to convey a powerful story. Carter watched her and wondered why she'd never made it big as an actress. She had the looks and the talent. It was part of her DNA, he figured, being the child of two multitalented parents.

He'd be a fool to ever think she belonged in his world of cattle auctions, small-town life and simple pleasures. Sure, Carter had wealth. He'd built an empire and had money to burn, but down deep inside, he was still a country boy. He liked rodeos, John Wayne Westerns and eating apple pie at the county fair.

Before he lost sight of his mission and talked himself out of apologizing, Carter stepped up to the gazebo. Macy had been so deep in character, she hadn't noticed him until Rocky gave three short, quick barks of greeting.

She froze in place when she finally noticed him.

Those violet eyes did a number on him. Something powerful surged through his system.

"You caught me in the act," Macy said, trying damn hard to keep her voice haughty, but the glow in her eyes gave her away.

"You're good."

"I'm…fair."

"You had me fooled then."

"I wasn't trying to fool anyone. I was trying to be convincing."

The conversation was going down fast. Carter climbed up the first step and produced one single, healthy stargazer lily he'd been holding behind his back. "For you."

She blinked then and the corners of her pretty mouth lifted. "It's my favorite."

Mara had told him today and he'd made a quick trip into town to get her a bouquet, but his housekeeper had informed him that one single stem would have more meaning. He'd never figure out a woman's mind, but he had taken Mara's advice.

Macy fingered the pink petal. "How did you know?"

"I have my ways," he said. "I'm here to apologize for barking at you this morning."

She remained quiet, her head down, gazing at the flower. "Okay."

"I was harsh and I shouldn't have been."

She lifted her lashes and spoke softly, "You're right. It's none of my business, but I wanted—"

"To help. I know. You can't, and I won't change my mind. But I'm asking you to forgive me for taking you to task for it."

She tilted her head to the right and made a pretty picture, standing there in her white flowing blouse and blue jeans, her hair down in curls.

"How can I not forgive you? You gave me my favorite lily."

She smiled then and Carter took her hand and pulled her into his arms. Her body felt perfect enveloped in his, and he could easily work up a reason to drag her off to bed. But his apology wasn't over. "I have a peace offering," he said.

Her eyes fluttered and she peeked at his mouth from under her lashes. It was too much to resist. Carter lifted her chin with the pad of his thumb and lowered his head a fraction of an inch to her mouth. "This isn't it," he said, taking her in a kiss he'd been thinking about all day. As soon as their lips touched it was like floodgates opening. She was soft, sexy and eager when she returned his kiss, their bodies contouring and melding together in a natural fit.

Her lips parted and he drove his tongue into her mouth. Her sweet, erotic taste traveled down to the pit of his stomach. Kissing her was like a potent drug. He wanted more. He cupped her head and kissed her again, raking his hands over her slender body, caressing her shoulders and running his palms along the swells of her breasts. She squirmed with desire and whimpered a plea. No one was more surprised than Carter when he backed away, breaking off the heady, sex-inducing contact. He wanted her, no doubt. But he had more to say.

"I want to take you out tonight."

Macy gulped air. Her eyes lifted to his, heavy lidded and hazy. "Wh-what?"

"I want to take you on a date."

Her chest rose and fell in deep breaths, and Carter found himself staring.

With knitted brows, she repeated, "You want to take me on a date?"

"That's right. Tonight. I have reservations in Dallas at a first-class restaurant. I reserved a private room. It's part of my apology, so take care when you give me your answer."

"But...why?"

He shrugged and wouldn't divulge the half a dozen reasons in his head. He didn't want to admit them to himself, much less to her. "Why not?"

Her expression changed from confusion to determination, and she put the biggest smile on her face. "I'd love to go. Yes."

He felt a ripple of anticipation zigzag through his body. Then, almost as soon as she accepted, a frown appeared on her face and her brows knitted together. "But, Dallas?" she asked on a worried sigh. "We could be seen."

Carter shook his head. "We won't be." He lifted a lock of her hair. The natural wave wisped around his finger. He liked Macy best this way, curly haired and natural, but when she became that sleek, straight-haired woman, she was equally as beautiful and almost unrecognizable. "We'll stay overnight. In the morning, we'll stop at some small towns on the way back and—" he winced at the notion "—we'll shop for furniture for the inn."

Macy's eyes blazed brilliant lavender-blue. She was a dead giveaway when she was pleased. "Really?"

"I don't do anything half-assed, Hollywood. My apology rocks," he said, kissing her one last time. "Admit it."

Her chin went up ready to deny it, but then she had a change of heart. "You got me there, Carter. It's the best apology I've ever received."

Satisfied, Carter spoke quietly, "Be ready at six with your best disguise."

# Nine

It was worth all the trouble she went through to see Carter's eyes nearly pop out of his head when she entered the great room.

She wore red.

A sleek, bodice-clinging, low-cut crimson design that covered her thighs with only an inch to spare. She'd taken a good look at herself in the mirror, cringed at the daring dress and almost returned it to the closet. The Emilio Pucci had been a gift from her mother that Macy had brought with her to New York, as a keepsake to hold dear during the auction. But Macy had never tried it on. Until now.

Macy smiled as Tina's encouraging voice echoed in her ears. "Red's your color, honey. Wear it and knock their eyes out." Her mother had a knack for clothes and style and had never been out-done by her competition.

It had taken Macy a long time to straighten out her barrel curls, but she'd actually won the fight with the hair blower, and now it fell in a shimmering sheet down her back. Next, she'd dazzled her mouth with ruby-red lipstick and accented her cheekbones with bronzer. Her eyes she couldn't do much about. She didn't have colored contacts; she'd always thought they looked strange on people and drew attention rather than detracted from it.

Carter had been holding a large manila envelope in his hands, looking it over carefully, but the second he'd spotted her, he'd tossed it onto the sofa and approached her. "Wow," he said, mimicking her, a case of imitation being the best form of flattery. "Beautiful," he murmured with a gleam in his eyes.

"Thank you."

Yes, definitely worth all the trouble she went through.

It was like the pot calling the kettle black though. Carter, in a black Western suit coat and a white silk shirt, minus the tie earned him "wow" status, as well. "You're not looking too shabby tonight, either, McCay."

Carter puffed out his chest and winked. "I aim to please, ma'am." His hand to the small of her back, he asked, "Are you ready for a drive to the city?"

His touch curled her toes. "I am."

Carter had ushered her a few steps toward the door then stopped abruptly. "Wait." He turned and strode over to the legal-size envelope he'd tossed on the sofa. "I almost forgot. This came for you today."

"For me?"

He handed it over, and Macy stared at it.

"It's the first piece of mail that's come for you. Who knows you're here?"

"Just my friend Avery and my attorney. This is from him. Barton Lowenthal."

"Is it important?"

Macy was standing next to a dreamy man, ready to go out on the town. Nothing was more important than that right now. "No, it's just probably more legal documents about my mother's estate."

Macy set the envelope on the end table by the entry. "I can look at it later."

She turned her attention back to Carter, Stetson in hand, waiting for her by the door. Her life here at Wild River was so far removed from Hollywood that it was laughable. She understood that she was Carter's rebound woman—someone to make him forget about his almost-fiancée's rejection. They would have no real future together. Macy shouldn't forget that, but for tonight at least, she could pretend that all away.

On the drive to Dallas, Carter made small talk and tried his best to make up for the way he'd treated her this morning. She'd been hurt and properly put in her place, but she wasn't giving up on his relationship with his dad. She could be stubborn, too, when she had to be.

Carter kept taking his eyes off the road to look at her. She, too, was pulled by his magnetism, glancing at him in quiet moments, marveling at his good looks and confidence. Finally, halfway into the drive, he reached over and laid his hand on her leg, just above the knee. His touch sent spiraling tremors clear down to her belly. She forgot all about being stubborn. He made her forget everything but the desire pulsing like wildfire in her veins. His capable fingers applied pressure, and she broke out in goose bumps. She sucked in oxygen when he slid a hot hungry look her way. "I might not make it through dinner."

She gulped, and images of him covering her body flashed in her mind. She relived the heady sensations from last night and wanted more. She wanted Carter. "We could shoot straight for dessert."

A wicked smile graced his face. "I like the way you think, Hollywood. But I owe you a nice dinner." He sighed from deep in his chest and removed his hand from her leg.

She missed his touch already and wondered how she'd make it through dinner, too.

As promised, Carter had arranged for them to be ushered into a trendy new restaurant on the top floor of the Majestic Hotel by way of an employee elevator. The secrecy made the evening only more exciting. Soft music played as dinner was served in a cozy room with a private bar and dance floor.

After ordering filet mignon and spinach soufflé, they were served shrimp scampi appetizers and champagne salad. Macy picked at her food. Her appetite waned. Not even steaming-hot loaves of French bread whet her taste buds. She sipped red wine and focused on the man sitting across from her, looking dazzling and sexy.

Between courses, Carter asked her to dance, making every effort to make this date memorable. Macy curved her body to his as they moved in step with a romantic tune.

"How am I doing with my apology?" He tightened his arms around her, and she leaned her head on his shoulder.

"I've forgiven you for the next five things you're bound to do," she said with a breathy sigh.

He threw his head back and laughed. She loved the sound of it and the deep baritone of his voice. "You're sure I'll blow it again?"

"I'm giving you rain checks I'm so sure."

He tightened his hold on her and spoke quietly into her ear. "But, darlin', where's the fun in that?"

The warmth of his breath made her shiver. With his rock-hard body pressed against her and his musky scent surrounding her, she was swept up with consuming desire. The privacy and the intimate way he held her seemed to charge the air around them. She lowered her lashes to focus on his generous mouth.

Carter shook his head with a warning glint in his eye. "Keep that up and our meal will have to wait."

He brought his mouth to hers and took her in a breathtaking kiss. From there, things moved fast. The kiss that started slowly turned to a frenzied melding of lips with arms and legs reaching, adjusting, their bodies desperately searching for satisfaction and relief.

Carter squeezed her hand then and pulled her off the dance floor. "Grab your purse," he ordered as he led her to the table. She clutched it and he entwined her fingers and then tugged her out of the private restaurant. The trip in the special elevator to penthouse rooms was another hurried affair, and once Carter put the keycard into the lock, they ducked into the suite.

She glimpsed the luxurious room. "Nice pl—"

Carter kissed the words from her mouth and backed her up against the wall. He murmured all the things they were going to do in this room, and Macy's face flamed as hot as her body burned. The Pucci dress was an easy target for a man with roaming hands, and Carter made sure he touched every part of her. His sweet assault made her moan his name over and over, and she knew they'd never make it to the bed.

His kisses moved from her lips and down her throat, his chin pushing material away so that his mouth could cover her breast. She arched for him and closed her eyes to the sensual sensation. Then he rode his hand up her thigh, and within seconds her clingy dress was hiked up to her waist. Impatient, he groaned when his fingers met with her hot, wet center. He pleasured her and little moans of ecstasy huffed out of her throat.

It was a whirlwind from then on, Carter taking time only to sheath himself before he brought her the most exquisite, erotic, exciting sexual encounter of her life.

Afterward, she slumped against him breathless and sated from head to toe. "Is…that…all…you…got?"

A deep, satisfied chuckle rumbled from his throat before he lifted her into the circle of his arms and carried her to the bed. "Just wait, sweet darlin'. Just wait."

Macy woke to air-conditioning cooling the hotel room. She lay on a luxurious bed of silken sheets, completely naked with sunlight streaming into the suite. She reached for a plush comforter and met with Carter's hand. He brought the covers with him as he rolled toward her, setting his hand possessive and firm on her hip. Warmth seeped in immediately.

He kissed her cheek. "Mornin'."

"Mmm, morning." She gave him a smile, and her heart surged when his dimples appeared as he smiled back. She felt things for Carter that went beyond her simple fascination for a Stetson-wearing hunk. She cared for him, and heaven knew she admired him. But anything more than that would just be suicide on her part, a head-on collision waiting to happen.

"You still tired?" he asked, rubbing her hip in ways that sparked illicit thoughts. Last night, once they'd made it to the bed, Carter had shown her the stars of Texas without ever looking out the window.

"Not too tired to…shop." She grinned.

He flung himself onto his back and groaned. "I was afraid of that."

She gathered herself up, covers and all, turning to face him. "A promise is a promise, McCay. Not to mention it was part of your apology."

He studied her through thick lashes, his mouth angling down. "I thought maybe the two 'apologies' I gave you last night would do the trick."

He did have a persuasive argument. He'd given her two mind-bending orgasms last night. But, Macy *gave* as good as she got, and Carter knew it. They were evenly matched sexual partners. "You're not getting out of it, Carter. Cowboy up."

Carter's mouth opened then shut. He lifted up and grabbed her around the waist, bringing her down on top of him, tickling her until she giggled uncontrollably.

"No! No! Stop it…stop it!"

He stopped and his mouth spread into a big grin. "Don't ever say 'cowboy up' to a Texan. We invented the term." He kissed her then set her down beside him.

Macy's laughter finally ebbed and she sank deeper into the bed, gazing up at the ceiling. "You don't play fair."

Carter put his arm around her shoulder and brought her close. "I know. I like to win."

Winning was important to Carter. He'd worked hard to build a business and succeed without trampling anyone on the way up. He was honorable and decent. He had confidence and knew how to make everyone feel at home. Macy envied him a little, even though she admired him.

The room went silent, Macy deep in thought. "You know who you are, Carter McCay. I like that about you."

"You say that as if you don't know who you are."

"Sometimes… I'm not sure. I know I'm an actress by default, the daughter of a legendary screen star. It was sort of expected of me, more by the public than pressure from my parents. I know how to read lines from a script. Acting pays the bills." Except that now she was a two-time lawsuit victim who had paid off her debts and was flat broke. "But I have dreams I've never realized. Dreams that one day I'd love to come true."

Carter turned to her, seemingly intrigued. "Such as?"

She lifted a shoulder in a shrug. "I want to open a drama school for kids. I want to teach. It's what I know. Unlike my mother and father, I'm happier behind the scenes than on camera. And I love children."

"So, why not do that when you go back to Hollywood?"

His suggestion unnerved her. Raw pain worked its way to her belly and made her ache inside. Not that she'd expected an open invitation to live at Wild River, but she didn't want to think about leaving. She needed the respite and to continue whatever she had going with Carter for however long it lasted. At the moment, going home to Hollywood wasn't even on her radar. "I can't...not right now."

Carter became quiet, and his silence was another jolt to her nerves. He stared out the window, and every so often his eyes flickered with an emotion she couldn't name. "You're right," he said finally. "You don't have to make that decision right away."

They left it at that and checked out of the hotel an hour later.

On the way home Carter drove them to several local antiques shops bearing rusted signs outside and musty wood paneling inside, and together they perused furniture, looking for the best fit for the Wild River Inn.

They made their fifth stop at a little out-of-the-way shop off the highway called Addie's Antiques. Macy had to smile at Carter when they entered the place. He'd become really involved in the decorating process and walked straight over to the one selection Macy would have chosen.

"This armoire could be refinished." He studied the piece from the forties with chipped edges and a broken hinge but made from sturdy wood.

Macy examined it closely and nodded in agreement. "I love the footed legs and the way it curves like an *S*. It has just the character I'm looking for and would go perfectly in the third bedroom."

"Sold," Carter said to Addie, who turned out to be the twenty-something granddaughter of the original owner.

Usually when Carter McCay entered a room, female heads turned in his direction and they would repeatedly cast him admiring looks. But Addie kept her eyes trained on Macy nearly the entire time they were shopping. Her curious stares were making Macy a bit uneasy. Carter completed making the arrangements for the sale as Macy continued to browse. Afterward, the antiques dealer followed Macy outside to the dirt-paved parking lot and finally asked, "Excuse me, but have we met?"

Macy dreaded that question. She'd heard it a thousand times, and it usually led to someone figuring out who she was. Standing near Carter's expensive sports car, she wished they'd taken the Jeep, which garnered a lot less attention as they traveled through small towns. She sighed silently and shook her head. "No, I don't think so."

The girl's face contorted, as if trying to place her. "It's just that you look so familiar. You actually look like that actress—"

Carter came up beside Macy to kiss her cheek. "Hurry now, darlin'. You know our boys are gonna drive Mama to drink if we don't get on home soon."

Macy caught on right away. When Carter took her hand, Macy followed his lead. She sent Addie an apologetic look. "Sorry to rush off, but he's right. Toby and our little Kenny are a handful of mischief. It's hard for his mama to handle our boys on a good day, but our littlest one is teething, and well, you know how that can be."

Addie's expression wavered. "Oh, uh, not really. I don't have kids."

Carter opened the door for her, and Macy hurried inside and fastened her seat belt. Carter gave Addie a quick smile then got behind the wheel of the car, and the powerful engine roared to life. As they pulled away, Macy waved to the young girl. "Bye now!"

Carter drove down the road, leaving Addie standing there with an odd expression on her face. He slid Macy a sideways glance, his mouth twitching in amusement. "Toby and Kenny? Are those the names of our children?"

Macy let go a small rumble of laughter and then confessed

"They were the singers of the last two songs we heard on the radio."

"Ah," Carter said, still smiling. He reached for her hand and gave a little squeeze. "Fast thinking."

The sensation of his tender touch ripped through her. Her heart pounded as she envisioned holding Carter's sons in her arms. *Their sons.* Thinking like that could get her in trouble. But for a few seconds while leaving Addie's Antiques, the notion didn't seem so far-fetched. Then a thought struck. "She'll probably guess who I am anyway once she thinks about it. People usually do. And she knows where you live."

Carter shot her a smug look. "No, she doesn't. I paid cash and arranged for Henry to pick up the furniture."

Macy felt somewhat relieved. "Well, that was fast thinking, too."

She should have known Carter would have all angles covered, just in case. Not that Addie would go running to a tabloid just because she recognized her. Of course, if the antiques dealer had seen the internet news lately, she might realize that Carter McCay was the mysterious cowboy whom Macy Tarlington had run away with that New York night. There wasn't much she could do about it, but she hoped to prolong her anonymity a little while longer. If she was ever discovered here, the media would come down on Wild River with cameras blazing.

They spent the next few hours shopping and found a dresser, a side table, two lamps and a hammered-iron queen-size bed. Once again, Carter paid cash and arranged for the furniture pickup in order to protect Macy's identity.

As they arrived at the ranch, Carter announced matter-of-factly, "We're home."

Macy glanced at the beautiful ranch house as a sense of belonging settled into her system. It was a beautiful, tranquil place, despite the occasional pungent scent of cow dung and raw earth that wafted to the main house. Entrenching sadness stole over her and her heart dipped as she realized how much she loved living at Wild River. But Macy couldn't allow herself to think behind the here and now. This was Carter's home, *not hers*. She was a temporary guest, and she'd always be grateful to him for inviting her here. And for making her feel welcome.

"I think we made a lot of progress today," he said, turning to her as he parked the car.

She smiled at him, though her heart wasn't in it. He was speaking of furniture. Macy thought the progress went deeper than that. "I think we did, too," she replied softly. "I'm hoping it all fits in the rooms the way I envisioned it."

"It will." Carter leaned across the seat toward her, cupped her head and pulled her close until his lips were an inch away. "Hollywood, you're good at what you do." Then he took her in a long, sweet kiss.

Macy came up for air seconds later and stared at him. He was deadly handsome and hard to resist. Joy entered her heart just being near him, and it frightened her how quickly her feelings for him were developing. She tried for levity to keep those feelings at bay. "I'm good at spending your money."

He chuckled and kissed her again. "You're good at a lot of things," he murmured, nipping at her throat. "I wish I didn't have a dozen things going on today. You could show me more..."

Carter walked up the steps to the house, holding her hand. Macy was floating in a sea of contentment and couldn't remember another time she felt this happy. Carter brushed a quick kiss to her lips. "I've gotta talk to Henry and get some work done. I'll see you later, okay?"

When? How much later? she wanted to ask. He handed her overnight case to her. "Okay."

She'd spent the night and a good part of the day with him, and she already missed him. She watched him retreat, his strides long and confident as he headed toward the bunkhouse. He had an impressive backside with broad shoulders, a perfect butt and long legs fitted into faded blue jeans. Macy walked into the house just as Mara was coming out of the great room. She was holding the manila envelope Carter had shown her yesterday.

"Oh hi, Mara."

"Good afternoon." Mara's gaze went to the overnight bag in

her hand. Never one to pry, she didn't say a word, but the inquisitive look on her face said it all.

Mara had always been kind and nonjudgmental, and Macy missed having female companionship while at the ranch. She shrugged and smiled at the older woman. "We went on a…a shopping date," she explained. "We bought some beautiful antique pieces for the inn."

Mara's free hand went to her hip. She spoke with a charming Texas drawl. "I'm glad Carter's finally come around to renovating that place. If you influenced him in any way, *good for you.* Henry and I have been hinting for him to get that place up and running for quite some time. I remember when it shined. It was a looker back then."

"When I'm through with it, I hope it'll measure up to your memories."

"Well, I bet you make it even better."

It was a kind thing to say.

"You said Carter took you shopping?" Mara asked.

"Well…it was more like I took him. I think he really enjoyed it though."

Mara looked at her with newfound admiration, her gaze drifting over her in a pleasant sweep. "Any woman who can get Carter to furniture shop has my vote."

Macy chuckled, and a part of her was glad she had Mara's approval. From the few conversations she'd had with her, Macy picked up on the faintest innuendos about Jocelyn Grayson that didn't paint her in a good light. But then, after the way she'd hurt Carter, Macy figured not too many people at Wild River Ranch held Jocelyn in high regard. Macy did a mock curtsy. "Well, thank you for that."

Mara smiled and handed over the envelope. "I saw this on the table. It's addressed to you. I thought it might be important since you don't usually get mail here."

"Yes, it's probably important," she said. "Thanks."

Macy tucked it under her arm. She didn't want to spoil her good mood by opening the envelope right now. She'd seen enough legal paperwork in the past few months to cover the entire square footage of the ranch house. For just a little while longer, she wanted no reminders of her life back in Hollywood.

"I have lunch waiting in the refrigerator. Chicken casserole. I can heat it up."

"Oh, I'm not hungry right now, but I appreciate the thought. I think I'll head over to the inn in a little while. I'm kind of excited about the new purchases. I want to make sure everything is ready."

"I'll give it a look when it's done. I know it'll be a big improvement," Mara said before she walked away.

Macy dropped her overnight case in her room and set the attorney's papers down on her dresser. She moved to the window and looked out over Wild River Ranch. The land lay flat and stretched wide for acres and acres. Cattle grazed and she heard horses whinny from the corral. Off to one side, she noticed Carter McCay talking to a few men. He was easy to spot. She could pick him out of a crowd. She was that attuned to him now.

With a sigh, her shoulders slumped and she allowed the mad rush of emotion to overtake her. For a little while longer, her life would be pure bliss.

"Have you seen Rocky?" Macy asked Bill Fargo as they sat down on the steps of the gazebo together. She handed him a cup of iced tea. "Usually, he's practically tripping over my boots keeping me company on the walk over here. I miss him today."

Bill thought about it a few seconds. "Come to think about it, I haven't seen him today, either. That's strange." He had a quizzical look on his face.

"That Rocky's not here?"

"Yeah. It's probably nothing, but I ran into Mr. McCay at the diner in town this morning. He was spouting off to the waitress and he—"

"Mr. McCay? But I was with Carter… Oh," Macy said, when it dawned on her, "you're talking about Carter's father, Riley."

"Yeah, it was Riley McCay, all right. Everyone in the diner seemed to know him, though they were trying their best to ignore him. He was complaining about his son and his high and mighty ways, spouting off that he wasn't allowed to step foot on Wild River Ranch or see his dog anymore. I remember hearing him mutter something about getting his dog back."

Macy swallowed, fighting off the impending dread creeping up her spine. "Does Carter know?"

Bill sipped his tea and then shook his head. "Not yet. At the time, I didn't think anything of it. The old guy just seemed to be letting off steam, but now it appears Rocky might actually be missing."

Macy rose from the steps, worried. "You don't really think he took him, do you?"

"I haven't seen the dog anywhere on the grounds this afternoon."

"But, you didn't see any intruders on the property last night, right? And you start work later in the day, so maybe Rocky is just taking an extra long nap somewhere in the shade." Macy tried to convince herself that was the case. The alternative, that Riley had taken Rocky, would cause only a bigger rift between Carter and his father.

Bill gave her a slow nod. "Maybe. Of course, if the old guy did snatch the dog, your boyfriend will have him arrested."

"He's not my...*boyfriend*."

Fargo rolled his eyes and then sent her a wise, knowing smile. "If he's not, then what's the holdup?"

Macy shook her head, unable to answer him. The lines that had once been so clearly defined were beginning to blur in her mind. She didn't have an answer for Bill because she didn't know where she stood with Carter. Their relationship was fragile and new right now. "I don't...know."

"You didn't see the look on his face when McCay thought you were in danger the other night," Bill said. "Believe me, that man wasn't concerned about anything but getting to you."

"Really?"

"I think you know that, Macy."

Macy's heart warmed. Was that really true, or was Carter just being Carter? He had a protective streak a mile long. He was protective about the dog, too. If Riley McCay had come onto

the property and taken Rocky, Carter's blood pressure would
explode. And he'd have his father arrested.

"What I know is that I have to find Rocky." Macy closed her
eyes briefly. An idea bounced around in her head. It was risky
but Macy never let that stop her before when right was on her side.

Bill pursed his lips and spoke with fatherly concern. "Macy,
whatever you're thinking about doing, please consider the consequences. You know I have to tell Carter what I heard this morning."

"I understand. But I have to do what I feel is right, too." She
reassured him with a smile and then kissed his cheek. "Don't
worry about me. We're not even sure Rocky is missing."

But Macy had a strong suspicion that he was, and finding the
dog would serve two purposes. Even if it meant facing Carter's
wrath, she had to try to bring the dog home.

# Ten

Macy sat in Riley McCay's small, tidy kitchen, the only room in the tiny house that looked kept and clean. Two rooms off the parlor were boarded up from the recent fire, and every so often a draft of hot air would bring the scent of charred wood into the room.

"I apologize again, miss, for scaring you the other night. I swear to the almighty, I didn't know anyone was staying at the place. I wasn't thinking straight."

The man looked sincerely contrite, and Macy saw Carter's younger image on Riley's weathered and beat-up-by-life face. He was graying at the temples and wrinkled from excessive abuse to his body, but Macy held hope for him. And suddenly she understood Carter's frustration and anger with his father. His dad was the one person Carter couldn't save.

"Mr. McCay, I've accepted your apology. But you should have spoken with Carter and tried to reason with him instead of breaking into the inn."

He gestured with a wave of his hand. "I wasn't planning on breaking in. I know a secret way onto the property, and I take me a visit every so often. Then it started storming real hard. I got mad as hell being locked out of that place and all. It should have been mine in the first place, but my son decided to get bull-headed. Damn it."

He worked himself up in anger, and Macy sat back in her chair, uneasy. Rocky sat at attention by her side, and she laid her hand on his back, stroking him gently.

"I'd like to help you, Mr. McCay, but you can't go sneaking onto Carter's property anymore. And you can't take Rocky again, either."

"I didn't take him. He followed me home."

"Mr. McCay," Macy said with a stern but soft voice. "I told you about my father's drinking problem. I've heard all the excuses and all the lies. You can't fool me. You took Rocky. You have to promise me you won't do that again."

Head down, he shrugged his shoulders. "I miss the ole boy."

"You miss Carter."

His eyes flashed. He began to shake his head in denial, but Macy looked straight at him, refusing to let him get away with anything but the truth.

Riley backed down and sat in silence.

Macy reached across the table and laid her hand gently on his arm. "If you want to see Rocky or your son, all you have to do is call Carter."

"That boy doesn't want to see me."

"He would, if you started acting like his father. Maybe you could—"

A car pulled up and Macy lifted her head to peer out the window. It wasn't Henry or Bill Fargo. Darn. It was Carter, and he wasn't out for an afternoon stroll. He bounded out of the car and barged straight into the house through the unlocked door. His eyes blazed hot fury when he saw her sitting at the kitchen table with his father. His voice tight, he spoke through gritted teeth. "Macy, damn it. What the hell do you think you're doing?"

Riley rose from his seat, unbending his body to stand as tall as Carter. "Now, boy. Don't you go talking to Macy that way."

Carter ignored his father. He glanced at Rocky by Macy's side and his jaw twitched. Normally, the dog would have raced over to him, tail wagging, sniffing at his boots. But Carter's sharp tone kept the dog frozen in place. "I'm asking you, Macy. What are you doing here?"

"I'm having a glass of tea with your father." She tipped her chin.

Carter glanced at the empty table and arched a brow. "Really? Are you acting it out? Because I don't see any tea."

"I was just about to get the pitcher out," Riley said. "Why don't you sit down a spell?"

Carter looked at his father as if he'd sprouted wings. "For *tea?*" He kept his anger in check long enough to say, "I don't think so."

Riley frowned and took his seat, folding his arms. "Fine with me," he said stubbornly.

Carter focused on Macy again. "How'd you get here?"

Mara had driven her across town under slight protest until Macy had explained it was all in her plan to get Carter and Riley speaking again. It turned out that Mara was an old softy at heart, so she'd agreed for both the men's sakes. "It doesn't matter."

"You're not going to tell me?" His face burned with recrimination.

Macy sucked in a breath. She wouldn't let him bully her, though she had a sinking feeling her idea was going down faster than a pinpricked balloon. She looked straight at him and shook her head.

Carter stared at her a long time. Then he blinked once as if banking his anger. "Let's go."

Macy rose from her seat, fearful she'd gotten in over her head. She'd never seen Carter behave so hurtfully. She braced her hands on the edge of the table and leaned forward to make her point. "Maybe you didn't hear me, Carter. I'm staying to have iced tea with Riley."

Something flashed in his eyes. "Fine. You stay if that's what you want. Rocky comes home with me."

"He's my dog." Riley's voice rose in indignation.

Carter clenched his jaw, his impatience almost tangible. "You lost your right to him, *Dad.* You almost got him killed. I can't prove that you took him, but I know you did. Don't ever do it again."

Carter changed his tone when he crouched down and called to Rocky. "C'mon, boy."

Rocky got up and ambled toward him. The poor dog looked confused, but once he reached Carter he was lavished with a few loving pats on the head and all was peachy in dog world.

Carter strode to the door and then turned to Macy. A shiver ran up her spine from the cold, unyielding look he cast her. "I'll send a car for you in an hour." He glanced at the threadbare kitchen, the masked filth in the other rooms along with the broken furniture. Then on a deep frustrated sigh, he walked out taking Rocky with him.

Macy watched him get in the car and pull away. She slammed her eyes shut and was hit with a hard dose of reality.

She hadn't helped matters. She'd probably just made things worse.

Carter was nowhere around when she returned to the house. Soft, late-evening light cast her bedroom in relaxing hues, and the hot, humid air had finally cooled down a bit with the help of the air-conditioning, but Macy wasn't feeling calm or comforted at the moment. She still believed that Carter's relationship with his father could be saved, but she might have gone about trying to fix it in the wrong way. Judging by the look she'd witnessed in his eyes when he'd walked out of Riley's house, Carter thought of her as a traitor.

He was the last person she'd ever want to betray. Macy had his best interests at heart, but she may have overstepped boundaries in trying to help.

"You blew it, Macy," she said to herself.

She should have taken Bill Fargo's advice.

*Consider the consequences.*

Maybe if she had, she wouldn't be feeling so miserable right now.

She glanced at the large manila envelope sitting on the top of the dresser and let out a quiet groan. She'd been deliberately ignoring it since the darn thing had arrived. She should open it, she really should. But going over more legal mumbo jumbo didn't appeal to her at the moment. It reminded her too much of losing her mother and the financial mess she'd been in. It reminded her too much that she didn't really belong at Wild River. She wanted to pretend a little longer that she did.

She sank down on her bed, feeling lonely and heartsick and not at all ready to face the night by herself. When her cell phone rang, Macy snapped her head up and looked toward her purse sitting on her nightstand. Only a handful of people knew her number. She rose from the bed, grabbing her phone from the deep recesses of her handbag, and before the third ring, peeked at the screen. She smiled when she saw the call was from Avery. She was just the friend she needed to talk to tonight.

"Hi, Av," she said. Her shoulders relaxed. Tension oozed out of her the second she heard Avery's voice on the other end of the receiver.

"Hello, Macy."

"Oh boy, how'd you know I needed a friend right now?"

"I guess because I need one, too. We must be on the same wavelength."

"Usually that's a good thing," Macy said. "But, it doesn't sound like you're too happy right now. What's the matter?"

"I'm a little upset. It's nothing too drastic, but there's this persistent man—"

"Already, it sounds interesting," Macy said. Avery had led a sheltered life. She could use a little excitement, whereas Macy had the opposite problem. Her life was anything but boring. "Go on."

"No, no. It's not anything like that. He's an art expert and quite smooth, if you ask me, and he's been calling, trying to persuade me to sell my father's impressionist art collection."

"Really. Who is he?" Macy asked.

"His name is Marcus Price. He's from Waverly's."

"Oh, wow. I've met him. Ann Richardson introduced me to him during our negotiations for my mother's auction. He's pretty dreamy looking, if you like tall, confident men with attitude."

"I've spoken with him once," Avery said. "To tell him no thank you, but he keeps calling. I'm dodging his calls and emails."

"Would you ever consider selling, Avery?"

"No. I won't even think about it. That collection is the only thing I have left of my father. He was the only one in my family that showed me any love. I adore those paintings because they were his. He nurtured them and added to the collection year after year. I can't...I truly can't part with them."

Macy had the impression that Forrest Cullen hadn't been the kind of father that Avery needed. He'd been distant at best, though he loved her and now, her dear friend was clinging to his memory with an art collection that her father had treasured.

"Well, if you're adamant about it," Macy advised, "why not meet with Marcus Price one time to give him your answer in person? Trust me, you'll appreciate his good looks. And you can make your position crystal clear to him."

Avery hesitated then released a deep sigh that carried over the receiver. "Maybe, I will. Thanks for listening. So, tell me, what's happening over there with your Wild River cowboy?"

Macy wasted no time launching into an explanation of the latest events of her life, including her misguided attempt to help bring Carter close to his father. "I'm sure I'm not Carter's favorite person right now. And, Av, he's been so good to me while I've been here. We've...gotten closer." Macy paused. The image of his stone-cold expression when he'd walked in and spotted her at his father's place flashed in her mind. He'd seen it as a betrayal, plain and simple. "I might have ruined everything."

"Maybe not. Why not talk it out with him?"

"Carter is pretty stubborn. I don't think talking is going to work. Not this time. And he's told me before...uh—" Macy cringed as she revealed the truth to her friend "—that it's none of my business."

"Then apologize to him. If he's a good man, he'll accept it."

Macy couldn't apologize to Carter. She still felt she was right. Carter shouldn't give up on his father. But she was afraid that, by pressing her point, she'd destroyed their budding relationship. "I don't know. I'll think of something, Av."

After she bid her friend goodbye, Macy sat on her bed, deep in thought. Her frank conversation with Avery made her realize how deeply she cared about Carter. Aside from finding him sexy and gorgeous, she liked him. More than she'd liked any other man who had come before him. While living at Wild River, she'd managed to keep her emotions on an even keel. Barely. Because she didn't really believe in love anymore and because Carter McCay owned the Love Curse Diamond. He'd already fallen victim to the bad fortune that ring symbolized, and Macy would be a fool to think a relationship with Carter would turn out any differently.

While her heart said other things, her mind steadied those thoughts with practicality. She wanted to be on good terms with Carter during her time here. She wanted to finish the project she'd started and see it through to the end. She didn't want an argument about Carter's father to taint her days here at Wild River.

She was going to fix that.

Soon.

The pool was cool and refreshing against Carter's skin as his arms sliced through the water with even, steady strokes. Moonlight reflected on the water's edge. He took a deep breath and ducked his head, swimming with finesse and efficiency. He'd mastered the technique from swims in Wild River as a young boy. Back then, it was all for fun, a way a poor boy had to enjoy himself on a hot summer day. He and his friends would jump off tree branches that overhung the rushing river. They'd yell and holler and hoot with laughter, sometimes egging each other on, sometimes daring each other.

Nowadays, swimming wasn't so much recreational as it was a means to an end. He swam laps to burn off excess energy. He swam laps when he needed to clear his head for business. And he swam laps to simmer down his rising temperature.

Carter's temper had skyrocketed this afternoon when he'd found out Rocky had disappeared. After speaking with Fargo, Carter had gone straight to his father's house, certain the dog would be there. And he'd been right, but he hadn't expected to find Macy there. That had come as a complete surprise. If Fargo knew Macy was there, he'd given him no indication.

Macy wasn't held hostage on the ranch—she could go wherever she wanted—but butting in to his personal affairs was another matter, and she'd crossed a line today. He was angrier at her than he was at his father. Why in hell was that? And why in heaven's name did he feel so damn betrayed?

Macy had good intentions, he reminded himself. But his anger didn't ebb. Instead his strokes became more deliberate, more intense as he cut through the water.

After a good thirty minutes in the pool, Carter climbed the steps and got out. Water dripped from his body as he reached for a towel on the chaise longue. The midnight air was cool against his heated body, his pulse beating hard from the vigorous swim. He dried himself off and wrapped the towel around his waist then headed inside the house.

Macy should be asleep by now, he thought. It didn't stop him from pausing behind her bedroom door. He sighed heavy and shook his head. He wasn't ready to forgive her. He wasn't even close. Part of him hadn't wanted her getting involved in his dealings with his drunken father, and another part of him hadn't wanted Macy to see how shabbily he'd grown up. Shame and humiliation were difficult things to overcome. Even though Carter had become successful and wealthy, that house and that man represented a scarred and painful childhood. He hadn't wanted Macy to witness that. To see how pathetic his young life had been.

He forced himself to move on, to take the steps that led to his own bedroom. Once inside, he showered and put on his boxer briefs. Climbing into bed, he grabbed the remote and turned on the television. Maybe, by the grace of all things holy, there would be a taped-delay baseball game on.

Five minutes later, a soft knocking sounded on his door. He clicked off the television, rose and went to the door. When he opened it, Macy stood before him in a tight spandex skirt and a sheer white tank top. It was sexier than a thousand-dollar silk negligee. His heart pounded and raw desire bolted through his system. He took a swallow and looked into her gleaming violet eyes. They glistened with so much emotion, he couldn't turn away.

He offered his hand, palm up, letting her make the choice. "It's just about sex tonight, Hollywood. I'm still madder than hell at you."

# Eleven

Macy knew what she wanted. An angry Carter was better than no Carter at all. She didn't want to spend the night alone and wake up in the morning with an awful sense of loss and guilt. She didn't want awkward moments between them when they saw each other on the ranch. Carter's anger was evident on his face and the stony set of his eyes, so if it meant a Wham-Bam-Thank-You-Ma'am night, it would still be the better alternative.

She gulped past a lump in her throat and placed her hand in his. His hand closed over hers instantly and he tightened the hold. A warning shone in his hard eyes and then his brow rose in challenge, but Macy didn't back down. Carter looked ready to devour her whole, but Macy didn't fear him. Instead, excited shivers tingled up and down her spine. Carter's wrath could be thrilling. She knew he'd never hurt her physically, so tonight he would be in charge. He would make love to her, and it would be about raw, hot-blooded, unabashed sex.

He entwined their fingers then led her to the bed. He sat down first, and as she stood above him his gaze bore into her with intense scrutiny. Those steely eyes were not caressing, but rather a pillage of her most private body parts. Her breasts flamed, and below her waist powerful throbbing had her squirming for his touch.

Spreading his legs wide, he drew her between his thighs and clamped his legs tight so that she was trapped and standing over him. "Undress."

Macy didn't blink. With trembling fingers, she found the hem of her top and she lifted it up for Carter. "Slow it down, Hollywood."

Macy took a breath. She thought of the harlot she'd once played onstage in an off-Broadway production. Her character hadn't undressed, but every movement she'd made on that stage spoke of raw sensual passion. Fortunately for Macy, being with Carter lent itself to sensuality on the highest level, so being a sex kitten for him wasn't a far stretch. She wanted to please him. She wanted this night to be memorable. For both of them.

She slowed down her movements, rotating her hips with each tug of material, and once the top was off and her breasts were free, another slight movement had them bouncing on her chest.

Carter drew in oxygen, and Macy knew a measure of satisfaction.

"Now, the skirt."

As soon as Macy reached behind for the zipper, Carter's hands met her there and he gripped her hips to swivel her around. The unzipping took a second, and then he pulled the skirt down past her hips. Cool air hit her bare bottom first, and a long few seconds passed. Macy looked over her shoulder and caught Carter admiring her backside. Before she could turn around, he placed both hands over her cheeks and his roughened palms stroked her with such finesse that goose bumps broke out all over her body.

She'd never done this before. Given a man free rein over her body. She'd never trusted anyone the way she trusted Carter, but it was more than that, and Macy didn't want to think about what that *more* was.

Her nipples hardened. The throbbing between her legs intensified as everything else melted into softness.

Next, Carter splayed his hands on her hips, the spread of his fingers nearly encircling her entire waist. Then he pulled her down onto his lap. She landed with an unladylike thud. "Oh."

Carter kissed away her surprise. It was a long, leisurely kiss that filled her mouth, their tongues peeking out and touching. When Carter was done, Macy blinked from the thoroughness of his kiss. She felt partially devoured.

He kissed her again and toyed with her breasts, flicking the peaks with his thumb, first one then the other, until she wiggled with tortured delight. It was painfully pleasant, and she was glad Carter hadn't decided on giving her a quickie before sending her away.

No, this was far more enjoyable. She was completely at his mercy. Not a bad place to be, Macy thought.

"Touch me," he rasped, as if craving her hands on him.

Macy dug her fingers into the sprinkling of hairs on his chest. He was strong, sturdy, and her explorations grew more and more demanding. She loved stroking his shoulder blades and feeling the power beneath her fingertips. She loved feeling the tight muscles underneath his skin and his flat, tapered torso. She kissed his chest and stroked her tongue over his nipples, moistening them and then blowing them dry until Carter's mouth twisted with a pleasured groan.

His erection poked her side from underneath his boxers. Macy's heart raced, and the warmth in her body started to flame.

Carter picked up on her need and lowered her in his arms until she was angled back, held by his one arm. Her backside was stretched across his thighs and her legs rested on the bed. Carter watched as her hair dangled onto the bedsheets, the tresses fanning out beneath her. Then the hand that had played her wonderfully above the waist slid down to the center of her womanhood. She jerked when his flattened palm rubbed against her most sensitive spot. A moan slipped through her lips as he continued to rub her back and forth. Her breaths coming in short, uneven bursts, she rotated her body and jerked in his arms. He was relentless and masterful, and when he slipped his finger inside her, she was gone and lost by the erotic thrusts of her body.

Her release was loud and necessary to her sanity. When she

opened her eyes, Carter was there gazing at her with a look of satisfaction and awe. By far, he was the best lover she'd ever had, and she wanted him to think of her in that same way.

He lifted her off him quickly to undress and returned with a condom. He sat in his place on the bed again and set her back on his lap, this time facing him. With his guidance, she straddled him, her legs curled around both sides of his torso.

His voice was heavy, urgent as he kissed her throat and whispered, "Do me, Macy. I can't wait another minute."

Macy gave Carter all that she had. She brought her body to his, and their joining was thrilling and beautiful in the way their sensual rhythms matched. Macy gyrated with hips that found their own pace, and he pumped into her with a natural, powerful force. They melded and meshed, frenzied with hot, moist kisses and tender touches that roughened at the height of their release. And then came a long, low groan of completion, a guttural song of satisfaction.

When it was over and their heartbeats returned to normal, Carter lifted her and kissed the nape of her neck as he set her down beside him on the bed. He whispered, "You amaze me."

Macy was spent and exhausted, but his words spoken in awe already began to renew her hunger for him. He remained on the bed, a sheet of sweat coating his bronzed body and his hair askew from Macy's roaming hands. "You amaze me, too," she said softly.

He nodded and stared into her eyes. There would be no basking in the afterglow of lovemaking tonight. No cuddling under the sheets, no hand-holding and sweet words. A deal was a deal, and Carter was still angry with her. She'd come to him tonight for sex. He'd let her inside his room for sex.

He turned to peer straight ahead to a wall that held no particular interest, his profile set with a stubborn slant of his jaw. He was waiting for her to leave, and Macy got the hint. She kissed his shoulder, licking away a moist bead of perspiration with her tongue, then rose from the bed. "Good night, Carter."

She stepped by him and bent to retrieve her clothes on the floor. As she unfolded her body, her garments gripped in her

hands, she felt a slight tugging on a lock of her hair. Before sh
could turn around, Carter was there, pressed against her back
His voice rough, his fingers gently weaved through the strand
of her unruly curls. "Where do you think you're going?"

"To bed."

His breath caressed the sensitive skin behind her ear. "You
bed's right here."

"But, you're still angry."

"Furious."

She whirled around. "I think you're making a mistake."

"With you?" He chuckled as he circled his arms around he
bare waist and cupped her cheeks. He covered her soft flesh wit
both hands and fondled her possessively. "If that was a *mistak*
then sign me up for a thousand more."

They were coated with perspiration and carried the scent o
lovemaking. "That's…not what I, uh…mean." Macy was losin
her train of thought.

Carter kissed away her words. "We'll have to agree to dis
agree, Hollywood," he said. "And not discuss it anymore. Nov
come back to bed, sweet darlin'. The night's far from over."

There were days when Carter didn't think about Jocelyn at a
Not that he'd ever forget her betrayal or her clever manipulatio
It was just a simple fact that Jocelyn Grayson didn't matter any
more in his life, though the lessons he'd learned from her woul
last him a lifetime. It wasn't that far of a stretch for him to giv
up on the idea of marriage. For one, his parents hadn't set a goo
example. His mother had to endure life with his father. And a
he'd grown to his teen years, Carter would often ask his uncl
why she'd stayed with Riley. His uncle had but one reply—she
loved him. As if that made all the difference. As if that was th
definitive answer.

For Carter, that hadn't been a good enough reason. Ther
had to be something better out there that didn't cause heartach
and destruction. Love surely wasn't all it was cracked up to b

Carter had a good thing going with Macy. They'd fallen into
rhythm together, and he couldn't recall a time in his life when he

een happier. Because he had smart, loyal employees he trusted, Carter was able to spend time with Macy just about every day. He'd meet her for lunch at the inn and they'd go over her plans and ideas for decorating. The furniture they'd purchased on their venture to Dallas had been picked up and had filled the rooms nicely. Sometimes, when the mood struck, Carter would coax her into an upstairs bedroom to make love. And the mood struck often. He smiled thinking of those stolen few afternoon moments.

During the past week, they'd made love so many times that he'd lost count. Macy's giving body and sweet smiles had tamped each one of his memories. Their daytime encounters excited him, but during the night they'd continually found out new things about each other.

He was smitten with Macy, finding her like an addiction, a drug he couldn't seem to kick. Ever since that night when she'd come to his bedroom and they'd agreed not to talk about his father, he couldn't stop thinking about her. He wondered when that would change and when the blazing heat would simmer between them. No one could sustain a raging fire forever.

Macy's life was in Hollywood. It's all she'd ever known. Her dreams were there, whether she wanted to admit that or not. He'd rescued her and given her temporary sanctuary from the glitz and glamour, but he knew she would eventually return.

But for now, she was his.

"Excuse me, Carter?"

He shook those thoughts loose, wondering where his concentration had gone. The annual inventory numbers were in, and he had worked from sunup into the late afternoon today, going over the books with his accountant. He'd postponed a trip to the Dallas office, insisting that his accountant drive out to the ranch instead. He wouldn't fool himself into thinking it was for any other reason than he wanted to be close to Macy for the time she remained on the ranch.

"Carter, did you hear what I just said?" Jacob Curtis snapped his briefcase shut and rose from his seat at the desk.

"Yeah…uh, I did. You'll be in touch to clarify those few duplicate payments on the books."

The hotshot accountant with roots near Wild River had known Carter for a long time and now eyed him carefully. "You're a little distracted today, Carter. Is everything all right?"

"Better than all right," Carter assured him, rising from his seat to shake his hand. "Thanks, Jake. I appreciate you driving out to the ranch today."

"It's what you pay me for. But, if I didn't know better, I'd think you had a better offer than coming into the city for business."

Carter twisted his mouth into a wry smile. "Maybe. You've known me a lot of years."

Jake gave him a gentle slap on the back. "Whoever *she* is, have a great time."

Carter didn't even try to deny it. "I plan to. C'mon. I'll walk you outside."

After the accountant took off, Carter climbed into the Jeep and headed toward the inn. The drive over took only minutes and when he arrived he was disappointed to see that Macy wasn't alone. Bill Fargo sat with her on the steps of the gazebo. They were shaded by ancient oaks whose branches swayed with the late-afternoon breeze.

Their snack break was a daily occurrence and something Macy enjoyed. "Hey, you two," he said, stepping out of the Jeep and approaching. The gazebo was an eyesore, but he'd pretty much given up on the idea of tearing it down. "What did Mara make for you today?"

Macy slid over on the step, giving him room to sit right next to her, and that gesture made him silly with happiness. He took off his hat before sitting.

"Red velvet cupcakes with cream cheese frosting and fresh-squeezed lemonade. Can you believe it?"

"Sounds like a celebration," he said, glancing at her then at Fargo.

"It's nothing special," Bill said with a wave of his hand.

"It *is* something special. It's Bill's birthday. I wouldn't have known, because he didn't say a word to me, but Mara has ways of finding these things out." She giggled and the engaging sound

pulled at something sacred in his heart. "I've invited him to dinner tonight. If that's okay with you?"

Carter had hoped for some alone time with Macy tonight,
but he couldn't refuse the older man a celebration. He'd become
a good friend to Macy and to some of the hands on the ranch.
"Sure thing."

"It's not necessary," Bill said, his face flushing red. "I don't
like a big fuss."

"No fuss at all," Macy replied. "I thought I'd make homemade
pasta with all the fixings."

"You cook?" Carter asked.

Macy spoke with confidence. "I have been known to sling
together more than a sandwich, you know."

"I didn't know," Carter said.

"Pasta's one of my favorites," Bill said, "but I've got a shift
tonight."

Macy gave Carter a beckoning glance, and he picked up on
her long look. "You've got the night off. Consider it a birthday
gift," Carter said, because he liked the guy and because he had
to see what homemade pasta with all the fixins tasted like when
cooked by a Hollywood starlet.

"The lady can cook." Carter smiled at her, handing her his
empty plate.

"It was delicious," Bill said and Macy beamed from the compliments, taking Bill's plate from his hands, too.

"I'm glad you enjoyed it." She set the plates in the sink and
turned to the men as she returned to the range top. "There's a lot
more. I can fix you both another plate."

She stirred the simmering sauce, proud of herself and what
she'd accomplished. Granted, she was rusty in the kitchen, and
it had taken her three hours to prepare the meal, but from the
satisfied looks and the second helpings the men had requested,
she knew her Pasta ala Macy was a big hit.

Bill rubbed his stomach. "I'll get a paunch if I eat another bite.
I've already had enough for a small army."

Carter shook his head, too. "I need to swim fifty laps to work off what I just ate."

Macy shut off the burner, covered the pot and took a seat with the men. They shared a glass of wine and toasted Bill's birthday. She enjoyed the rest of the evening and the steady flow of light conversation.

Carter wasn't kidding about swimming laps. Shortly after Bill took his leave, Carter tried to coax her into the pool with him but Macy insisted on cleaning up the kitchen. She didn't want Mara walking into a mess the following morning. When Carter offered to help, she gave him a playful shove and told him not to sap all his energy in the pool.

She had plans for him that involved his stamina.

That comment earned her an earth-shattering kiss that left her completely breathless. "Be ready for me in an hour," Carter rasped. "I've been dying to get you alone all day."

Macy was a clean-as-you-go kind of girl, so it didn't take her long to get the kitchen back in shape. Afterward, she went to her room and took a long, refreshing shower, washing the heat of the day and the slight smattering of spaghetti sauce stains off her body. Fully refreshed and dressed in a pale violet negligee that Carter had given her last night, she took a brush to her hair. Carter had said the nightgown's color was the perfect match to her eyes, and as she looked at herself in the mirror, she had to agree.

Macy was in a good mood. So good that she picked up the manila envelope that had been collecting dust on the dresser. She weighed it in her hands. It wasn't really that thick. Maybe the envelope contained only a few copies of the settlements she'd signed. She didn't think they were that important because her attorney hadn't called her about them.

Confident that nothing could possibly mar her contentment, Macy sat down on the bed, crisscrossed her legs and opened the envelope flap. She pulled the papers out, scanning over them briefly. She was right. It was nothing but copies her efficient lawyer wanted her to have in her possession. She closed her eyes and sighed.

*That wasn't too bad, Macy.*

But her relief was short-lived. Something hit her leg and her eyes snapped open. A small sealed envelope slipped out of the larger envelope on her lap. "What's this?"

Stuck on the front of the letter was a large chartreuse Post-note.

*Macy,*
*I found this while going through your mother's Santa Monica office. It's sealed and addressed to you from Tina. If you need further legal counsel, don't hesitate to call.*
*Barton Lowenthal*

Macy pulled off the Post-it note and saw her mother's handwriting beneath. She had the most unique style of writing, with perfectly spaced vertical lettering that could be mistaken for typeset, it was so symmetrical.

*My Sweet Macy*

Macy took a big swallow and stared at the envelope she held in her lap, touching the edges with shaky fingertips. The letter had obviously been mixed up with her mother's business papers. For all she knew, it was a grocery list or lines in a new script she'd wanted Macy's opinion on. It could be a receipt for a gift she'd given Macy. It could be a hundred frivolous things, and part of Macy hoped that was the case. But the other part, the one that gave her stomach the trembles and caused her nerves to jump, told her this was something important.

"Open it, you coward," Macy murmured as she continued to stare at the envelope.

Macy found the strength to gently pull the flap away from the glued edge of the opening. On a deep breath, she lifted out the stationery that had been creased in thirds. She unfolded it and saw a full page written by Tina.

"Mom," Macy said, tears welling in her eyes.

She noted the date. Her mother had written this letter during the time of her illness, in those last few days of her life.

Macy shook again with renewed force. Her tears were ready to fall. It wasn't the letter so much as the shock of seeing her

mother's handwriting again and knowing this would be the ver
last communication she would have from her. She'd already dor
this, she thought. And it was hard to say goodbye. Now, she woul
have to do it again.

She forced herself to read the words so delicately and pe
fectly written.

*My Sweet Princess,*
*I know I haven't been a traditional kind of mother to you,*
*but I hope you know how very much I love you. I always*
*will. If you are assured of that, then I can rest in peace.*

*You were the best daughter a mother could have wished*
*for. You brought joy and love into our house. Both your*
*father and I were so proud of you. Clyde would have done*
*anything to make his little girl smile. Always remember*
*that.*

*I suppose it wasn't fair of me to vent to you my anger at*
*him for leaving both of us. I never intended to taint your*
*view of him. Clyde was a good man and a wonderful father.*

*I must confess, selfishly I was angry with him all those*
*years after his death. And I was lonely, missing him so very*
*much. I made bad choices after I lost him, and I knew in my*
*heart no man could ever take his place. Those impetuous*
*marriages were mistakes of my own doing. It was foolish*
*for me to have even tried to replace your father. I say this*
*now, so that you will know that I have always believed in*
*true and everlasting love.*

*I had that with your father. He was the love of my life,*
*Macy Genevieve. He truly was. I will never regret loving*
*him, and I hope one day you will find a love so strong,*
*so steady and so overpowering that it simply takes your*
*breath away. That's what I want for you. That's all I've*
*ever wanted for you...to love and be loved by someone*
*worthy of you.*

Tears blurred Macy's vision and trickled onto her cheeks a
she sobbed quietly. She set the letter aside and lowered her hea

down, covering her face with her hands. The devastating pain that touched her soul was overwhelming. Her mother's words resonated and her heart broke like fallen glass, the tiny pieces scattered. "Oh, Mom."

Three light taps on the door snared her attention and she looked up. Carter walked into her room, wearing nothing but a pair of worn jeans riding low below his waist. "Macy, darlin', it's past midnight. You coming to bed?"

The sight of the tall, tanned, handsome cowboy walking into her room as if he belonged there struck her like a bolt of lightning. She loved his drop-dead body, his hazel eyes and the sensual tone of his Texas drawl. She loved everything about Carter McCay. And the clarity that only her mother's letter could draw out finally dawned on her.

She was in love with Carter.

She loved him from the very depths of her being.

And she realized, too, that her fears were never about leaving the ranch to go back to her "real" and insane world. She'd dreaded leaving Carter.

Her perfect, stubborn cowboy.

She slammed her eyes shut. *Oh, God.*

"Hey," he said tenderly, coming over to the bed. "What's the matter, sweetheart?"

She held it together long enough to lift the letter she'd let fall into her lap. "It's the last…the last l-letter from my m-mother."

Carter's sympathy reached his eyes. He climbed onto the bed and wrapped an arm around her. "Don't cry, Macy."

She set her head on his shoulder and sniffled some more.

"Or maybe, do cry." He seemed out of his element, but the comfort of his solid strength helped. He was always trying to protect her. "I don't know."

She raised her head to meet his eyes. She knew she probably looked a mess with a tear-stained face and red, blotchy eyes. "It's just that I thought I knew everything. And now, I find out I was wrong. About a lot of things. It's crazy, you know."

"I don't know," he said tenderly. "Why don't you tell me?"

Macy didn't hesitate to unburden herself. She'd wanted to

share this with him for a long time. "Those rings I sold at Wa verley's, well, I thought they were cursed. I started thinking c them as the Love Curse Diamonds. And then when we ran int each other outside the restaurant—"

"When you were almost mowed over by the press?"

She sniffed. "Yes, then. I found out you had proposed to Joce lyn with that ring, and she refused you. I felt so bad that you ha gotten hurt."

Carter didn't react. He didn't even flinch at the mention c Jocelyn's name. She derived some relief and, selfishly, a littl bit of pleasure from that. Maybe Carter had gotten over Jocelyı

She went on, "I believed that anyone who held on to thos rings would never be happy. I mean, my mother had been ma ried three times. All three marriages brought her nothing bı hard luck. First, my father died in a horrific crash. And the there was Amelio Valenzuela. He was some sort of prince wh told my mother after the wedding he was duty-bound to rule h small country. He left her after three weeks and there was a bi scandal. Then there was Joseph the Jerk. He was a fashion phc tographer who adored my mother. He gave her everything sh wanted until he put that ring on her finger. That was the ring yo bought," she added. Macy felt guilty enough to duck her hea down, even now, after she realized she'd been mistaken abou the diamonds. "Joseph cheated on her so often and so blatantl after they were married that she walked out on him a few montł after their wedding."

Carter listened to her and nodded. "So, what happened? Di your mother tell you something in the letter to change you mind?"

"Yes, and with her explanation I'm seeing things more clearl Now I understand. I know why she did the things that she did

"And you don't believe the rings are cursed?"

She shook her head and drew a deep breath to steady her sha low breathing. Her crying had drained her energy. "I sold thos rings at auction because I needed the money. My mother didn have a head for business. She was broke when she died, and the I made those errors in judgment."

Carter kissed her forehead, distracting her. His arms around her lent her the strength she needed. "Which ones?" he asked.

"You remember me telling you about that nude scene I wouldn't do?"

"Yeah," he said, squeezing her shoulder, his voice a little lighter. "I don't think I'll ever forget that."

"I was sued over that. And then there was another occasion more recently when I signed to host a television special about my mother for Spotlight Entertainment. I was still grieving and was led to believe that hosting the show was a way to honor my mother's life. Halfway through, I realized it was a bash fest about Tina Tarlington's love life, with her daughter at the helm. I walked out when they wouldn't change direction and they sued. I didn't want to settle the lawsuit, but my attorney cautioned me about the expense involved to fight it, but more importantly, the media frenzy a court battle might create. I finally decided to settle and let my mother's film legacy speak for itself."

"So you sold off the rings you thought were cursed, because you needed money." He was clarifying the statement, more than asking a question.

"Yes, but I *wanted* to be rid of them." It felt good to finally reveal the truth to Carter. "It seems silly to me now, but all this time I thought those diamonds caused my mother's heartache. I thought they were the source of so much misery, including yours."

Carter's mouth pulled down for an instant. "That's not true, Macy. The diamonds weren't to blame. It was probably my own fault for thinking I was in love with someone like Jocelyn. That whole thing was a mistake."

Macy nodded, reassured that he wasn't still in love with Jocelyn. That he'd realized she wasn't the right woman for him.

"Are you sorry you sold the diamonds?" he asked.

"Not the other two. I'm too practical for that, but I, uh…wish I had held on to the ring my father gave my mother. I'm afraid I'll never see the Tarlington diamond again." Tears dripped from her eyes and fatigue caused her shoulders to slump, even while being comforted in Carter's arms. "I'm sorry. I didn't mean to ruin your night."

"You're not ruining my night, sweetheart. In fact, stay righ here. Don't move. I have an idea."

He got up and left the room. Macy dried her eyes with th bedsheet and ran a hand through her long hair. She felt awful Her stomach ached and her head pounded, but she also felt re lieved to have finally told Carter the truth about the ring, and about herself.

And mostly she was relieved to have finally realized her lov for him. She adored him and she wouldn't deny it another second How could she not? He was her perfect cowboy, stubborn and all

When he returned, he came bearing a plush black velvet ring box. He sat down beside her on the bed and offered it to her. "Thi is for you, Macy Tarlington. If you want it."

# Twelve

Macy took the ring box from Carter's hand. Joy burst through her heart and all of her fatigue, weariness and heartache melted away. She peered into the depth of Carter's beautiful eyes, and when he gave her an encouraging nod, she opened the box.

"Oh wow." She stared at the diamond ring Carter had purchased from the Waverly auction. The diamond's lustrous facets reflected under the light with a brilliance that only matched the beautiful glow Macy felt inside.

Carter had offered her a ring. She was waiting for the words to come along with them, the words that would seal her fate with happiness. She was so much in love with Carter now that she could barely contain herself. She wanted to jump into his arms, scream at the top of her lungs and make love with him until the early morning dawned.

"I have no use for it now," Carter said in a sincere tone that, once the words actually registered, burst her hopeful bubble. His next words nearly destroyed her. "I'm never going to propose to a woman ever again. Why don't you take the ring and sell it? You can open up that drama school you've been dreaming about when you go back to Hollywood."

Everything inside her went limp. Her hopes were instantly dashed, replaced by deep, wrenching disappointment. Pain sliced sharply through her entire body, cutting her like the blade of a dagger. She'd finally given in to her feelings for Carter. She'd finally realized that love was inevitable. And that it yielded great, uncontrollable power.

The Love Curse Diamond had struck again.

*Silly her for daring to believe in love again.*

She thought her time at the ranch had meant something to Carter. She thought that he might actually fall in love with her. She thought—and this particular notion hurt the most—that Carter hadn't viewed her as his rebound girl, a temporary solution to his heartache.

*Silly, silly her.*

He waited for her reply wearing a satisfied expression. He thought he'd found a way to ease her pain. It was his way of protecting her.

The cure will kill you, they say and surely Carter's solution would slowly, systematically cause her to die at least a thousand deaths. If only she hadn't fallen in love with him.

Her heart sank yet the pain that blistered her would never see the light of day. She would hide her heartache and lift her head with pride. There wasn't anything else Carter could do or say to her to make her feel any worse.

"If it's not enough money to start up a school, I'll invest in you, Macy. I'll become your silent partner."

"You'll invest in me?" She'd been wrong. She did feel worse. He wanted to go into business with her, not pledge his undying love.

She stared at the ring and bolstered her courage. Concealing her destruction would be the hardest thing Macy would ever have to do. She had no more tears to shed, but keeping her voice steady and her body from collapsing in grief wouldn't be easy. Summoning up her acting ability, she got into character and pretended to be a woman with more pride than smarts. Macy used every trick in her arsenal to bring him a performance worthy of a standing ovation.

"Carter, thank you. It's very generous of you." She smiled wide with gratitude plastered on her face and touched his cheek tenderly. "There's no need to go into business together." She took a silent swallow. "The ring will bring me enough money to see my dreams come alive."

She held her head up and kept the smile on her face. "I can't thank you enough for letting me stay here at the ranch and for, well...*everything*."

"No problem, darlin'."

"I, uh, I guess this is a good time to tell you. As soon as the work is finished on the inn, I'll be leaving."

Carter frowned and his brows knit tightly together. "When?"

"It's just a matter of putting on the finishing touches now."

"When?" he asked again.

Macy plunged ahead. The pain would be sharper and the knife twists far more gutting if she prolonged her stay here. "I've been in touch with my agent," she fibbed. "There's a role that's perfect for me, and I'll need something current on my résumé before I take a stab at opening a drama school. Success breeds success, as they say. I need to be in Hollywood before the weekend for an audition."

"*This* weekend? That's in three days."

She hid her dismay well, yet her mind screamed for mercy. Three days left at Wild River. Three days left to be with Carter McCay. The thought made her stomach knot with tension, but she forced herself to continue with her charade. "Yes, I know. It's time for me to face my life head on."

He pierced her with a long, unblinking stare filled with intense regret. She met his regret with bold determination, and he let out a deep sigh of resignation. He wouldn't try to change her mind. He wouldn't say a word to stop her. They'd both known this arrangement was temporary. She wondered if he would miss her. She hoped so. She wouldn't want her time here to have been so easily forgotten.

Carter brushed her hair to the side and kissed her forehead, her cheeks and then brought his lips to her mouth. His intoxicating kiss made her heart bleed.

That night, he made love to her with great passion. He touched every part of her body with his hands and his tongue and his mouth. He stroked her until she cried his name, and he pleasured her as if she was the most desirable woman on the planet.

And with each loving embrace, each sensuous kiss and each powerful release, she fell more and more in love with him.

Macy stood on her terrace, looking out over her neighborhood as Pacific breezes whipped at her hair. The salty sea air freshened an otherwise smoggy day. Sometimes on a clear day, from one angled view on her terrace, she could actually see the ocean. Today wasn't one of those days.

Since she'd left Wild River, she'd pretty much stayed isolated in her three-bedroom condo in Brentwood. Her only contact had been with a grocery store clerk, a gas station attendant and her neighbor Ella, who had come by to drop off her mail. She'd felt so odd, so out of place, that it had taken her several days to finally reacclimate to living in Los Angeles again.

Carter had insisted on driving her to the airport and had given her a goodbye kiss that buckled her knees. He held her in a tight embrace afterward, and she thought maybe he wouldn't let her go. That maybe he'd realized he couldn't live without her. That maybe he could take one more chance on a woman, the right woman. But Carter had let her go and forced himself to step away from her, though with great reluctance. That was something she could hold on to when she thought back on her time at Wild River. Carter hadn't said the words, but at least, his actions told her, he wasn't ready for her to leave.

"I'm here if you ever need me," he'd said. "Wild River is only a plane flight away."

But there was no true conviction in his voice. He was so certain that she'd step into her old way of life, paparazzi and all, without a look back. He had her pegged all wrong, but it wasn't up to her to inform him. He'd pretty much laid his cards on the table the other night.

*I'm never going to propose to a woman ever again.*

She asked herself why couldn't she have stayed and allowed her fiery fling to flame out? Since when had Macy become such a stick-in-the-mud that now, suddenly, she held dear traditional values? Since when had she wanted the clichéd husband and family and white picket fence?

Since she'd met Carter and fallen in love, that's when. With him, she wouldn't accept anything less than having his love.

She'd kissed Carter one last time in front of the airport's security gate, then brought her mouth to his ear and whispered, "I'll never forget you, Carter. And please reconsider about your father."

She hadn't waited for his reaction. She knew he wouldn't be happy with her last words, but she had to say them. She'd whirled around with her overnight bag in hand and made her way through the security line without ever once looking back.

Memories of Carter consumed her thoughts. She kept going over the irony in her mind. For the time she'd lived at Wild River, she'd thought that Carter's ownership of her mother's cursed ring meant there was no hope for the two of them. She'd believed that no good would actually come from Carter falling in love with her, or her him. Their fate was cast. But the staggering truth was sharper and more painful. Carter simply *didn't* love her. It had nothing to do with a curse or the diamond rings.

Thoughts of her gorgeous white-clad cowboy, astride his stallion, racing into town to sweep her up and ride into the sunset would be left for the late show in her dreams. It was the only place for them. And as soon as Macy realized that, her heart would stop aching, her stomach would stop clenching and she would get her head back in the game.

Carter had worked from sunup to sundown for the past eight days. He made appointments he really didn't need to make, had meetings in his Dallas office with each one of his employees that were unnecessary and worked alongside his capable ranch hands in the barns and on the land. He dove into his work with uncanny vigor. His actions caused attention, garnering raised eyebrows and a few tactful questions from those close to him.

None of his attempts helped him shake the feeling that he'd lost something valuable, something that couldn't be replaced. This afternoon, as he stood by the corral fence watching the new colt lumber around the arena, separated from his mama and trying to find his own way, Carter felt one with him. Just like Midnight, he faced the uncertainty and stumbled around.

Earlier today, Carter had looked up an old girlfriend's phone number. He'd stared at the screen that, with one tap of his finger, might have hooked him up with a woman, and then he cursed at his own stupidity.

"What the hell." Instead of making that call, he'd grabbed a cold beer and strode outside.

He took a few gulps quickly, letting the foamy brew slide down his throat, and thought about how often in the past week he'd been tempted to call Macy. He'd thought about her at least twenty times a day. He wondered if she'd fallen right back into step with the Hollywood scene. And the more he thought about her, the more it irked him that she'd left the minute after he'd given her back that ring. Maybe that was all she'd ever been after. Maybe she saw her opportunity to play on his generous nature with well-rehearsed tears. She'd admitted she was broke. Just maybe, she'd played him for a fool. She might, at this very minute, be going after the other diamonds she'd sold at the Waverly auction.

Carter winced at his own suspicions. He'd been tainted by Jocelyn's deception, and because of her he'd vowed to keep up his guard around women. His wavering trust was as thin as a split horsehair.

He swore an oath and told himself he was right to let her leave. They'd had a brief affair with no talk of a future between them, no talk of anything beyond the here and now. That night in New York, he'd seen a woman being hounded and pursued against her will and he'd intervened. His protective streak had kicked in big-time, and he told himself that's all it was. He couldn't watch Macy being badgered like that, and another round of protectiveness had kicked in when he'd seen the extent of her vulnerability. He'd invited her to Wild River because she'd needed an escape, a safe place to hide out, and not because she was beautiful and witty and the distraction he'd needed at the time.

"Hey, Rock," he said when the golden retriever ambled toward him. "How's it going, boy?"

The dog plopped his forlorn body down beside him. Rocky had been a victim of Macy's departure, too. He'd spent the first five nights in her bedroom, waiting eagerly for her to appear. He'd sniffed in her closet, under her bed, in the bathroom, and when Carter would pass by her room, the dog would look up with a question in his disappointed caramel eyes. It was one thing to work through his own sense of emptiness with Macy gone, but seeing it expressed so damn desperately on the dog's face was like a sucker punch to his gut.

"Yeah, I miss her, too." Carter had been insane to think that he wouldn't.

He polished off his beer in one quick gulp and strode to his Jeep. "C'mon, Rock."

He knew the dog would follow in hope that Carter would lead him to Macy. That wasn't going to happen. Rocky would just have to forget her, and in time he would. Carter might not be so lucky.

He sped off with the dog in the passenger seat. Rocky stuck his head out the window, and the warm August air hit his face and ruffled his whiskers in the breeze.

Though he didn't have the first clue why, Carter drove across town and slowed as he approached his father's house. He parked the Jeep in front. On a deep, unsteady breath, he turned his head to face the shack where he'd grown up, and he stared for a long while. He didn't really see a broken-down porch with wood planks missing or window shutters loose on their hinges. He didn't really see the dirt and neglect. He looked beyond that this time, to see something entirely different.

A chance.

He got out of the Jeep with Rocky at his side. "It's a ten-minute visit," he said to the dog. "And then we're outta here."

An hour later, Carter's restlessness and jumpy nerves got the better of him. He powered the Jeep along the highway that led to Wild River Ranch and took the turnoff that led to the inn. He thought about that mysterious Gold Heart Statue, and whether his friend Roark was in any danger. He went over the facts on his mind about that text Roark had sent... Anything to keep him from thinking about Macy.

Rocky's ears perked up when he heard Bill Fargo's call of hello. Carter pulled the Jeep alongside Fargo as he walked the grounds. "Hey there, out doing your rounds?"

The old man smiled. "That's what you pay me for."

Carter nodded. "Got time to take a break?"

The old man looked at his watch. "I was just about to."

Carter parked by the front of the inn and climbed out. He walked with Fargo to the shaded gazebo steps and they sat down. Rocky sniffed all around first, his nose down as he moved along the perimeter, picking up Macy's scent. When he finally looked up, it was with recrimination.

*Where the heck is she?* the dog seemed to be asking.

Carter ignored him and stretched his legs out, his boot heels scraping the cracked stone steps that surrounded the gazebo. "How's it going?"

Fargo looked out across the field. "Fine. No sign of trouble. Everything's been kinda peaceful—too peaceful actually, without Macy stirring up trouble."

Carter swiveled his head and caught the man's knowing gaze. "Yeah."

"Haven't seen you here for a while," Fargo said. "Not since Macy left."

"I've been busy."

"I bet you have. Busy ignoring the truth. Maybe even afraid of dealing with it."

Carter should take offense. The man worked for him, and though his tone wasn't disrespectful, his words certainly were. "What do you think I'm afraid of?" He gave Fargo a pass due to his age. Carter was curious to hear what he was getting at.

Fargo took his hat off and ran his hand through his shock of graying hair. "I was *busy* like you once upon a time. So busy, in fact, that I let a woman slip right through my fingers. The perfect woman for me. It was a messy thing, it was. And I'm sorry I ever let her go."

"What happened with her?"

Fargo's self-deprecating laughter touched the very ends of Carter's soul. "I lost her. Oh…it was a long time ago, but in some ways it was yesterday. I've been lonely for her all my life. I'd hate to see that happen to you."

"Me? That won't happen to me. I'm never going to let it."

"You're too busy, Carter," he said with a shake of his head. "Ignoring what's right in front of you. Too busy denying what you're feeling in here." He thumped a finger into Carter's chest right over his heart. "And letting what's going on in here," he said, pointing to Carter's head, "make the wrong choices for you."

Carter drew a deep breath.

"Don't let pride stand in your way, son. If you care about Macy—"

"How do I know she feels anything for me?" Carter asked. "And how can I believe her? She's an actress. As soon as she got the ring back, she left the ranch."

"Did she get what she really wanted? If you think she was after that diamond ring, you're thinking with your ass."

Carter's eyes snapped to his.

"Pardon me. I'm an old man, and I tell it like it is. That girl was devastated when she left the ranch. I heard it in her voice. I saw it on her face. Maybe the only acting she was doing was when she pretended it didn't kill her to leave Wild River. I know one thing, it'd be a shame to let your fears and suspicions hold you back from finding out the truth."

Carter drew a sharp breath. The old man was confusing him, and when he got that way he became cautious. Carter didn't need someone telling him how he should feel and what he should do. He'd done all right for himself so far, with only a misstep or two in his life. But who could blame him? He'd had a rotten upbringing and was proud of what he'd accomplished under the guidance of his uncle.

Carter changed the subject abruptly and spoke with Fargo for only a few minutes more before taking his leave. He couldn't

let Fargo persuade him into making another blunder. He wasn't
about to go after Macy, hat in hand, only to have her turn a cold
shoulder to him and laugh in his face. Though a large part of him
said she wouldn't do that, Carter couldn't be sure, and he wasn't
good at taking foolish chances.

The next day, he wandered around the ranch with no real sense
of purpose. His work was all caught up and his desperate restlessness couldn't be ebbed. He'd taken off on his favorite mare
and rode roughshod over the terrain, pushing his horse hard and
coming back exhausted and spent. The day after that, he paid
his cousin a visit to shoot the breeze and drink hard liquor until
he couldn't see straight. Brady had driven him home that night.

That next afternoon, Carter sought Bill Fargo out to finish the
conversation they'd begun the other day. But Fargo didn't answer
his phone or respond to the text message Carter had sent him.
Henry hadn't seen him today, and neither had Mara.

Carter strode into his bedroom, frustrated. He had to shower
and change for a business dinner in Dallas he'd rather not at-
tend. As he slipped his shirt off, he noticed a plush velvet ring
box sitting on his dresser. His heart leaped in his chest. It looked
like the same box he'd given Macy. There was a note attached.

Carter opened the box first. To his amazement, the legendary
Tarlington diamond caught the light and reflected back at him
with a twinkle. There was no mistaking the iconic ring with the
T-shaped configuration. Its brilliance was matched only by its
uniqueness. Mystified, Carter set the ring down and lifted the note.

*Dear Carter,*
*You bought a very expensive ring at Waverly's during the*
*Tina Tarlington auction. I outbid you, or rather, my assis-*
*tant outbid you for Tina's prized ring from the man con-*
*sidered her one true love. I adored Tina's work and once*
*spent time with her. I'd hoped she'd run away with me, but*
*it wasn't to be. In any case, I've had my eye on you, Carter,*
*and think you are a good man. You have fallen hard for*
*Tina's daughter, without a doubt. I'd like you to give this*
*ring back to her. Whether you return it to her as a favor*

*to me, or give it to her as a pledge of your love, it's up to*
*you, but I wouldn't be a fool if I were you. Macy is worth*
*far much more than a mere diamond ring.*
*Bill*

The words sank in as the questions flew. Carter's wary nature
had him looking at an attached bill of sale that appeared absolutely
authentic from Waverly's. And inside the ring, he squinted to read
the loving inscription from Clyde Tarlington, *With love to my Tina.*

Carter was shaken to the core. His suspicions had vanished.
He didn't need any more proof that this diamond ring was the
genuine article. He had the actual Tarlington diamond in his possession, and there was only one person on earth who deserved
to wear this ring. There was only one person on earth who deserved everything he had to give.

Carter closed his eyes briefly, acknowledging the potent emotion sweeping through him. He'd denied it, stomped on it and
disregarded it for too long. Now, it swelled in his heart and made
him feel giddy inside. He didn't have a clue who the heck Bill
Fargo really was, but he knew one thing—he owed him a giant
Texas-size thank-you.

Macy stared at the cowboy who stood on the grassy hill, his
black felt Stetson shading his eyes and his manly physique accented by tight Wrangler jeans and a red Western shirt. When
the director called "Action," Macy took her cue and rode on
horseback over to him.

The cowboy was a pretty boy who was cocksure of himself,
strutting around the Hollywood set, getting into character by
spitting tobacco and dusting up his shiny new leather boots. The
irony of Macy landing this role in the Rugged Cologne commercial was almost laughable, but she needed the work and it
paid well.

The cowboy spoke his lines, his Southern drawl too drawn
out to sound authentic. In a grand sweep, he lifted her off the
horse and stumbled backward attempting to carry her weight.

Desperately, he clutched at the material of her calico dress while trying to keep his balance and ruined the take.

It seemed the Rugged cowboy needed some more time in the gym.

Macy couldn't help making comparisons. Ronny Craft was trying, but he needed a few more years of maturity and a complete personality adjustment to pull off being the real cowboy deal. He'd been hitting on her all day, asking her out on a date, and hadn't quite gotten the hint no matter how many times she'd told him no.

Carter *was* the real deal, and she missed him like crazy. Just being on horseback again reminded her of the time she'd spent at Wild River Ranch. Working on a set with wranglers and watching them care for the horses brought images of the night Midnight was born. This silly cologne commercial had stirred up memories of Carter that Macy had tried desperately to lock away.

The diamond he'd given back to her would go a long way in helping her achieve her drama school dream, but Macy's heart wasn't in it anymore. She couldn't force herself to sell the ring. She couldn't force herself to find a location for the school. Every day she found an excuse to put it off.

And every day she hoped her love for Carter would diminish. Every day she'd tried to talk herself out of loving him until she finally realized that she would probably love him until her dying day, in the same way her mother had loved her father.

It hurt to think her love was one-sided. But the hurt also helped to remind her that he had never loved her back. He hadn't put up even a mild protest when she announced she was leaving the ranch.

"That's a wrap!" the assistant director shouted an hour later. The crew, who'd been quietly hovering behind an invisible boundary in back of the director, scattered and scurried to clear away the equipment.

Later that day, Macy stopped at the grocery store to buy eggs and vegetables. A veggie omelet was on the menu for tonight's meal. Macy pulled the scarf from her head, tired of the disguise, and let her black curls fall freely. The media frenzy surround-

ng her had died down now that the Tina Tarlington auction was
over, and Macy could actually drive in her own neighborhood
without being followed. She had Whitney Wynds to thank for
that. The rising new starlet had stolen the spotlight for her high
crimes in fashion. She'd taken a scissor to a designer's original
work, making it all her own for her first Hollywood premiere,
and the style police from all across the nation wouldn't let it rest.

Macy enjoyed the peace as she walked the brick pathway that
ed to her condo. But her small smile faded as she glanced down
at the sidewalk and saw the shadow of a man looming long and
tall behind her. A Western hat outlined by the late-afternoon sun
old her who it was.

"Ronny," she said, gripping her grocery bag tight. "I told you
on the set, I won't go out with you."

"Who's Ronny?"

She recognized that voice. Macy whirled around so fast she
dropped her bag of groceries. "C-Carter?"

He grinned, a devastating grin that made her breath catch.
"Hello, Hollywood. I've missed you."

"I've, uh, missed you, too." Macy blinked. Her heart thudded
heavily against her chest. And her legs went wobbly at the sight of
him standing in front of her home. "Wh-what are you doing here?"

Carter took a few steps forward and then bent to pick up
her grocery bag, sneaking a peek inside. "I bet half those eggs
didn't break."

She blinked again, trying to get with the program. Carter was
here, in Hollywood, and more important, on her doorstep and
she wasn't dreaming. "No, I, uh, guess the grocery boy packed
them really good."

Carter rose, holding the grocery bag in one hand while the
other hand touched her arm lightly. His beautiful hazel eyes
turned serious. "Do you have time to talk?"

Talk? He wanted to talk?

She nodded, wondering what brought him here. "Okay."

"I'm not interrupting anything…with Ronny?" he asked, his
brows lifting.

"Ronny? Oh no…he's not—" *He's not a cowboy. He's not* you.

"'Cause if you've got something going with him," Carter said his voice menacingly low, "I'd have to knock him ten ways to Sunday."

Macy actually laughed. And so did he. "May I come in?"

Macy let him inside her home and immediately wondered what he thought about her decor. She had good taste but loved to bargain shop. Her home was an eclectic display of design on a budget.

"Nice," he said as she grabbed the grocery bag from his arms. He walked around, taking a look out her terrace window while she put her grocery bag on the kitchen counter. She was so nervous having him here that she fidgeted with the plastic bags of vegetables and actually counted the unbroken eggs. Carter was right, she'd lost only half of them.

She shoved the carton in the refrigerator, her nerves jangling and when she turned around Carter was there, standing three feet away.

He looked massive inside her small kitchen and handsome wearing a Western jacket over a pressed white shirt. His jeans were comfortably worn and fit him to perfection. He took his hat off and a lock of his dark blond hair fell onto his forehead. It was so endearing, Macy had to hold herself back from rushing into his arms. She didn't have a clue what he was doing here.

"I paid a visit to my dad the other day. We…talked for a while."

Macy swallowed past a big old lump in her throat. "That's good."

"Rocky came along."

She bit her lip, holding back her satisfaction. "I bet Riley was glad to see both of you."

Carter shrugged. "I think so."

It was a start, Macy thought, and she wondered if the two of them had actually gotten along during the visit. Still, she was glad Carter had made the effort with his father. But she wondered if that was the reason he was here—to tell her about his progress with his father? She waited for him to say more about it, but his expression changed and she knew that conversation was over.

"I, uh," he began, then stopped to brush invisible dust from the brim of his hat. Macy had never seen Carter looking so nervous. "I never thought I could do this again."

Macy's throat constricted and her voice came out small and fragile. "Do what again?"

His gaze fastened over her right shoulder, as if he was searching for the right words. He seemed determined to get something off his chest. "You know that Jocelyn made a fool out of me and it hurt my pride and my ego. She'd been trying to make Brady jealous the entire time we were together. I didn't see it. That kind of manipulation works on a man's trust."

Macy nodded.

"I guess I really didn't know her, and I certainly didn't love her," he said. "I know that now."

"You do?"

Carter's gaze shifted back to her. He pierced her with an intense look. "Yeah, I know it for fact. Because I'm crazy in love right now. With you, Macy."

Macy slumped back against the refrigerator door, floored by his admission. Joy instantly leaped into her heart. "You are?"

"That's right. I am. I love you. I never thought I'd let myself feel this way. I never thought I could trust anyone with my heart again. I wanted no part of marriage or long-term relationships. I was done. And then I saw you on that New York street—"

"And you rescued me."

"It was fate, Macy. I might never have met you otherwise."

Macy looked him straight in the eyes. She knew how hard this was for him. He was taking a giant leap of faith in revealing his feelings. And she should make him sweat it out longer after what he'd put her through. But she didn't want to tempt fate. And she'd been waiting her entire lifetime to say these words. "I'm pretty crazy in love with you, too," she said. "For the record."

Carter closed his eyes to her declaration, as if he was absorbing her words. As if he was reaffirming them in his mind. When he opened his eyes again, she was standing toe-to-toe with him. She looked into his beautiful hazel eyes. "Are you going to kiss me now?"

Carter took her into his arms and Macy melted in his embrace. "Not yet, sweet darlin'. There's more."

"I'm listening." Macy circled her arms around his neck and watched his mouth move, watched his strong stubborn jaw relax and watched his Adam's apple bob up and down. Every motion, every nuance that was Carter brought her happiness.

"I'm having the gazebo rebuilt. It's going to be magnificent. And I want the Wild River Inn to house your drama students. They can come for summer sessions and weekends during the school year. I want you to teach, Macy. I want you to be my wife and live with me at Wild River Ranch until the sun sets for the last time on both of us."

"Oh, Carter." It was more than Macy had ever dared to hope, yet it was what she'd been secretly wishing.

"There's more," he said, "and believe me, if I thought I could wait another few hours, I'd do this much better. But I can't. I've wasted enough time."

Carter bent down on one knee and took a red paisley neckerchief out of his pocket. He unfolded it carefully and presented her with a diamond ring. "There's only one place this ring belongs," he said reverently. "And that's on your finger."

Stunned, Macy's hand came to her mouth. She stared at the sparkling diamond, eyeing the ring that had bound her parents' love. Then finally, she managed to whisper through thick emotion, "The Tarlington diamond? I never thought I'd see it again. How did you…?"

"It just came into my possession, sweetheart. I'll explain later," he said tenderly. Then he took her hand in his, holding it steady while the rest of her body trembled in anticipation. "Macy Tarlington," he began, "I'm promising to love you and keep you safe and happy for the rest of our lives. I'm promising you this from the bottom of my heart. And I'm asking you to become my wife and have my children. Come live with me at Wild River. Come *home*."

Macy didn't hesitate. Wild River was her home. She loved Carter with everything she had inside and she belonged by his side. "Yes, Carter, I'll be your wife." She didn't know how he'd done it, but the proposal and the ring together went beyond her most cherished dreams. Her voice softened to a hush. "I love you so much, Carter McCay."

He slid the ring on her finger and happy tears spilled down her cheeks. "It fits."

Carter laughed along with her and then finally brought his mouth down to claim her in a bone-melting kiss that knocked her knees out from under her. Carter was there instantly, protecting her from the fall. He lifted her and carried her out of the kitchen. "Show me your bedroom, darlin'. I've missed you something fierce."

Macy grinned, touched a loving hand to her cowboy's cheek and pointed the way.

Afterward, once the sun had set and they lay facing each other, sated and cocooned in the cozy embrace of their love, Carter told her about their mysterious benefactor, Bill Fargo. His explanation left more questions than answers, but Carter said he was grateful to Fargo, or whatever his name was, because the old guy managed to break through his stubborn pride and make him see the love he had for Macy.

"Thanks to Bill," Macy said softly, "I'm getting a wonderful husband."

Carter kissed her cheek. "And I'm getting a multitalented, beautiful Hollywood starlet, uh, *serious actress* for a wife." He winked. "There aren't too many Texans who could make that claim."

Macy thought she was definitely getting the better end of the deal, but she'd never admit that to her Stetson-wearing gorgeous hunk of a cowboy.

She wasn't that stupid.

Just incredibly lucky.

\* \* \* \* \*

*Turn the page for another exclusive story revealing the history of The Golden Heart Statue by* USA TODAY *bestselling author Barbara Dunlop. Then look for the next installment of THE HIGHEST BIDDER, A SILKEN SEDUCTION, by Yvonne Lindsay, wherever Harlequin books are sold.*

# THE GOLD HEART, PART 2
Barbara Dunlop

*Rayas, 1912*

The sharp clatter of the prison door closing reverberated through Princess Salima Adan Bajal's very bones. The uneven stones were icy cold through her soft shoes, and the dampness of the gray walls seemed to penetrate her silk robes.

"How much farther?" she whispered to the hulking, turbaned guard walking beside her. Her throat had gone dry. Her heart was pounding. And her muscles ached with taut-stretched nerves.

The guard, Zaruri, had taken possession of his bribe, her priceless Gold Heart statue, before letting her into the prison. It occurred to her now that giving up her only leverage might have been a mistake. He could just as easily kill her here as keep his end of the bargain.

"Downstairs," he announced in the guttural tone of the Rayasian language, dragging open an aged, wood plank door.

"How do we get out again?" she couldn't help asking. She dreaded the thought of going yet another floor downward into this dank dungeon. It had been built over a hundred years ago, during the Barbary Coast War. Only the thought of her beloved Cosmo Salvatore, chained to a wall, condemned to death, propelled her forward.

She'd met Cosmo in Istanbul while she was visiting cousin and he was on leave from the Italian army in which he served as a captain. She'd kept her identity a secret, and they'd fallen in love like two ordinary people. If only he'd let her go. But he tracked her down to Rayas and kissed her exuberantly in public

The palace guards had immediately arrested him. She'd begged her father, King Habib, to free him. But her pleas had made her father only angrier. He'd offered no leniency and instructed the judge to impose the maximum penalty.

Someone cried out from the depths of the prison. A guard shouted, and another door clanged shut. It had been long minutes since she'd had a glimpse of daylight. But if she was going to die here, at least her fate was linked to Cosmo's. She'd die knowing she'd done everything in her power to save him. That was something.

She raised her head and squared her shoulders, ready to face whatever was to come.

But suddenly, Cosmo was in front of her, held firmly by another guard as he blinked in astonishment.

"Salima," he rasped. "What are you *doing?*"

"I've come to rescue you." She reached for him, but he jerked away.

"Leave," he commanded in a harsh tone. Then he looked to Zaruri. "Take her away."

She grasped Cosmo's tattered sleeve. "It's all right."

"It's not all right. It's not safe for you here."

Zaruri grunted and started forward, propelling Salima with him. "There's no time for this."

Cosmo's guard turned him along the narrow passageway.

"We're getting out of here," she whispered to Cosmo.

"They're going to kill you," he whispered back.

She shook her head. Despite her earlier fears, she refused to believe that. If they were going to kill her, they'd have done already.

"I love you," she told him.

"Salima," he ground out.

"It's my fault you're here."

"It's *my* fault I'm here."

"If I'd told you I was a princess."

"If I'd listened when you asked me to stay away."

Zaruri growled as he jerked her to a halt. Using an iron key, he unlocked a door, yawning it open, shoving her outside.

She chafed at being handled so roughly. As a member of the Rayas royal family, Salima was never touched by commoners. But seconds later, Cosmo was beside her, and they were breathing the clean night air and nothing else mattered.

"The horses are at the river," Zaruri informed them.

Salima drew herself up, forcing herself to hide her relief. She was a princess. "You are sworn to secrecy," she reminded the men.

"You are a fugitive," Zaruri returned, his yellowed teeth showing in the moonlight. He hoisted the statue that was tucked under one arm, wrapped in gray cloth. "And I am a king."

Salima bit back a retort. The Gold Heart statue might be one of the most prized possessions of the royal family, but Zaruri would never be anything but a commoner. Then again, from here on in, neither would she.

Cosmo's strong arm snaked around her shoulder. He took a step backward, then another, drawing her with him, eyes warily watching the guards. Then she and Cosmo were walking away, then running along the path that led to the river.

They found horses tied there. But, as Salima would have mounted, Cosmo pulled her against him, stepping back into the shelter of the trees, where his arms wrapped tightly around her.

"I stink," he groaned in apology.

"I don't care." She hugged him back, pressing her body full length against his. It was something she'd never dared do in Istanbul.

"You shouldn't have come."

"I couldn't let them kill you."

Cosmo drew back in obvious confusion. "Kill me?"

"You were sentenced to death."

"I was sentenced to two years, Salima." His hands engulfe
hers. "I'd have made it two years."

Salima digested the information. Had the court lied to Cosmo
Or had her father lied to her?

"I was told they were going to behead you."

"For kissing you?"

"I'm a member of the royal family."

Cosmo's hands moved up to cradle her face, their warm ca
luses cupping her cheeks. "I'm not saying it wouldn't have bee
worth it."

"How can you joke?" she whispered, her knees still shakin,

He bent toward her, his hot, tender lips taking possession o
hers. Desire flowed through her veins. Her arms wound aroun
his waist, and she came up on her toes, wanting desperately t
get closer. The silk scarf slipped off her head, her black hair lif
ing in the breeze.

After long minutes, Cosmo drew back. "I love you, Salim
I was going to wait it out, then come for you. One day I'll be
general. I can protect you."

The precariousness of their situation rushed back. "We hav
to get away, very far away."

"Will they come after you? Try to take you back?"

A complicated question. "Only until you defile me." She w
useless to her father after that.

Cosmo's eyes darkened, and he kissed her again, harder th
time, deeper and longer, his body straining against hers.

"And then what?" he rasped, as hidden desires boiled up i
side her.

"They'll either disown me or kill me," she answered.

"Do we get to pick which?"

She couldn't believe he was joking again. "It doesn't wor
that way."

"How does it work?"

"We disappear forever."

"I can live with that."

* * *

Salima's head was bare, her dark hair upswept and interwoven with tiny white flowers. Her arms were barely covered in wispy sleeves of white lace and satin. The dress itself was a sheath that nipped in at her waist, dipped down to her cleavage and brushed the toes of her heeled shoes. She felt very Western, nothing of a Rayas wedding in evidence.

It had taken weeks to cross the Mediterranean, and then to Europe and England, where they'd boarded and ocean liner. They'd barely made international waters, on route from Southampton to New York, when Cosmo had her in front of the ship's captain saying their vows. The ceremony was swift, witnessed by the first mate. They'd kissed and signed the register, then dashed down the passage to their compact stateroom. Cosmo pushed open the door and scooped her into his arms.

As he carried her across the threshold, she battled the vestiges of fear that had constantly cramped her stomach while they traversed the Mediterranean and Europe.

"We used our real names," she couldn't help pointing out. Misdirection and subterfuge had become second nature to her over the past three weeks.

He kissed the tip of her nose, kicking the door shut behind them. "That's so we'd really be married."

"What if they check the ship's manifest?"

Her father and her three brothers would have agents fanning out across the Middle East. They'd certainly be in Italy. Eventually, they'd move farther north in Europe.

Cosmo set her on her feet, gazing softly into her eyes. "I'm going to defile you now."

She drew back. "In the daytime?"

He traced the soft skin of her neckline. "Absolutely."

"But…" She wanted Cosmo, wanted him in every way a wife wants her husband. But there were passengers in the hallways, the ship's crew wandering around the decks.

Cosmo obviously guessed her thoughts. He reached behind him to flip the lock on their stateroom door. "No one will bother us, sweetheart."

He moved closer, imposing, wrapping his arms around her waist. "I've waited weeks, Salima. Months if you count Istanbul."

"I know."

He tugged her more tightly against him, and she could feel his arousal. His dark gaze bore intensely into hers. His voice was harsh, guttural. "I *need* you to be my wife."

She understood. She wanted that, too.

They'd known each other only a few months, but she couldn't imagine her life without him—married off to a sheik or a prince from a neighboring kingdom, used as a bargaining chip to further her father's influence in the region. If she'd followed Rayasian tradition, she would have never laughed, never shouted, never run barefoot on a beach, never felt the wind rustling her hair. She'd have borne a stranger's children, walked two paces behind him, sat silently through state dinners and withered away behind the palace walls.

Instead, her new husband kissed her, passionately and thoroughly, starting a throbbing pulse that fanned out from her belly, tingling when it reached her skin.

There was a sudden, sharp rap at the door.

Somebody shouted in Salima's native language, followed by a protest in English.

Cosmo turned, placing himself between her and the door as it crashed open, banging back on its hinges.

A tall, swarthy man barged into the small room. He held a seaman in front of him, a knife to the man's throat.

"You are a disgrace to the House of Bajal," he shouted at Salima. "You have blackened your mother's memory and cut out the heart of your father."

Salima felt herself shrivel. Shame washed over her at the truth of his words. The queen had been dead for more than ten years, but Salima had adored her.

Cosmo circled sideways, drawing the Rayasian man's attention. "Don't you dare speak to my wife."

"You have married this dog?" the man spat.

The seaman's eyes were wide, his gaze darting from Salima to Cosmo to the open door. But the hallway was silent and empty.

The Rayasian man kicked the door shut. He threw a rope to Salima. It bounced off her wedding dress and dropped to the floor.

"Tie him up," he demanded, jerking his head toward Cosmo.

"Don't listen to him," Cosmo ordered.

The man clamped the knife tighter against the seaman's throat, and a small trickle of blood leaked out.

The seaman gasped, and Salima clamped a hand over her mouth, afraid she might throw up.

"Tie him up."

"Sweetheart," Cosmo whispered, his feet inching farther away from her. "You have to trust me on this."

Salima whimpered. She knew that if she helped the Rayasian man, he would surely kill Cosmo. Then he'd haul her back to Rayas to face her furious father. But she couldn't let him kill the innocent seaman.

She bent toward the rope.

"Salima," Cosmo warned.

The Rayasian man gave a cold chuckle, switching to his native tongue. "You were a princess long before you were his wife."

He was right. She *was* a princess.

She rose, squaring her shoulders, speaking in the most imperious tone she could muster. "I am your princess. And I order you to let him go."

A brief hesitation flashed through the man's eyes. Were they in Rayas, he would be instantly arrested for disobeying.

But they weren't in Rayas. And his surprise quickly turned to a lecherous smirk. "Very soon, we will be alone, you and I. And you will not like my rules."

"What's he saying?" Cosmo demanded.

"You would not dare touch me." But her stomach clenched, and she could feel the blood drain from her face.

A salacious smile curved the man's lips. "Who would believe a lying traitor like you?"

"What is he saying?" Cosmo repeated.

"That he's going to rape me." She looked directly into Cosmo's eyes. "But he's going to have to kill me first."

In fact, he was going to have to kill her before he got to Cosmo, or to the seaman.

She rushed boldly forward.

Cosmo shouted something unintelligible. He jumped in front of her, his fist connecting with the Rayasian man's face, dislodging the knife, sending it clattering to the floor.

The seaman lurched forward, knocking Salima onto the bed. The Rayasian man's fist connected with Cosmo's chin, sending him reeling. Cosmo recovered, and they squared off. Salima eyed the knife on the far side of the room.

The man hit Cosmo in the side of the head. He wrapped a beefy arm around Cosmo's neck, pulling hard, tightening the noose.

"Cosmo!" Salima heard herself scream. She scrambled to her feet.

But before she could reach them, Cosmo broke free. He dove for the knife, grasping it, rolling onto his back as the man lunged. The knife plunged into the man's heart. His eyes went wide. His mouth opened in shock. And he went immediately limp.

Cosmo shoved the Rayasian off as Salima rushed to his side.

The seaman came to his feet. "That was clear-cut self-defense," he asserted.

Cosmo rose, speaking distinctly and concisely to the seaman. "I don't want to have to explain this."

After a moment's silence, the seaman nodded. "I'll take care of it." Then the seaman reflexively rubbed his throat, his palm coming away with a smear of blood. "Let me take you to another cabin."

Salima buried her face in Cosmo's shoulder as they made their way down the passage and up three flights of stairs.

The seaman unlocked a door, showing them into a spacious stateroom. "A last-minute cancellation," he told them. "This is one of *Titanic*'s finest first-class cabins."

Salima couldn't seem to stop shaking. There was a roaring in her ears as Cosmo spoke to the seaman, and unshed tears blurred her eyes. She barely noticed the opulent furnishings, the giant, canopied bed, the picture window and the rich red-

and-gold wallpaper, decorated with dazzling light fixtures and carved wood accents.

She was vaguely aware of the door closing and locking, a popping sound and then Cosmo's arm supporting her once more.

They moved to an emerald-green sofa. He sat, drawing her down onto his lap. Then he placed a glass of champagne in her hands.

"Drink," he instructed.

Her fingers felt numb on the long stem of the glass, and her voice quavered when she spoke. "He was trying to kill you."

Cosmo stroked her hair. "I'm a soldier, Salima. People have been trying to kill me half my life. So far, no luck."

"You're joking again."

"It's the truth. Stop worrying."

"I can't." But she took an experimental sip of the champagne. Rayas women didn't drink alcohol, so she didn't know what to expect. The liquid was sweet on her tongue and soothing to her dry throat, and she downed the rest.

"Take it easy," Cosmo advised.

"It's all my fault." She spoke as much to herself as to him. She'd known the risks. "I gave away the Gold Heart statue."

She held out her glass, and he poured from the bottle. "The statue is what got me out of jail," Cosmo said.

"But now it's cursed."

"Drink slower this time," he advised.

She nodded, then downed the glass.

Cosmo chuckled, resting his forehead against her hair. "I adore you."

"The curse has doomed our love." She'd heard the stories, the legend of the three statues. Her eight times great-grandfather had presented them to his daughters with a warning. Subsequent generations had protected them, and their luck had held.

Cosmo slowly opened a front button on her wedding dress. "It's not doomed from where I'm sitting."

She watched in fascination as his square hand moved to the next button, and the next. Her bodice gaped open, revealing her lacy white bra. He slipped his hand beneath her dress, around her waist, drawing her into a passionate kiss.

The champagne glass slipped from her fingers to bounce against the thick carpet. Her pulse tripped to double time, her arousal combining with the buzz of the champagne. Shyness vanishing, replaced by a sense of urgency, she pushed off his suit jacket, struggling with the buttons of his shirt, needing to feel his skin against hers.

He groaned her name, his hand closing over her breast. A sensation jolted through her body, zipping to the apex of her thighs, leaving a glow in its wake.

She gasped, and he stroke his thumb across her nipple.

*"What—"*

"Trust me," he urged while his other hand slipped up her thigh, coming to the lacy panties beneath.

Cosmo's hands were traveling to the most intimate places of her body, and she didn't care. He stroked her through the flimsy silk. She held her breath, cataloging the new and amazing sensations his touch evoked.

He kissed her deeply, and she met his tongue, her body awash in heat and need. Her hands gripped his shoulders, trying to steady herself. He stripped off her panties. Then his fingers explored her moist flesh, pushing deeply inside.

"So hot," he murmured against her mouth. "I want you so much."

He pushed up her voluminous dress, revealing her nudity. The bodice gaped open. She didn't care. She arched against him, desperate to feel his touch.

He loosened his pants, shifting her to sit astride him. His sex pressed intimately against her.

"Like this?" she gasped in astonishment.

"Like this." His hand moved between them.

White-hot jolts of sensation quivered her thighs. She could feel him against her, stretching her body, pulsing, invading. He felt enormous.

"Don't," she tried to protest.

But he silenced her with a kiss, clamping her tight against him as he slid home.

It hurt. A little. Maybe. But then the ache was miraculously replaced with need. He moved inside her, and sparks showered her brain. She jolted back in shock, her eyes flying open.

He was watching her, eyes midnight dark with passion.

He stroked again, causing another shower of sparks.

Her mouth formed an O.

He smiled, flexing his hips once more.

"Oh, my," she breathed, arching her hips as a growing pulse gained strength between them.

"If this is doomed," he groaned, capturing her mouth and increasing his rhythm, "then I'll gladly take it."

Look out for
**Mills & Boon® TEMPTED™ 2-in-1s,**
from September

*Fresh, contemporary romances
to tempt all lovers of
great stories*

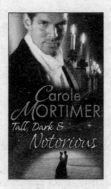
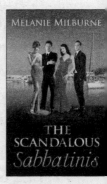

# MILLS & BOON® *Book Club*

# *Join the Mills & Boon Book Club*

---

Want to read more **Modern**™ books?
We're offering you **2 more** absolutely **FREE!**

---

We'll also treat you to these fabulous extras:

- 🌹 Exclusive offers and much more!

- 🌹 FREE home delivery

- 🌹 FREE books and gifts with our special rewards scheme

*Get your free books now!*

## visit www.millsandboon.co.uk/bookclub
## or call Customer Relations on 020 8288 2888